SLAYERS

THE DRAGON LORDS

OTHER TITLES
BY CJ HILL
(AKA JANETTE RALLISON)

Slayers (under pen name CJ Hill)
Slayers: Friends and Traitors (under pen name CJ Hill)
Slayers: Playing with Fire (under pen name CJ Hill)
Erasing Time (under pen name CJ Hill)
Echo in Time (under pen name CJ Hill)
Son of War, Daughter of Chaos
Blue Eyes and Other Teenage Hazards
Just One Wish
Masquerade
My Double Life
A Longtime (and at One Point Illegal) Crush
Life, Love, and the Pursuit of Free Throws
The Girl Who Heard Demons
How I Met Your Brother
Playing The Field
The Wrong Side of Magic
My Fair Godmother
My Unfair Godmother
My Fairly Dangerous Godmother audio book
All's Fair in Love, War, and High School
Fame, Glory, and Other Things on my To Do List
It's a Mall World After All
Revenge of the Cheerleaders
How to Take The Ex Out of Ex-boyfriend
What the Doctor Ordered (under pen name Sierra St. James)
Just One Wish audio book

SLAYERS

THE DRAGON LORDS

C.J. HILL

To all of the people who have patiently waited for book four to come out.

It's here!

Unfortunately, I must now inform you that you'll have to wait for book five. I know, I know. I'm not happy about this turn of events either. Next time I write a book, I'll choose characters who can tell their stories in fewer chapters.

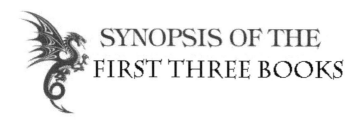

SYNOPSIS OF THE FIRST THREE BOOKS

Brant Overdrake was a man of ambition and ego—always a dangerous combination. His family had kept dragons on the remote island of St. Helena for generations. He was a dragon lord, a man able to connect to a dragon's mind and make the animal do whatever he wished.

His family had cared for the dragons in secret, but Brant had other ideas. He planned to use the dragons' electromagnetic pulses as weapons. When dragons screeched, they sent out an EMP (electromagnetic pulse) that destroyed electronics, rendering cars, phones, computers—most technology—useless.

He moved to Virginia and started laying the groundwork for a future takeover of America's government.

When transporting a pair of dragon eggs, his wife had unexpected early labor and he was forced to make an emergency detour to an airport near DC. (Labor comes at inconvenient times. If you don't believe this, ask me about my last labor, which lasted eighteen hours. It was *quite* inconvenient.) While the dragon eggs were at the airport, the general population was exposed to their signal.

This was unfortunate for Overdrake because the dragons had a natural enemy—Slayers. Slayers were descendants of the knights who killed dragons in the Middle Ages. If a person with Slayer genes came in contact with a dragon or dragon eggs while in utero, the person's genes were activated, turning them into a Slayer. The child then grew up with an innate interest in dragons and inborn athletic skill.

The summer before her junior year of high school, Tori Hampton, a senator's daughter, enrolled in Dragon Camp in the hopes of understanding her obsession with dragons. (She was a socialite, yes, but not a *spoiled* girl, despite what the hardcover book flap of Slayers claims.) Jesse and Dirk, the blessed-with-good-looks captains of the camp teams A-Team and Team Magnus, introduced themselves at registration and took her to the camp's secret secondary location. (I'm not kidding about the good looks part. I based Dirk on Dirk Benedict. If you don't know who that is, google his pictures from *Battlestar Gallactica*. You see what I mean?) At the secret camp, Tori met six other teens, all close to her age. She found out that they were actually training to fight real dragons and that she herself was a Slayer.

When Slayers came within five miles of a dragon (or the dragon simulator that Dr. B developed to help the Slayers train and complete missions) their powers turned on. The Slayers always had highly attuned senses, but when their powers were triggered they had extra strength, night vision, and the ability to leap ten to fifteen feet in the air. They also had an individual skill. Jesse could fly, Bess threw shields up, Kody could throw both freezing blasts and fireballs, Dirk saw what the nearest dragon saw, Shang and Lilly extinguished fire, and Rosa and Alyssa healed burns.

Slayers who had the same skill set were counterparts, which meant they could read one another really, really well. Also, when in the same vicinity, Slayers could tell where their counterparts were without looking. It was a skill that helped while fighting and made the group more tight-knit.

Two days into camp, Tori discovered she could hear

what the nearest dragon heard. It seemed like a useless and disappointing skill as dragons didn't generally hear much that would help the Slayers fight them. She also found out that she was Dirk's counterpart. Their skills weren't exactly the same, but close enough to give them the counterpart abilities.

Dirk developed feelings for her; she developed feelings for Jesse. (I did mention that Jesse was hot too, didn't I?)

When Tori overheard vets near a dragon give information about the dragon eggs' location, she realized her skill was not as useless as she first imagined. She and the other Slayers planned a surprise attack on the location in order to destroy the dragon eggs. Because, as the old saying goes, it's easier to kill your dragons before they hatch. Okay, that isn't actually an old saying, but it should be.

Where was I? Oh yes, telling you about the ill-fated surprise attack. It was a surprise, although mostly the Slayers were surprised because they were ambushed. If you haven't read the first book (and you should, because it's awesome) I'm going to have to disappoint you here and tell you that Dirk is actually Brant Overdrake's son, a traitor who was sent to camp to spy on the Slayers.

However, as the Slayers were being ambushed, and were trapped in Overdrake's enclosure, Dirk had a change of heart about betraying his friends. He then double-crossed his father by helping Tori save the others. At this point Tori found out she could also fly.

It was a surprise to her, but not to Overdrake, because he already knew what readers won't learn until the second book—that Tori is actually part dragon lord. Her ability to hear what the dragon hears—that's not really a Slayer skill, it's a dragon lord one.

This, by the way, was supposed to be the big reveal in

Slayers: Friends and Traitors. And would have been quite a surprise to many people if the publisher hadn't given away that plot twist on the back blurb. Which they did. Yeah, authors generally don't have any control over what goes on the back of the book.

Anyway, I keep getting off track. So after the Slayers escaped, Overdrake set a dragon on them. Dirk's dragon. He had to help his friends fight and kill it in order to save their lives. In case you haven't figured it out yet, Overdrake isn't a very nice person.

In book two, camp ended and the Slayers went back to their homes. Tori heard the eggs hatch, got together briefly with Dirk, and had her father search for Ryker, the missing Slayer.

I haven't mentioned him yet, even though book one starts out and ends with him. (Hey, it's hard to summarize hundreds of pages.) When Dr. B first told Ryker's parents that their son was going to be a Slayer, instead of letting Dr. B train him, Ryker's parents moved without a forwarding address. Well, you can't blame them, really. Would you let your son fight huge, flying carnivores that breathe fire?

Tori's father was able to track down Ryker's address, because he worked for the government and let's face it; you can't disappear from the government. They know where you are.

On Halloween, Overdrake kidnapped Alyssa as a way to lure the Slayers into another ambush. He knew they'd go after her. As the Slayers met for the mission, Tori let Dirk know that her father had tracked down Ryker and she told Dirk that he lived in Rutland, Vermont. While Dr. B prepped the Slayers for the mission, Tori sensed Dirk's anxiety about the mission—he was plagued with guilt for betraying his friends—and she figured out who Dirk was.

What follows is an awesome chase scene through DC,

which you should read sometime. Plus, you should visit DC because it's a cool place. (And when you go to the Jefferson Memorial, you can imagine me stepping off the area between the columns to see if a dragon would fit through them. This is the sort of dedicated research authors do.)

The Slayers retrieved Alyssa, although sadly, her memories and powers were gone. Slayers had an Achilles' heel, so to speak. If they were drugged to the point of unconsciousness, the pathways in their brains that gave them powers were destroyed. The Slayers not only lost their powers, they didn't even remember being Slayers.

It was a sad and yet funny scene because Alyssa thought they were all crazy.

Moving right along. Tori realized she had put Ryker in danger by revealing his address to Dirk. This is probably a good example of why you shouldn't trust hot guys. Just saying. The Slayers then flew to Vermont to find and convince Ryker to join them. Overdrake's men reached Ryker's house at roughly the same time and a fight ensued. When you read that scene, please appreciate it because I had to rewrite it like, six times.

The Slayers found out that not only was Ryker a Slayer, but his cousin Willow was too. Their addition was especially good news because the Slayers' numbers had been dwindling. They just lost Alyssa, and in the backstory of book one, they'd lost two other Slayers, Leo and Danielle. You need to know about them because they come into play in book five. At this point, you may be wondering if I regret writing a book with so many characters. *Yes.* I mean, of course I don't—although I will never *ever* write a series with so many people in it again. The poor audiobook reader had such a hard time doing different voices for them all.

Back to the storyline. Dirk realized that his father was going to attack the Slayers' plane. As they were flying home, he warned Tori. The Slayers were able to jump out of the plane before the dragon ripped the thing apart. Another author's note here: I wanted to make that scene as authentic as possible, so I went skydiving. If you read that book, imagine me thousands of feet above the ground trying to convince the skydiving instructor that I'd changed my mind and didn't want to jump after all. They don't listen to you at that point. You're strapped onto them and they just pull you right out of the plane. But I digress.

Anyway, another fight ensued and in this one, Tori was briefly able to enter the dragon's mind. She couldn't influence the dragon at all. Overdrake had too firm a control on it, but he was angry that she tried and told the dragon to ignore the rest of the Slayers and kill her.

As you may have guessed, the dragon wasn't successful. Because if the dragon was, the book would have ended very badly, and I would have gotten angry emails from readers. I'd rather not get those.

In book three, *Slayers: Playing with Fire*, we learn that Bianca—Overdrake's first wife and Dirk's mother—was secretly pregnant when she left her husband twelve years ago. She didn't want her second son sacrificed to Overdrake's upcoming war the way Dirk would be. She knew if she left with Dirk, Overdrake would hunt her down to get him back—but her second son would have a chance to live if she separated from her husband and hid the baby's existence.

Poor Bianca. Her secret doesn't stay a secret because when Aaron turns twelve and his family is in financial straits, he sells some of the dragon scales that his mother had absconded with.

I will not go into detail about the scenes where the Slayers track the dragon scale back to Aaron, but I will say that I posted this question on Facebook: How would you get an unconscious body out of a Renaissance Festival? And I was surprised and a bit worried when many of my friends immediately had complete, workable plans for that venture. This should tell you something about the quality of people writers hang out with.

By this point in the book, the Slayers suspect that in order for Dirk and Tori to be counterparts, not only is Tori half dragon lord, but Dirk is half Slayer. Since his Slayer power is flying and dragon lords can also fly, neither he nor his father realized this fact. But Bianca definitely passed down Slayer genes to her sons—evidenced by the fact that her third son by a different father has Slayer powers. (Overdrake doesn't know about him either.)

Aaron realizes that when Overdrake attacks the nation with his dragons, his younger brother, Jacob, will be drawn into the fight. He wants to do everything he can to stop Overdrake, and asks Tori to leak his location to his father. That way, he can live with Overdrake and work as a mole for the Slayers.

Tori tells him absolutely not. Which means you know this is going to be an important plot point. Aaron tells her that if she doesn't help him, he'll find a way to see Overdrake on his own—and Overdrake may suspect his intentions then. She tells Aaron she'll give him a week to change his mind.

After a conversation with her father, Tori suspects that Senator Ethington may be working for Overdrake. In what are the funniest scenes in book three, Jesse and Kody bug the senator's phone. They get information about an incoming arms deal, and tip off Tori's father so he can put a stop to it. Which he does.

Understandably displeased, Overdrake wants to send a message to Tori. (Or perhaps he's doing his own version of matchmaking, I'll leave it to you to decide, Gentle Reader.)

He steals Tori's dog, Brindy, then feeds a dog to a dragon while threatening Tori that her family will meet the same fate if she interferes with him. (I never said he was a *good* matchmaker.)

Tori calls Dirk, more than a little upset, and Dirk confronts his father—because his father had promised he would leave Tori and her family alone. Overdrake then reveals that Tori's dog is fine. He hadn't needed to kill Brindy to make his point.

Dirk tells Tori he'll give Brindy back if she'll meet him late at night in a deserted location. She agrees. Yes, he's the enemy, but you can't blame her for being an animal lover. And besides, Dirk is good looking, so there's that too.

Dirk takes the opportunity to slightly kidnap Tori and brings her to see Khan, one of his dragons. Dirk believes that if she sees a dragon when it isn't attacking, she'll appreciate her dragon lord side. He tries to convince her to leave the Slayers and join him.

Tori enters Khan's mind because she wants to learn how to control dragons. The knowledge could help her the next time one attacks. When Dirk starts kissing her, she doesn't stop him because she wants to stay in the dragon's mind. Personally, I would totally kiss a Dirk Benedict lookalike if it meant saving the country. Wouldn't you? No? And you call yourself a patriot...

At the end of the night, Tori sends Dirk a message about Aaron and his location. The next morning, she also tells Jesse that she kissed Dirk. He isn't very understanding about her patriotism.

The last scene of the book is Overdrake's men chasing down Aaron at the Renaissance Fair. And that's how it ends. On a cliffhanger. Which is why I've been getting emails since Aug 2016 asking me when the next book is coming out.

By the way, this was my second book where I've had to use the word Renaissance repeatedly and I still spell it wrong. Every. Single. Time.

So, that pretty much should bring you up to speed. Oh, one more piece of information you need. Dr. B lived on St. Helena with Overdrake. In fact, his father worked for Overdrake. His younger brother, Nathan, was a Slayer who was killed by Overdrake's father.

PROLOGUE

YOU SHOULD NEVER MAKE
PROMISES YOU CAN'T KEEP

Fifteen years ago

Alastair Bartholomew was about to make a deal with the devil, or at least a deal with his own father—which felt like the same thing. Alastair hadn't even asked for the loan yet, but he knew there would be a price to pay, a little bit of his soul thrown in with the bargain.

He glanced over the maps, brochures, and realtor flyers he'd spread over his kitchen table. Buying land was the first step to building the Slayer training ground. He'd been looking at properties for the last six months. A stack of construction bids for the facilities sat next to the brochures. He would also need money for research. He not only had to figure out what sort of electric pulse a dragon's heart put out, he would need to build a machine to replicate it. There were so many expenses.

Alastair turned his attention to the maps of Virginia, Maryland, Delaware, and Pennsylvania. Was a secluded location more important in a campsite or accessibility to the DC area? The closer his camp was to DC, the more expensive the land would be.

Shirley, his wife, had put their daughter, Bess, into her favorite pajamas and was now patiently waiting for the toddler to finish her bottle.

Even though Bess was almost two, it was a battle of the wills.

"Aren't you done yet?" Shirley cooed. "It's time for a story and then bed."

Bess regarded her mother while taking slow sips of her bottle. In her fuzzy white footie pajamas, she always reminded Alastair of a baby polar bear. Bess's hair was a wild disarray of curls. Her blue eyes were much too alert for this time of night.

Shirley bent lower to be on Bess's level. "Don't you think it's time for your bottle to go bye-bye? You're a big girl now. Big girls use sippy cups."

Bess popped the bottle out of her mouth. "No," she said, "Ba-ba mine." Then she inserted the bottle back in her mouth.

Shirley sighed, checked the kitchen clock, and turned to her husband. "I'd better put her to B-E-D before you-know-who comes, or we'll never get her to sleep."

Bess let the bottle drop from her mouth. Her blue eyes lit up with happiness. "Icecweam twuck!" she exclaimed and toddled to the front door.

Instead of going after her, Shirley narrowed her eyes at Alastair. "How come every time I use the term 'you-know-who' Bess thinks I'm talking about an ice cream truck?"

He kept his gaze firmly on the stack of septic tank bids in front of him. "I have no idea."

Shirley put one hand on her hip. "You shouldn't feed Bess ice cream. She won't eat healthy food if you give her junk."

The doorbell rang, saving him from further discussion of what he and Bess did while Shirley was gone.

"That's probably my father," Alastair announced and went to the front room. Bess was already on her tippy-toes doing her utmost to get around the child-proof handle on the doorknob. She loved opening doors. Unfortunately, she also loved dashing outside and shedding her clothes on the sidewalk.

Alastair opened the door. His father—Roderick Bartholomew to people who knew him in the States—had his hands thrust into his jacket pocket. Years of managing a ranch had given him a lean, muscled build that was only now giving way to the softness of middle age. He'd always had a stern expression and the lines in his face had grown increasingly deeper in the years since they'd fled St. Helena. Alastair never asked how often his father thought of Nathan. It was clear his father thought of him every day. The evidence was there in the grooves of his face.

Now that Alastair had a child of his own, he better understood the force of that emotion. You didn't forget when someone killed your child.

Bess saw her grandpa and lifted her small hands up in glee. "Bampa!"

The sternness on Roderick's face melted. He bent down and swooped Bess into his arms. "How's my princess?"

He snuggled his face into her neck, a move that always made Bess shriek with laughter. After he'd caused enough shrieks to ensure that Bess wouldn't sleep any time in the near future, Roderick carried her into the living room and sat down on the couch with Bess on his lap. She immediately began rifling through his pockets to see if she could extract treasures such as keys, pens, or lint. Alastair and Shirley sat down on the adjoining loveseat.

"So," Roderick said, "You want a loan." He always got right to the point.

No one would have known by looking at Roderick's plain clothes and worn jacket that he was a wealthy man. His businesses—some of which he discussed with Alastair, some of which he didn't—were quite successful. Roderick had a talent for making money, perhaps because he didn't let things like rules, laws, or ethics stand in his way.

"I need a loan for the Slayer camp," Alastair clarified. He stayed away from his father's money for the most part. Any time his father paid for something—usually lavish gifts for Bess—Alastair felt vaguely like he was condoning insider trading. He had only decided to ask for his father's help because there was nowhere else to turn. He could get a bank loan that would cover the price of land and a few cabins, but he couldn't very well explain to financial institutions that he also needed to build a second specialized camp that would serve as a secret training ground. Not many people wanted to bankroll superheroes.

"It's our best way to stop Overdrake," Alastair told his father. "When he attacks DC, we'll have a group of Slayers who are capable of killing his dragons."

Alastair had mentioned his idea of a training camp to his father before but he'd never asked for funding. The weight of the request felt like a yoke around his neck. The camps would require more than two million dollars to become functional, and who knew how long it would take for the regular camp to start returning the investment.

Roderick didn't speak for a moment. Alastair was used to his father's silences. He waited.

"You only know where one Slayer child is," Roderick finally said. "One. And that's Bess. How can you build an entire camp on the hope that more Slayer kids will somehow find their way to it?"

"It'll be a dragon-slayer-themed camp," Alastair pointed out. "I'll advertise with knights taking on fire-breathing beasts. The right children will be drawn to it."

Bess had pulled a penny from her grandfather's pocket. He took it from her before she could see how it tasted. "They'll be drawn to it? That's a long shot, and you know it."

Shirley and Alastair exchanged a look. "I'll show him," Shirley said. She walked out of the room. A minute later she came back with a bag of stuffed animals.

She sat down in front of Bess and took out a cat. "What's this?"

Bess dropped the pen she had just liberated from her grandpa's jacket and glanced at the cat. "Ki-ki."

"That's kitty," Shirley interpreted for Roderick. She pulled a stuffed dog from the bag. "What's this?"

Instead of answering, Bess made barking noises, jumping up and down with each bark.

"Right. A doggy." Shirley reached into the bag again. "What's this?" She slowly took out a stuffed dragon.

Bess's posture stiffened and she scowled. "Bad dwagon!" She slid from the couch, grabbed the toy and flung it on the floor. "No, no!" she yelled and stomped on the toy several times.

Roderick watched, his mouth slightly ajar. "You taught her to do that."

"We didn't," Shirley said. "You should see what she did to the fairy tale picture books I checked out of the library. I didn't realize they had dragon pictures in them until it was too late." She shook her head at the thought. "I had to pay the library thirty-eight dollars to replace them."

Bess stepped off the toy and watched it, seemingly studying it for signs of life. She waved a scolding finger at the animal. "No, no, bad dwagon!"

Alastair regarded his daughter with a sense of resignation. "I have to keep all my dragon research books on high shelves. Otherwise I'm afraid she'll impale them."

Satisfied that the dragon toy would not be bothering the family again, Bess picked up the stuffed animal, trotted across the room to a garbage can, and dropped the toy inside. "All bedder!" she chimed and padded back over to the others. She tried unsuccessfully to climb onto the couch by herself until Roderick picked her up and put her on his lap. "Conquering dragons before you're potty trained, eh princess?"

"All bedder!" she said again.

It wasn't all better. Alastair couldn't stand the thought of his daughter ever seeing, let alone fighting, a real dragon. And yet, that's what he was planning. That's what he was asking his father to give him a loan for.

Alastair didn't let himself dwell on the implications of what that meant for Bess's future. He had time until the dragons attacked. Fifteen to twenty years. He would find and train so many Slayers, his daughter would only bear a small portion of the danger.

"Slayers are natural dragon fighters," Alastair reminded his father. "Any Slayer children in the area will want to come to camp. My goal is to have the regular facilities open in three years. That way when the Slayer children are old enough to go to camps, mine will already be well-established. I'll offer scholarships for families who can't afford the cost. We'll find and train all of the Slayers."

Roderick turned his attention to Bess. She was busily shoving his car keys between the couch cushions. He didn't give his disappearing keys any notice. Instead he ran a hand over Bess's wispy curls. "She reminds me of Nathan."

"I know," Alastair said. Bess was determined, mischievous, and exuberant. Just like Nathan had been.

Roderick's gaze swung back to Alastair, all his former sternness restored. "I don't want her anywhere near a dragon. Brant Overdrake can't even know she exists."

Alastair gave the answer he told himself every time he had the same thought. "All of the Slayers, including Bess, will be safer from both dragons and Overdrake if they're trained."

His father couldn't argue with that. If Nathan had known that he was a Slayer and that Overdrake was a dragon lord, his brother would probably still be alive.

Roderick brushed one of Bess's curls behind her ear. His hands looked rough and worn against the little girl's smooth skin. "You can train Bess," Roderick conceded. "But I don't want her anywhere near a battle."

"None of us do," Shirley said. She had been uncharacteristically quiet and somber during this conversation. But then, how could anyone talk about their child's future battles lightly?

"We'll hope for the best," Alastair added. "However, we have to prepare for the worst."

With the keys now swallowed by the couch, Bess sat down beside her grandfather and tried to pry his wedding ring from his finger.

"Fine then," Roderick said in a tone that indicated he'd made up his mind about the issue. "I won't give you opinions or platitudes, I'll just tell you my terms for funding your camp. You can train Bess, but when Overdrake attacks, she stays out of it."

"I don't want her to fight," Alastair reiterated. He glanced across the room at the garbage can and the dragon tail that stuck out. "But how am I going to keep her out of it?"

"You're the parent," Roderick said. "You'll figure something out. And speaking of parents, don't tell your mother any of this. It will make her worry."

Over the years, Alastair and his father had kept a long list of things from his mother.

Unable to pull off her grandpa's ring, Bess bent down to bite it. Roderick gently moved his hand away. "No, no," he told her.

Bess laughed and tried to bite his finger again.

Shirley stood up, walked over, and picked up their daughter. "No biting, sweetie."

Bess chomped her teeth together. "I a cwocodile."

Shirley made a tsking noise and carried Bess into the kitchen, most likely to have a talk with her about appropriate animal behavior.

Alastair watched them go and inwardly sighed. "We can't even keep her from biting people. What makes you think we'll be able to control her when she's a teenager?" He lifted one hand in frustration. "Has anyone figured out yet how to control them?"

Roderick leaned back against the couch. "I'll give you ten million to build your camp and buy equipment clear and free. It won't be a loan. It's a gift."

A gift, as long as Alastair went along with his father's demands. Alastair didn't answer right away. He knew his father wanted the Slayer children found and trained as much as Alastair wanted it, more maybe. Avenging Nathan's death wouldn't be complete until Overdrake was defeated.

"I could go to the government for funding," Alastair said, attempting to force himself into a better bargaining spot. "They might help me."

Roderick only shook his head. "You have no way to prove anything to the government. Dragons and dragon lords—they'll think you're crazy. Probably put you on one of those watch lists so you're frisked every time you go to an airport."

A silence stretched out between them. Alastair looked at the ceiling then back at his father in aggravation. "It will take years to train the children. They'll trust me. They'll depend on me. How am I supposed to tell them I'm sending them into a fight that I won't let my daughter go to?"

"So don't tell them," Roderick said. "When the time comes, Bess can call in sick."

"And what will Bess think of me for making this sort of deal?"

Roderick pulled his phone from his breast pocket. "I don't care what she thinks as long as she's alive." He tapped his phone screen. "Give me your bank account number, and I'll have the funds to you by Monday."

Ten million dollars. Alastair could buy the land within the week and start the zoning process. And would it really be such a bad thing to keep Bess out of the fight? Wasn't a part of him already breathing a sigh of relief at the thought?

"Well?" his father asked. "Do we have a deal?"

Alastair thought of the stacks of bids and lists of expenses sitting on the table. What other choice did he have? If he depended on outside financing, maybe the camp would never get off the ground. Wasn't it better to assure that the rest of the Slayers were trained to fight instead of standing on principle and having none be trained at all?

Alastair nodded at his father. "All right." A part of him felt like he had sold out, that he had compromised himself. Another part felt a reprieve had been granted. Bess wasn't allowed to fight. He wouldn't lose her the way he'd lost his brother.

Alastair would just have to come up with a way to tell her about this stipulation before the battle began.

CHAPTER 1

Tori put a stack of *Hampton Means Leadership* flyers into a box, only half seeing them. She and her sister Aprilynne were at their house with a few people from their father's office putting together campaign kits for volunteers. Aprilynne was the one running the show. Even at nineteen years old, she had no problem ordering staff members around. She was poised, beautiful, and blonde—a younger version of their mother.

Tori worked mechanically. It was hard to keep her mind on mundane things like packing door hangers when Aaron was in danger—danger that she had put him in.

He was only twelve. So many things could go wrong with their plan to have him work as a mole. What would Overdrake do if he suspected Aaron's intentions? Beat him? Threaten his family? Or perhaps Overdrake would act with more finesse. He'd undoubtedly try to convince Aaron that his upcoming attacks on America were warranted, just like he'd convinced Dirk.

Tori grabbed a stack of Hampton T-shirts, dropped them in the box, then checked her phone. She half hoped Aaron would text her that he'd changed his mind and hadn't gone to the Renaissance Festival after all.

No new messages.

"Is someone missing in action?" Aprilynne asked as she brought a stack of empty boxes to the dining room table where Tori stood.

"What?" For one shocked second Tori wondered how her sister knew about Aaron.

Aprilynne set the boxes down. "Jesse," she said. "You've been checking your phone every five minutes and have been in a bad mood since you got home."

Tori had been at a journalism project with Jesse that morning. The reminder of their conversation made her heart squeeze painfully. "Yeah...he's angry with me." It was the truth, and talking about him was easier than coming up with a different reason for her anxiousness.

"Because?" Aprilynne opened up one of the boxes and began filling it.

Tori and Aprilynne stood apart from the rest of their father's staff, but Tori still kept her voice low. "I saw an ex last night. I mean, it wasn't a planned date or anything, but we ended up hanging out, and um..." She had no way to explain that she'd kissed Dirk in hopes of getting information about the dragons from him.

"What happened at the 'and um' part?" Aprilynne counted out yard signs for her box and placed some inside. "Because Jesse has no reason to be upset just because you talked to an ex."

"I kind of let Dirk kiss me."

"Oh," Aprilynne said. "In that case, yeah, I see Jesse's point."

Tori closed her box and ran tape across the flaps. "I wasn't cheating on him. I wouldn't have told him about it if I had."

Aprilynne blinked at Tori in disbelief. "You told Jesse you kissed another guy? How did you expect him to react?"

Not as strongly as he'd reacted. "I wanted to explain what happened. I was trying to be honest and come clean." Wasn't that the right thing to do? She'd thought so at the time. "But Jesse wouldn't accept my apology and I don't know how to make things right." She glanced at her phone again. No word from Aaron or Jesse.

"First off," Aprilynne said, "this isn't something you can fix with a few texts. You need to talk to him in person." She gazed around at the other staffers who were all busy either filling boxes or carrying them outside to a truck. "Go to Jesse's house and apologize again. Sincerely and a lot. This is also a good time to employ feminine charms. If Mom comes by to check on us and asks where you are, I'll cover for you."

Tori slid the box on the floor and picked up an empty one. "I can't. I don't know where he lives, and his address isn't listed." It wasn't listed because Dr. B had moved the family and given them new identities.

"You've never been to your boyfriend's house?" Aprilynne asked in surprise.

Tori shrugged. "His mother teaches at my school. It would be weird going to his house."

"Not any weirder than him coming to our house." Their house was frequented by an assortment of bodyguards.

"Which is why Jesse has never come to our house," Tori said.

"What's his mom's name?"

Tori counted out yard signs for the next box. "Ms. Richardson. You didn't have her. She's new this year."

Aprilynne went to Veritas Academy's website on her phone. "Laura Richardson." She examined the faculty photo. "She looks nice enough."

"Obviously the result of Photoshop. She's cold, prickly and doesn't like Republicans."

"In that case you'd better change out of your vote-for-my-dad T-shirt before you show up on Jesse's doorstep." Aprilynne began texting someone. "I bet I can find her address. The school must have that information."

"You don't need to look for it," Tori said.

The Slayers weren't supposed to know one another's personal information. That way, if any of them were captured by Overdrake, they wouldn't be able to divulge anything. Tori and Jesse had already broken the rules by exchanging phone numbers. She didn't want to know his address too.

Aprilynne kept texting. "You'll feel better after you talk to him."

Tori went back to filling boxes. She shouldn't worry about Aprilynne's sources. Her sister wouldn't be able to come up with much information about a fake name and the school wouldn't give out personal details about the staff.

After Tori finished her box, a message from Dr. B appeared on her Slayer watch.

Her mouth went dry. Even before she opened the text, she knew it was about Aaron. Time to face the music and hope it wasn't a funeral dirge.

Aaron has disappeared. He went to the fair to sell a scale and may have had problems with a dealer, a customer, or Overdrake. Bianca has notified the local police but he hasn't been gone long enough to worry them. She'll keep me posted.

Tori read and then reread the message. Overdrake must have Aaron. Why didn't Bianca already understand what his disappearance meant? Had she missed the note Aaron left her? But no, she must have read it or she wouldn't know his cover—that he'd gone to sell a scale.

Tori taped up the box and set it on a stack with others, trying to make sense of the situation.

Another message from Dr. B lit up her watch. This one sent only to her. *Any possibility you could go to North Carolina with me? Your skill as a counterpart may be able to help locate Aaron.*

Counterparts could sense each other if they were within a few dozen yards and Tori was counterparts with both Dirk and Aaron. The skill wouldn't be much help in this case. Aaron was long gone from the fairgrounds.

It's a slim hope, Dr. B went on, *but Bianca is distraught and it's all I have to offer her. She's worried someone knifed Aaron, stole the scale, and now he's lying in a ditch somewhere.*

A tight ball of recrimination formed in Tori's stomach. Bianca didn't know what Aaron had done. Was it possible he hadn't been clear in his note?

Tori needed to talk to Dr. B in private. She picked up her phone, held the screen so Aprilynne couldn't see it, and pretended to read a text. "Jesse wants me to call him. I'm going to head to my room for a minute."

"You're better off talking to him in person," Aprilynne called after her.

As soon as Tori reached her bedroom, she called Dr. B on her watch phone.

He answered immediately. "If you can go, I'll have the jet ready by the time you reach the airport."

She'd known she would eventually have to tell Dr. B what she'd done, but his worry for Aaron made the truth harder to admit. She took a deep breath and pushed her words out. "I'm pretty sure Aaron is with Overdrake. At least, that's where he meant to go. He was supposed to explain everything in a note to Bianca."

"Wait," Dr. B said, confused. "Aaron didn't say anything about going to his father. Quite the contrary. And how do you know where he meant to go? Did he contact you?"

"Yes. He got a hold of me through my father's office." Why hadn't Aaron explained things to his mother? Had he changed his mind about what he was doing? "What did his note say?"

"I've got a scan of it. Hold on." A few moments later, Dr. B read, "I'm going to find a buyer for the scales. I've got to do it to protect our family. I don't want to leave any evidence in the house that could let Overdrake know the truth about me."

Tori rubbed her forehead in frustration. She'd given Aaron one stipulation—that he tell his mother he'd decided to work as a mole—and he hadn't done it. The last sentence of his note was most likely written for Tori, not Bianca. Aaron had told her in a roundabout way that he wasn't giving his mother an explanation because he didn't want to leave any evidence that Overdrake could find.

Whatever his reasoning, he'd left Tori to break the news to Dr. B and his mother.

"What did he tell you he was doing?" Dr. B repeated, an uncharacteristic sharpness in his voice.

"We had a plan. His plan, actually. He said he'd go to Overdrake by himself if I didn't help him."

Perhaps it was cowardly of Tori to emphasize how little choice Aaron had given her, but she wanted to let Dr. B know she hadn't forced him to offer himself up. "You have to understand—Aaron grew up hearing stories about your brother, about how Nathan was drawn to the dragons on St. Helena, and Overdrake's father killed him because of it. Aaron is afraid that when Overdrake attacks, the same thing will happen to his brother."

Aaron had inherited both dragon lord and Slayer genes, but his eleven-year-old half brother Jacob was only a Slayer. And therefore a potential threat to dragons.

"Aaron asked me to leak his location so Overdrake would come for him. He's going to pass information to me."

Since Tori didn't know which dragon she was connected to, Aaron would have to repeat any information he got to all four dragons. It was by no means a foolproof system but it was better than nothing.

Dr. B's voice came through her watch, crisp with judgment. "You sent a twelve-year-old to spy on a ruthless tyrant? What sort of information do you think Overdrake would give a child? The name of his government contacts? His battle plans?" Dr. B had never yelled at Tori before. She'd always thought the man was made of solid patience. His anger, although not loud, cut twice as deep.

"No," she said quietly, "but Aaron was determined to go and he might be able to give us important information—like Overdrake's location. Overdrake will train him to be a dragon lord, so eventually he'll have access to the dragons. When he does, he'll be able to pass along information about how to control them. Isn't that worth something?"

Dr. B didn't answer. He was either considering her point or was too furious to form words.

Tori paced across her room. "Both times when we fought dragons, luck saved us as much as skill—that, and

Dirk's help. Next time, we might not have either. But if I can control a dragon, or even if I can break Overdrake's control of one for a little while, that might be the difference between life and death for all of us. So yes, I thought sending Aaron to Overdrake's was worth the risk. Tell Bianca I'm sorry."

"I won't tell her that." Dr. B voice was mostly controlled again, his temper back in check. "At this point, telling her the truth will only further wound her. She can't know that Aaron chose to leave her because he thought her so incapable of protecting Jacob, he decided to take on Overdrake himself."

Guilt twisted through Tori. "Aaron didn't want to hurt her. I can reassure Bianca of that."

"You'll do no such thing. We need her as an ally and right now she trusts us. I won't ruin that by making her think we're willing to sacrifice her children to our cause. I'll tell her we have reason to believe that Overdrake has Aaron and promise that as soon as we have more information about him, I'll call her."

"Okay," Tori said. Even Dr. B seemed to be insisting that honesty wasn't always the best policy, or at least not the best strategy. "I'll let you know when I hear anything from Aaron." It was a small offering but it was all she had.

"Your actions in this affair," Dr. B continued, "are unacceptable, to say the least."

Tori sank down onto her window seat, leaning against a row of pillows there. "I only—"

Dr. B didn't let her finish. "Not because you helped Aaron enact this plan, but because you did so without any consultation from the rest of the Slayers. Sending Aaron in may prove to be a valuable strategy, but you shouldn't make far-reaching decisions without any debate or vote.

Doing away with democracy is Overdrake's plan, not ours."

That stung. Granted, Dr. B always made the Slayers discuss any important mission beforehand, but he'd also taught her that being a captain meant that sometimes you had to make hard decisions alone. That's what she'd done this time. "I didn't tell the other Slayers because they're predisposed to distrust dragon lords. Jesse doesn't want me to even try to learn how to control dragons." It was one of the things they'd fought about this morning. "The Slayers refuse to see the potential of training Aaron."

"And you refuse to see the danger. Twelve-year-olds are impressionable and easily influenced. What if Overdrake converts Aaron to his side? If Dirk and Aaron both help their father during an attack, we'll have to simultaneously fight three dragons. What will our chances be then?"

She didn't answer. As it was, they hardly had a chance against two.

"Captains can't function without the trust of their team and I'm afraid this bit of subterfuge will cost you the other Slayers' trust. You've left me no choice but to put you on probation."

The words clanged in Tori's ears. Her fight with Jesse and her worry about Aaron had made her overly emotional. Otherwise, tears wouldn't have sprung to her eyes. Probation meant she'd be temporarily demoted from being A-Team's captain, not kicked off the team. Still, hot tears spilled onto her cheeks. She felt as though Dr. B had told her he no longer liked her and doubted the Slayers would either.

"Ryker will be captain until I reassess the matter," he said. Ryker was the other flyer on A-team. He'd only been with the Slayers since Halloween, less than a month.

Tori's voice lodged halfway in her throat, making it hard to speak. "I understand."

Dr. B said his goodbyes and Tori slumped against the back of the window seat, exhausted.

It was stupid to feel so hurt. She hadn't wanted to be a captain in the first place, but having the position taken away from her as a punishment made her feel small and breakable and completely wrong about everything she'd done. She kept trying to do the right thing, so why did everything seem to turn out horrible?

Aprilynne peeked her head into the room, then came over and sat next to Tori. "I take it the conversation with Jesse didn't go well?"

"No." Another lie. For someone who'd always prided herself on her honesty, she'd become nothing but an assortment of untruths.

Aprilynne put her arm around Tori's shoulder. "I told you that you should have talked to him in person."

Tori nodded.

"We'll find a way to fix things," Aprilynne said reassuringly.

Hopefully her sister was right about that. Surely after Jesse's anger simmered down, he'd realize she'd been acting with good motives. He'd realize that the two of them belonged together. They'd gone through so much—meant so much to one another. He couldn't really want to throw everything away because of a few strategic kisses.

Tori leaned against her sister and shut her eyes. She enlarged her dragon hearing as far as it could go, hoping to hear Aaron's voice in the background, some reassurance that he was okay. All she heard was the slow rattle of the dragon's breath.

Where was Aaron right now?

CHAPTER 2

When Aaron woke up, he lay on the floor of a small living room, one that vibrated with a loud hum. He sat up quickly, heart racing. His head felt like it weighed ten pounds. He shook it, trying to clear his mind. Part of his brain was screaming at him to get up and run. He'd meant to meet his father and go with him—but not like this. He hadn't planned on being drugged and kidnapped.

As his vision focused, he realized he wasn't in a living room. He was on an airplane, a moving one. Not the sort of commercial plane he'd flown on before. A smaller private jet.

The oversized chairs and coffee table were bolted to the ground. Dirk sat in one of them, a calculus book open in his lap. It was odd to see Dirk—and not just because he was the older brother his mother had always spoken about with so much wistful reverence that the guy might have been a mythological being instead of a person. It was odd because everyone had told Aaron how much he looked like Dirk.

They had the same blond hair, blue eyes, and their features were similar enough that Tori and Dr. B had pegged them for brothers as soon as they'd met Aaron. Dirk was taller with broader shoulders and a squarer jaw, but that was because his brother was almost eighteen.

When Aaron reached the same age, he'd probably have those things too.

Maybe everyone was right. Maybe looking at Dirk was like looking at his own future.

Dirk only gave Aaron a passing glance, then went back to writing equations in a notebook next to his calculus book. Somehow seeing him calmly do math problems bothered Aaron. If you were going to kidnap someone, you shouldn't do something as normal as homework while it was happening.

"You're awake," a voice behind him said. "Good."

Aaron turned and noted Brant Overdrake sitting on a couch. Aaron had seen pictures of his father taken when his parents had still been married. His dark hair was streaked with gray, and he had more wrinkles around his brown eyes, but other than that, he hadn't changed much. He was tall, fit, and stern-looking. The sort of person who could dissect you with a gaze.

Overdrake eyed Aaron with smug approval. "It's hard to keep a dragon lord drugged for long. We have a resistance to drugs. The fact that you're up already is a piece of proof that you're my son. Although we'll need to go to my compound to see for certain." Overdrake gestured to the seat next to Dirk's, inviting him to sit. "Your mother told you about me, I assume. You know who I am?"

Aaron got to his feet, still feeling clumsy and tired from the drug. He slumped into one of the leather chairs. "Yeah, you're Brant Overdrake." Aaron brushed his hand against his pocket, checking for his phone. Gone. "Where is my phone?"

"In a safe place."

Aaron kept his voice even. No point in losing his temper. "Can I have it?"

"Later. How is Bianca these days?"

He sounded so polite, so civilized. It was hard to believe this was the guy who'd had men chase him down and sedate him. "Why did you drug me and where are you taking me?"

"Didn't I make that clear? I'm sorry. You'll be going to my home for a paternity test. You resemble Dirk, true, but for all I know you could be some look-alike the Slayers found so they could try and track me."

Aaron rubbed his forehead. "Dude, they sell paternity tests at Walmart. You don't have to fly me anywhere."

Overdrake picked up a glass from a cup holder and took a casual drink. "I drugged you because you ran away. Which, I assumed meant you knew I wanted to talk with you but you weren't willing to come with me peacefully. Sometimes parents have to use force with their children. You understand that." He said this as though drugging and kidnapping him was the same as sending a five-year-old to his room. "Besides, if you happen to be a Slayer, drugging you will have taken away your powers and a chunk of your memory."

Aaron had heard the story of how his grandfather drugged a Slayer to take away his powers and had ended up killing the kid. And now his own father had drugged him? The thought made him feel sick.

"Are you looking at me blankly," Overdrake drawled, "because you've forgotten everything you knew about Slayers?"

Had he forgotten things? He was part Slayer so the drug might have affected his brain. He remembered making plans with Tori. But he'd done that as a dragon lord. Maybe other parts of his memory had just been wiped clean. How would he know?

Overdrake swirled the liquid in his glass. "You do know what a Slayer is, don't you?"

"Yeah," Aaron said. "Mom told me about them. They're people programmed to kill dragons and fight dragon lords."

"You ran into some at the Renaissance Fair?" Overdrake prompted.

Dangerous ground. Aaron had already worked out his story and he wouldn't even have to lie much about what had happened, but he still had to worry about slipping up. "The Slayers didn't run into me. They attacked me because they thought I was one of your men." He didn't have to fake the irritation in his voice. He was still ticked they invaded his house and scared him and his mom half to death. His home hadn't felt safe since.

"And Tori was one of them?" Overdrake asked.

"They didn't give me their names." Aaron said the words as though the question was ridiculous—which it was. Tori hadn't given him that sort of information. He'd figured out who she was afterward. "I don't remember how many Slayers there were," he went on, steering the subject away from her. "Five, maybe. They wore helmets so I couldn't see their faces. They wanted information about you and the dragons. After they realized I couldn't tell them anything, they didn't stick around long."

"Did they hurt you?" Overdrake asked.

"They grabbed me and threatened me." He paused. "It doesn't sound like a big deal, but it was."

A muscle pulsed in Overdrake's cheek. "I believe you. For all of their supposed ideals, they're willing to break the law or intimidate others when it suits their purpose." He set his glass into the holder and laced his fingers together. "Tell me, what are your feelings toward them?"

Aaron let out a disbelieving cough. Was he serious? "My feelings about the nameless, faceless guys that attacked me? Uh, I'd have to say anger and fear." He'd felt enough of both emotions during the attack. "Slayers are dangerous and I want them to leave me and my family alone." Especially Jacob. He didn't want them ever recruiting his brother.

Overdrake's gaze went to Dirk. Aaron hadn't thought Overdrake cared about Dirk's opinion on the conversation. His brother had hardly acted like he was paying attention, but he nodded in approval before returning to his homework. Whatever he was doing, it required lots of numbers.

Overdrake leaned back in his chair, more relaxed. "I'm glad Bianca warned you about the Slayers and things didn't turn out worse. What did she tell you about me?"

Aaron ran his hand along the chair's arms, thinking over what to say. "She doesn't talk about you much. She told me you had dragons and you were going to use them to take over the government. She didn't want me to be a part of it, so that's why she left when she was pregnant with me."

The bottom half of Dirk's pencil snapped in two like he'd been pressing it too hard. Dirk flicked the broken half away and reached into a backpack for another.

"Did your mother teach you about dragons?" Overdrake asked.

"She told me some things, but I didn't pay much attention. It's not like I've ever run into one."

Overdrake picked up his glass again. "No, she made sure you wouldn't. She stole you from me and tried to keep you from your heritage." He smiled at Aaron. "We'll set that right."

Aaron shifted uncomfortably in his seat. *Keep calm,* he told himself. *You wanted this.* But it was hard not to be freaked out. Before, when he'd thought about contacting his father, it had always been a choice, something he could back out of if he wanted. Now that option was gone. "Did you tell my mom you were taking me?" he asked. That's what any normal kid would ask in this situation. "She's going to freak out if I just disappear."

"She disappeared with you thirteen years ago," Overdrake said, taking a drink. "You know what they say, turnabout is fair play."

"She'll call the police and tell them you kidnapped me."

Overdrake waved his hand, dismissing the protest. "This isn't a kidnapping, it's a custody dispute. They happen every day in America and the police don't do much about them. Really, considering she denied me custody for twelve years, I think my turn with you is long overdue."

"You didn't let her see Dirk," Aaron pointed out. That got his brother's attention. Dirk's posture stiffened and he frowned. He didn't look up, though. He was concentrating firmly on his equations.

"It was unfortunate but necessary," Overdrake said. "Bianca knew when we married that I needed sons to help me. You can't imagine how upset it makes me to know she's hidden you away from me all this time. And, no doubt, she's told you horrible things about me."

For the first time, Aaron wondered if his mother had lied to him about his father. "You're not going to use the dragons to attack cities?"

"See, this is exactly what I mean. She's poisoned you against me. I'm going to use the dragons to set cities free."

Uh huh. "Does setting them free involve burning things and killing people?"

Overdrake laughed. "Is that the sort of person you think I am? Someone who enjoys destroying things?" He shook his head. "A leader builds things, not destroys them."

What did he mean by that? "So you're not going to attack with the dragons?"

Overdrake sighed as if Aaron was a little kid asking whether Santa was real. "This is what you need to know. I plan on building a great future for this country. Think of me as an architect with blueprints for an amazing palace. Whenever a builder creates a new structure, he needs to clear the ground first. Get rid of the rubble and weeds. Things that shouldn't be there to begin with. Clearing them takes work and effort, but what he builds is so much better, it's worth the effort. Do you understand?"

Not really. But Aaron suspected that the answer to his earlier question was: yes, Overdrake did plan on using the dragons to attack. Aaron nodded uncertainly.

"Good," Overdrake said, "Now tell me about yourself. I assume you play sports."

Aaron didn't just play sports, he was the best athlete in his grade. "Yeah. Football, basketball, and some soccer."

Overdrake nodded as though he expected as much. "Dirk's always been varsity. Your grades?"

"As and Bs." More Bs than his mother liked. She wanted him to get straight As.

"Where do you live?"

Aaron tried not to swallow. Swallowing would make him look guilty. "Charleston." His family had vacationed there enough times that he could fake it. No way was he going to tell Overdrake his real address. "You're going to give me my phone so I can call my mom, right?"

"I'll let her know you're safe. Did she ever remarry?"

"No. She's single." It was partly true. She and Wesley, his stepdad, were separated. Aaron didn't want Overdrake to consider that she might have any Slayer children.

"Really?" he asked. "I always imagined she would remarry quickly."

Aaron swallowed despite his best efforts not to. She'd married Wesley not long after Aaron was born.

Overdrake didn't seem to notice his discomfort, or at least didn't press the subject. Instead he spent the next twenty minutes asking about Aaron's hobbies, his school, and bits of his life.

Aaron answered them carefully, making sure not to accidentally give information about his mom or brother.

After the plane landed, Overdrake turned to Dirk. "So, was he lying about anything?"

Aaron froze. Tori had said counterparts could sometimes tell when the other was lying, but Aaron had assumed he would have to be talking to Dirk for him to detect a lie. But maybe that wasn't the case. Earlier, when Aaron was talking about meeting the Slayers, he hadn't told any lies. He'd just left out a lot of the truth. The look that Overdrake had shot Dirk—he'd been asking if Aaron had answered honestly. Dirk had nodded in reply.

Would Dirk know he'd lied about their mother remarrying? If he did, he might figure out why. And his address—he'd lied about that too.

Dirk picked up his homework. "As far as I could tell, the kid was telling the truth."

Overdrake smiled, happy with that piece of news.

Aaron just stared at his brother because he could tell Dirk was lying. Somehow he felt the dishonesty as strongly as if he'd been the one uttering the words. This was both good and bad news. Good news, because Dirk didn't rat him out. Bad news, because it was apparently a lot easier to tell when a counterpart lied than Aaron had hoped.

***

Overdrake blindfolded Aaron before he led him off the plane. Aaron remained blindfolded for a car ride that must have been at least an hour long. He didn't know whether to be worried or to think all the cloak and dagger stuff was lame. He wasn't allowed to take off the blindfold even after Overdrake led him out of the car. They walked down an uneven path for ten minutes, maybe more. Then they went into a building, climbed down several flights of stairs, and walked through a hallway.

It didn't matter how many times Aaron asked, "Where are you taking me?"

Overdrake always answered in a variation of, "You'll see when you get there."

Aaron didn't see though, he smelled it: something like old car parts. A door opened, Overdrake towed him through it, and then the door shut with a loud metallic clang. Were they in some sort of mechanic's shop? Aaron's adrenaline spiked. Something felt wrong, ominous.

"This," Overdrake said, "Is where we'll administer your paternity test." Finally, he took off the blindfold.

They stood in some sort of dimly lit cave. It was several stories high and as wide as three or four basketball courts. It had the echoing feel of a basketball court too. A pond sat by an outcropping of boulders with a hill of boulders behind that. Smaller boulders lay near Aaron's feet. The odd thing about the cave was that they'd come through a door to get here. Weirdest place ever. Creepy. Dirk and Overdrake stood beside Aaron, looking bored.

"Can you see?" Overdrake asked him.

"What am I supposed to see?" Aaron asked.

Overdrake grunted like he wasn't pleased with the answer.

And then Aaron saw that the black shape he'd thought was a hill of boulders wasn't rock at all. It was alive and moving toward them. A huge, slinking beast. Aaron took a step backward, almost tripping over his own feet. "Is that a dragon?"

"It is," Overdrake said, his voice sounding pleased again. "Meet Khan. He'll most likely kill you if you can't protect yourself, so you have three options." He pointed to a small opening in the ceiling of the cave wall. "You can fly up there and hide, you can go into the dragon's mind and control it, or you can pick up those rocks at your side and use them as weapons."

Aaron took another step backward. "Are you insane?" He should never have come here; should have never told Tori he'd do this.

"If you're my son, the dragon's fire won't hurt you. If you're an imposter, well, you'll die. But you'll have learned an important lesson before you do, which is that you shouldn't impersonate someone."

The man *was* insane. He was standing there calmly talking about the dragon frying him like this was all some game that didn't mean anything.

Why did Aaron have to prove himself? He hadn't come to Overdrake claiming to be his son. The man had kidnapped him from the fair and brought him here. Aaron wanted to yell at Overdrake, but Khan was coming closer. He needed a plan. He needed to *do* something—fight or hide.

But all Aaron could manage was to stand motionless, gawking at the dragon. With its dark scales, it looked like a shadow that had come to life, some sort of inky nightmare. The thing was so huge it could have easily ripped an elephant apart. It lifted its long neck, glared at him with a pair of golden eyes, and growled, showing rows of dagger-like teeth.

Aaron didn't know how to fly or control a dragon. The boulders to his side were the size of large ice coolers. Too heavy for him to normally pick up, but he must have his dragon lord strength now. The dragon was closer than five miles—it was almost closer than five yards. Aaron hefted up the corner of a boulder, and it lifted into his hands as easily as a pillow. He held it over his head, stepped into the throw, and launched it at Khan's throat.

The dragon dodged easily enough and in return, shot a blast of fire in Aaron's direction. Long churning flames. Instinct made him leap sideways, a motion that took him higher and farther than he'd planned. When he landed, he was a good fifteen feet away from the boulders, his only weapons.

A stupid move. He searched around for something else to throw. There wasn't anything. He'd have to leap back there.

Fly, he told himself *Fly!*

Nothing happened. His feet didn't leave the ground.

The dragon turned and took a threatening step in his direction.

Overdrake held up his hand. "Enough," he said, and the dragon halted. Within the span of a few seconds, it went from attack stance to calmly sitting, eyes half shut.

Overdrake clicked something on a remote and the lights in the cave brightened. "You passed your test. You do indeed have powers when you're near a dragon. Although I must mention that of the three options I gave you, attacking a dragon is the most foolish one. But then, we have plenty of time to work on your education."

Aaron planted his hands on his hips, his breaths coming out fast. "You call this a test? Hey, I'll tell you what you can do with your education." He then spat every swear word he knew at his father. He was still shaking from the fear and adrenaline and his heart felt like it was about to hammer its way through his chest.

Overdrake shook his head. "You'll need to work on your temper. I don't stand for that sort of disrespect from my sons."

"I could have been killed!" Aaron yelled and added a few more swear words.

Dirk rose a half a foot into the air and glided over. It was weird seeing him levitating off the ground that way. He took hold of Aaron's arm and pulled him toward the door they'd come in. "I'll show Aaron around and take him to his room."

The door was steel and looked like something that belonged in a prison, but Dirk opened it easily enough. Aaron was still cursing when Dirk dragged him out into the hallway and shut the door behind them.

"Calm down," Dirk said, landing on the ground again. "You were never in any danger. My father had control of the dragon the whole time."

"It shot fire at me!" Aaron shook off Dirk's grip. He could do that now that he had extra strength. "If I wasn't a dragon lord, I would have been burned alive. What sort of psycho test is that?"

"Khan only shot fire at you after you'd thrown the boulder. By that point, it was clear you were legit, and dragon lords don't burn." Dirk motioned for Aaron to follow him down the hall.

Aaron didn't really have a choice. He didn't want to be standing in the hallway when Overdrake came out. He grudgingly followed Dirk. "He's crazy, isn't he? Like, legitimately mental."

"No," Dirk said. "He just likes to make a point. And the point he was making today is that he's in charge and there are consequences for anyone who crosses him. Once you've learned that lesson, everything will be much smoother." Dirk said the words like they didn't bother him. "Oh, and by the way—welcome home."

Home. They both knew this wasn't his home. Aaron wasn't sure if Dirk was trying to be friendly or just ironic.

They kept walking down the hall, their footsteps clanging on the floor.

"Back at the fair," Aaron said, "when you saw me, you told me to run. Why?"

Dirk looked unruffled by the question, but his voice had a note of bitterness. "Because my mother gave me up in order to protect you—in order to keep you from being trained as a dragon lord." He opened a door and went up a stairwell. "Seemed like a shame to have that sacrifice be for nothing."

Aaron let out a sharp breath and followed after Dirk. He suddenly felt like he'd betrayed his mom, done something horribly wrong.

Instead of walking, Dirk lifted off the ground and flew over the steps. Aaron leaped up a few stairs, bumped into the stairwell, did the same thing at the next bend, and gave up the idea of using his powers to shorten the climb. He trudged up them the normal way.

Dirk checked over his shoulder to see if Aaron was keeping up, saw he wasn't, and waited for him. "Don't look so depressed," he said. "Being a dragon lord isn't a bad thing. You'll get the hang of leaping eventually. Plus you'll get to control dragons and fly."

Aaron kept trudging up the steps. "Is this like good cop/bad cop, and you're the good cop?"

Dirk chuckled, then stopped himself. "Sorry for laughing. I've just never thought of myself as the good cop sort." He landed on the steps beside Aaron and resumed climbing the stairs with him. "You'll be staying at the dragon enclosure for a while. Once my dad," he paused amending the term. "Once our dad feels he can trust you, you'll move in with the rest of the family at the house."

"Who's the rest of the family?"

"Cassie is our stepmother. Bridget, our half sister, is seven, and we've got a baby brother on the way. How about your family? Do I have any half siblings there?"

Aaron didn't answer the question. He didn't want to tell the truth and worried Dirk would be able to tell if he lied. He glanced around the stairwell. Cinderblocks lined the walls. The whole place had the atmosphere of a penitentiary. The sooner he figured out exactly how things were going to work here, the better. "How are you going to keep me from leaving? Is someone going to be guarding my room?"

Dirk shook his head. "You've already forgotten the point of today's lesson. Dad is in charge and if you cross him, there will be consequences."

"So he'll hurt me if I try to escape?"

"You're too valuable for that. He'll find other ways."

"What do you mean?"

Dirk scoffed. "Do you have to ask? Look, I'm ticked at my mom for leaving me when I was a kid. I won't pretend I'm not. But that doesn't mean I want to see her hurt. So do both of us a favor and don't give our father any reasons to track her down to make his point in a bigger way, okay?"

Aaron's stomach lurched and a feeling of dread pressed into him. He held his chin steady, though. He didn't like being threatened. "He won't be able to find her."

"Please. He's got your cell phone with her number in it. Do you think he can't figure out a way to get to her? He's probably already noticed that none of your contacts have South Carolina area codes. Where are you really from, North Carolina?"

Aaron didn't answer, just grit his teeth and followed Dirk down the hallway. He should've thought to erase his contacts.

Dirk exhaled slowly, and Aaron could feel his sympathy mixed with concern. "None of this will be as bad as it seems right now. I'll give you some advice for dealing with Dad. Don't bother fighting him. He'll make sure he wins. The best way to sway him is to bargain. What do you want—well, besides a new dad and a plane ticket home?"

"I want to call Mom."

"Okay. So tell Dad you're willing to stay as long as you get to call home once a week and he buys you a Ferrari."

"I'm twelve. I can't drive."

"That doesn't matter. Ask for a car anyway. He'll buy one for you because he understands people who can be bought. It's the ones that can't who make him nervous."

A Ferrari would be cool. "Any other advice?"

Dirk glanced over at him with a sad smile. "Yeah, next time I tell you to run, make sure you do."

That advice had come too late. Aaron swept a hand along the cement walls. How far below the surface were they? This whole place made him feel claustrophobic.

They reached a metal door. Dirk opened it and motioned for Aaron to go inside.

Instead of cement, the walls were a dull gray metal that blurred his reflection. A simple bed, dresser, and desk sat in the room. No windows. Amazing how much a bedroom looked like a cell when it didn't have sunlight. An alarm clock perched on the dresser and small TV hung on the far wall. A doorway stood in the back. A bathroom?

"This is where you'll live until we decide we can trust you." Dirk pointed out a plate of food on the desk: a sandwich, chips, apple, and a bottled water. "Cassie left some stuff for you in case you're hungry. Don't stay up too late. Dad believes in being an early riser so you'll start training at seven every morning."

"Is there some reason all the walls are metal?"

"They'll keep the dragon signal from reaching you so your powers will wear off. Otherwise you'd have too much energy to sleep."

The metal walls probably also made the place harder to break out of. Real cozy.

Aaron wandered over to the bed. A crayon drawing lay on his pillow.

"That's a welcome gift from Bridget," Dirk said. "A self-portrait."

Dirk had told Aaron that they had a little sister, but she hadn't seemed real until now. He had no idea how to treat sisters or seven-year-olds. Did they cry easily? Throw temper tantrums?

Aaron picked up the drawing. It showed a dark-haired girl smiling and reaching her stick figure arms up into the air. *To Aaron* was written on the top. "Is she doing yoga or surrendering?"

"She's reaching out to hug you."

"Oh. Good." Aaron looked around the room again. "I wasn't sure what the norm for your family was. Glad yoga's not expected."

Dirk laughed and shook his head. "I can tell you're a lot like me, which means we'll probably get along." He put his hand on Aaron's shoulder. It was a friendly gesture until he fixed him with a penetrating gaze. "But I need to tell you one more thing. If you ever do anything to hurt Bridget, I'll know, and I'll make you suffer."

Aaron dropped the picture back on the bed and stepped away from Dirk's grip. "Give me a break. I wouldn't hurt a little kid. What sort of person do you think I am?"

"I think you're fine which is why I'm willing to let you go near Bridget." Dirk paused as though realizing he'd forgotten something. "I should have clarified that the last message was Cassie's that she wanted me to pass on to you." He shrugged in apology. "She's pregnant so she goes through frequent periods of hormonal snippiness." Dirk casually slipped his hands into his back pockets.

"You don't want to know what I'd do to you if you hurt Bridget."

Aaron held up his hands. "I won't even talk to her."

"You'll have to talk to her. She'd be crushed if you didn't. She also loves to play Uno and Wii, so plan on getting drafted into several games a day." Dirk smiled and then walked to the door. "If she likes you, she might let you win sometimes."

CHAPTER 3

Overdrake glided from the enclosure, humming with satisfaction. Such good news. He had another son. A boy with strength, intelligence, and bravery. A boy who would grow up to be every bit as tall and handsome as Dirk. Perhaps Overdrake was foolish to take so much pride in his sons' appearance, but why not? Their good looks were more proof that he fathered superior children.

He flew across the property that separated the enclosure from his house, still humming. Later he would let himself feel the fury of Bianca's betrayal. Right now he would bask in fortune's generous gift to him. Aaron was old enough to be of real use and yet still young enough that he could be molded. And Overdrake would train him right, wouldn't make the mistakes he'd made with Dirk. Sending Dirk to the Slayer camp, for all its advantages, had been an error. Dirk's friendship with the Slayers had made him soft, soft and reluctant to do what needed to be done.

He didn't worry that Tori might have heard the scene between Aaron and Khan play out. She was linked to Vesta. He knew this because he'd checked the time stamps from Tori's messages to Dirk with the door logs at the dragon nursery. Whenever Dirk had been in the enclosures during their conversations, he was always with Vesta—even though Overdrake routinely switched Vesta's and Jupiter's locations. Hatchlings couldn't be left in the same place for too long or they became overly territorial. Overdrake had even tested his theory of Tori's connection to Vesta. He'd fed a dog to the dragon while warning Tori that if she crossed him, her family would meet the same end. Tori had heard him just fine.

Dragon lords felt the presence of whichever dragon was closest but could choose to stay linked to any dragon they were familiar with, even if that dragon flew hundreds of miles away. So whether Tori consciously knew it or not, she was choosing to stay joined to Vesta unless one of the other dragons came much nearer. Most likely, Vesta's signal was the one that turned on Tori's powers when she was a baby. She went to that dragon by default.

Still, Overdrake would take precautions while he trained Aaron. He'd limit Aaron's exposure to Vesta and only give him information outside of all the dragons' hearing.

As Overdrake went into the house, he pulled Aaron's phone from his pocket. Finding Bianca's number wasn't hard. He scrolled through the contacts until he came to Mom. By the time he sat down in his den chair, he had it memorized. He used his computer to make the call. It automatically rerouted his IP address through a dozen cities in countries around the world, making the call untraceable.

The pressures of his job were many, as were the frustrations, but being a dragon lord did have a few perks, and he planned on savoring this one: crushing your enemies.

Bianca picked up immediately. "Hello?"

"Hello Bianca," he said. "It's been a long time, hasn't it?"

She gasped and didn't speak for a moment. "Who is this?"

"It hasn't been *that* long. You recognize my voice. Don't say you don't."

"Where's Aaron?" she demanded. Even when she was upset, her voice had that melodic, feminine tone.

"He's with me, that's why I rang you up."

"Where are you?" A tone of desperation made its way into her voice. She knew, yes, she already knew she'd lost. "Let me talk to him. Please."

He leaned back in his chair. "You hid him from me. That was unwise."

"Brant, please." Her words became shaky. "We can work out some sort of arrangement. Where is he?"

Overdrake had planned on letting her grovel for several minutes before he hung up, had looked forward to it as one of the spoils of the war, but her voice pulled at his sympathy. That was his problem. He'd always had a weak spot for her. Apparently, it was still there. "He's fine. That's all you need to know."

"Don't do this," she pleaded. "You already took Dirk from me."

He gripped the armrests, leaving imprints of his anger in the fabric there. "I didn't *take* Dirk from you. You can't take something that is already rightfully yours." He ended the call with a sharp, final keystroke.

He'd done her the courtesy of letting her know where Aaron was. That was more than she'd done for him. This was so typical of the way their marriage had been—he'd always done more for her, and she'd never appreciated it. She'd never understood family loyalty. But his sons would.

CHAPTER 4

Dr. B called Tori at six on Sunday morning. She picked up her watch from her nightstand and answered it, groggy from a lack of sleep. "Yes?"

She'd already called him last evening and confirmed that Overdrake had Aaron. She'd heard it all play out in Khan's enclosure—the fear in Aaron's voice and then the anger. It felt like she'd lived it with him, not just the first time, but a dozen more times as she lay in bed trying to sleep.

Had she made the right decision to send him? Did "rightness" even matter if it ended badly? Overdrake hadn't sounded as though he trusted Aaron. Or even liked him, for that matter.

Really, what sort of parent threw a child in with a dragon and then calmly waited around to see if the child could defend himself? Was that what Overdrake had done to Dirk when he was younger?

The thought made her ache for Dirk as well as Aaron.

Dr. B's voice came over Tori's watch speaker. "Brant called Bianca last night to gloat. As you can imagine, she's quite distressed."

"I'm sorry," Tori said automatically, but then felt a pinch of anger toward Dr. B. He'd taught the Slayers how to make decisions but hadn't ever taught them how to deal with the guilt that came with those decisions. Guilt had thick, cold spikes that embedded themselves in your chest. Ones that felt as though they would never go away. Perhaps the only way to deal with them was to wait until all feeling left you, until you were hard enough inside that the spikes couldn't stab you as much.

"Bianca wants to know if you can contact Dirk and ask for his help to get Aaron back home."

If Aaron was in danger, that might be their best option. But was he? Overdrake knew he was a dragon lord now. If Aaron wasn't being harmed, it would be a shame to abort the mission before they gave it a chance to work.

Dirk might not realize Tori knew about Aaron's kidnapping. He didn't know she had any contact with Bianca, and if Tori hadn't been connected to Khan, she wouldn't have heard Overdrake take Aaron into a dragon enclosure. Perhaps it would be easier to get information from Aaron if the other dragon lords didn't know she knew his whereabouts.

So many angles to consider.

"Asking Dirk for help won't do any good," she pointed out. "He either changed his mind about involving Aaron and told his father about him, or Overdrake has a way to spy on my messages to Dirk. If the first is the case, Dirk won't help us. If the second is the case, Overdrake will see my request and make sure Dirk doesn't help us."

And Overdrake would most likely use the information to set some sort of trap for them.

"Granted," Dr. B said, "you couldn't plan anything without hearing Dirk. You'd have to make sure he was telling the truth…" Dr. B's voice drifted off in thought.

Tori waited. He didn't speak. It was unlike him to be unsure about what actions to take, unlike him not to plan out options as though life was a chess game and he'd already thought through every possible move.

Dr. B sighed. "I was on the phone with Bianca for an hour last night. She was practically hysterical. I told her I would ask for your help. I need to offer her some hope."

Spikes of guilt again. It was more important to comfort a worried mother than to hope for an advantage by pretending ignorance of Aaron's capture. "Fine, I'll message Dirk and find out how Aaron is doing. That way you'll at least be able to reassure her."

"Good. Let me know when you hear something."

Tori pushed her covers off. No point in trying to go back to sleep now. "Did you tell the other Slayers what Aaron and I did?" She'd expected to get a barrage of messages on her watch phone last night but they hadn't come. The silence was almost worse, the waiting. She'd spent half of last night wondering if the other Slayers were still speaking to her.

"I told them," he said. "They were, of course, upset that you acted without their input or consent, but on the whole, they understand your motives."

He was probably minimizing their reaction. Lilly, A-team's fire quencher, hardly trusted Tori because she was part dragon lord—and that was after Tori had fought with the Slayers and helped kill two dragons. Lilly wouldn't be happy about anything that could end up benefitting Overdrake.

"I informed them of your probation," Dr. B continued, "and emphasized that we need to move on from this incident. Infighting will destroy our team."

"You told them not to message me about it, didn't you?"

"I decided it was best if they cooled down before they spoke to you."

Oh. It was that bad. What had Jesse thought? That realization hurt the worst—that he might think less of her because of this.

Dr. B's voice softened. "They know you meant well. They're still your friends."

Hopefully he was right about that.

After Dr. B hung up, Tori pulled herself out of bed and switched on her light. Time to figure out what to write to Dirk. If she hadn't planned on Aaron being taken and then heard Overdrake threatening him in the enclosure, she'd be mad about it, outraged. She had hoped Dirk would have a nice chat with his brother, and instead, Aaron was missing and his mother was devastated.

As Tori sat down at her desk, she groaned in aggravation at herself. Last night she'd been so torn up with guilt and worry that she hadn't been thinking straight. She should have messaged Dirk right after she heard Aaron in the enclosure. That would have been her natural reaction. When she'd thought Overdrake had fed her dog to a dragon, she'd texted Dirk right away.

So she ought to pretend she hadn't heard it. But then, what explanation would she give Dirk for knowing Overdrake had Aaron?

She had to tell him something. Bianca was waiting.

Was it safe to tell Dirk that his mother had contacted Dr. B? Or would that be as good as admitting that the Slayers had talked to her?

Tori sifted through the options and implications while she opened her phone and went to the site where she messaged Dirk. A note was already there waiting.

Dirk had written some small talk about the weather getting colder and then added: *I've got a sore throat. The medicine isn't working. I'll have to try some more later.*

The last three phrases were Slayer code that meant *Don't try to talk to me. I'll contact you when we need to communicate again.*

She knew what this most likely meant. When Overdrake decided to kidnap Aaron, Dirk had figured out his father spied on the site and now he was warning Tori against using it.

Either that or Dirk had figured out that she'd sent Aaron to spy on them and he didn't want to talk to Tori again. Aaron might be worse at keeping secrets from a counterpart than Tori had hoped.

Was there anyone she knew who wasn't mad at her right now?

She stared at Dirk's words as though they would change, as though they might tell her something different. After a minute, she exited the site. Closing it seemed so final, like shutting a door to your only escape route.

She left her desk and lay back on her bed with a thud. She couldn't assure Bianca that Aaron was all right. And worse, she had no way to contact Dirk.

She hadn't realized how much that door meant to her until it had been shut.

CHAPTER 5

Aaron woke up at six fifteen, even though he hadn't set his alarm clock. Prisoners shouldn't have to set alarms. He'd planned on making that point by still being in bed at seven when training time started, but in the end, he got up. No reason to tick off Overdrake, not when he wanted to earn the man's trust.

Once Aaron's anger and fear had faded, the desire to learn about dragons became a tangible thing, an energy swirling through his brain that had kept him up long after his powers faded. Dragons were real: huge, powerful, flying beasts. And Aaron would be able to control them. Almost as cool—when dragons were nearby, he would have superhero strength and eventually be able to fly.

Who wouldn't want that? All he had to do was put up with his father's enormous ego. The man obviously had plenty of that. Aaron still couldn't believe his own father had men chase him through the Renaissance festival, drug him, and then set a dragon on him. Seriously, it was no wonder his mother left.

Aaron wanted to talk to her now, to tell her he understood why she'd never let him see his father. But he couldn't. Aaron was locked up and completely cut off from the rest of the world. No phone. No computer.

Even though he didn't want to escape, he went to the door and tried the handle. Still locked from the outside. He took a shower then rifled through the dresser for clothes. Several sizes of jeans were folded there along with an assortment of T-shirts, boxers, and socks. Whoever had stocked the thing, hadn't been sure what size he was. He got dressed, then sat on his bed and watched TV. His gaze kept going to Bridget's crayon drawing. Seemed so incongruous. His father was keeping him a prisoner, and his half sister was drawing him pictures.

At seven o'clock, with only a short knock as a warning, Dirk unlocked the door and strode in carrying a plate with eggs and bacon. Aaron's stomach flipped at the smell.

Dirk set a glass of milk on the bedside table. "Sleep well?"

"No."

Dirk handed him the plate. "Well, that doesn't matter. I still have to teach you about dragons. I'm supposed to give you safety facts while you eat. Try to pay attention so you're not killed quickly. If you die today, it will look like I have sibling rivalry issues."

Aaron picked up his fork and dug into the eggs. Waking up early had taken its toll and he was starving.

Dirk dropped into the desk chair and watched him. "I'm also supposed to report on your anger level." He cocked his head. "I'm not picking up as much hatred as I'd expected."

"I can hate you more if you want."

Dirk continued to stare at him, eyes narrowed. "Aren't you going to ask me to help you escape?"

"Nah, I've decided I want to study dragons. They're kinda cool. And eventually I'll be driving a Ferrari."

"Keeping up a brave front. Good. Dad respects that sort of thing."

"Maybe I really am brave." Aaron had meant to sound tough. It came out petulant.

Dirk just laughed. "Good. Because you'll need all the bravery you can get."

CHAPTER 6

On Monday, Tori tried to find Jesse before first period so they could talk, so she could apologize again. She'd called and texted Jesse the day before—overtures which he'd completely ignored. Perhaps she deserved his anger, but she also deserved more consideration than he was giving her.

She'd bought Jesse a stuffed donkey—a politically themed peace offering. On Saturday before she ruined things between them, he had given her a stuffed elephant.

Jesse wasn't anywhere in the hallways. No sight of his dark hair or broad shoulders anywhere. At six foot two, he was tall enough that he was hard to overlook among the sea of students. She finally had to put the donkey in her locker and go to class.

He came in late for journalism, didn't ever glance back at her, and then made a beeline for the door as soon as the bell rang. By the time she followed the crowd out of the room, he'd disappeared in the hallway.

At lunch, he sat at the table with the other basketball players, ignoring her.

How long was he planning on acting this way? Hours? Days? The school week was short due to Thanksgiving, and she didn't want to wait until the next Monday to work things out.

After school, instead of heading outside to meet Lars, her driver, she waited for Jesse by his locker. She opened her phone to a social media site, but couldn't concentrate on it. She kept scanning the crowd, kept trying to pick out his footsteps in the cacophony of others.

Finally Jesse appeared. He walked over with an air of determined nonchalance, said a curt, "Hello," then twirled his combination, keeping his attention there.

Tori slid her phone into her pocket. "I realize you're angry with me, but it would help to know whether you're angry because of Dirk or because of Aaron."

"Both." He still didn't look at her.

"I'd like to remind you, that in each situation, I was aiming for a better strategic position for all of us."

Jesse let out an incredulous huff. "The kid is twelve."

She leaned closer and lowered her voice. "You were eleven when you became a Slayer. You still knew what you were doing, didn't you?"

Jesse opened his locker with more force than the task required. "If Overdrake brainwashes Aaron like he brainwashed Dirk, we'll have to fight three dragons at the same time. You didn't think the rest of us deserved a say about that?"

"Aaron won't join Overdrake. He wants to protect his brother by helping us. I could tell that about him."

Jesse turned to her, disbelief in his brown eyes. "I'm not sure I trust your judgment when it comes to knowing what guys are like."

She decided to ignore that jab. "Overdrake has more dragons than we could ever fight. If I can learn to control them, that knowledge could save us. Isn't that worth taking some risks?"

"And what about the fact that going into a dragon's mind makes killing them harder?"

Dirk had let her use her dragon lord powers to explore Khan's mind, encouraged it even. The knowledge had cost her. "Harder doesn't mean impossible."

"Even hesitating could cost lives."

Couldn't he at least try and see her point of view? She picked up her backpack from the floor and slid the strap onto her shoulder. "When I made decisions about Aaron and about Dirk, I did what I thought was best. I'm sorry if I was wrong. Really. I am."

He considered her silently for a moment. Some of the hardness left his expression, pushed away by emotion. "Do you have feelings for Dirk?"

"He's my counterpart. Of course I have feelings for him." She cleared her throat uncomfortably. "But only counterpart feelings." Was she blushing? Why did her cheeks suddenly feel hot?

Jesse looked far from convinced. "So, you're saying you didn't enjoy kissing him?"

"No," she said too quickly. The answer was a knee-jerk denial.

"No, you didn't enjoy it, or no you can't tell me you didn't?"

"I didn't..." He was staring at her with so much scrutiny she couldn't help but flush. "I was...it was just...I mean..." She was speaking gibberish. She knew that, but she was suddenly having flashes of memory—Dirk's arms around her. And the last time she'd kissed him, she hadn't needed to. Not really. Did that mean she *had* enjoyed kissing him? "It wasn't like...it was just, I mean..." and now she was repeating the gibberish she'd already said.

Jesse folded his arms, his open locker forgotten. "That's convincing."

"It's not that simple."

"It should be."

The words stung because he was right. She still had feelings for Dirk and she shouldn't. But that didn't mean she'd been lying to Jesse about her feelings for him. It didn't mean she'd wanted any of what had happened last Friday to happen. She'd stopped Dirk at first and then only let him kiss her for strategy sake. "Jesse…"

He put up a hand to stop her. "Until you figure out what you want—who you want—the two of us should go back to being just teammates."

All of the air fled from her lungs. "You're breaking up with me?"

"No, I'm pretty sure you did that on Friday when you made out with another guy."

That wasn't fair. He couldn't mean it. "You know very well why I kissed him."

"Yeah, because you haven't decided whether you're a Slayer or a dragon lord. That's another thing that you ought to figure out."

He turned and strode away, leaving her staring after him, stunned.

He didn't think she'd decided she was a Slayer? He'd broken up with her because she'd been trying to get information from Dirk?

Okay, so maybe she had enjoyed kissing Dirk a little, but she hadn't kissed him because she wanted to cheat on Jesse. She'd done it to save lives. Could she help it if Dirk was a good kisser? Jesse should be more understanding. She could have kept the whole event a secret, but she was trying to be honest.

She pushed her way through the crowded hall, walking fast and blinking back tears. No, she wasn't going to cry about this. She would let herself be angry instead. She had new plans for the stuffed donkey in her backpack. It was going to become Brindy's next dog toy.

***

On Tuesday, Tori didn't try to talk to Jesse and he didn't talk to her. She felt as though she was walking through water. Everything felt slower and more difficult. On Wednesday, his gaze wandered to her a few times, but he always looked away before she had a chance to speak to him. In journalism, he seemed happy enough to chat with Tacy, the class's residing ultra-blonde cheerleader. He smiled at her as they talked, the sort of smile that usually just belonged to Tori.

Fine. Let him be that way.

She didn't need him. She could function just as well with half her heart torn away.

On the ride home from school, she got a text from Aprilynne with an address. Tori read it, puzzled, and then texted Aprilynne asking if she'd sent it by mistake.

It's the Richardsons' address, her sister replied. *I told you I could get someone at the school to give it to me. Now you can go see Jesse and work things out.*

No, now she could call Dr. B and tell him she'd inadvertently found out Jesse's address. If Overdrake ever captured her, his family needed to move again.

On Thursday, Tori helped her mother make Thanksgiving dinner. A nice leisurely dinner with her family would have been nice—the sort where everyone played a few card games or watched a movie afterward, but Thanksgiving was never that way at her house. A lot of the staffers and interns at her father's office didn't have family close by, so her parents always invited at least a dozen people over. And her mother prided herself on providing a home-cooked meal.

The visitors couldn't all fit at one table, so her parents dragged the kitchen table into the dining room and then Tori and Aprilynne were supposed to play hostess for all the people that hadn't managed to get seated at her parents' table. This was never fun because the guests wanted to sit near her father, so basically, Tori spent the meal trying to make small talk with a bunch of disappointed social climbers.

It wasn't like she had anything in common with her father's employees anyway. They saw her as an uninteresting high school kid and usually talked among themselves and ignored her.

This year, since Aprilynne had started working at her father's office, she was bound to know all their inside jokes and gossip, and Tori would be the only one silently waiting for it to end.

Usually Tori didn't mind the work that went into Thanksgiving dinner, but right now the last thing she wanted to deal with was hours of cooking, cleaning, and then eating with strangers. Couldn't her family for once be like all the other families, slobbing around and just being with each other?

When her mother cheerfully called her into the kitchen, Tori stood in the doorway and didn't take the apron her mother offered. "Please, can we go to a restaurant, buy the stuff, and pretend we made it? I'll drive."

Aprilynne snorted. She was at the far counter turning sweet potatoes into a dish that more closely resembled a brown sugar casserole than an actual vegetable. "Nice try. Like I don't suggest that every year."

Tori's mother strolled over and draped the apron around Tori's neck. "We need to get the mashed potatoes going."

"It's a holiday. We're supposed to relax."

"Our guests work hard for your father. This is the least we can do for them." Tori's mother stepped behind her, took hold of the apron strings and tied them. "You're a Hampton. That should mean something to you."

"Yeah, it means Thanksgiving dinners always suck."

Tori's mom hefted a bag of potatoes off the counter and handed them to her. "We give our guests our best. The work is part of the gift."

Tori had heard this before. Sometimes this little truism even convinced her that the work wasn't so bad. Today it just seemed like a trite excuse to make her suffer. "After I go to college," she announced, "I'm never coming home for Thanksgiving. I'm going to enjoy a peaceful meal in the cafeteria."

"The peeler is by the sink," her mother said and breezed off to cut up celery for the stuffing—her homemade specialty stuffing. Because, obviously, the kind from the box wasn't good enough.

Tori peeled, cut, and boiled the potatoes. Maybe her mother would let her pretend she was sick so she could watch a movie in her bedroom. Surely there would be enough fake smiling and mindless flattery going on that hers wouldn't be needed. But of course, she was a Hampton and that meant there could never be enough fake smiling and mindless flattery.

She was draining the potatoes when she heard noises in her mind, a voice in the dragon enclosure. She maximized the sound, letting it grow louder.

"I shouldn't need to remind you," Overdrake said, "but I will. You should watch what you say."

Was he speaking to Tori? Was this some sort of threat?

"Why do I have to watch what I say here?" Aaron's voice. She relaxed. Overdrake was talking to him.

"I thought Tori only heard what Vesta heard," Aaron continued.

Tori heard what Vesta heard? That was news. And apparently wrong. Which dragon was she listening to now? Khan still? She'd been connected to him when Overdrake had introduced Aaron last Saturday.

"We can't be certain Tori will always be linked to Vesta," Overdrake answered. "Do you need a refresher on the necessity of precaution?"

"No." And then as though Aaron was repeating a motto, he added, "If I make a mistake around a dragon, it might be my last."

"Precisely. Don't ever treat them like pets. They're not."

"Yeah, I know."

Tori put the drained pot back on the stovetop and went to the fridge for the butter and milk.

A pair of footsteps approached the dragon and Overdrake murmured, "Here you are, boy. We saved the bones and dark meat for you."

Ah, even though Khan wasn't a pet, he still got Thanksgiving leftovers. Tori supposed that was better than feeding the dragon stray dogs. One faint crunch sounded in her mind—the noise of Khan biting into bones. Didn't take much effort for a dragon to swallow something as small as a turkey.

Tori dropped a cube of butter into the pot, measured out the milk, and waited for Overdrake and Aaron to walk out of the enclosure. Instead, Overdrake spoke again. "I've been giving your inability to fly some thought, and the only reason I can see for it is that you need an added incentive." Words with a cool sharp edge.

"I'm making progress," Aaron protested. "I can fly twenty feet at a time. Sometimes thirty."

"That's not flying; that's leaping. Perhaps the problem lies in your practice sessions. You haven't sufficiently felt you were in danger. There is, of course, an easy way to remedy that."

Aaron groaned.

"Look," Overdrake said, "Khan is staring at you and he doesn't seem pleased."

"Oh, come on," Aaron said, his voice picking up anger. "I'm trying to fly. It's not my fault I always land instead."

"Your choices are the same as when you were here last. You can throw the boulders—a bad choice. Control the dragon—which won't happen as long as I'm in his mind. Or fly to that hole in the ceiling."

Overdrake was setting a dragon on his own son again? Wow, Aaron was having an even worse Thanksgiving than she was..

The dragon made a low rumbling sound in his throat, a warning.

"I'll check back in a half an hour and see how you're doing," Overdrake said.

"Don't!" Aaron said. "You can't—" He didn't finish, and for a horrible moment Tori wondered if the dragon had killed him. No, Overdrake wouldn't let it go that far.

Tori stood in front of her pot, the masher gripped in her hand like a weapon and breathlessly waited.

The next thing she heard from Aaron was a stream of swear words. For a twelve-year-old, the kid had a mouth on him. And he had some creative ways to use his swear words. Not necessarily grammatically correct ways, but creative.

Overdrake made a tsking sound. "You've already forgotten to watch what you say. I hope my other instructions are more firmly rooted in your mind."

She heard the door clang closed. Overdrake had left Aaron alone in the enclosure with Khan.

She felt sick for him, wished she had some way to talk to him. *Overdrake told you he had control of the dragon,* she wanted to say. *That means he won't let it kill you.*

Of course, that didn't mean the dragon wouldn't hurt him. It had probably been instructed to do just that.

"Tori?" Her mother walked by on the way to get a mixing bowl. "Are you all right?"

Tori startled and realized she'd been standing there frozen, the potato masher still lifted like she was going to stab something with it. "Yeah. I'm fine." She pushed the masher into the potatoes, half stirring them, while she listened for Aaron.

Her mother watched her. "You'll never get the lumps out that way."

"Uh huh," Tori said.

Her mother sighed and went back to seasoning the stuffing.

Aaron had stopped swearing and was panting, takin deep breaths. "Stay away from me," he yelled at t dragon. "Stay back!"

Khan roared, the kind that involved fire. Had Aaron managed to jump out of the way? She knew from experience that although fire wouldn't burn him, the heat was still painful.

"Back off!" Aaron called. He was trying to control the dragon. It wouldn't work as long as Overdrake had hold of Khan's mind.

Fly, she thought. *Your body knows how.* He was probably overthinking it. Flying wasn't like riding a bike that took coordination, balance, and practice. It was instinctual. You needed to go somewhere high, you leaped up, and you soared there.

A thudding sound in the enclosure made her wince. She'd heard the sound before—a dragon's tail smacking something—hopefully the ground and not Aaron.

"If you can hear me," Aaron said, "I'm saying right now, that my Ferrari had better have a sunroof."

Ferrari? Tori supposed Aaron wasn't talking to her. Man, Overdrake was buying him a Ferrari?

"I've done everything you asked," Aaron continued, "and you haven't let me talk to my mom, you haven't let me go outside—you haven't even told me where I am!"

Hold on, maybe Aaron was letting Tori know he didn't have any information yet.

Another thud. "You know, Child Protective Services would have something to say about this!"

A sound like a rock shattering echoed through the enclosure. "Despite what you think, I do remember the stuff you tell me. I know to enter a dragon's mind, I'm supposed to follow my senses and let them pull me in.

After I'm there, I split my focus so I can enter the dragon's second level of consciousness and find the control center. See, I've been listening."

Aaron *was* talking to her, passing on Overdrake's instructions. Tori already knew how to enter a dragon's mind. And she'd figured out when she was with Dirk that to get to Khan's control center, she needed to envision herself walking through his mind. What else had Overdrake taught Aaron? She shut her eyes, leaned forward, all her attention focused on the enclosure.

"Once I'm in the control center, I'm supposed to envision the dragon's will like it's an actual object and clutch it in my hand. It's not my fault I can't do it. You're always there controlling it first."

If another dragon lord wasn't already there, could she envision the dragon's will as an object and take control that way? Did it matter what object she envisioned? Did it have to be the same object every time?

She couldn't ask, and it didn't sound like Overdrake had actually given Aaron a chance to practice it.

The dragon roared again, and the sound of fire crackling filled her ears. She was familiar with that noise, could almost feel the heat creeping along her skin.

Aaron let out a yell that made Tori flinch. Had the dragon done something—swiped him with his claws? Bitten him?

And then the yell turned into a laugh. Aaron wasn't screaming in pain; he was whooping happily. "Sweet!" he said, still laughing. "Check out this action. This ain't no leap!" More laughter, joyful and unbridled. "I'm freaking Peter Pan."

Khan had gone quiet. All Tori heard was the sound of Aaron's laughter zooming farther and then closer to the dragon. The door opened and then there was the sound of clapping.

"You did it." Overdrake's pride was evident. "I knew you would." He stopped clapping. "However, if I hadn't commanded Khan to stay on the ground, he would have caught you within two wingbeats. You were supposed to fly to the hole to escape, not circle around the enclosure like it's a skating rink."

"Sorry!" Aaron called back. "I couldn't help myself. Flying is awesome. Look—double flip!"

Tori expected Overdrake to be angry or at least give him a reprimand for making mistakes around dragons. Instead he laughed, a deep, affectionate laugh. The sort you expected from fathers.

"You were born to fly," Overdrake went on, pride ringing. "You're my son, after all."

"How do I stop myself?"

"One of three ways. You run into something, you run out of energy, or you will yourself to stop, just like you willed yourself to fly. I suggest the latter."

"Willpower isn't working. But hey, watch this spin."

Overdrake laughed again. "I'll keep Khan calm while you practice. Take as long as you'd like. And then we'll talk about your sunroof."

Tori minimized the sound so it wasn't as loud. She had thought listening to Overdrake talk to her was bad. His voice always dripped with disdain if not outright hatred. But listening to this was somehow worse. Hearing Overdrake praise Aaron—hearing him so happy—it was chilling.

Tori mashed the potatoes harder, smashing anything that hinted at lumpiness.

Aaron...what else was happening to him? Her counterpart sense told her that he was exultant, not just because he was flying, but because he had Overdrake's approval.

Aaron shouldn't want that. He should be repulsed by Overdrake's fatherly pride and the suggestion that sports cars could buy his loyalty. But Aaron wasn't. She could tell he wasn't.

Her stomach clenched with worry. What had she been thinking to send a twelve-year-old to Overdrake? Were twelve-year-olds' brains even done developing?

She wished she had a way to remind Aaron that before Overdrake was clapping and talking about sunroofs, he'd locked Aaron in the enclosure with a fire-breathing, fifty-ton carnivorous animal. Aaron seemed to have forgotten that fact.

Aprilynne strolled over on her way to the oven. "Are you trying to mash the potatoes or beat them into submission?"

Tori looked down at the pot. Bits of potatoes had splattered over the stovetop, polka-dotting the whole thing.

Tori's mom swept up to check the potatoes. "I'm sure those are..."

"Pulverized," Aprilynne supplied.

"Done now," her mother said. She picked up the pot and whisked it away before Tori could do more. "Why don't you, um, set the tables?"

A task she couldn't mess up. Really, when had Tori become *that* child? The difficult one. The one that her parents needed to make allowances for?

CHAPTER 7

Dirk sat in the family room, ignoring the football game on the TV in front of him. Instead, he listened to the noises in the kitchen.

Norma, the housekeeper his father had hired from the Philippines, was clanking plates into the dishwasher. Bridget sat at the kitchen table drawing pictures and chatting away to Norma, oblivious to the fact that the woman didn't understand a quarter of what she said. With Bridget, that sort of thing didn't matter. Cassie was in the kitchen as well, washing the china she didn't trust anyone else to handle.

After the first couple days, their father had moved Aaron to a room in the house and had been purposely lax about guarding him. Aaron had agreed to stay, and his freedom was a test to see if, given the chance, he would bolt. So far, he hadn't.

His father had taken Aaron to the enclosure over an hour ago. They'd gone to feed Khan the turkey carcass but obviously, his father had more planned. It took about ten seconds for a dragon to eat something that small. They weren't big on chewing.

Dirk tapped his thumb against the remote control, nervous for Aaron and irritated all over again that his father had abducted the kid.

It wasn't only the wrongness of the kidnapping that bothered Dirk. He'd had an unwanted sense of responsibility thrust on him. Now he had to worry about Aaron, had to act as an intermediary, and most problematic, he had to figure out whether he should help the kid escape.

Back when he'd first seen Aaron, scared and trying to get away at the fair, Dirk had decided he couldn't stand by and see his brother shanghaied. He could ask Tori to meet him somewhere and hand Aaron off to her. She would help Dirk if he asked her. And as an added benefit he would get to see Tori again. Although with a twelve-year-old around, the meeting wouldn't end like the last had.

But now Dirk didn't know. Aaron didn't appear all that eager to leave. After his first burst of outrage at being taken, his anger had fizzled into sporadic resentment, occasional homesickness, and a stubborn insistence that his cell phone be returned.

Most of the time, he acted happy enough to be here. He was interested in the dragons, wanted to learn everything about them, and was almost equally curious about their father. Every time Aaron was with their dad, he peppered him with questions about his life, his likes, his dislikes, and his plans to take over.

Their father never answered questions about his attack plans, but over the last five days he'd talked more about himself and told more stories about growing up in St. Helena than Dirk had ever heard. His father was lapping up the hero worship.

Aaron loved the fact that he'd inherited superpowers, was in awe of their father and was more than willing to be bribed. But Aaron was also keeping secrets. Dirk could sense that. Aaron was a bad liar—too nervous, too unused to lying to be casual about it.

Some of the lies Dirk understood. Aaron had lied about where he'd lived to protect their mom. He'd lied about being an only child to protect whatever siblings he had. Dirk would have done the same thing.

But at other times Aaron seemed to be hiding things Dirk couldn't even guess at. His deception was there in his questions, some lurking agenda that Aaron was always trying to shuffle away from Dirk's notice. And every time Aaron called their father "Dad" there was a little bit of a lie mixed in with the word.

Which didn't make sense because the one thing Dirk was sure about was that they shared a father.

Dirk set down the remote. Maybe he should go to the enclosure and see what was taking his father and Aaron so long.

Before he got up, his father's voice boomed through the kitchen. "You're looking at a boy who can fly—not twenty feet, not thirty feet—but miles."

"Oh, that's wonderful!" Cassie said. When she talked to Aaron, her voice was always too sugary. She apparently hadn't made up her mind about whether having Aaron here was a good thing or not and was overcompensating.

Bridget said, "Yay! When can you take me on a flying piggyback ride?"

"Not for a while," their father answered. "He needs to work on his landings before we saddle him up and make him haul around little girls."

"Can you take me then, Daddy?" Bridget asked.

Hopefully their father would say yes because now that she'd gotten the idea of flying into her head, she wouldn't be happy until someone took her. And Dirk was the only other someone who could fly.

"In a few minutes," their father said. "I've got to give Aaron something first."

Aaron and their father came into the family room. Their father sauntered over to the end table where his tablet was charging and handed it to Aaron with a flourish. "I've connected you to a site that you can use to call your mother and tell her about your new achievement."

Aaron brightened. "Awesome! Thanks!"

Awesome? It was like the kid had already forgotten that talking to his mom didn't used to be a privilege.

"However," their father went on, "I'll take the tablet back after I'm done with Bridget, so don't waste your time calling your friends. They wouldn't believe you about flying anyway."

Aaron hesitated before putting in a phone number. His gaze went to Dirk. "If I make the call, will anyone be able to track it?"

His father picked up Bridget with one arm, making her giggle and grab onto his neck. "No need to worry about that. My IP address is automatically rerouted."

Dirk answered the question Aaron was really asking. "No one will be able to tell where your mom is either."

Satisfied with the answer, Aaron tapped in her number and flung himself on the couch, half leaping, half flying. He crashed into it so hard the piece of furniture wobbled and nearly fell over.

"No flying in the house," their father called over his shoulder and left the room.

"Sorry, Dad," Aaron called back.

Dad. Liar.

Aaron turned his attention to the phone. "Hey Mom, it's me. I'm fine—"

Dirk hadn't expected that he'd feel a pang of anger when he heard Aaron say the word 'mom' but he did, sharp and strong. He wasn't sure who the feeling was directed at—his father for not letting Dirk talk to his mother all these years and then allowing Aaron to do it after five days, at his mother for skipping out on his life and choosing to raise Aaron instead, or at Aaron for being the one that she chose.

Dirk was caught between the desire to storm out of the room and the urge to stay and listen to half of his mother's conversation. She was so close. Close enough that if Dirk turned off the TV he might be able to hear her voice.

"I have no idea," Aaron said. "I've only gone from the house to enclosure. The weather seems normal so I guess I'm not in the tropics or anything."

Dirk turned up the TV a couple of notches. He didn't need to hear his mother's voice. He'd gone long enough without it, without her. And he was perfectly fine. Perfectly. Fine.

"It's not like I'm locked up or anything," Aaron said. "Everything's cool. I'm learning about dragons, and today I figured out how to fly. You should have seen me. I'd send you video, but I'm not allowed to take pictures of the dragons or myself flying."

A pause.

Aaron lowered his voice. "There aren't any other houses around. And besides, if I did something like that he wouldn't trust me anymore. I want him to teach me dragon lord stuff. I'm fine, really."

Bianca must have instructed Aaron to leave the house and find help so he could go back to her. How sweet. How motherly. She was telling Aaron to leave but she'd made sure Dirk stayed.

Dirk turned off the TV and headed out to the front porch for some fresh air. His mother could tell Aaron how much she missed him in private.

Once outside, Dirk leaned against the porch railing and looked out over the mile of property they'd lived on since last month. The place was filled with all sorts of fresh air but he still felt like he was suffocating. The house didn't feel like home. He hadn't even unpacked all his boxes yet.

He tried to see the property the way Aaron saw it— the tangle of trees that surrounded the yard, an entire forest that ran up the surrounding hills. The carpet of discarded leaves browning on the ground around them. No sign of civilization.

Aaron wouldn't be able to escape without help. Fifteen-foot fences surrounded the property, the doors and windows were alarmed, and the yard was riddled with motion sensors. The nearest neighbors were miles away.

If Aaron knew and planned to circumvent those things—which would be easy enough with the power of flight and a good excuse to go outside—he still wouldn't make it far. While he'd been unconscious on the airplane, their father had injected a tracking chip into his left hip. As long as it was in place, their father would always be able to find Aaron.

Minutes went by. Dirk saw no sign of his dad flying nearby with Bridget. The two must be on the other side of the property. Dirk had gone outside without a jacket and the cold November air was pushing through his shirt like it wasn't there. He tucked his fingers under his arms to keep them warm and leaned against a porch column. He didn't want to go back inside yet.

The door swung open and Aaron stepped out, tablet in his hand. "Mom wants to talk to you." He held out the tablet.

For a moment Dirk stared at it, anger fighting with a decade-old longing to hear her voice. "She wants to talk to me?" he repeated, buying himself time to decide whether or not to speak to her.

What would she say? Did she want to apologize? Maybe she just wanted to ask him to help Aaron escape.

"Yeah." Aaron kept holding out the tablet.

Dirk took it. He would at least give her the chance to explain why he hadn't been good enough, why she'd chosen a baby she'd never even seen over him.

"Hello," he said.

"Dirk, is that you?"

He'd thought he would recognize her voice. He'd heard it enough times on the videos from his early years. But her voice sounded lower, breathier.

"Yeah, it's me."

She didn't say anything else, and he wondered if he'd lost the call. Then he heard her crying.

Crying.

It should have moved him. And maybe it did. But it also frustrated him. You were supposed to comfort crying people and he wasn't ready to do that yet. She hadn't given him any sort of explanation.

"Sorry," she said. "It's just that you sound so grown up."

He recognized her voice then, the lilt of it. "Well, it's been twelve years."

"I know. And I've thought of you every single day."

Thinking of him was probably easier than being there for him. "Have you?" he asked.

"Of course. And every birthday I wondered where you were and what you were doing."

Well, that made two of them. She wasn't apologizing and she wasn't explaining. Man, that meant she was just going to ask him to help Aaron.

"I want to know everything about you," she said. "Tell me about your life."

A memory flashed through his mind from the night she left. He hadn't understood what her absence meant back then, only that his dad was furious about it. His father had picked up his Mom's china cabinet and flung it into the dining room wall. The cabinet shattered, then lay in a heap of splintered wood and bits of dishes.

Dirk had known broken glass was dangerous, but he saw an undamaged teacup resting in the wreckage. He'd wanted to save it. After his father stormed out of the room, Dirk waded through the shards. A jagged piece of wood scraped across his ankle and when he put out a hand to steady himself, he sliced his fingertip. But he didn't cry out because he knew if he made a sound, his father would return and take the cup from him.

He hid it in his toy room and waited for his mother to come home. He'd figured she would be upset that his father had broken her dishes, but Dirk would be able to produce a piece of her china and make her happy again.

Eventually Dirk forgot about the cup. Years later, one of the housekeepers found it and brought it to the kitchen. As soon as his father saw it, he threw it in the trash. Dirk hadn't protested. By then he'd realized he couldn't make his mother happy.

Now, with the tablet clutched in his hand, Dirk could find no words to tell his mother anything about his life. He stepped away from the porch column, ready to go inside. "I don't want to take up your time. Aaron only has a little while to talk. I'll let you get back to him." He handed the tablet to his brother.

Dirk knew he shouldn't leave Aaron outside, unsupervised. He would be too tempted to listen to their mother's advice and make a break for it. If the kid wanted to run, he needed to know what he was up against and do it right.

As Dirk opened the door to go inside, he said, "Don't go anywhere. You're not supposed to know this, but you've got a tracking chip in your left hip."

There. He'd done his duty by his mom. He'd helped Aaron so he didn't make a mess of his escape.

Dirk went inside, marched upstairs to his bedroom, and stayed there the rest of the night.

***

The next morning while Dirk was still asleep, his father strolled into his bedroom and announced, "I've got work to see to. Take Aaron out on the grounds and help him with his flying. He's got a lot to learn. He should practice most of the day."

Dirk didn't get up, didn't even open his eyes.

One handed, his father picked up the side of the bed and toppled Dirk onto the floor.

There were definite drawbacks to having a parent who got extra strength every time he visited the dragons.

Dirk groaned and sat up. "Fine. I'm awake."

"Good. Aaron is up too. Make sure he has breakfast before you go out."

Ten minutes later, Dirk was dressed and downstairs in the kitchen. Bridget had made toast and was putting a thick layer of jam on her bread. Aaron sifted through the cereal cupboard. "Don't your parents believe in sugar cereal?" "Why does every box in here have the word bran on it?"

Dirk opened the fridge, took out a piece of pumpkin pie and an apple, then motioned for Aaron to follow him. "Come on. We'll eat while we walk to the enclosure."

Outside, clouds covered the sky, a white backdrop against the gray-brown of the trees. Their bare branches reached upward, skinny and scrawny and brittle. Everything looked dead, but it wasn't. The trees were just smart enough to keep their energy deep inside where winter couldn't destroy it. They'd learned they didn't have to fight the cold, they only needed to endure it.

As Dirk headed down the stairs, he handed Aaron the pie. "Breakfast. It's the most important meal of the day."

Aaron narrowed his eyes at Dirk. "You know you're a complete jerk, right?"

Dirk switched the hand he held out. "Fine. Have the apple if you want it."

Aaron took the apple but hardly seemed to notice it. They shuffled across the wet leaves on their way to the enclosure. "Do you know how long Mom has waited to talk to you? Do you know how badly she's wanted it? You didn't even speak to her for an entire minute. What's wrong with you?"

Dirk took a bite of the pie and felt the tang of cinnamon on his tongue. "My problem is I'm scarred from a bad childhood. You see, my mom left me when I was six."

"Only because Dad wouldn't let her take you. She didn't *want* to lose you."

"She didn't *lose* me," Dirk said. "I didn't wander off in the woods. Kids aren't like car keys and spare change that you misplace. She took off. She's got to live with that now. I can't undo it."

Aaron stared at him, dumbfounded, noting not just Dirk's words but the emotions behind them. Apparently, it had never occurred to his brother that Dirk would feel so strongly about being abandoned.

How nice to be twelve and think your parents loved you.

"It wasn't like that," Aaron said, begrudgingly taking a bite of the apple. "She wasn't to blame. You should talk to her."

Dirk bit into another piece of pie but hardly tasted it. "Maybe next time when you call her." He only said this so Aaron would drop the subject.

"She didn't want things to be this way," Aaron said, but he didn't push the issue. Not while they finished the walk to the enclosure or trudged down the stairs, even though his sullen footsteps said the subject hadn't completely left his mind.

The two went into the enclosure to charge their powers, then Dirk flew with him around the property showing him how to dive, turn, and land. Before their powers wore off, they flew back to recharge them. At noon, sack lunches waited for them at the enclosure door.

Aaron was a quick learner. Mostly because he was fearless. He didn't worry about knocking into trees or hitting the ground wrong during a landing. Speed didn't faze him. By the end of the day he was bruised, cut, and had done considerable damage to some trees, but he'd learned a lot—enough that it would be easy for him to fly off the grounds and go halfway across the state before his powers wore off. Had to be tempting. The idea tempted Dirk sometimes, and he didn't have as many reasons to run away.

Before going back home for dinner, Dirk took Aaron to some thick branches in an old maple to rest for a bit. Dirk liked this spot. From it, you could see a stream that cut through the forest. Some still-green bushes lined the water, stubbornly refusing to abide by the rules of autumn.

He and Aaron would have to go home soon or Cassie would complain about them coming late for the meal. She had a thing for punctuality. But Dirk had to take care of one thing first. "You heard me when I told you about the tracking chip, right? You realize if you take off, you'd better find a way to gouge that thing out first or Dad will track you down. And when he finds you, sunroofs will be the least of your worries."

"Yeah." Aaron flicked a piece of bark with his fingernail. "Thanks for the warning."

Dirk waited for the obvious question, but it didn't come. "You're not going to ask me how to get it out?"

Aaron shrugged. "I don't want you to think I'm planning on leaving. You might tell Dad."

Aaron was testing him, trying to see how loyal Dirk was to their father.

"I wouldn't tell Dad, because then I'd have to admit I told you about the chip in the first place. He wouldn't be happy about that."

Aaron's gaze darted to Dirk. "Is he keeping you here somehow? Is he forcing you to do what he wants?"

How should Dirk answer that question? Should he mention that he'd tried to run away last year and his father had sent a dragon to bring him back? Should he admit that the only reason his friends were still alive, especially Tori, was that Dirk was doing everything their father asked him to do?

Dirk leaned back against the tree trunk. "Nah, I just like Ferraris."

Dirk felt the flash of disappointment—disgust really—that went through Aaron. Well, fine, let the kid be judgmental. That was easy when you were twelve. Besides, it wasn't like Dirk wanted Aaron to look up to him anyway. He wasn't role model material.

Aaron shifted on the branch. "Won't EMP from the dragons destroy the chip?"

"I'm sure it's been radiation hardened." Instead of explaining the science behind that, Dirk said, "Which means, no. An EMP won't affect it."

"So," Aaron said slowly, "just out of curiosity, and not because I'm planning on leaving—how do I get the chip out?"

"I don't know."

Aaron swore and shook his head.

Dirk laughed, not because it was funny, but because Aaron had taken such careful precautions to guard his emotions when he insisted he didn't want to leave, and then had completely ruined the effect by swearing in frustration.

"Can you tell where it is?" Dirk asked. "Do you feel the chip?"

"I can't feel it, but I know where it is. There's a red bump on my skin that didn't used to be there. But I can't go digging around in my hip with a knife. What if I hit a major vein or something?"

Yeah. Probably not the best idea. "I'll research tracking chips," Dirk said. "Maybe we could find a way to block its signal or something."

Aaron considered this. "You would help me leave?"

Dirk didn't answer for a moment. On the stream, images of tree branches rippled along the surface of the water, refusing to stay still and straight. "Dad wants you here so you'll help with the dragons. That way instead of attacking with two dragons, he can attack with three. He wants it so badly he thinks he can make it happen. And maybe he can. If he can't convince you that a revolution is needed, or buy you off with promises of power and possessions, then he might abduct a few of your friends or family and threaten to leave them in the dragon enclosure. He has ways of getting what he wants."

Dirk had expected Aaron to be repulsed by this statement, or if Aaron really had begun to idolize their father, be defensive on his behalf. But Aaron didn't even register any surprise. He already knew what was expected of him in the revolution and apparently, he'd worked out the consequences if he didn't help.

"Personally," Dirk went on, "I think you're too young to be involved, and even if you weren't, well, if Dad has to coerce you to stay here and take part, you'll be more of a danger than an asset. If you're a danger, we should let you leave before you can do any damage."

Aaron tilted his head. "So, are you saying you'd help me if I decided I wanted to leave or are you just saying that you'd tell Dad that he should let me go?"

Committing to that answer was best done in degrees, carefully. "I'll decide that when you tell me you want to leave."

Dirk could feel Aaron drawing back, hiding behind his walls again. He stared at the fallen, decaying leaves instead of at Dirk. "I don't want to leave, but I still want to know how to get rid of the tracking chip. It makes me feel like I'm cattle or something."

"I know. After I found out about your chip, I did a thorough check on myself, just in case."

Aaron's gaze returned to him. "Find anything?"

Dirk sighed for effect. "My muscles are so massive, it's hard to find something that small."

Aaron rolled his eyes. The kid was too used to being the top dog at his school—confident he would always be the strongest and the fastest. Dirk had been that way too until he'd gone to camp and met the Slayers.

"Think you could take me on?" Dirk challenged.

Aaron at least had the intelligence to shake his head. "Nah, but someday I will." With a grin, he added, "and I'll win."

Dirk took Aaron's arm and held it up, comparing their biceps. "Well, today ain't that day. Break is over. Practice your diving on the way back to the house."

***

On Saturday, Dirk went to the mall by himself. He told his father he was going Christmas shopping, and he did pick up some presents to make the story believable, but the real reason he went was so that he could buy a new phone. That way he could set up an untraceable account on the dark web and use it to text Tori.

That night he went into Vesta's enclosure to tell Tori what he'd done. The fledglings didn't have large spaces like Khan and Minerva. Their habitats were only the size of a basketball court—large enough for them to fly around a bit but small enough for them to understand that they lived in captivity, that they were dependent on humans, and should obey their rules.

Asleep, Vesta looked like a rhino-sized boulder. She didn't stay that way for long. As soon as she caught Dirk's scent, she lifted her wings, spreading them like enemy flags raised before a charge. Vesta was still young enough that she challenged anyone who came in her vicinity. She hadn't learned yet that there was no point fighting a dragon lord. Her gray scales hung on her loosely, armor that was too big. She was still growing so fast that her body overcompensated by giving her room.

Before she could shriek, he took control of her mind. Hearing the dragons screech bothered Tori. Besides, Vesta was finally getting big enough that every once in a while her shrieks produced EMP, and he didn't want to risk having his new phone fried. The dragon's EMP was a good thing, in that regard. Dirk was relatively sure his father didn't bug the enclosures. No point in paying a lot of money to make the place EMP-proof when Dirk could just talk to Tori when he was outside exercising the dragon.

Time to take Vesta for some fresh air and practice. He put on her harness and saddle, then opened the door in the roof. As usual, she bolted upward, full speed, convinced she'd find freedom if she rushed at the sky fast enough. He always let her tire herself out a bit before he reined her in and put her through her paces.

The wind rushed past him, roaring in his ears. Hearing and seeing were so much easier when he was inside a dragon's mind. Then the landscape came alive.

The sky was a sea of stars, the rustle of trees a constant hum, and everything smelled of leafy decay and the crisp possibility of snow.

"Tori," Dirk said. "I've set up a new site where we can talk. It's untraceable so you don't have to worry about me finding you and I don't have to worry you'll send the Slayers after me." He gave her the site name and password. "My dad hacked either your account or mine so we can't use our regular site anymore. At least not for real conversation. You should still contact me on it every once in a while, though, so my dad doesn't figure out I've got a new site and start looking for it."

Dirk leaned back in the saddle as Vesta made a sharp upward turn. "You could go on and on about how awesome I am. That would be believable. You could also tell me how much you miss me; that sort of thing." He repeated the site address and password a few more times, then waited a couple of minutes and checked his phone to see if she wrote anything to him. She didn't. But that wasn't entirely a surprise. Sometimes she was at places where she couldn't access the internet. She would write soon. Probably by the end of the night.

CHAPTER 8

Friday night, Jesse drove to Georgetown University. He'd told his parents he was going to a movie with friends. In reality, Dr. B had sent him a message that he was needed for a mission. Non-urgent. No other details. For smaller jobs, Dr. B generally only used a couple of Slayers.

Tori probably wouldn't be there tonight. And Jesse shouldn't hope that she was. He was trying to spend less time thinking about her. That had been his one goal this week—not to get over her, not to rid himself of the pain that seemed to have found a permanent place in his chest—he just needed to stop thinking about her so much. He had to stop conjuring up her face, stop rereading her old texts, and stop imagining her in Dirk's arms. He also needed to stop second guessing whether he should have done something differently; maybe done everything differently.

Was he being petty and jealous to keep Tori at an arm's length, or was he being smart to get off her merry-go-round-of-indecision-about-Dirk? Whatever the case, Jesse was doing a miserable job at keeping himself from thinking about her.

In his defense, he was reminded of her every day at school, where half of the guys eyed her and flirted with her. And then there was Slayer stuff—he had to work with her there. And as if that weren't enough, everywhere he went, someone was talking about Senator Hampton, Tori's father.

If the man won the presidency, Jesse would have four solid years of Tori reminders. Maybe eight.

When Jesse pulled into the parking lot next to the library, he automatically searched for her car. Wasn't there. He was disappointed, despite himself.

He spotted Dr. B's truck, even though the camp director had a way of changing vehicles and never used the same license plate twice. Jesse recognized it because the simulator lay in the truck bed. The machine was covered by a tarp, but he knew the thick, rectangular shape well enough.

So, it was going to be a mission where he needed his Slayer powers. That meant he would either need to fly somewhere or be ready for a fight. He parked his car and walked over to the truck for details. Dr. B got out, peered around the lot to make sure they were alone, then motioned for Bess to join him at the back of the truck.

Although they were father and daughter, the two didn't look much alike. Granted, they were both tall, had blue eyes, and Jesse supposed that Dr. B's unruly gray hair must have once been brown curls like Bess's. But Dr. B had an air of perpetual intellectualism and seriousness, as though he was always pondering some significant matter. If Bess ever pondered anything, it was probably her next practical joke.

"What's up?" Jesse asked.

Bess zipped up her jacket. "My dad's hopes."

Dr. B gave her a sharp look, which she ignored. "I've been working with Shang," he said, "trying different methods to help him regain his memory. I can't say for certain that anything we've done has actually helped. He's recalled a few vague things, but I'm not sure whether he's remembering things because the pathways in his brain are regrowing or because he wrote a novel about his experience and is making logical correlations."

Excitement flickered inside Jesse. "But he might have remembered some things?" It was the first good news he'd had in a while. "What has Shang done to improve his memory?"

"Meditation," Dr. B said, "revisiting places we've been, and practicing things we practiced. He still has quite a bit of muscle memory. He may not consciously remember our plays but when confronted by a mechanical dragon, he instinctively follows them—or at least tries to. It's harder without his powers."

Jesse raised his eyebrows. "Wait, you've had him practice with the heli-dragons?" They were like six-foot hummingbirds that shot out fifteen-foot flames.

"Not with the flames running," Dr. B said. "Just normal harmless routines." He said this as though it were normal to dodge moving blades. "Shang has also been eating Ling Zhi mushrooms. They're an herbal supplement that's been used medicinally in China for two thousand years to promote long life and boost spirituality. For all I know, the original Slayers could have used them to help regain their memories."

Not much was recorded in historical documents about how Slayers could regain lost powers but Dr. B had spent years researching the subject. If Slayers kept away from mind altering substances, eventually the damaged pathways in their brains would regrow and both memories and powers would return. But the medieval records also talked about a quicker way to recover—an instantaneous method.

"Lately, Shang has added powdered Ling Zhi to his food," Dr. B continued. "Although the benefits are inconclusive, I feel Shang's improvement is enough for us to try the powder on another Slayer. Leo, as a shielder, is especially important."

"Because we're MVPs," Bess put in. Shielders could protect people not only from dragon fire but from bullets.

Dr. B opened his briefcase and produced a large vitamin bottle and a Ziploc bag full of what seemed to be shredded brown Styrofoam. Not exactly appetizing. "I'm hoping the two of you can convince Leo to try this."

Jesse inwardly sighed. This mission was nothing but wishful thinking. The mushrooms *might* help but might not. Leo didn't have any memory of his lost powers, Overdrake, or what was at stake. How were Jesse and Bess supposed to convince him to eat ancient Chinese mushrooms every day? The two of them were going to look weird, and not just a little weird, but crazy, laugh-about-you-later weird. Leo wouldn't go for it.

Unlike Shang and Alyssa, who'd lost their memories and abilities when Overdrake had drugged them, Leo had lost his Slayer identity because he started drinking and at some point had drunk himself unconscious. He'd either been too careless to protect his powers or he'd decided he didn't want to fight Overdrake. Even if he regained his skills, he might not want to rejoin the Slayers.

Still, Jesse took the bag and bottle from Dr. B. He couldn't refuse. Despite being mad at Leo for abandoning the rest of the group, Jesse still wanted him back. If there was even a small chance that eating ancient Chinese mushrooms could help, Jesse would do his best to convince Leo to do it. And not only because Leo was a shielder, but because he'd been a friend.

Jesse put the bottle into one pocket and tried to shove the bag into the other. It didn't fit right, too bulky. "How are we supposed to get him to eat these? What's our story?"

Bess helped him wedge the bag into his pocket. "I'm doing a science fair project, and I need test subjects who are willing to take Ling Zhi and record their energy levels. I've already enlisted your help and I gave you a supply tonight, which is why you have the stuff with you."

"Okay." Coming from Bess, the request would seem almost normal. Jesse relaxed a bit. Maybe this had a chance of working.

Dr. B took a remote from his coat pocket and pressed the button. "In case that doesn't work, I'm giving you permission to tell Leo about the Slayers and to prove you have powers."

The trailer behind his truck let off a faint hum, the simulator turning on. A moment later, a surge of energy hit Jesse, sharpening his senses. The night seemed brighter, as though the moon and stars had been on a dimmer switch and had just been cranked up. He could hear the music playing from one of the buildings. The smells from the parking lot intensified: spilled oil, lingering exhaust, and old tires. He no longer felt cold. He was strong, powerful, and had to quell the urge to take to the air and fly. He wasn't here for recreation, no matter how much he longed for that weightless feeling of sailing through the sky.

Dr. B handed Jesse and Bess maps of the campus. "Leo texted his friends about going to a party in Village A. He should be there by now."

A party at a university. Did his friends realize Leo was only a high school senior?

Dr. B glanced around the parking lot again, a habit of surveillance. "I was able to call in a favor from a professor friend. If anyone questions your invitation to the party, tell them you're friends of Brock Booher. One of my associates is adding twenty points to his last test in exchange for getting you in."

Dr. B had been a professor at Georgetown for years but had gone on sabbatical after he learned that Overdrake knew who he was. The Slayers weren't the only ones that had to worry about Overdrake finding them.

Jesse surveyed the maps. The first was a layout of the nearby buildings. The Village A apartment complex was circled. It was about a dozen buildings, separated into blocks. The second was a map of the complex itself—or rather four maps, since the footprint of each story in the main buildings was different. Catwalks connected five of the central buildings. Staircases sprouted throughout the complex like weeds. Could there really be that many stairs scattered around? Why? The place looked like a maze.

Jesse turned the paper even though he knew seeing it from a different angle wouldn't help. "Who built this thing?"

Dr. B slipped the remote into his pocket. "Someone who was trying to steer away from the usual sort of floor plan, I'm afraid."

Bess only gave the papers a glance. "The place was obviously designed by someone trying to replicate King

Minos's labyrinth. Which means we may have to fight a minotaur once we go inside."

Jesse turned the map back around. Usually he tried to memorize a place's layout, but this time it was impossible. He wasn't sure he could decipher it, let alone remember it. "How are we even going to find the right apartment?"

"The party is on the rooftops." Bess pointed to some horizontal lines on the drawing. "A catwalk spans the length of the buildings on the fourth level, so once we get there, we should be able to stroll along here until we spot the party."

"You understand this map?" Jesse asked.

"Nope. Dad took me around yesterday so I'd have a feel for the place."

Good. At least they had a chance at figuring it out that way.

Dr. B lowered his voice. "If you have to show Leo your powers, check for security cameras, and make sure no one else sees you. We don't want odd videos of you turning up on the internet. Also, be on the lookout for any of Overdrake's men. He may have someone watching Leo."

Jesse folded up his maps. "Why would Overdrake waste manpower on Leo? He isn't exactly a threat anymore."

"Because Leo could regain his powers," Dr. B said. "But more importantly, Overdrake knows the other Slayers might visit him. Therefore, Leo is effective bait."

Bess tucked her papers into her pocket. "That would be a cushy job: Getting paid to watch some kid on the off chance his old camp friends stopped by."

If Overdrake wanted to use ex-Slayers as bait, he would have had someone tailing Alyssa as well. He knew where she lived. But Dr. B had never mentioned any sort of suspicious surveillance there and he'd done recon on her house more than once so Lilly and Rosa could visit her.

"Nothing has ever turned up with Alyssa, has it?" Jesse asked.

"That doesn't mean Overdrake isn't watching Leo." Dr. B folded his arms behind his back, undeterred in his opinion. "He knows how valuable shielders are."

"True," Bess said with a smirk. "It's like I said, we're the MVPs."

Jesse put his maps away. "I think you mean: MVSs. At any rate, you have my vote. We have plenty of flyers, and we usually botch things." Neither said what they both knew. The flyers carried most of the burden of killing the dragons. They were the ones who confronted them in the air, avoiding fire and teeth in order to remove the Kevlar shield that protected the one vulnerable spot on a dragon: its underbelly.

"Lastly..." Dr. B reached into his breast pocket, then handed Jesse and Bess each a small dart. Tranquilizers to attach to the bottom of their watches. Once loaded there, they could be shot by pushing a button.

"I'm hesitant to provide such scant protection," Dr. B apologized, "but it seems unwise to try and gain entrance to a party while armed. If anyone checked for weapons, you'd find yourself in serious trouble."

Jesse and Bess both loaded their darts into their watches.

"Any questions?" Dr. B asked.

"Yeah," Bess said, pushing her sleeve away from her watch. "What sort of parties did you go to in college that you're worried about pat-downs and metal detectors?"

"If you wish to take handguns," Dr. B answered patiently, "I'll get them from the truck, but we'll need to go over reminders about shooting near crowds."

Bess held up her hand to stop him. "We'll be fine." Their heightened senses and extra strength were more than enough protection from drunken frat boys.

"Very well," Dr. B said. "I'll wait here unless you request backup. If you need a police distraction, I can always call and report underage drinking."

Jesse adjusted his watch making sure it would fire straight. "I doubt we'll need backup." It would be his luck to be caught in a raid, dragged to the police station, and then have to call his parents to pick him up. They wouldn't let him out of the house again.

As Jesse and Bess turned to go, Dr. B gave them a fatherly smile of encouragement. "I'm glad we're doing this. It's time we reminded Leo who he is."

If only it could be that easy. *Hey Leo, you're supposed to fight dragons...*

Jesse and Bess headed across the parking lot, walking close together. The lampposts cast tangled shadows of the barren trees across the pavement.

"Leo will ask why we're at a college party," Jesse said. "We need a story."

"I thought of one on the drive here," Bess replied. "We're out on a date and I wanted to go to a chick flick but you wouldn't take me because you're a guy and therefore hate all movies that aren't peppered with weapons. You thought we should go paintballing, but hello, I spent time doing my hair. I obviously don't want it covered in paint. Your friend Brock told you about the party and you wanted to check it out. I may or may not be so annoyed that I'll ditch you and go off with Leo."

Perhaps Bess had too much time on the drive to concoct a story. "Why do I have to look like a jerk in this scenario?"

She fluttered a hand at him. "Sometimes it can't be helped. The necessities of plot and all that."

They came to the walkway that led through the red brick buildings. Fall leaves, turned gray by the night, littered the ground. "How about we're together tonight because my girlfriend dumped me for another guy. You're not seeing anyone, so we decided to hang out."

The part about his girlfriend dumping him was true, even if Bess didn't know it yet. Or maybe she did. Tori might have told her about Dirk. Jesse wasn't about to ask. He already regretted not coming up with a different story. Thinking about Tori made his chest feel like he'd been punctured and his soul was slowly seeping out into the atmosphere. Which was why he was supposed to stop doing that.

"Speaking of me not seeing anyone..." Bess let her sentence drift off uncertainly. "Do you and Ryker ever talk about girls?"

They'd talked about Tori. More specifically, Ryker had told him, "You're way too invested in her. She's Senator Hampton's daughter. She's going to dump you, go for someone rich jerk, and you'll be carrying your heart home in confetti-sized pieces."

And that's pretty much what had happened last Friday. Tori could claim she kissed Dirk for strategic reasons, but she and Dirk had a history. They'd gotten together last September. For that matter, they'd gotten together her third day at camp. The two apparently couldn't be alone together for long without their lips meeting up.

"And if you do talk about girls," Bess said, bringing him back to the present. "Does Ryker ever talk about anyone in specific?"

"We mostly talk about training," Jesse said.

"Have you ever talked about me?"

Oh, that's where this was going. He should have guessed as much. Whenever Bess was around Ryker, she always got either flirty or demure. She'd even started wearing makeup to practice.

"He's not seeing anyone right now if that's what you're asking."

"I know that much. Willow and I talk." Ryker and Willow had stayed at Dr. B's house when they first became Slayers. Might still be. Dr. B kept those sorts of details secret. "I was wondering," Bess continued, "since you're his counterpart, if you knew what he thinks of me."

"He thinks you're an amazing Slayer and he likes you."

She cocked her head, trying to read more from his expression. "How much does he like me?"

"I don't know."

She let out a sigh. "You're his counterpart. If he liked me, you'd know, which means he must not like me that much."

"It's not that." Ryker was just smart enough to realize that girls made confetti out of your heart. "He's too busy thinking about dragons to think about girls."

Bess kicked a loose stone in their path, sending it skittering down the walkway. "That's one more reason to hate dragons."

The music grew louder, percussion and angry electric guitars. They'd reached the Village A apartment complex. From the outside, the structure looked normal enough, boxy red brick buildings interspersed with terrace patios and the occasional balcony. A sign on the sidewalk read: If you SEE something SAY something, then gave the number of the Georgetown police department. Hopefully no one would be calling about the two of them.

"There's a staircase this way," Bess said and strode to some concrete steps that led to the main level. Once there, they walked to a set of narrow metal stairs that zigzagged up the side of the building. Even from down here the scent of beer was overwhelming. He'd be able to smell it even without the help of his Slayer senses.

Bess went up the stairs, taking them fast. They passed so many discarded red Solo cups, they might have been left as a trail by Hansel and Gretel in their later, drunken years.

A few people were coming down the steps in various stages of soberness. Jesse and Bess remained silent when anyone was nearby, but after they'd passed by the last couple, Bess said, "Let me do the talking to Leo. I'm his counterpart. There has to be some part of him I can reach."

"If anyone can bring him back, it's you."

Leo had been the quietest Slayer, but he'd also been the first to notice if anyone was homesick so he could lend a listening ear. He'd been the last to insult anyone and the easiest to make blush. The one who was so unlike Bess, at least until the two of them got together. Whenever Leo had been around Bess, he was quicker to smile and laugh. The two of them always had some running inside joke that lasted all of camp.

Bess's pace increased. "I keep wondering if I could have done something to stop Leo from losing his memories. Maybe I should have warned him more to be careful. Maybe I should have broken the rules and kept in contact with him."

"It wasn't your fault," Jesse said.

"I know. But knowing something and feeling it are two different matters."

They turned from one staircase, twisted around and went up the next.

Finally they reached the top floor and the main catwalk which had not one, but two railings—a simple tan one that resembled a picket fence and a sturdier gray one that had obviously been added later when the first proved unsuccessful at keeping students on the right side.

From up here, the map of the complex made more sense. The footprints for the stories were different because the building in front of them was only three stories, the one in front of that was two, and on the other side of the road where the land sloped downward was another line of two-stories.

The view was worth creating buildings in a stair-step fashion. Past a row of trees, the Potomac River flowed by like a wide dark street. Beyond that, the city lights of Rosslyn glowed.

Jesse pulled his gaze away from the attraction of the landscape to the apartments on his other side. Each building had two apartments side by side that shared a large deck. The catwalk connected them all, leaving ten-foot gaps between the terraces.

Several people jostled by Bess and him on the catwalk. More than one party was going on up here. Looked like three. The one in the middle had a table set up and a group of people gathered around, cheering on a couple of guys who were playing beer pong.

"Do you see Leo anywhere?" Jesse asked.

"Not yet, but if he's here, I'll find him." Counterparts could always find one another when they were close.

They wandered past the first party. Bess shook her head and kept going. "If he's not on any of the terraces, we'll have to go inside the apartments to search for him."

They reached the middle party. A food table sat between apartments and a few people milled around it. A couple of guys were filling cups from the keg at the end of the table. A row of space heaters did their best to warm the area.

"This one," she murmured, and they strolled that way.

Two upperclassmen guys stood nearby monitoring the traffic. Jesse smiled at them in a casual manner. "Hi. Brock Booher invited us."

"Great," the first guy said, friendly enough. "Cover charge is ten dollars."

Jesse pulled out his wallet, but Bess beat him to it with a twenty. "Thanks."

She and Jesse made their way onto the terrace, trying to spot Leo among the people talking there. He was tall and thin with shaggy brown hair.

"There he is," Bess said, pointing to the food table. She hurried that way and Jesse followed, still not seeing Leo. He couldn't be either of the guys filling glasses at the keg. They were too short and stocky. The only other guy nearby had hair past his shoulders and wore a trench coat.

"Leo!" Bess called.

The guy in the coat turned. Jesse had to blink twice before he recognized him. Quiet, reserved Leo had turned goth. A swath of hair swept across his face, nearly hiding one of his eyes. He wore skintight black jeans, a T-shirt with skulls, and…was he wearing eyeliner?

Bess squealed in surprise. "Leo, it *is* you!"

He startled at the sight of them, then grinned. "Bess! Jesse!"

Instead of answering, Bess launched herself into his arms, nearly plowing him into the table. "It's so good to see you!"

He hugged her back then held her at arm's length to look her over. "I can't believe you're here. What brings you guys to Georgetown?"

"I'm thinking of applying," Jesse said, changing his story on the spot. "I wanted to check out the place."

"Cool." Leo's gaze bounced between the two of them, still taking them in. "Are the two of you dating?"

"Yes," Bess said at the same time Jesse said, "No." They'd never decided on that point. Something, Jesse now realized, they should have done on the walk here instead of talking about Ryker.

Leo cocked his head at them in confusion.

Bess pursed her lips and made an aggravated grunting sound at Jesse. "No? Is this your way of breaking up with me? So classy."

"Um, I..." Jesse stammered.

"First the paintball fiasco and now this." Bess folded her arms with the air of a martyr. "Men."

Leo laughed and shook his head at her. "You're such a liar. You haven't changed at all."

Bess laughed then too, letting her arms drop to her sides. "I've definitely changed. My lies are more interesting now."

Leo had seen through Bess's story so easily. Were his counterpart senses still working? Jesse shouldn't have gotten his hopes up. The lie hadn't been a good one. But a part of him hoped anyway.

"What about you?" Bess asked Leo. "How are your lies coming along?"

"I'm an expert, of course. I lie so well even I believe myself most of the time."

She flipped a strand of hair off his shoulder. "Your hair is longer."

"So is yours," he said with a note of defensiveness.

"I didn't say I didn't like it." She tilted her head, considering him. "I'm sure those bangs will come in handy should you ever need to hide your identity from surveillance cameras."

Leo made a tsking sound. "I was almost about to say how much I've missed you. Now I'm rethinking."

She playfully swatted him in the arm. "And you told me you were a good liar. You've missed me like crazy. Admit it."

He grinned. "Fine I admit it, but only so you won't hit me again." He glanced behind Bess and Jesse, his gaze sweeping the terrace.

"We didn't bring Rosa with us," Bess said.

Leo's eyes snapped back to Bess in embarrassment. "I wasn't... I didn't ask if you had." So easily flustered. He was actually blushing. Maybe he hadn't changed as much as Jesse had thought.

"You were wondering it," Bess said with mock offense. "I swear the only reason you ever hung out with me at camp was because I was Rosa's friend. She's doing fine, by the way. She's as sweet and adorable as always and as far as I know, single."

Leo brightened. "Good. You'll have to give me her number. I've been kicking myself that I never got it at camp."

Well, that was the first problematic request of the evening. With the exception of Tori and Jesse, the Slayers didn't have each other's phone numbers. They communicated through their watches. Dr. B had made this a rule so that if Overdrake ever captured any of them, he wouldn't be able to locate the other Slayers by tracking their phones.

Tori and Jesse probably shouldn't have exchanged numbers but after they'd started dating, they'd needed a way to communicate. They weren't about to set up dates through the Slayer channels.

Bess dug through her jacket pocket and pulled out a pen. "I don't have my phone with me, but give me your number and I'll text you Rosa's." She put the pen tip on the back of her hand, ready to write. When Bess did text him, the number would be from a computer with an untraceable IP address. Ditto for Rosa's contact information.

Leo rattled off his number, then added, "We should all get together again—have a camp reunion party."

"Absolutely," Jesse said. Taking Leo to some of their old practice spots might shake a few memories loose.

"You know what would be even better?" Bess's eyes widened as though an idea had occurred to her. "You could be one of the volunteers helping me with my science fair project."

"How would that be better than a party?" Leo asked.

"You'd get to see more of me. It will be super easy. You just need to eat Ling Zhi."

Leo flicked his bangs away from his eyes. "Ling what?"

"Ling Zhi mushrooms. They're an herbal supplement the ancient Chinese used to increase the immune system and promote long life. I'm having people take them for two months and track their energy level and illness rate."

Leo made a face, showing his distaste for the idea. "You know I hate mushrooms. Remember how I always picked them off my pizza?"

"Don't be a wuss," Bess said. "You can take Ling Zhi in capsules and won't even have to taste them, although you'll have to take a lot to get the same results."

Leo's expression of distaste didn't change.

Bess blinked her lashes innocently. "Don't you want more energy and less illness? Some people claim Ling Zhi even helps with cancer."

Leo cocked an eyebrow at her. "Are you doing a science project or starting a multi-level marketing company?"

Bess ignored his question and turned to Jesse. "Can you give Leo the Ling Zhi I just gave you? That way I won't have to make a special trip to Leo's house until his supply runs out."

"Sure." Jesse produced the bottle and the Ziploc bag. He shook the bottle making the capsules rattle. "This is the version for wusses."

Leo pushed Jesse's hands down, then glanced around the terrace. "Don't pull that stuff out here. People will think you've got drugs."

Oh. Jesse hadn't even considered that possibility. "It's not that sort of mushroom," he clarified.

Bess took the items and put them in the pockets of Leo's trench coat. "The powder is good in smoothies. One heaping tablespoon three times a day."

Leo rolled his eyes. "You want me to drink mushroom smoothies for two months?"

"This is for science," Bess insisted.

Leo shook his head. "Look, we both know if I say yes, I'll gag down some for a day or two and then forget about the whole thing until you call for my results. I don't want to ruin your science project and have you mad at me. I'd better pass." He reached into his pockets to retrieve the Ling Zhi.

"I'll call daily and remind you." Bess put her hands behind her back, refusing to take the mushrooms.

Leo shook his head again. "I'm sure you can find some people at your school who want to help you cure cancer."

Strike one. "Rosa is part of the experiment," Jesse put in. "If you're taking part too, you'll have something to talk to her about when you call."

Leo rocked back on his heels, unimpressed by the suggestion. "I know I used to be shy, but I've changed since camp. I can come up with something to say to Rosa that doesn't involve mushroom smoothies." His gaze traveled around the crowd. "But if you need another participant, my friend Ryan is a health nut. Runs cross country. He'd probably eat pinecones if you told him it would help his time on the mile."

Leo would probably give him the Ling Zhi before the night was over. Plan B it was, then. They'd tell Leo the truth about who he was and show him some proof.

"It's kind of loud out here," Jesse said. "Let's go somewhere and talk. We've got a lot to catch up on."

"You want to leave already?" Leo asked. "You haven't even gotten any drinks yet."

Cups of beer sat lined up on the table next to the potato chips and dip. Leo picked up a couple and turned back to Bess and Jesse.

Jesse had known that Leo drank, but somehow seeing the proof, casually held in his hands, still stung. It was a reminder that he'd chosen to leave them.

"We don't drink," Jesse said.

Leo shrugged. "No worries. There's soda in the ice chest." He put one of the drinks back on the table and took a sip from the other.

"You shouldn't drink," Bess said, perhaps too sharply.

Leo took another sip and smiled, goading her. "Why not?"

Bess stepped over to him nonchalantly. "Because you're underage, it's bad for you, and..." She knocked the cup from his hand before he could bring it to his lips again. "It's too messy."

The beer spilled down the front Leo's shirt. He swore and pulled at his shirt while arching his back. "What the— why did you do that?"

"Because I care about you," Bess said, still sweet. "This is what love feels like."

Jesse grabbed some napkins from the table and handed them to Leo. "Sorry. Sometimes Bess is just..." *too emotionally involved in your choices.* "...is just Bess."

She folded her arms. "Right. So let's go somewhere and talk."

Leo pressed the napkins to his shirt. A hopeless task. He was standing in a puddle. "Only if you know a place with a Laundromat."

Jesse gave Leo a few more napkins. "We really need to talk to you."

Leo kept dabbing at his chest. "And I've really got to get out of this wet shirt."

There was one way to fix this. Jesse slipped off his jacket, handed it to Bess, then took off his shirt. "Here," he said, holding it out. "I'll trade you."

Leo waved Jesse's offering away. "Nah, I'm not going to take your shirt."

"It's fine," Jesse said. "I'm not cold." Perks of having his Slayer powers on. "I still have my jacket.

"You don't have to do that." Leo kept wiping his shirt with napkins. Most of them were ripping into wet shreds.

Bess rolled her eyes. "Just take Jesse's shirt so we can go somewhere else. Seriously, every girl on the roof is staring at him now."

Jesse glanced across the terrace. Yep. Quite a number of girls were eyeing him. Some with blatant approval. One swirled her drink invitingly and winked.

Bess took the shirt from Jesse's hand and shoved it at Leo. "Take Mr. Eyecandy's shirt before one of the gawkers decides to come over and attach herself to him. We have something important to tell you."

"Fine." While Leo peeled off his shirt, Jesse put his jacket back on. The girls, he noticed, were still watching him.

Leo handed Bess his shirt. "Where did you want to go?"

She put Leo's shirt on the back of a folding chair to dry off. "Down by the library," she said. "No one will be there."

"Just a sec," Leo said. "Let me tell Ryan where I'm going. He's my ride." He craned his neck, scanning the terrace until his gaze landed on the beer pong table. "Ryan!" he called.

No one there paid attention to him. Too noisy.

Leo marched toward the table. "Yo, Ryan!"

One of the spectators turned. He was average height, beefy, with thick arms and a neck that seemed too big for his head. His hair had been cut so it looked like a dark halo. "What?" he called back and then noticed Jesse and Bess standing there.

That's when everything changed. Because it only took that single look for Jesse to realize Ryan was going to be a serious problem.

CHAPTER 9

As Jesse stared at Ryan, the back of his neck tingled with a warning. When Slayers' powers were turned on, they picked up on the adrenaline levels of the people around them. Fear, anger, and aggression all transmitted as strongly as smells and sounds. Jesse hadn't sensed any of those emotions at the party, but suddenly all three spiked from Ryan.

Not normal emotions. Not normal levels. The only times Jesse had felt that sort of hostility was when Overdrake's men were attacking.

"Crap," Bess muttered. She'd felt it too. Turned out, Dr. B had been right about Overdrake watching Leo. The guy must be on Overdrake's payroll and he'd recognized them.

Ryan reached into his jacket pocket. Was he going for a gun? "Shield," Jesse hissed.

He'd barely finished saying the word before he figured out where Bess put the forcefield. A guy strolling away from the beer pong table smacked into it and fell backward. His drink splashed on a couple of girls who stood nearby. Both shrieked in annoyance.

Ryan kept his gaze on Jesse. When his hand lifted from his pocket, he held a phone, not a gun.

He must be calling for backup. In the span of two seconds Jesse analyzed his options. He could tell Bess to drop the shield, rush over, grab Ryan's phone, and crush it. But he might not get to the phone fast enough to prevent a warning, and crushing a stranger's phone would cause a scene. Leo especially wouldn't understand that sort of thing.

Jesse could shoot Ryan with the tranquilizer dart. But he wouldn't go unconscious for a minute—too long to prevent him from warning whoever was on the other end of the phone. Besides, once he started staggering around, Leo would worry about him and refuse to leave. He'd probably insist on staying until the paramedics arrived.

In fact, any sort of altercation with Ryan would only drive a wedge between Jesse and Leo.

Man, Jesse hated when the only option was fleeing.

"We've got to go," he told Bess. Ryan hadn't produced a weapon, but that didn't mean he didn't have one. He might be refraining from using it around so many witnesses. "Keep your shield between us and him."

Bess's hands fisted at her side. "We can't leave Leo."

Leo probably wasn't in danger. Still, Jesse didn't like leaving him either—vulnerable and unaware that he was friends with the enemy. It felt like letting Overdrake win. "Leo," Jesse called and waved to him. "Let's go."

Leo was still on their side of the shield. He'd momentarily stopped his march toward Ryan, distracted by the guy who'd fallen and showered girls with beer. They were wiping angrily at their hair. Leo turned his attention back to Ryan and gestured behind him at Jesse and Bess. "Hey, I'm going to chill with some old friends for a while. Don't leave without me, okay?"

Ryan plastered on a smile that did nothing to decrease his adrenaline levels. He held the phone away from his mouth to talk to Leo. "Have them stay. The party is just getting started."

Right. Ryan wanted to keep them here until more of Overdrake's men arrived. He probably didn't realize that Jesse and Bess knew what he was. Either Overdrake hadn't told his surveillance men about the Slayers' powers or Ryan didn't think they were turned on right now.

"We'll be back," Leo assured him.

No, they wouldn't. While Ryan and Leo spoke, Jesse tapped the side button on his watch, sending Dr. B his own distress message: Enemy nearby.

"You've gotta stay," Ryan insisted. "Hold on a sec." He muttered something into the phone, then slipped it into his pocket. "I just told Amelia you were here and she's on her way over to see you. If you leave now, she'll think you ditched her."

"Amelia?" Leo repeated, his resolve wavering.

"You know what would be fun?" Bess called. "We should go see Rosa."

Jesse nodded. "She lives nearby." He had no idea where she lived.

His watch lit up, Dr. B asking for more details and reporting that he would call the police. It would take law enforcement a few minutes to get here. Fortunately, it would most likely take Overdrake's men even longer to arrive. He probably didn't have men stationed nearby.

Leo ambled back to Jesse and Bess. "I'd love to go with you but I probably should stay. Amelia is a friend who has been having a hard time. I owe her."

Amelia hadn't been on the phone with Ryan unless she was also working for Overdrake.

Time for a new strategy. Jesse shrugged. "No problem. We can stay."

Bess shot him a sharp look. She knew they shouldn't stay and Jesse had no way to tell her he was lying to Leo.

Jesse motioned in the direction of the catwalk. "Let's go where it's quieter and we can catch up on old times while you wait for your friend."

"Okay," Leo said. "But let me get some food first. I'm starving." He edged past them to the food table and picked up a paper plate.

Bess leaned over to Jesse and whispered, "This isn't a good place for a shield. I'm already sliding it all over the place to avoid more accidents."

Ryan shuffled over to them, pretending casualness. "So how do you guys know Leo?"

"We're his age," Bess said. "How do you know him?"

Ryan laughed and shoved his hands into his pants pockets. Not enough room there for a gun. If he had one of those it would be in his jacket. "I'm only a year older than Leo," Ryan said. "We went to the same high school. I'm trying to convince him to come to Georgetown."

Ryan seemed older than a freshman. Had Overdrake discovered where Leo went to high school and hired someone to infiltrate the place or had Overdrake just convinced one of Leo's friends to work for him? In the end, it didn't matter. The result was the same.

"I don't recognize you from school," Ryan said, still questioning them about how they knew Leo.

No point in denying where they met. Overdrake already knew the information, and Leo would answer if Jesse didn't. "We went to camp together." Jesse matched Ryan's casualness. "Every summer since junior high."

Hopefully Ryan didn't realize that he and Bess were onto him. Ditching him would be easier that way.

Leo finally finished filling his plate and returned to the group, eating potato chips. "Dragon camp," he said. "Back when I was a nerd."

"You were never a nerd," Bess protested. Her gaze only shot to Leo for a moment then returned to Ryan. Her shield must be right in front of Jesse's face. If Leo walked forward, he'd knock into it.

Leo put his hand on the side of his mouth as though letting Ryan in on a secret. "Bess's dad ran the camp. She's a little biased."

Ryan forced a grin. "Dragon camp. Sounds interesting. What sort of thing did you do? Paint ceramic dragons?"

He was trying to keep them talking until his backup arrived. How long would Overdrake's men take? Twenty minutes? Longer? Were any stationed in Georgetown?

"We did normal camp stuff," Leo said. "Archery, horseback riding, running around and nearly burning down the forest."

They'd also leaped from tree branches and dodged fireballs. Did Leo remember any of that? Jesse would have to ask him later. Right now, he needed to get rid of Ryan and take Leo someplace where he and Bess could explain the situation. If they showed him their powers, maybe they could convince him to leave with them. At the very least, they needed to warn him about Ryan. The guy was being paid to watch him.

While Leo was telling Ryan about all the jogging they'd had to do at camp, Jesse broke into the conversation. "We should let Ryan get back to his beer pong." He took one of Leo's potato chips and bit into it. "Nice meeting you."

"I was done watching the game," Ryan said. "I don't mind hanging with you guys."

Bess smile apologetically. "Sorry, but we need to talk to Leo privately. He can get back to you in a few minutes." She hooked her hand through Leo's arm. "Let's go downstairs."

"You can't leave the party." Sharpness edged Ryan's words. "The tenants don't want strangers roaming around."

"We won't go far," Bess said, already pulling Leo with her.

"Seriously," Ryan said. "Don't leave the rooftops."

Leo glanced over his shoulder at Ryan. "Relax. I'll be back soon."

Not if Jesse could help it. He shadowed Bess as she towed Leo toward the right side of the building. He hoped they'd find stairs there. Otherwise they'd have to use the main catwalk and it was crowded and in plain sight.

"What did you want to talk to me about?" Leo asked, his pace too slow.

"It's hard to explain without sounding crazy," Jesse said. "but we want you to come back to the Slayers."

"You mean camp?" Leo shook his head. "I've got to work during the summer."

Bess let out a huff. "Leo, you used to have superpowers and you need to get them back."

Jesse smiled at her stiffly. "Remember how we weren't going to sound crazy?"

"I'm sorry," she said. "I don't have the patience for subtlety, and I can't pretend it doesn't matter."

The music was too loud to hear footsteps following them. Was it Jesse's imagination, or did he sense them anyway? Jesse looked over his shoulder. People were strolling around, but no one seemed to be directly following them. Ryan was watching them, eyes narrowed. If he had a gun, would he come after them and use it once they went around the side of the building? Even with silencers, gunshots were loud. Probably louder than the music. Might not be that kind of gun, though. Shang had been hit with a tranquilizer. Those didn't make a lot of noise.

"We need you," Bess kept her voice low. "I've already fought two dragons. Me. One shielder. Do you have any idea how much we need your help?"

Leo pressed his lips together and turned to Jesse. "What is she talking about?"

"And that's another thing," Bess said, waving her free hand at him. "You just forgot our entire mission. How could you think that wouldn't matter? If it was only your life at stake, okay, then be an idiot if you want, but you knew it wasn't just your life. It was all of our lives. And it was the lives of people across the nation. Why would you do this?"

Leo shot Jesse another look. "Does she need some medication or something?"

Bess narrowed her eyes at Leo. "I need you to remember who you are for two minutes."

"Bess," Jesse broke in, "this isn't helping."

They rounded the corner. A walkway wound across the building giving way to narrow metal stairs. A matching set lined the next building over.

Walking down them two at a time was snug fit, so Bess maneuvered Leo in front and propelled him forward. Jesse followed. Leo went down a half dozen steps, nearly stumbled, then swatted Bess's hand. "Stop pushing. You're going to make me fall."

"Hurry," she told him. "We need to get away from Ryan. He's not who you think he is."

Leo planted his feet. "What are you talking about?"

Bess didn't keep pushing him. If she had, he might have toppled downward. "Your friend works for Overdrake."

"Who's Overdrake?" Leo asked.

"A terrorist," Jesse said.

"Right," Leo said with a scoff. "Is this some sort of joke?"

Bess turned to Jesse. "Should I carry him?"

Before Jesse had a chance to answer, the sound of clanging footsteps echoed below them.

Ryan's backup couldn't be here already, could it? One glance confirmed Jesse's fears. Three guys were on the bottom floor, rushing upward. He doubted they were students in a hurry.

In a few minutes, he and Bess would have two fronts to contend with. If they ran back to the terraces, Overdrake's men could spread out, attacking them from even more directions. And these guys would definitely have weapons.

Bess drew in a sharp breath. "Let's go to the rooftop catwalk."

The stairs leading down from there were their best bet of escape. They didn't wind through the complex like these ones did. She took hold of Leo's arm to tug him upward.

He tried to shake off her grasp, oblivious of danger. "You couldn't carry me if you tried."

A noise sounded near the top of the stairs. Footsteps. Jesse turned to see Ryan rounding the corner. He looked down at them, smug and self-assured. "I told you that you weren't supposed to leave the party."

He sauntered over to the stairs, hands behind his back. Was he carrying a weapon? Jesse hesitated before telling Bess where to put her shield. If she put it in between Ryan and them, she would block their escape.

Leo glanced from the men running up the stairs to Ryan questioningly. "What are you doing?"

"I'm getting a bonus." Ryan swung his arm forward, pointing a gun in their direction.

"Plow him," Jesse told Bess.

Instead of keeping her shield stationary, Bess pushed it into Ryan, fast and hard. He fell to the ground like a bowling pin and the gun clattered from his hand.

Jesse gestured at the staircase on the adjacent section of the building. "We'll use those stairs. I'll take Leo."

Leo had frozen, gaping open-mouthed at Ryan. Bess jumped onto the railing and then leaped the ten feet separating the staircases. Leo's mouth fell further open. "What the—"

Jesse hooked his arms underneath Leo's and sprung into the air, half leaping, half flying across the gap. Leo let out a startled scream of protest. When they landed on the other staircase, Jesse released Leo. He nearly fell forward, not because he didn't have footing, but because his knees gave out.

Leo grabbed hold of the side of the building for support. "I can't believe you did that! Next time you want to risk your life, don't drag me with you!"

Jesse, Bess, and Leo were at the next section of buildings—closer to the stairs at the rooftop catwalk, but far from safe. Ryan got to his knees and was crawling to the gun. In a moment, he would shoot at them. Bess could only protect against gunfire until Overdrake's other men came up behind them.

Bess bounded up the remaining stairs, taking them three at a time.

Jesse couldn't leave Leo, not with Overdrake's men closing in. Ryan had dropped his façade and openly pulled a gun. Leo might not be safe from him anymore. Maybe Overdrake's men would think he'd seen too much.

Jesse grabbed his friend by the middle, flung him over his shoulder, and flew up the remaining stairs. When he reached the top, he put Leo down, but only so bystanders wouldn't think he was kidnapping someone. He took hold of Leo's elbow and yanked him into a run. "People will start shooting at us soon, including your buddy Ryan. If you don't want to be hit, move faster."

Leo stumbled along next to Jesse, glancing over his shoulder. "Why would he—what's going on?"

Bess darted around some lawn chairs. "We were trying to tell you before, now we don't have time."

They were almost to the end of the terrace, almost to the catwalk. "You'll just have to trust us," Jesse said.

That's when his attention was drawn to the far end of the catwalk. On the right, two police officers had emerged from the elevators.

Jesse should have felt relieved. Dr. B had called the police and now they were here. Overdrake's men wouldn't shoot into a crowd if police could return fire. But the relief didn't come. Instead Jesse's adrenaline ratcheted up a notch. It took a moment for him to realize what his senses were telling him. Something wasn't right. One of the policemen was walking at a normal pace—looking at the students like a father who'd caught his children up past their bedtime. Disapproving, but not alarmed. The other was hurrying, trying to get around people.

The man's aggression, fear, and adrenaline were too high. He wasn't here to help. He was on the hunt.

Overdrake had at least one man in the police department. He'd known Dr. B had been a professor at Georgetown. Maybe he'd concentrated men here because of that. Jesse didn't like the other explanation that came to him—that Overdrake had men planted in all the cities surrounding DC.

Bess slowed. "Police on both sides. Where do I put my shield?"

Jesse caught sight of the second pair of policemen on the left side of the catwalk, both calm. Didn't matter if those were legitimate cops, as long as one of them was crooked, Jesse and Bess were in trouble. Clusters of people were standing on the catwalk, blocking the policemen's path, but that wouldn't last long. Already, students were moving out of the way.

"Put the shield behind us," Jesse said. "We're going straight."

"Straight?" Leo repeated. He dragged his feet, refusing to move.

"I've got him," Jesse told Bess. "Go."

Leo tried to break Jesse's grasp. "No way, man. You'll break our necks."

Leo shouldn't have worried so much. The roof below them wasn't that far down.

Bess streaked forward, and Jesse ran after her, dragging Leo along. People stumbled out of their way, muttering angry exclamations. More and more heads turned to watch them. As Bess hurdled over the railing, a collective gasp went up from the crowd.

"Stop, stop, stop!" Leo cried and kept repeating the word as Jesse propelled him to the railing. Jesse leaped into the air, hauling Leo with him. They landed on the roof below, sliding on the gravel that peppered the roof. Leo pitched forward and almost fell. Jesse didn't let go of him. They had more terraces and roofs to run across before they made it to the street.

A whooshing noise came from behind him, something spinning through the air. Two dark objects smacked into Bess's forcefield.

"Come on!" she called. She stood at the end of the roof ready to jump down to the terrace below.

Jesse ran, forcing Leo forward. He wanted to fly, but at this point, a dozen students were probably videoing the event. It was better to pretend he was a normal person or at least a normal person with good leaping skills.

They landed on the terrace and Jesse kept pulling Leo. His protests had subsided into gurgled moans. Another leap. As they ran over the next roof, Leo panted out, "Now what are we going to do? We're stuck." The roof was two stories high, too far to jump down.

They only had one choice. "We're going to fly."

Jesse dragged Leo—who was now cursing and trying to yank his arm free of Jesse's grasp—to the side of the building where Bess waited.

She took hold of Jesse's back and he grabbed Leo around the waist. "Don't scream."

Leo didn't listen to this piece of advice and screamed not only as Jesse leaped over the edge but the entire time they sailed to the sidewalk. Fortunately, no one was on the street to see them, and they were close enough to the building to be shielded from view from of anyone watching from the top, so Jesse continued to glide along toward the parking lot. Not the most comfortable way to travel, but it was faster than forcing Leo into a run.

Leo stopped screaming and clutched Jesse's arm, gaping at the ground that slid by under their feet. "How is this happening?" he demanded, and then immediately added, "Someone slipped something into my drink, didn't they? None of this is real."

"It's real," Bess said. "And it's not even the first time you've flown this way."

Leo shut his eyes. "I'm never going to another college party," he muttered.

Dr. B's truck came into sight. He sat behind the wheel, motor running. "I'm dropping you off with Dr. B," Jesse told Leo. "He and Bess can explain things to you." The sooner they all left the better.

Jesse deposited Leo on the ground and Bess joined him.

As Jesse turned to go to his car, Dr. B opened the door for Bess and Leo to get in. "It's good to see you again," he said to Leo as though he were making a polite social visit. "Do get in. We've things to discuss."

***

Half an hour later, Jesse was sitting with Dr. B, Bess, and Leo at a café in DC. Leo's hands shook as he took sips of coffee. Dr. B had ordered sandwiches and fries for all of them, but most of it sat on the table untouched. Jesse wasn't hungry. Bess was only playing with her fries.

Dr. B and Bess had explained everything to Leo on the drive here, but he seemed too stunned to take it in. So they had reiterated most of the information again while watching Leo drink coffee.

"We need to decide how to best protect your safety," Dr. B said. "Even though Overdrake probably doesn't see you as a threat, you're still a potential liability to him. And now that you know of his existence, he might not be so willing to leave you alone."

"I don't know of his existence," Leo said with frustration. "I only know what you've told me, and I'm not sure how much to believe about that. I'm just supposed to accept that my memories are wrong and all this stuff happened that I don't remember?"

Why was it so hard for him to believe? Jesse leaned forward over the table. "I flew with you down on the street. You saw Bess's shield knock into Ryan. How can you doubt what we're telling you?"

"Okay, granted," Leo held up a hand, "I saw you do some weird stuff. But I've also seen magicians saw women in half and make people disappear. Just because I can't explain it, doesn't mean you're telling me the truth."

Bess folded her arms. "If you like, I can hit you with my shield again."

He glared at her. "Don't do that anymore. It's annoying."

Again? Apparently, a few things had happened at the restaurant before he got here.

"You saw Ryan pull a gun on us," Jesse said. "Doesn't that tell you something?"

Leo picked up a fry and took a bite. "Maybe he was trying to protect me because the two of you were dragging me off somewhere. I know him a lot better than I know you. You're completely different people than I thought."

Bess let out a long breath. "You do know us, Leo. We've been your friends for years."

"According to you, the friends I knew from camp weren't the friends I actually remember. You expect me to believe I had a completely different forgotten life." He finished the fry and took another. "How much food do you need to have in your stomach to dilute the effects of alcohol?"

"I don't know," Bess said, "but I think you've had enough coffee. You're shaking."

"The caffeine isn't why I'm shaking."

"We need to discuss your safety," Dr. B said, gently turning the conversation back to his original topic.

Leo made a sound that was half grunt, half laugh. "I'm supposed to trust you with my safety? You're the ones that were running from the police and jumping off rooftops." He leaned back in his chair and ran a hand through his hair. "Man, am I going to be charged with fleeing from the police?"

"I doubt it," Jesse said. "There's probably video to show that you weren't acting on your own accord."

Dr. B steepled his fingers on the table. "We can move your family and provide you with a new identity so that Overdrake won't know how to find you. However, you'll have to break ties with everyone you know. As we've seen from Ryan, some of them could be operatives for Overdrake.

Leo lifted his hands, protesting the idea. "You want me to give up my whole life?"

Pretty much, Jesse thought. That's the cost. That's what we've all had to do. But confirming this wouldn't make Leo feel better.

"I want you to give up your life," Dr. B said, "in order to protect it."

Leo's lips pressed together, far from convinced with this line of reasoning. "Until you showed up, I was protecting my life just fine." He held his hand out, palm upwards, to Dr. B. "Now if you give me my phone back, I'll call for a ride home."

Dr. B. reached into his pockets, taking Leo's phone from one and the battery from the other. He handed them both to Leo. "Once you've had some time to think about what we've told you, we'll contact you again."

"Right," Leo pushed his chair back from the table and stood. "I'll watch for the bat signal."

Jesse rubbed his forehead. This had all gone so badly and now Leo was leaving, still unconvinced about everything they'd told him. How could he ignore the facts?

Leo took three steps then thudded against Bess's shield. He cursed and rubbed his nose. "Would you stop that?"

"At least start taking the Ling Zhi," she said.

"Fine," he said, still facing the door. "Just let me go."

She picked up a fry. "You know, I can tell when you're lying."

"I'll take them," Leo said louder then marched forward, one hand lifted in front of him to check for shields.

Bess leaned toward her father and lowered her voice. "We can't let him leave. Do something."

Dr. B stared at Leo's retreating back with the mournful expression. "He has a choice in the matter. I can't make him choose us."

"But his life is in danger," she persisted. "Sometimes you have to kidnap someone for their own good."

Dr. B shook his head. "If we forced him to come with us the FBI would investigate and we would put our whole operation at risk. And what for? Leo would hate us." He let out a heavy sigh. "I'll have some of our people keep an eye on him and help him if he's in trouble. We can't do more than that."

Leo opened the café door and strode outside, phone in hand, without looking back at them.

He was gone and they might never see him again. Overdrake could make sure of that.

Bess opened her mouth to speak, then swallowed the words instead. She put her elbows on the table, buried her face in her hands, and began to cry. Jesse reached over and rubbed her back in consolation.

The way Leo had stalked off and left—it felt like losing him all over again. They'd failed. Jesse hated that he couldn't change that fact, and he hated that he couldn't do anything to make Bess feel better.

CHAPTER 10

Tori didn't hear from Jesse over Thanksgiving break, didn't hear from Dirk either, for that matter. Although she did hear from Bess and Rosa, her closest Slayer friends. Dr. B didn't like the Slayers to use their watches for personal communications, but Tori ignored this rule and messaged both of them. *Whether you agree with what I've done or not, please understand I did it to help—because I'm trying to keep us all safe. Don't be mad.*

Back when Tori had agreed to join the Slayers, she'd known she might face death, and she'd accepted that. But she'd never thought about how much her life itself would change. Not just because of the secrets, but because her knowledge of the danger and dragons set her apart from her family and friends in a way she hadn't expected.

So many things seemed different now. She knew of Overdrake's threat and had faced and fought him and his men more than once. She'd flown through the sky, ridden on dragons, and delved into the mind of one. She wasn't the same person anymore—was stronger, deeper and more intense—but she couldn't explain any of it to other people. Really, only the other Slayers understood her. A small group. And she couldn't bear the thought that she'd disappointed them.

Rosa had written back right away. Tori had known she would. Rosa was too sweet, too kind to ignore an apology.

I understand and I'm not angry anymore. But next time, talk to us first. You've got to learn to trust us.

Bess didn't reply for a few hours—perhaps she had to think over her response, or perhaps she was out somewhere busy with her social life. Or both.

We're cool, she finally wrote. *Either your gamble will pay off and everyone will be forced to agree it was brilliant, or we'll be dead and it won't matter. Well played, my friend.*

Typical Bess. She refused on principle to take most things seriously.

When Tori walked into journalism class on Monday, Tacy was as beautiful and perky as always, and nearly draped over Jesse's desk. Jesse didn't seem to mind. He was chatting with her.

Jealousy spiked through Tori. She supposed that was Jesse's intent. He was showing her how easy it was for him to move on and forget about her.

Tori was *so* not in the mood for this. She ignored him through class and through lunch too.

Dr. B sent a private message to her watch during last period.

I've called a Slayer practice after school. Have your driver drop you off at Jesse's house for a study group. Jesse will tell his parents that the two of you are going out on a date and he'll drive you to the practice grounds. Let me know if you can't comply.

Well, that was just what she wanted to do—spend time in a car with Jesse, then face the Slayers. How many of them were still angry at her?

But there was no getting around it. She'd already missed too many Slayer practices and she was on probation. Time to face them. She phoned her mother and told her about the study group.

After school, Tori gave Jesse's address to Lars and he dutifully drove her there.

Jesse lived in an average suburb: narrow streets lined with cars, homes made of brick and clapboard siding, yards with bare trees and the occasional forgotten toy laying on the grass, soon to be buried until the spring thaw.

Jesse's house was a boxy, one-story brick with black shutters and a sit-down porch that attempted charm, but didn't quite manage it. Too sparse. The chairs sitting there looked like an afterthought, as though they hadn't fit in the kitchen and had therefore been relegated outside.

Lars scanned the area and opened his door. As he got out, his hands never strayed far from the gun he kept tucked in his holster. He doubled as a bodyguard, making sure she got where she needed to go.

Tori climbed out of the car. "You don't have to see me to the door."

He marched up the walk beside her anyway, swaggering as though attempting to intimidate the surrounding shrubbery. "I take orders from your parents, not you."

Okay, maybe she *had* ditched him once too often, but she'd had good reasons. Now he made a habit of giving her curt little lectures or pointedly asked her if she was trying to get him fired. You wouldn't think a six-foot-four war veteran would be so touchy. But yeah, he was.

When she reached the door, she rang the bell.

After a few moments, Jesse's mother answered. She was a middle-aged woman with straight dark hair cut in a no-nonsense bob. Her brown eyes were similar to Jesse's but her other features seemed to belong solely to her. Crisp, professional, unforgivably competent. Tori had to pretend she didn't know the woman's real last name was Harris. The family went by Richardson now, just as Jesse went by Jonathan.

Mrs. Harris-now-Richardson looked from Lars to Tori with surprise. "Hello," she said. Tori could tell she meant, "Why are you standing on my doorstep?"

Hadn't Jesse told her they were going on a date? Then again, maybe it was for the best that he hadn't. Lars thought she'd come to do homework.

"Hi," Tori said. "I'm here to see Jonathan."

Mrs. Harris stared at her blankly.

"We're studying," Tori added.

Mrs. Harris's eyes turned to Lars, a question forming on her lips.

"Lars isn't staying," Tori assured her. "He just drives me around and makes sure I'm not kidnapped on the way to people's doorsteps." She waved a goodbye at her bodyguard. "See, I'm fine. I'll give you a call when we're done."

Jesse had apparently been changing out of his school uniform. He sauntered into the room wearing jeans and pulling a T-shirt over his head. "Hi, Tori."

The sight of him—that flash of his abs—shouldn't have made Tori stare. She'd gone swimming with Jesse a dozen times during the summer, and besides, at camp most of the Slayer guys had considered shirts optional. But months had passed since then. Her immunity to chiseled abs had worn off.

Mrs. Harris moved out of the way to allow Tori entrance. "Come in."

Tori's gaze snapped back to Jesse's mother. Had she seen Tori gawking at her son? "Thanks," Tori murmured and tried not to blush as she walked inside.

Mrs. Harris smiled, but it was decidedly forced and a bit horrified. Back when Jesse had first introduced them, his mom had pretty much disliked Tori at first sight. Her feelings didn't appear to have changed since then. "The two of you are studying?"

"Yeah," Jesse said. "We're going out to eat and we'll do some studying afterward."

"Oh," Mrs. Harris said. "How nice." To her credit, by the time she said the last sentence, her disapproval was hidden in politeness. "Don't stay out too late. It's a school night."

"Might take a while," Jesse said. "We've got a lot to go over." He crossed to the window and glanced out—no doubt checking to make sure Lars hadn't stationed himself out front—then he motioned for Tori to follow him through the house to the garage.

His home was about what she'd imagined it would be. Worn furniture spread through the rooms, the kind that looked comfortably lived in. A large family picture hung on the wall. Jesse smiled in a way that was more posed than natural. His real smile lit up his eyes, made everything about him seem warm and shining. But even his posed smile was nice. It was probably hard to take a bad picture of Jesse.

The bookshelves in the living room told her that this family took reading seriously. That was bound to happen when both parents were teachers.

It was odd to see this part of Jesse's life, to see the place where he was just a normal teenager and not a Slayer captain. And it was especially odd to be alone with him after they'd spent the last week ignoring each other.

In the garage, an aging silver Prius waited for them among stacks of moving boxes. Tori climbed in the passenger side and wished she'd been able to change out of her school uniform. Her fireproof pants and jacket were much more comfortable when worn over jeans.

Jesse got in beside her, opened the garage door, and drove onto the street. The grass in the yards they passed was a faded green. Patches of fallen leaves clumped together along the roadside. Everything looked tired and dismal.

Neither of them spoke for a few minutes. The silence that hung between them was thick, filled with things that still needed to be said. Tori glanced at Jesse from the corner of her eyes, taking in the sweep of his bangs lying against his forehead, his tan skin, his brown eyes fringed by thick lashes. His profile was so familiar and now so untouchable.

He'd had enough time to cool down, hadn't he? Did he still want things to be this way between them?

"So," she began as though this were any other conversation, "why didn't you tell your mom we were going out?"

Jesse's gaze stayed on the street. "I told her I was going out. I just didn't specify who I was going with."

"Oh. Does she dislike me because my dad is a Republican or for some other reason?"

"She doesn't dislike you." He barely stopped at a stop sign before turning onto another street. "I told her she shouldn't vote for Senator Ethington, and so now she thinks you're converting me to the Republican Party."

Tori scoffed at the idea. "I can't even get you to listen to my Slayer strategies. I doubt I'd have much luck with politics."

"I listen to you about Slayer stuff. I just question the dragon lord stuff."

Ever since Thanksgiving, whenever Tori had thought about Aaron, she'd felt a sense of dread well up inside of her. She wasn't about to admit to Jesse that Aaron had wanted Overdrake's approval, that Aaron wanted to please his father. "You're the one who told me that in battle you can't play it safe. You've got to take chances. That's what I did by sending Aaron in. I took a chance."

Jesse shook his head, jaw tight. "It was Dirk who always said you can't play it safe. I tend to err on the side of caution."

Jesse was right. It *was* Dirk who encouraged her to take chances. She'd heard the advice so often, she'd thought it came from Jesse too.

He was still shaking his head. "I can see how you'd get us mixed up, though."

She didn't miss the barb in his words. "I kissed Dirk for a strategic advantage. If kissing some girl gave you a strategic advantage against Overdrake, you'd do it, wouldn't you?"

He didn't answer. Which meant he knew she had a point. "And I would be more understanding about it," she added.

"How attractive is the girl in question?"

"Why does that matter?"

"I think it would matter in how understanding you were afterward."

He was determined to be difficult. "I would be understanding either way. I'd just be less happy if she was hot."

Jesse tapped his fingers against the steering wheel and put on a contemplative expression. "Tacy might have dragon lord information."

"She doesn't."

"You never know."

He was teasing her. Was that a good sign or a bad one? If his anger had faded and he was still keeping his distance from Tori, where did that leave her?

"The last time we talked," she said, "you told me I needed to figure out if I was a Slayer or a dragon lord. But I think I can be both. Our best bet during a fight might be if I'm down on the ground, hidden somewhere, while I try to get control of the dragon. At the very least, I'll be able to distract Overdrake."

"Distracting Overdrake isn't enough. We need you in the sky as a flyer." He said the words earnestly, which made them feel like a compliment. "We wouldn't have killed either of the last dragons without you."

"If I can control a dragon, we won't have to kill it."

"And if you try to control it, you might not be able to kill it." Jesse shot her a quick glance. "Dirk obviously thinks that if he turns you into a dragon lord, you'll switch to his side. How do we know he's not right?"

She refused to let her mind wander to Dirk's techniques. "I guess you'll have to trust me."

Jesse huffed out a breath, one that mixed with the hum of the tires on the road. They'd come to the highway and the Prius rattled slightly while attempting higher speeds. "No one ever thinks they're vulnerable. But sometimes people aren't as strong as they imagine."

She thought of Aaron again, of the pleasure he'd felt on the day he'd learned to fly and he'd earned Overdrake's approval. Aaron had thought he wouldn't be vulnerable to his father's influences, but maybe he was.

Tori wasn't vulnerable, though. She couldn't be won over by Ferraris. Or dragon rides. Or Dirk's kisses. "You'll have to trust me," she said again, and added more quietly, "If I wanted to date Dirk, I could. I don't, though. I want you." She wished she could slip her hand into his and scoot closer. Doing that would make everything feel normal again. But he was keeping both hands on the wheel and she was belted in. And besides, things weren't normal between them.

Jesse's gaze went to hers and she saw a flash of happiness in his eyes that was quickly replaced by caution, perhaps mistrust even. He returned his attention to the road. "Are you going to see Dirk again? Because we both know he'll be willing to offer you as many chances for that sort of strategic advantage as you'll take."

Tori leaned back in her seat with a sigh. Jesse made the issue seem simple, but it wasn't. "No. I mean, probably not." Dirk had helped the Slayers before. Shouldn't she be on good terms with him? "I can't just...things might happen, so I don't know." Why did she always sound like she was spouting gibberish when she talked about Dirk?

"Well," Jesse said slowly, "as long as you don't know the answer to that question, I don't think we should be a couple."

He was giving her an ultimatum? She was supposed to cut Dirk off even though he'd turned against his father more than once to help the Slayers? Her heart cracked a little right then, but sadness didn't seep through the fissures, frustration did. "You're telling me to forget what's good for the country and put our relationship first?" Jesse had always, always put what was good for the country first, but now he wasn't going to do that?

"No," he said, his tone matching hers in frustration. "I'm telling you I'm not going to sit by while you see Dirk again. The guy is our enemy and you keep making out with him. Sorry, but I'm not that understanding."

She looked out of the window, out at the cars on the highway they were passing. "I should have never told you the truth about Dirk." It was a petty thing to say, but she didn't care. Her choices had been to break into tears or be petty, and she didn't feel like crying.

Jesse's grip on the steering wheel tightened. "Eventually, you're going to have to fight Dirk face to face. You realize that, don't you? When Overdrake attacks, Dirk will be there too, shooting at us and telling his dragons to attack us. If you can't fight him, you'll end up dead."

Part of her knew that what Jesse said was the truth, but another part of her couldn't believe it. Dirk wouldn't kill her. He wouldn't. She couldn't imagine him shooting at any of the Slayers, let alone commanding a dragon to attack them. Overdrake was their enemy. Not Dirk. She didn't argue the point, though. She had no proof to offer. Maybe she was just deluding herself.

Jesse's voice softened. "I know this is hard. Really, I do. When we're done fighting Overdrake, things will change."

Of course things would change. Overdrake had four dragons and ten eggs. Even if the Slayers were lucky and managed to kill the next two dragons he attacked with, he would eventually whittle their numbers away.

One of Dirk's lessons on World War Two came to mind, a joke he'd told her about a German and an

American soldier talking after the war. The American said, "I heard that in a battle, one German Tiger Tank was worth ten of our American Sherman Tanks."

"You heard right," the German said.

"Then how did we win the war?" The American asked.

"When we had a battle, you always brought eleven tanks."

Overdrake certainly had enough dragons to kill the Slayers. And flyers were the most vulnerable, the ones that Overdrake targeted first. She and Jesse might not both make it out alive and then the whole dating point would be moot. Jesse must know this, but he still wanted to spend their remaining time together as nothing more than teammates.

He shifted his grip on the steering wheel. "I'm not saying all of this because I don't care about you. I'm saying it because I care too much. When we argue, I can't think straight. Neither of us can afford to be that way."

How was she supposed to respond to that? Tell him to care about her less? His words were just an easy out. A more noble sounding version of: It's me, not you. So she didn't respond at all. Her throat felt too tight for words. She pulled homework from her backpack and worked on it—firmly, stiffly, and without being able to concentrate on it.

Five miles before they reached the practice field, Tori's powers kicked in—the simulator's doing. Her senses grew sharper and her energy picked up. Soon she would be soaring and gliding in the sky—it almost made up for the rest of practice.

A few minutes later, Jesse's car reached the driveway of the old farm where they trained during the school year.

An overgrown orchard surrounded the place, hiding it from the main road. It's once orderly rows had been overrun with unruly trees intent on turning the land back into forest. Sam, the unknown patron of the Slayers, had bought it a decade ago and surrounded the whole place with a fifteen-foot barbed wire fence.

Jesse pulled up to the gate and punched in the code to open it. Then the Prius jiggled down the uneven road and over to the stretch of dirt where the Slayers parked. Before Jesse had even completely turned off the car, Tori got out and slammed the door harder than she intended. With her powers turned on, things broke easier. She stormed off toward the stable to get her horse.

Within a few steps, Jesse caught up with her. "Listen, I shouldn't have laid all of that on you right before practice. We should have waited until afterward to talk."

"I'm fine," she said, steeling her voice to make it sound truer. *Breathe*, she told herself. *Just breathe.*

He knew she wasn't fine. She could see the concern in his eyes. "Really," he said, "I'm sorry."

Two words that didn't change anything. They were little stitches that couldn't hold together the wounds between them. "Yeah, I'm sorry too. The problem is I think we're sorry about different things." She headed to the stables so she didn't have to keep hearing him apologize for not caring about her enough—or for caring about her too much. In the end, it worked out to be the same thing.

She had to get through this practice—no, not get through it. Even though she felt horrible, she had to prove to the other Slayers and Dr. B that she was ready to be a captain again, that she deserved it. She was going to slay her dragons faster and better than she ever had—or at least faster and better than Jesse did.

 # CHAPTER 11

Tori went into the barn, a weathered red building that was quaint enough for a country-themed calendar. The quaintness had happened completely by chance, she supposed, since Dr. B only cared about function, not beauty. The inside was almost industrial: gray divided stalls and a sterile-looking tack room.

She was met with the familiar scent of hay mixed with horse and manure. A comforting smell. Probably because for years it had been the smell of long rides through wooded trails with her sister and parents. Nature. Freedom.

All of that seemed so long ago.

Booker, Dr. B's usually-silent and frequently grumpy right-hand man, stood by the stalls saddling up the extra horses. Two were always kept ready in case one of the Slayers' mounts had a problem during practice. Most of the other Slayers were still in the barn cinching on saddles or putting their gear on. When she walked in, everyone turned and looked at her.

And that's when she remembered Jesse wasn't the only one angry at her. Most of the Slayers were too.

She held up her hands to gather their attention and took a deep breath. "Hey guys, I'm sorry I didn't let you know what I was doing with Aaron. I know I should have but he didn't want me to tell anyone. I had to make the call alone."

Ryker stopped brushing his horse and fixed her with a gaze. Since he was six foot four, his gazes always carried extra weight. "You weren't supposed to—" he made air quotes, "let us know. You were supposed to let us have a say in the matter. Adding a third dragon lord to Overdrake's arsenal affects all of us."

Her shoulders stiffened. "Aaron is on our side. He can help us, but I knew the rest of you don't trust him because he's a dragon lord."

Ryker went back to brushing his horse. "We don't mistrust Aaron because he's a dragon lord, we mistrust him because he's a child."

Lilly, Tori's blonde-haired nemesis, hefted a saddle on her horse. "*I* mistrust him because he's a dragon lord. By nature, they're power-hungry and back-stabbing."

"Thanks." Tori made her way to the tack room. "I appreciate that opinion. If I ever decide to stab someone in the back, you're making the choice a lot easier."

Bess left her horse tied to a post, intercepted Tori, and gave her a hug. "I'd tell you not to listen to Lilly, but since that's been standard policy for years, I won't bother."

For a moment, Tori melted into Bess's hug, lived on it. As long as she still had friends here, everything would be fine. Even after Bess let her go, Tori kept a tight hold on that knowledge.

Booker led the backup horses to the door. "Listen up! You'll have time for chatting when you're dead. Get your horses ready and get on out of here."

He most likely meant they would have time for chatting after they'd been symbolically killed during practice and were sitting out waiting for the next round. But with Booker, it was hard to be sure.

Tori took Bane from his stall. He was a black gelding, a beautiful creature who seemed to dislike everyone but her. He gave her a welcoming whinny and nudged her with his velvety nose. She petted his neck and murmured to him, then led him to the far end of the barn so she could brush his coat and see to his hooves. Despite her familiarity with the routine, everything felt disconnected, like she was watching someone else prepare the horse.

After she saddled Bane, she suited up in her fireproof gear. Usually she hated wearing her helmet because it was hot and stuffy. Today she hoped Dr. B would keep the pre-game instructions short so she could put it on. That way, she wouldn't have to work on keeping her expression stoic.

She picked up her pellet rifle, then left the barn and rode Bane across the grassy field. The area was about the size of a football field, but felt larger, perhaps because hopeful bushes and saplings dotted the land. They wouldn't last long. If the horses didn't trample or eat them, the practice dragons—small remote helicopters that shot out fire—would eventually burn them.

Booker had already set out an assortment of civilian-shaped plywood pieces around the field. They represented bystanders that the Slayers were supposed to avoid killing during the course of practice. Each fallen or damaged cut-out cost the team a hundred points from their score, and the losing team had to muck out the stalls afterward.

At the far end of the field, Dr. B surveyed the practice from the silo headquarters. He controlled one heli-dragon while Theo, Dr. B's resident tech genius, ran the other. Theo was a twenty-something guy who took way too much pleasure in trying to blister the Slayers, a fault Dr. B never fully paid attention to.

Tori rode to where the Slayers were gathered and took a spot beside Rosa. She was petite with long dark hair, gentle brown eyes, and features that made her look closer to fourteen than her seventeen years. One would never assume she could shoot a rifle with deadly accuracy, which was why the Slayers always used her when they needed to case out a place.

"Are you doing okay?" Rosa asked Tori.

"Yeah," Tori said.

"Are you lying?" Rosa asked. She worried too much, which balanced Bess out, who didn't worry about anything.

"A little," Tori said.

"We all still love you."

Hardly the truth, since Lilly had never loved her in the first place. But Tori didn't argue the point. Rosa thought the best of everyone, and at the moment, Tori appreciated that quality.

Bess and Ryker were mounted and talking intently, oblivious to Tori's arrival. Bess's crush was understandable. Ryker was custom-made to invite crushes: black hair, blue eyes and the ability to fly. He was almost as attractive as Jesse.

Tori inwardly sighed. She had to stop thinking things like that. He wanted a platonic relationship, and anyway, she couldn't afford to be distracted today.

Jesse joined the group a minute later, stationing his horse by Willow's and Lilly's. The two girls were both blonde, but their similarities ended there. Willow's hair was long and curly. Lilly's was bleached with a new blue streak. Willow was tall and soft-spoken. Lilly was about as short as Rosa, although no one would have ever described her as petite. Petite implied delicate and sweet. Lilly was an in-your-face, flip-you-off, prima donna.

Ryker looked at Jesse, tilting his head in question. "Dude, what's wrong?"

"Nothing." There was only a little stiffness in Jesse's voice.

Everyone turned their attention to him. He seemed calm enough, ready to fight dragons and crush opponents.

Ryker's eyes flicked in Tori's direction. "Oh," he said with understanding.

Which made everyone turn to Tori.

"Did I miss something?" Willow asked, her gaze bouncing between Ryker and Jesse.

"It's a counterpart thing," Bess said. "You can't expect counterparts to make sense or explain themselves to anyone else."

"I wish I had a counterpart," Willow said.

"We all wish we did," Rosa said sadly.

Ryker and Jesse were the only counterparts left. The thought made the group seem so small and doomed. They'd lost half their fighters.

Kody was the last to join the group. He'd been by a pile of firewood, tossing the things up in the air and sending freezing blasts at them that sent them spinning; his own personal warm-ups. He could also send out fireballs but didn't do that nearly as often. Fire didn't damage dragons.

He gave the group one of his usual smiles. "All right, y'all. Ready to get her done?" Perhaps it was his southern charm, but Kody seemed perpetually optimistic and good-natured. Which was probably fortunate for the guys he went to school with. Even without his Slayer powers,

Kody had enough muscle to do serious damage to anyone who got on his bad side.

No one said more because Dr. B was driving up on a souped-up golf cart, one that went so fast it could probably be classified as a small jeep. He lurched the thing to a stop in front of them and climbed out. "Everyone here? Good." He picked up the tablet that he used to take notes about their performances. "I have some things to go over before we start."

The Slayers turned and maneuvered their horses into a tighter circle around him.

"The bug on Senator Ethington's phone has provided some information of note. It appears the government has granted Venezuela permission to perform some military exercises near the east coast."

Several Slayers groaned. They'd already learned that Overdrake had allies in Venezuela who'd help him, most likely by providing troops.

"Overdrake also has ties to Colombia," Dr. B went on, "and they'll be delivering shipments of supposed goods on the west coast at the same time Venezuela is sending ships to the east coast. The tentative date is the end of April. It may or may not be the time Overdrake chooses to attack, but we'll need to be ready, just in case." His gaze turned to Tori. "Hopefully we'll be able to record Senator Ethington saying something that gives us a reason to alert your father of his doings, but so far he's been careful to speak using euphemisms."

Dr. B turned his attention back to the others. "The good news is that Senator Ethington's relationship with Overdrake is becoming strained. In his own words, he's tired of Overdrake acting like he's his boss. Perhaps before long, the senator will be less willing to carry out his bidding."

Lilly snorted. "He's a politician. That means he has no backbone."

Usually Tori let those sorts of comments slide. She wasn't in the mood today. "Honestly, Lilly, do you ever think about what you're saying?"

Lilly looked at her with surprise. "Since when did you become a Senator Ethington fan?"

"I'm not talking about Senator Ethington. I'm talking about all the other politicians, including my father, who have a backbone."

And that was pretty much how practice started.

After three rounds of fighting against the heli-dragons, Tori had spent a total of about fifteen minutes alive. The rest of the time she sat out as one of the dead. Her emotions were making her careless. She'd only managed to shoot her dragon once, and truth be told, that was because Ryker had disabled the chains and Kevlar vest from the dragon, allowing her to get the shot in before the dragon could kill her.

Before the start of round four, the Slayers rode their horses to the troughs that dotted the playing field. The other Slayers usually let Tori have a trough to herself since Bane tended to nip at the other horses, but this time, Jesse rode up.

General, Jesse's horse, kept a good distance from Bane while he got his fill. Jesse took a drink from his water bottle as he considered Tori. "Are you all right?"

He no longer had the right to ask her those sorts of questions. "I'm fine," she said airily.

He screwed the lid of his water bottle back on. "You're not concentrating."

"Oh, I'm concentrating. I'm just concentrating on all the reasons I'm mad at you."

He sighed—the sort of sigh he'd used when she'd first joined the Slayers and he thought she was missing some horribly obvious point. "I know you don't want to take instructions from me right now, but I'm telling you this because I don't want you to die during a real attack: You've got to be able to set your feelings aside when you fight."

"Yeah, that's one of the top reasons I'm mad at you. You don't have a hard time setting your feelings aside."

"I have plenty of trouble." He tucked his water bottle back into his saddle. "But when it's important, I at least make an attempt."

He might have continued his pep talk, but Willow rode up to their trough. She pulled off her helmet, letting her curly hair spill out onto her shoulders. "I'd like to make an official complaint."

Willow wasn't one to complain—at least not seriously, and Tori wasn't sure whether she was serious now. "What's wrong?"

Willow pulled out her water bottle and took a swig. "I'm tired of being killed. Just once, I'd like to do some damage to the dragon before it eviscerates me."

"Join the club," Tori said.

"It's not the same," Willow protested. "You die in the sky because the dragon attacked you before you could kill it. I wander around aimlessly, following after the rest of you, until Dr. B or Theo decides to terrorize me with their helicopters of death."

"Willow—" Jesse started.

She raised a finger at him. "Don't you dare tell me I'm a valuable team member. My life doesn't seem valuable to anyone but me."

"Willow—" Tori tried.

Willow didn't let her finish either. "And, Tori, I know you're busy, but you've got to stop missing practice. Every time you're not here, Ryker sends me out as bait to draw out the dragons."

Tori hadn't realized this. She looked at Jesse for confirmation. "He does?"

Jesse shrugged. "I'm sure he wouldn't do it in a real battle."

"Then he shouldn't do it in practice." Willow sent a glare over her shoulder in her cousin's direction. "Seriously, what is even the point of having me practice? I can't do anything. Tell Dr. B to let me do civilian triage on the sidelines."

Dr. B had assured Willow that eventually her extra power would manifest itself. But a month later, it still hadn't happened. Tori supposed all the Slayers had begun to wonder what none of them would admit: Maybe Willow didn't have an extra power.

Bane flicked his mane in annoyance. He didn't like the other horses standing too close. Tori patted his neck to calm him down. "This time you won't die," she told Willow. "Your assignment next round will be to stay by Rosa and protect her."

Rosa could heal burns. In a battle, she would be what kept a lot of them alive. They usually had her stay far away from the dragon.

"Protect her how?" Willow moaned. "She's a better fighter than I am."

"Not true," Jesse said. "You're a good fighter. Rosa is just more experienced. And she became experienced by practicing. That's why we're here: to get better."

Willow huffed dramatically. "*Fine.*" She twisted her hair into a coil and put her helmet back on. "I'll go stick by

Rosa and wait for the helicopters of doom to find me again." She gave her horse a nudge and trotted back to where the others were assembling.

Jesse leaned toward Tori and lowered his voice. "In a real battle, have Willow work crowd control."

"She's not that bad," Tori said, immediately defensive.

Jesse tilted his chin at her. "I'm saying that because I don't want her in over her head. I don't want her to get hurt."

He was right, but Tori still felt the need to defend Willow. Not that long ago she'd been the new girl without combat experience or a decent power to help her fight. "She just needs time to get up to speed."

Jesse didn't comment on that. She knew what he was thinking anyway. They might not have much time.

"She can protect me while I try to take control of a dragon," Tori offered.

Jesse shook his head. "We need you in the air fighting."

A helicopter shot above the trees and hovered there, ending the conversation. Round four had officially started. It was Jesse's turn to lead the teams until the second heli-dragon showed up.

"Positions!" Jesse yelled to the others. Before he left, he turned back with a half-smile, the teasing sort he used to give so freely. "Hey, if you're going to be mad at me, at least put your anger to good use. Show me up. Kill your dragon so fast that you put me to shame."

That had been her original plan. She wasn't about to admit she'd failed miserably at enacting it. She tugged Bane's reins, turning him to the field. "Thanks, but I don't need tips on how to be angry at you."

"Good," he said, his smile turning into a full blown smirk. "Now channel that resentment at the dragon."

She would have told him what he could do with his advice but he rode off, focusing on the heli-dragon. She put her helmet back on, leaned forward on Bane, and the horse was off before she even tapped his flanks. A-team was heading south to circle the dragon. Time to concentrate. The worst part of Jesse's advice was that if she did manage to kill her dragon first this round, she'd look like she'd followed his counsel and he'd been right. If she didn't kill hers first, she'd look like she hadn't managed the art of mastering her emotions.

Man, it was going to be such an uncomfortable ride back to Jesse's house.

Across the field, Kody whooped and charged the dragon.

Ryker, who seemed to be in his own personal competition to determine who had the most testosterone in the group, answered with his own war-cry. Guys. Seriously.

Tori did a quick search of the sky for the second helicopter. Didn't see it. Once it arrived, A-team would break off to engage it. She urged Bane into a cautious trot. Training with horses always made Tori feel like she was playing a game of polo—with things that wanted to kill her.

Dr. B claimed the Slayer horses were descendants of the stallions bred by the original Slayer Knights and used to defeat the dragons of the Middle Ages. They were fearless, obedient, and strangely willing to charge at large carnivorous beasts. To Tori's mind, this made the horses more foolish than the regular, more cowardly variety.

Animals should instinctively know to run in the opposite direction of fire-breathing death.

As they rode across the field, Bane actually snorted angrily at the helicopter. It spurted a stream of fire at Tori as if answering the horse's challenge.

Ryker rushed at the helicopter from the opposite direction. He was close enough that he should have flown off his horse and gone after the copter in the air. Instead, he rode under it. "Behind you!" he called to Tori. "A-team, split!"

Tori still wasn't used to Ryker calling the commands and he'd been doing it for three rounds.

Tori gave Bane two taps on the haunches. This was the signal that she was leaving him and he should go to a safe place and wait. She was fairly certain Bane understood the direction. The fact that he usually wandered around eating shrubbery instead indicated that he was either too smart to be fooled by the mechanical dragon or not smart enough to avoid danger when food was around. She had no idea what he'd do in an actual attack on a city. Perhaps rummage through the garbage cans for leftovers.

Tori flew upwards, twisting mid-air to follow the helicopter. She felt weightless in the sky, as though gravity had lost its grip on her. Moving became instinctual here, more thought than effort.

She took note of each member of her team below. In their dark suits, they were hard to distinguish from each other, but if Tori hadn't recognized their horses, the symbols on the back of their jackets would let her know who was who. Kody rode to the south of the dragon. Lilly trailed behind him. Willow and Rosa waited with their horses by trees on the sidelines, watching.

With Rosa in reserve, Jesse and Bess were left to handle the first dragon by themselves. Two people. It wasn't enough. A-team had four fighters, five if you counted Willow. Dr. B would have to rearrange the teams soon. Probably the only reason he hadn't done it already was that he wanted to see what Jesse and Bess could do against impossible odds.

Today, they'd done pretty well. Or maybe it just seemed that way compared to Tori's dismal performance.

Ryker reached the helicopter first. He flew above it, diving toward the section that represented the Kevlar straps. He had to press the buttons that represented cutting them. The machine tilted upward, shooting a stream of fire that arced at Ryker.

A moment later the flames disappeared, leaving only a trail of smoke. Lilly had extinguished it.

Ryker swooped downward, in an attempt to get out of the line of fire. The helicopter swung that way, following him.

Tori wheeled upwards. She and Ryker had a system worked out. She flew in front of the dragon to draw its attention. Since her dragon lord abilities made her immune to fire, she could be hit by a stream that melted her flame-resistant suit and she still came out unblistered.

Hot, yes. Sweaty, definitely. And if she was really unlucky—naked. So far the naked part hadn't happened, but she worried one day it would. Anyway, when fire hit her, she felt like she'd walked into an oven, but she emerged from the flames unhurt.

Tori soared in front of the dragon, gun raised, and shot at it. Her airsoft rifle didn't damage the helicopter, just as a real rifle wouldn't do more than irritate a dragon. Its scales were bulletproof. The only part of a dragon that was unprotected was a soft spot on its underbelly, and Overdrake covered that part with Kevlar.

Theo had painted an angry face on the machine, complete with fangs. Tori took an extra shot, hoping to knock off some of the paint.

Fire spurted from a nozzle underneath the helicopter. She spun to the left but was too slow to avoid the reach of the flames. They hit her on the side, making her suit sizzle. The acrid scent of burning plastic enveloped her.

Well, that lovely smell was going to be hard to explain to her parents. Study group had just taken an ugly turn.

"Are you paying attention?" Tori called to Lilly.

"Sorry!" Lilly chimed back.

No, she wasn't. Since Lilly had found out that Tori couldn't be burned, she'd become slow to extinguish the flames that came in Tori's direction.

"I couldn't cut the strap," Ryker called, his frustration evident. "Sequel." That meant he was going to try again. Risky, as the dragon was no longer paying attention to Tori, but had turned to Ryker.

Instead of darting away, Ryker hovered in the air, letting the machine come nearer. She knew he would stay there, a stationary target, and then right before the dragon reached him, he would dart upward, putting himself above the dragon so he could take a shot.

But Theo and Dr. B knew the move too and would likely be planning for it. As would Overdrake when he actually attacked with dragons. Dirk had told him all their moves, strategies, and tactics.

Did Ryker not understand this? He had no caution when it came to fighting, which made Tori twice as wary. She felt like she had to watch out for him.

She pulled a paint bomb from her vest and called "Trident!" to tell Ryker she was about to use a sticky grenade.

If a paint bomb landed near the straps, they blew off both the chains and the Kevlar, and best of all, the flyers didn't have to get as close to the dragons to use them.

Ryker wheeled away from the dragon and out of the trajectory of Tori's grenade in case she missed. Which happened occasionally. Tori had good aim, but dragons were fast. If a grenade missed and exploded on the ground, it would most likely splatter a few of the people-shaped wooden cutouts.

She decided not to worry about civilians today. Life was hard, after all, and they should have noticed the dragon and taken cover somewhere else besides the playing field.

The dragon jerked downward to get away from her. Using explosives was more dangerous when the dragon flew low to the ground—higher chance of casualties even if the grenade stuck to the dragon—but Tori wanted to win this round quickly. She flung the grenade, fast and hard. It hit the target with a clang that made the copter shiver. Instead of sticking, it bounced off—right toward Kody.

"Freeze it!" she called.

His arms were already drawn back. "Got it!"

He hurled an icy blast to knock the grenade away.

Since A-team didn't have a shielder, Kody's bursts were A-team's only defense against rogue grenades. Usually he managed to swing the grenade away from the team. This time his first blast missed, and he had to shoot a second. A concentrated stream of cold air hit the grenade, sending it to the ground a few feet away from him.

Too close. An explosion of red paint splattered Kody, his horse, and a couple wooden civilians. He was dead until the round ended.

Kody wiped paint from his helmet. "I reckon that's another messy death."

"Happens to the best of us," Ryker called.

Kody rode off the field muttering. Tori muttered too. She couldn't afford to kill anyone else.

The helicopter swooped low, focusing on Lilly. She urged her horse into a gallop, in an effort to keep out of range. Lilly could avoid the dragon's fire but not its teeth or claws. Tori and Ryker flew over the machine's back, managing to push the buttons that signified they'd cut the Kevlar straps.

Now they had to shoot the buttons to show they'd blown through the chains. That was easier to do. They didn't have to be as close.

Willow rode downfield toward A-team. Jesse must have noticed Kody's untimely death and sent her to help out.

The helicopter noticed her. It rose with a lurch, then dived at her, zigzagging to prevent Tori and Ryker from getting a clear shot. Before the machine reached Willow, she bolted into the trees. The copter skimmed over the canopy, searching for her.

Tori and Ryker both tailed the helicopter. Before they reached it, the machine careened back to the playing field, going after Lilly again. Ryker followed, but Tori hesitated. A low buzz was coming from the direction of the road.

A motorcycle. She groaned. That noise meant Dr. B was sending in camp personnel to pretend to be Overdrake's men. Couldn't be a stranger. The fence kept out anyone who didn't know the gate code.

Now Tori would have to worry about guns and nets and whatever other devices Dr. B wanted to spring on them. And this after she'd already lost Kody, their only protection from guns. He could blast the weapons out of the owners' hands.

The motorcycle was far enough away that only Tori, with her more sensitive hearing, could pick up the sound. She looked over at Team Magnus's side of the field. Bess was still in play. Tori switched her mic to Team Magnus's frequency. "Bess, we've got an incoming motorcycle. He'll be armed. Can you help us out?"

Technically, Tori wasn't supposed to ask for help from Team Magnus unless they'd already killed their dragon, but Tori was hot, tired, and didn't feel like playing by the rules.

"Negative," Jesse called back on her earphone. "We'll have incoming over here too."

He was probably right. What one team got, they usually both got. But couldn't Bess help them out until another one showed up? In a real battle, Bess wouldn't be told to protect her own team and leave A-team to be picked off by a gunman.

Tori bit back that reply. She wasn't going to press Jesse for help. The motorcycle was louder now, closer.

Willow rode out of the trees, the bike trailing after her. A big man sat there, his identity hidden by his helmet and coat. Since the Slayers didn't use armor piercing bullets—they accidentally shot each other on occasion—she wouldn't be able to take the biker out of play with gunfire. Overdrake's men, on the other hand, used armor-piercing bullets, so a hit from this motorcyclist's pellet gun would still count as a kill.

The biker hadn't pulled out a gun yet, but Willow was so close, she was bound to be shot within seconds. Killing the dragon was Tori's first priority. She should concentrate on that—but she didn't like leaving everyone vulnerable to gunfire. Hadn't she told Willow she wouldn't let her die this round? Ryker could deal with the dragon for a few minutes.

Still high in the air, Tori circled behind the man to get out of his sight. She didn't recognize his build. He wasn't one of the regulars who played Overdrake's underlings. Probably some new sniper Dr. B had added to his cadre to show the Slayers they weren't invincible.

As though Tori's repeated deaths hadn't already taught her that.

Her choices in battle were always fight or flight. But flight meant something different to her and she chose that option.

She dived down to the bike, wrapped her arms around the man's chest, and plucked him from his seat. He jerked in surprise, hadn't seen her coming.

His problem. She shot upwards. The bike teetered then fell, wheels spinning while the engine uselessly hummed. The man thrashed in Tori's grip, then went still as he realized how quickly the ground was receding beneath them.

"I wouldn't recommend struggling," she said. "I might drop you."

His words came out as a growl. "Put me down!"

Dr. B's voice pinged in her earpiece. "T-bird, what's going on?"

Yeah, he was bound to be unhappy about this turn of events. She'd abandoned her main priority—dragon shooting—in order to protect her team. "I've never had my own prisoner," she said cheerily. "Maybe this could work out for me." She shifted the man in her arms slightly. "What kind of information, my captured minion, can you give me about Overdrake's location?"

"Take me to Alastair, immediately!" the man said, the growl still in his voice. He was not afraid and not amused by this.

Tori had never heard Dr. B swear, but he did then. It was an uttered exclamation of disbelief. "T-bird, don't hurt him. He's not part of the game."

Not part of the game? Impossible. This area was fenced off, locked up tight. No one got in here without knowing the gate code.

Out on the field, both helicopters descended onto the ground, signaling the round was over. That also never happened until the dragons or all the Slayers were killed.

Tori was so surprised that she just stood there, hovering a hundred feet above the ground, holding the stranger. "Wow. Who are you?"

The man let out a laugh. Not the happy kind. "You know me as Sam."

CHAPTER 12

Sam? *Oh crap*. The man who funded the camp. The man behind the Slayer operation, who Dr. B wouldn't talk about. He'd driven onto the playing field, and Tori had ripped him off his bike and held him hostage in the air.

Definitely not her best moment. Although on the plus side, at least she hadn't pulled him from his motorcycle and beaten him up.

"Sorry," she said. The word seemed inadequate. She suddenly wasn't sure whether she was holding Sam too tight or not tight enough. She began a slow descent, so gradual she wouldn't startle him further. "We were in the middle of a training session. I thought you were one of Overdrake's men."

"In a real attack," he said icily, "are you going to assume that every person you come across is one of Overdrake's men? Will you pull random fleeing strangers from moving vehicles and threaten them?"

"In a real attack, I imagine people will be fleeing in the opposite direction of the dragons." Tori was halfway to the ground. "Do you want me to take you to Dr. B? He's in the control tower."

"Tell him to meet me down here. I want to talk to all of you."

And by the sound of his voice, he wasn't delivering good news. Or maybe she was jumping to conclusions. Maybe his voice only sounded disapproving because he was angry at her.

Dr. B had undoubtedly heard the instruction through Tori's neck mic, but she repeated it anyway. "Dr. B, Sam requests an audience."

"Yes," Dr. B said. "Tell him I'm on my way."

Tori relayed that message as well.

A-team had also been listening on their earpieces and had overheard everything that had transpired. Seen it too. All of their heads were tilted up, watching the scene play out. Whatever questions or comments they had, either awe or worry was keeping them silent.

Willow dismounted and went to Sam's bike to set it upright. Lilly rode across the field toward the spot Tori would land, watching. Team Magnus was moving downfield as well, must have switched to A-team's frequency.

Dr. B used an override signal that broke into both teams' channels. "Please assemble midfield."

He didn't mention that their visitor was Sam, but Kody had left the dead zone and joined Team Magnus on their way across the field. He was pointing to Tori, most likely filling them in on any details they'd missed.

Tori set Sam gently on his feet, then stepped to his side, giving him space. "I'm Tori, but I suppose you already know who all of us are."

He glanced at her long enough to nod, then straightened his coat, pulling it down where it had ridden up. He didn't seem to have more to say to her. Was it better to apologize again or just pretend the whole thing never happened? Well, Sam might go for the latter, but the other Slayers were never going to let her live this down.

Ryker and Jesse landed not far from Sam, standing as straight as soldiers meeting a general. Kody, Bess, and Rosa rode over and joined the others forming a half circle. Across the field, Dr. B was speeding toward them in the golf cart, still a few minutes from reaching them.

Jesse removed his helmet, something the Slayers weren't supposed to do around anyone but Dr. B, Theo, and Booker. One by one the rest of the Slayers followed suit. It was an honor they wouldn't have bestowed on any other outsider.

Sam surveyed them silently but left his helmet on. Perhaps he meant to keep his identity a secret. Perhaps they would never know exactly who he was.

Had it been a mistake to take off their helmets? Instead of seeing the gesture as an honor, maybe Sam saw it as an indication they didn't take rules as seriously as they should have. Tori fiddled with the ridge of her helmet, wishing Dr. B was here already.

Jesse stepped up to Sam. His brown hair was mussed from sweat and smoke, and he'd managed to get a streak of dirt on his cheek, but his bearing was solemn, one of utter respect. "I'm glad to finally meet you, Sir. I've wanted to thank you for a long time for what you've done for us and for the nation."

Sam's posture stiffened at the compliment and his gaze turned in Bess's direction. "You're welcome. But I didn't do it for the nation. I did it for my granddaughter."

Bess's eyes went wide and her mouth dropped open in recognition. "Grandpa?" She dismounted from her horse and stepped to him for a closer look.

Bess was Sam's granddaughter? The surprise showed on each of the Slayer's faces. They couldn't have known, and yet as soon as the information was out, Tori felt as though they should have, as though it was a missing puzzle piece that had been sitting in front of them all along. Who else would want to stop Overdrake so fervently that he would have planned and invested in the Slayers for all of these years?

Brant Overdrake's father had killed Dr. B's brother, and now Dr. B's father was doing his best to make sure that Overdrake didn't succeed in his takeover attempts.

Sam pulled off his helmet and smiled at Bess. He didn't look like the sort of man who smiled very often. He was in his late sixties with weathered features and deep lines that spread across his forehead and down the sides of his mouth. His gray hair was receding and messy from the helmet. He didn't bother fixing it. "How are you doing, missy?"

She stood in front of him, her blue eyes bright. "*You're* Sam?" The name obviously wasn't his real one.

Sam—Mr. Bartholomew—reached out and pulled her into a hug. For a moment his whole countenance softened. He was not the gruff man who'd snapped at Tori or the stern one who'd brushed off Jesse's gratitude, he was a grandpa. "Are you really so surprised? You always knew I'd move heaven and earth for you."

Bess pulled away from him, looking embarrassed but happy. "Why didn't you tell me you funded the Slayers?"

He shrugged, a teasing gesture. "If you realized how much your old grandpa was worth, that second-hand Honda I gave you wouldn't seem like such a great birthday present."

Bess laughed and her gaze went over him again. "Yeah. Why don't we revisit that gift?"

Mr. Bartholomew shook his head. "Not a chance. All my extra cash goes to this place." He turned his attention to the helicopters that now lay placidly on the ground—innocent except for their menacing painted faces. "It goes to whatever those infernal contraptions are." He squinted, examining them more closely, taking in the blackened nozzles that shot fire. "Those blades could chop your head clean off."

"We know how to avoid them," Jesse said. His stance was still soldier-straight, but his expression was more defensive and less admiring than it had been.

"I'm with you, Mr. Bartholomew," Tori muttered. "The helicopters are unnecessarily dangerous."

Mr. Bartholomew tucked his helmet under his arm. "Well, at least I know it was the safety-conscious flyer who yanked me off my bike while I was going twenty miles an hour."

Dr. B reached midfield at last. He shut off the cart and hurried up to the group, his unbuttoned coat flapping out behind him like an uncertain flag. "You didn't tell me you were coming."

Mr. Bartholomew's earlier smile melted away. "Maybe if you'd answered my last dozen phone messages, I could have."

Dr. B swept his hands at the field and rocked back on his heels. "As you can see, I keep busy training the kids." He didn't seem to know what to do with his hands and finally settled on tucking them behind his back. "I apologize that Tori mistook you for an enemy. But you shouldn't come to a practice unannounced. You could have been hurt."

"More likely one of the kids *will* be hurt." Mr. Bartholomew jerked a thumb at the helicopters, his scowl much more impressive than the painted ones on the machines. "You have the flyers darting around moving blades."

Tori nodded. "They also shoot out fifteen-foot flames."

Dr. B gave her a sharp look. She smiled back at him. It was nice to hear from a reasonable adult for a change.

Mr. Bartholomew frowned at the scorch marks that crisscrossed the grass. "Camp was supposed to teach the Slayers to use their powers in order to protect themselves but this . . ."

"Is training them to do just that," Dr. B insisted. He glanced at his watch, a gesture too unsettled to be casual. "Let's go somewhere to talk while the Slayers finish the round."

Mr. Bartholomew didn't move. "Fine. We'll take Bess with us." The words came out as a challenge, although Tori couldn't guess what that challenge was.

Dr. B knew, though. It registered on his face—a mixture of discomfort and stubbornness. "Bess needs to practice."

Mr. Bartholomew shook his head. "Not anymore."

Bess's gaze traveled, unconcerned, between her father and grandfather. Her nonchalance made it clear she was used to seeing them disagree. "It's okay, Grandpa. I can see you when I'm finished with this round."

Mr. Bartholomew kept his eyes on Dr. B, not through with his challenge. "We had an agreement. It's time you told her about it."

Dr. B motioned to the cart and he lowered his voice. "We'll discuss this privately."

Tori's eyes circled to the other Slayers. They were all standing there, awkward and trapped, spectators stuck in an argument between their leaders. It wasn't polite to hear all of this but they had no choice.

Mr. Bartholomew folded his arms. Something about the stance reminded Tori of a bull right before it charged. He wasn't going to back down and could run over anyone who opposed him. "Enough is enough. She's already fought two dragons."

"We were attacked," Dr. B said in the weary tone one uses when the point has been made repeatedly before. "And her powers helped to not only save the lives of the other Slayers but to kill two dragons—dragons Overdrake would have unleashed on innocent people."

"I'm glad for it," Mr. Bartholomew countered. "No one wants to take Overdrake down more than I do, but not at the cost of Bess's life. I already lost Nathan. I won't lose her too." He pointed a finger at Dr. B, a sharp gesture. "We had an agreement."

Bess stepped in between the two men, hands raised. "What agreement? What are you talking about?"

Yes, what? Tori's heart was beginning to beat faster as though her body had already figured out what her mind hadn't.

Mr. Bartholomew waited for Dr. B to speak. He didn't. His lips remained firmly clamped together in either defiance or frustration.

Mr. Bartholomew turned to address the group. "I agreed to fund this camp on the condition that when Overdrake attacked, Bess would stay out of it. She could be trained so she would know how to protect herself, but that was all."

No. Mr. Bartholomew's words spun in Tori's mind. They couldn't be true. She hadn't heard right, and yet she couldn't have misinterpreted what had been said. Mr. Bartholomew was insisting Bess not fight.

Across from her, the other Slayers stared at Mr. Bartholomew, pale and stunned—worse, wounded.

Tori's gaze turned to Dr. B. He'd never shown favoritism to any of the Slayers, not even his daughter. He wouldn't have made a deal to exclude her from fighting when the rest of them needed her so much. And yet he stood there, not denying any of it.

Tori felt like something had come loose inside her. No, not inside her—some part of the world had come loose. Its neat stacks of order, logic, and moral codes were precariously swaying.

How could Dr. B—their leader—have done this to them?

And after everything the Slayers had accomplished, how could their funder come here and casually announce he was taking Bess away from them? They couldn't hope to take down Overdrake and the dragons without a shielder. The last time he attacked, he would have shot and killed them all if it hadn't been for Bess.

Lilly was the first to recover from the shock. With hands planted on her hips, she said, "So the rest of us are supposed to march off and face death, but not Bess. That was your deal?"

Mr. Bartholomew cast her an unconcerned glance. "I never claimed to be a fair man, just a rich one."

Several of the Slayers called out protests, all of them drowned out by Bess's own voice. "It's not your choice whether I fight. It's mine."

Mr. Bartholomew didn't budge. "No, Bess. Your father gave that choice to me when he took my millions. I'm sorry." His gaze traveled around the rest of the Slayers. "Believe me, I am sorry."

No, he wasn't. He obviously wasn't or he wouldn't put them in more danger by taking Bess.

And still, Dr. B stood there, jaw clenched, and said nothing.

Mr. Bartholomew turned back to Bess and held out his hand. "You'll be staying with your grandmother and me for a while."

Finally, Dr. B stepped forward. "You don't have parental consent to take her anywhere."

"You're right," Mr. Bartholomew retorted. "But I've got a few of these kids' parents on my payroll, not to mention salaries for Theo, Booker, and yourself. And let's not forget who's paying for the horses and all your equipment. You can't afford to lose my funding."

Bess smacked her helmet into the side of her leg. "Stop it. I'm not leaving my friends unprotected. You can't ask me to do that."

"Bess," Dr. B broke in. He was calm again. In an instant, he'd gone from an argumentative son to the same patient teacher who always oversaw their training exercises. "Go with your grandfather. We'll talk about this later."

Bess whirled on him. "You're giving in? Just like that?"

Dr. B ran a hand across his mouth and let out a long sigh. "It will be months, maybe years before Overdrake attacks. We have time to discuss this with your grandfather. For now, it's better if you go with him."

Bess took a step back, blinking back emotion.

Mr. Bartholomew didn't exactly smile, but he looked relieved, triumphant even. Apparently, he had no doubt how any future discussions would turn out. "Come on, Bess," he said, and without waiting for her answer, he stalked off to his motorcycle with quick determined strides.

Bess's hands shook, making her fumble with her helmet. "I thought you were better than the other parents, more sacrificing."

"Bess—" Dr. B started, but she went on as though he hadn't spoken.

"You're a hypocrite. You're asking the others to risk their lives when all along you knew I wouldn't be allowed to fight." She turned sharply and followed her grandfather, jogging to catch up with him.

Dr. B's face had grown a shade redder but whether from anger or embarrassment, Tori couldn't tell. When he turned back to the other Slayers, he couldn't keep the note of defeat from his voice. "Today's practice is over."

Jesse crossed his arms, his expression a mix of pain and disappointment. "How could you have made that agreement?"

Kody put it more bluntly. "You sold us out."

Tori still felt as though parts of the world had come loose and fallen to the ground. It was hard to speak when reason and fairness lay in shambles at her ankles. "I can't believe this."

Dr. B raised his hands to stop the protests, which at this point were coming from every single Slayer except for Rosa. She put her hand to her mouth. Her shoulders shook up and down, quick breaths that heralded tears.

Dr. B spoke over the top of them. "I made that agreement when Bess was two years old because I didn't have any other choice for funding this camp—for finding and training you. I needed to teach you how to use your powers so that when dragons attacked, you didn't all die quickly."

Lilly huffed. "Now we can die more slowly. Thanks."

Dr. B's hands were still up. "Did I keep Bess from fighting during the last two dragon attacks?"

No one answered. They knew he hadn't.

He let his hands fall to his sides. "Do you think I don't realize how important a shielder is? We'll get Bess back. And if I can find a way, we'll get Leo, Shang, Alyssa, and Danielle back too. Until then, we carry on the best we can. It's our only option." Without waiting for more discussion, he turned and trudged back to the cart, head bent as though he was dragging a weight behind him.

The Slayers silently watched him go. The silence was not because they didn't have more to say, but because they weren't going to say it while he was around.

The cart hummed to life and he headed toward the silo. Both helicopters lifted from the ground and whirred that direction as well. The horses had wandered off, busily grazing on weeds, but no one moved to get them.

Willow tugged at her bun until her hair fell back around her shoulders. "I wonder what other things Dr. B hasn't told us."

"He isn't like that," Rosa insisted. She'd stopped crying, but tears were still evident on her cheeks. "He loves us like a father."

"No," Ryker said bitterly. "He loves Bess like a father. He didn't make bargains to spare any of the rest of our lives. He's training us to fight and to die."

"He didn't have a choice," Rosa said. "He had to fund the camp."

Lilly let her helmet fall to the ground with a thud. Her expression spoke clearly of her intention. She hadn't dropped it by accident. The helmet lay in the charred grass like a resignation letter. "First Dirk and now Dr. B."

"It doesn't matter," Jesse broke in. His dark eyes flashed with intensity. "We've only ever had two options. We either fight or we sit back and hope someone else can stop Overdrake. Because if he ends up ruling, he's not only going to hunt us down, he's going to take out anyone who has Slayer genetics and that means our families."

Jesse's gaze traveled around the group, emphasizing his point. "Overdrake won't risk letting our brothers and sisters and cousins have children—one accidental exposure to his dragons and new Slayers would be born. He's probably already tracing our family trees so he can put our relatives on his hit list."

That thought had never occurred to Tori and judging from the others' reactions, most of them hadn't considered the possibility either. Her mother's side of the family— Dirk had already decided that's where Tori got her Slayer genes from—if Overdrake ruled, they could all be slaughtered.

"He wouldn't..." Rosa said. "People wouldn't stand by and let him do that."

"Rulers have done a lot worse," Kody pointed out.

No one argued that point.

"I'm going to fight Overdrake," Jesse said with firm determination. "Even if I'm the only one left, I'll do everything I can to stop him."

Yes, Tori thought, you'll be the first to sign up for a noble death. Should she admire his courage or cry in frustration because of it?

Kody tugged at the collar of his jacket. Due to his muscular build, his fighting clothes never fit him like they should. "Me too. I'm gonna whoop some dragons—no matter who else lets us down, betrays us, or turns out to be a dragon lord." His gaze cut to Tori. "No offense."

"Um, none taken," Tori said.

"Overdrake's already come after my family," Ryker said. "I'm fighting."

Lilly picked up her helmet. She looked like she wanted to chuck it, but she tucked it under her arm instead. "Fine. I still owe Overdrake for what he's done to Alyssa and Shang."

Rosa wiped at her cheeks. "When he attacks, I'm going to be there for all of you."

All eyes turned to Tori, waiting for her to chime in. The Slayers hardly had a chance against Overdrake, but what else could she say? She wasn't going to let her friends down. They'd already fought alongside her twice. "I'll be there too," she said.

"On which side?" Lilly muttered.

Seriously? Had Tori just been thinking that Lilly was worth fighting for? Clearly a mistake.

"Stop it," Jesse told Lilly. "We need to work together as a team, now more than ever."

Tori's eyes narrowed at Lilly. "Whatever else I am, I'm not one of Overdrake's tools."

Lilly snorted. "Then what do you call reuniting dragon lord junior with his despot daddy?"

"Need to work as a team," Jesse reminded her.

Tori hardly heard him. "I sent Aaron to help us. And he will. Criticize my genetics if you want, but I am and always will be a Slayer."

For once, Lilly didn't say anything, didn't even roll her eyes. She just stared at Tori as though she wanted to believe her. It was probably only a momentary lapse of ill-will, but it was there just the same, that flash of hope.

Lilly hesitated, then nodded, and the tension among the group seemed to melt away.

"Good," Jesse said, "We're all on the same team and the same page."

"Speaking of being a team," Willow put in, "I notice none of you asked if I was going to be there during the fight."

"What?" Jesse and Ryker asked at the same time. The question was also identical: not what did you say but what are you talking about?

Willow waved a hand at them. "None of you even noticed that I didn't join in your Slayer death pledge, did you? It's like I'm invisible or something."

"Of course not, Wills." Ryker said. He opened his mouth to say more but she didn't let him finish.

"I'm not completely useless, you know. Back when Overdrake's men attacked my house, I was the one who took out three armed thugs using nothing but household furniture."

"When Overdrake attacks," Ryker said with an air of patience, "are you going to be there for us?"

"Yes," she replied. "Thanks for asking."

Jesse put his hands together in a way that pronounced he was ready to move on from that line of conversation. "We're agreed then. We keep training no matter what."

Ryker, Kody, Rosa, Lilly, and Willow nodded.

They were so undermanned. A small group of teenagers on a darkened field agreeing to take on a man who commanded dragons, a man who knew them each by name. Willow was right; everyone was most likely pledging their deaths. Tori knew that and nodded with the rest of them anyway.

 CHAPTER 13

A week passed. Dirk still hadn't heard from Tori. Perhaps she hadn't been able to write down the site and password the first time he'd given it to her. The next time he was with Vesta, he repeated the information.

Another week passed, and still no word. Maybe Tori hadn't answered because she was investigating the site to make sure communications between them were actually untraceable. Could her silence mean she'd decided not to have anything to do with him? No, that didn't seem like her. She was too intent on persuading him to come back to the Slayers to give up their conversations.

While he was out with Vesta, he told Tori to post something on the old site, so that he knew she was okay. Gaining access to Vesta wasn't hard. Dirk worked with the dragons every day after he finished schoolwork. Some kids had to practice the piano, Dirk had to train two-and-a-half-month-old fledglings, taming them enough that they would retain orders even when their dragon lord wasn't close by. Eventually Aaron would take over some of the training, but not until Dirk had broken in Vesta and Jupiter.

Tori didn't post anything on the old site.

Was she mad at him? She might have found out about Aaron's disappearance and blamed him for that.

The next day, Dirk tucked his phone in his pocket and made his way to Vesta's enclosure. He walked across the room's cement floor, ignoring the scent of dragon dung mixed with disinfectant. The older dragons were trained to relieve themselves in the same area so Dirk or his father could subdue the dragons and the vets could clean up the place, but the fledglings seemed to enjoy making messes in as many places as they could.

Dirk stepped around a pile and breathed through his mouth. How did the dragons stand the smell?

Vesta turned to him, hissing and raising her wings in defiance. Her golden eyes glared at him and she bared a row of sword-like teeth. Pointless dramatics.

His father would have punished her by sending pain impulses through her body. Dirk didn't. Eventually Vesta would understand her opposition was futile. His method took longer, but the dragons hated him less during the process, so the extra time was worth it.

She shot a warning stream of fire that was too far away to reach him. Putting on a show. Which meant she was finally getting old enough—smart enough—to recognize that he wasn't prey. He was a dragon lord, someone to reckon with. Before long, she would realize that fighting against him was useless.

He slipped into her mind, today imagining her control center as a game console remote that he could pick up at will. His father liked to picture the dragon's control centers as beating hearts that he could grip and squeeze the life out of if he needed. Gaming remotes seemed less violent.

Come on, Vesta. Time to fly.

Her resistance evaporated as soon as she understood he was taking her outside. She was as happy as a dog going for a walk. He had to remind her to stay still so he could put on her saddle.

Once Dirk flew out of the enclosure, he spoke out loud to Tori. "Why haven't I heard from you?" She would know he was talking to her.

While Vesta circled the property, he took out his phone and checked it. No answer. He was getting used to that response. He ran Vesta through a set of drills, making her dip, turn, slow, and speed up.

Still no answer from Tori. She had to be home from school by now. She must have found out about the kidnapping and was upset with him.

"I didn't tell my father about Aaron," he said. "My dad learned about him from your message. If you're mad about that, you've been mad at the wrong person." Dirk slid from the dragon's back and flew beside her, skirting through trees.

At present, the fledglings looked more like overgrown gargoyles rather than sleek, beautiful dragons. In a month or so, new scales would begin to grow in. Either red, blue, black or green, depending on which genes Vesta had inherited from her parents.

"Besides," Dirk went on, "Aaron doesn't want to leave. He's having a great time. The only time he ever complains is when he has to stop practicing with the dragons in order to do schoolwork." Their dad was making Aaron and Dirk do online classes—accelerated, no less—because he was sure his children were brilliant, and if any of them weren't above grade level, they were slacking off.

No answer.
No answer.

"Talk to me," Dirk cajoled, "and I'll tell you a dragon lord secret."

That at least should get a response. He wasn't sure what he'd tell her, but he could think of something that wouldn't cause too much damage.

Still no response. Something was wrong.

Nothing serious could have happened to her, could it? The news would have reported on that. And he'd seen a photo of her on the internet a few days ago. Her dad had taken his family with him on the campaign trail and news sites had shown pictures of her smiling during a rally.

Tori might have been too far away for an uninterrupted link to Vesta during her campaign travels, but she should have heard some of his message over the last couple of weeks. She should be hearing this one now. Her family was back on the east coast, well within range.

Dirk landed on his lawn to practice controlling Vesta while remaining at a distance. He shut off his phone and then slipped it into his pocket. He wouldn't have been so worried about Tori's silence except he could think of one really bad explanation for it: His father had done something to her, maybe drugged her so she'd lost her Slayer abilities.

If that were the case, it would mean she'd forgotten everything about the Slayers, forgotten Dirk was her counterpart. Would any of her dragon lord abilities remain? Normally, drugging a dragon lord didn't affect their abilities but normally women weren't dragon lords at all. Neither Dirk or his father was sure how Tori's Slayer and dragon lord abilities were connected. Drugging her might make her lose both.

As Dirk considered the idea, the possibility seemed more likely with every passing minute. He impatiently ran

Vesta through the rest of her exercises. Instead of letting her strain against his will—allowing her to have some choice about whether or not to struggle and prolong the pressure of his commands, Dirk held onto her mind with a tight grip and left no room for disobedience. She performed fast, precise, and without mistakes.

Even though Dirk returned Vesta to her enclosure fifteen minutes earlier than usual, the dragon was exhausted and cross. Oh well. Maybe they'd both be in a better mood tomorrow.

Dirk returned to the house and made a beeline up the stairs. Bridget sat in the hallway, singing to one of her dolls. He ignored her and marched to the den. His father didn't like to be interrupted when he was working, but today Dirk didn't care.

He knocked loudly on the door. He wanted to storm in, but his father didn't allow anyone to come in without his permission. The den was where he kept private records, where he contacted his agents, and in general, brokered the deals to buy the nation.

A shuffling sound came from behind the door—things being moved on the desk—but no answer.

Dirk wasn't about to go away just because his father hadn't answered. He opened the door and strode in.

His father wasn't in the room. Aaron was. Which was odd because when their father wasn't in the den, he always locked the door.

His brother stood by their father's desk, an enormous cherrywood structure that was pushed up against the right wall so the computer screen wasn't visible from the door. Aaron moved to the door, probably trying to give the impression that he'd been on his way out when Dirk came in. The guilt and fear rolling off of him, however, suggested he wasn't in the room innocently.

Dirk cocked his head. "What are you doing in here?"

Aaron tapped his hand against the side of his jeans. "Same as you. Looking for Dad."

Dirk glanced around the room to see if anything was out of place. Nothing seemed to be, but he'd definitely heard things shuffling on the desk.

"I thought Dad was here," Aaron continued, trying a little too hard to be casual. "The door was open a crack, so I came in. But he's not here, so now I'm leaving. You probably should lock the door when you go. He wouldn't be happy if he found it unlocked."

Was Aaron offering to leave Dirk alone in here as a sort of bribe—a way of buying his silence?

Aaron tried to pass by Dirk to leave, but Dirk took hold of his arm and stopped him. "I'm impressed. How did you get past the lock?" The door had a keypad and his father didn't give out the code.

Aaron pulled his arm away from Dirk. "I told you, the door was open."

Hard to tell whether that was the truth or not. Aaron's main emotion was fear. Any guilt he possibly felt for lying didn't even make a dent in that sentiment.

Dirk still didn't let him pass. "What were you looking for?"

"Dad," Aaron said.

"If that were the truth, you wouldn't be so afraid."

Dirk could feel Aaron trying to control his emotions, trying to bottle up his fear. "I'm only afraid that you're going to tell Dad about this and make him think I was doing something wrong."

Aaron wasn't lying about that. It was exactly what he was afraid of.

"Look," Dirk said. "I don't want to get you in trouble. I know you were probably in here searching for a way to call your mom or something, but you can't ever come in here like this again. Dad has confidential stuff in here. Things he'd kill to protect. If he found you in here messing around—"

"Our mom," Aaron said, and some of his fear vanished, replaced by annoyance.

"What?"

"You said I was looking for a way to call *my* mom. She's *your* mom too. And you don't have a reason not to call her. Dad didn't take away *your* phone. I can give you her phone number any time you want."

Dirk dropped Aaron's arm. "I have plenty of reasons not to call her. Reasons you're too young to understand. And stop trying to get me off topic. We were talking about you breaking into Dad's den and how it's a really stupid idea."

"He's coming," Aaron said, hurrying to the door. "We've got to go."

"How do you know he's coming?" Dirk asked, more alarmed than curious. Being here when their father came in wasn't an option. He followed after Aaron.

"I saw his car out the window."

"You weren't looking out the window."

"Didn't have to. I saw it in the reflection of the picture frame."

Dirk wasn't about to stay and check to see what could be seen from reflections. He stepped out into the hallway and hit the lock button on the keypad. A moment later the sound of the garage door officially announced their father's arrival.

Aaron disappeared down the hallway. Dirk would worry about getting the truth from him later. Right now he was going to talk to their father. He still needed to find out what, if anything, his father had done to Tori.

Dirk located him in the kitchen, pulling leftovers out of the fridge. He wore a suit and tie but had already loosened his collar.

Dirk folded his arms and got to the point. "Did you do something to Tori?"

His father hardly paused while he took out a container of stir-fry. "Not today. Why?"

"Have you done anything to take her memories away?"

His father shut the fridge, suddenly interested. "Why? Did she lose her memories?" He sounded surprised, amused, but not like he was responsible.

"I don't know," Dirk said. "I haven't heard from her in weeks."

His father took in this information, nodding while he put the stir-fry in the microwave. "Well, that's troubling. You probably had plans for some sort of Christmas gift exchange, didn't you?" He went to the silverware and grabbed a fork and knife. "Maybe this is Tori's way of telling you she just wants to be friends, or in your case, enemies."

Dirk didn't say anything. He was judging his father's reaction. Could he read his father as well as he thought? Was he just feigning innocence?

"It's not you," his father went on, enjoying himself, "it's her. Her misplaced loyalty, her short-sightedness, and her inability to recognize a man of quality." The microwave dinged and his father took his plate out. "I'm beginning to feel quite offended on your behalf. Do you want me to find her and exact revenge?"

"No," Dirk said stiffly. "That's exactly what I don't want you to do." He stalked out of the kitchen before his father could suggest anything else.

Dirk would have to find a way to speak to her himself. Tori had tracked him down at one of his school events, he could do the same. Even though her family had moved houses, chances were she was going to a high-security private school in the DC area. Only a limited number of those were around. He'd start with the one she'd attended before her move: Veritas Academy.

Once he reached his bedroom, he checked Veritas Academy's website. They had an away game on Friday with Maret. If he hadn't heard from her by then, he'd figure out a way to go there and try to find her.

CHAPTER 14

Tori was at a political rally in New York when she heard from Aaron. She was sitting in her seat beside Aprilynne and her mother, trying to maintain an interested and supportive expression in case any of the cameras panned to her during her father's speech.

In the dragon lord part of her mind, she heard Aaron come into the enclosure and begin a training session with Khan. He did these every other day, sometimes with Dirk, sometimes with Overdrake, and most of the time he didn't say anything that was informative. Usually it was stuff like, "Hey dragon, you're looking especially big and fearsome today." Or, "Down boy," or, "Show me some respect, dude, because I can make you stand on your tiptoes and pirouette like a ballerina."

This playful talk always worried Tori because she could tell Aaron was enjoying himself. Perhaps too much. If Tori had gained a bond with Khan after one trip into his mind—an unwanted bond that would make it harder for her to kill him during a battle—what were Aaron's repeated excursions into the dragons' minds doing to him?

Would his loyalty to his younger brother always be enough to keep him on the Slayers' side? Perhaps before long, he wouldn't be able to bring himself to give Tori intel. Not when he knew she'd use it to kill the dragons.

Tori enlarged the sound from Khan's enclosure in her mind. She was listening for information but also wondering if Dirk was with Aaron today. It was always odd to hear Dirk's familiar voice, to hear him joking around with his brother. He never gave any indication that he thought she might be eavesdropping. He never spoke directly to her.

More than once, she'd gone to the website where they exchanged messages to see if Dirk had written anything new there. He hadn't. The code phrase about having a sore throat was the last thing there—the message not to contact him. Nothing else by way of an explanation.

She'd considered writing him anyway, but what if he'd put up the warning because Overdrake had found a way to trace what she wrote there? She couldn't risk her security or her family's just because she wanted to talk to Dirk.

But really, how long did he plan on being silent? Almost three weeks had gone by.

"Yo, Lizard Legs," Aaron called. "Your master is here."

The dragon made a growling sound. A rustling noise came next: the dragon unfurling his wings.

Dirk hadn't said anything today. Maybe he hadn't come with Aaron this time. That meant Overdrake was probably around.

"None of that salty attitude," Aaron said. "We've got work to do."

The dragon let out a roar so loud Tori winced and pulled her focus away, minimizing the sound. Her eyes swept over the cameramen. All were still focused on her father. Good. None of them had caught her wincing while her father expounded on the importance of education.

"If any listening devices were in here," Aaron said, "hopefully they're fried now. That's the best benefit of EMP as far as I can tell."

Wait, Overdrake must not be in the enclosure. Aaron was talking to her. She leaned forward eagerly and enlarged the sound again.

"I found out where the eggs are. Four are going to hatch in the next few years. Those are here in the compound so the vets can watch over the shell-thinning process. Although, I still don't know where here is."

Four. Even if the Slayers managed to kill all the dragons Overdrake was using now, four more would take their place soon enough.

"The other six eggs are being stored at 2045 Water Street, Lock Haven, Pennsylvania. The place has round-the-clock security guards. I'm not sure how many, but I don't think it's a lot. Overdrake is going to move them someplace closer before he attacks. I don't know where or when that is."

Tori hadn't expected such important information, at least not this soon. She needed something to write with. She repeated the words 2045 Water Street, Lock Haven in her mind as she grabbed her purse and searched for a pen.

Aprilynne shot her a sideways glance. "What are you doing?" she whispered.

Tori didn't answer. *2045 Water Street, Lock Haven.*

She didn't have a pen. All she had was makeup.

Aaron began speaking again. "As far as controlling dragons, I've learned a couple of things."

She wasn't ready to remember more things yet. She still had to write down the address.

"After I go into the dragon's mind, at first it feels like I'm just sharing the dragon's senses. I've got to go beyond that to control it. I picture a path that leads to its control center, and it's sort of freaky because once I think about the path, it appears in front of me—like it's a real thing. At first, Overdrake had to show me each of the paths while we were in the dragon's mind together, but now I can do it on my own."

She uncapped a blue eyeliner pencil and as inconspicuously as she could manage, wrote 2045 Water Street on her arm.

She wasn't inconspicuous enough. Aprilynne leaned over, horrified. "What are you doing?"

"Nothing." She added Lock Haven, in deep blue letters. The word almost reached her wrist.

Aprilynne's gaze darted to the camera. They were still trained on their father. "That's not nothing. That's an address written on your arm."

"Shhh," Tori said.

"... path is like wading across a dark, thick river," Aaron continued. Tori had missed the first part of his sentence. "Jupiter's is like finding a waterfall in a bunch of lights."

"You're shushing me?" Aprilynne hissed. "You're the one making a mess all over your arm. How are you going to keep people from seeing that?"

"Shhh," Tori said again.

"Vesta's is like pushing through a wall of rubber branches—sort of bumpy and jiggly. And Khan's path is more like walking through strings of seaweed."

Yes, that's what it had been like—seaweed that sprouted from the ceiling instead of the floor. Tori needed to jot down the others so she remembered them. Under the address, she wrote: V branches, J lights, which meant the dark river must belong to M, Minerva.

Aprilynne coughed in disbelief, then leaned back into her chair shaking her head. "It's these sorts of things that make Mom and Dad worry about your mental stability."

"Once you get to the control center, you give the dragon's will a shape by picturing it as an object. It can be anything as long as it's small enough to hold, but you should use the same thing each time until it becomes automatic. As long as you're holding the object, you've got control. If another dragon lord got there before you and has a control object, yours won't work. That's all I've learned so far."

Aaron was silent for a moment, then said, "I nearly got caught finding out the information about the eggs, so I don't know when I'll be able to tell you anything else."

Another, longer pause. "I don't know how long I can hide stuff from Dirk. I have to make myself not think about you most of the time. I have to...I don't know. Maybe I'll have to really be a dragon lord for a while so they don't catch me."

What did Aaron mean, he would have to *really* be a dragon lord for a while?

What exactly did being a dragon lord entail? Overthrowing a few cities? Plotting the Slayers demise?

Aprilynne nudged her. "Stop glowering or everyone will wonder why you hate Medicare."

Tori re-plastered her supportive smile on her face and tried to look interested again.

"I hope you're connected to Khan or Minerva," Aaron said with a sigh in his voice. "Because I don't know when I'll get time to talk around the fledgling dragons. Overdrake doesn't leave me alone with them. They're mean and unpredictable." His voice changed, turned into the sing-song voice people used when speaking to animals.

"Not like you, boy. You're just a big scaly dog, aren't you?"

Aaron was already too attached to Khan. Tori couldn't help frowning again.

After that Aaron didn't say anything else. Tori kept listening, straining to hear more, but the only sounds were those of the dragon's heavy footsteps and then wingbeats. The dragon was moving around the enclosure, probably obeying Aaron's unspoken instructions.

She should send the information about the eggs' location to Dr. B and then wipe off the eyeliner before anyone saw it. An address would be a particularly bad thing for the cameras to catch if Overdrake happened to be watching coverage of this speech.

Tori pushed the button on her watch that signaled she had a message for Dr. B, then began slowly texting out the address into her watch. Speaking into it would have been faster, but she didn't want Aprilynne to hear. Her sister wouldn't be reassured about Tori's mental health if she suddenly began to hold a conversation with her wrist about how the voice in her head had told her where the dragon eggs were hidden.

Once the address was sent, she put the other information in a text and sent it to herself. When she was done, she leaned over Aprilynne and asked her mother for a tissue. Her mother pulled two from her purse and handed them to Tori with barely a glance in her direction. "If you have to blow your nose, wait until you're sure the cameras aren't on you."

Aprilynne looked upward. "Oh, we're so beyond anything Miss Manners could fix."

Tori wiped the eyeliner off her arm as discreetly as she could manage, making sure the cameras stayed pointed at her father. While she did, she checked her watch for a return message from Dr. B.

No answer yet.

He'd called a practice for this afternoon and in all likelihood, it was still going on. With the Slayers already assembled, perhaps they were busy planning a mission to the address. The group would need to scope out the building first. If only a few security guards were around, taking them out wouldn't be too hard. Or at least it wouldn't be if Bess were with them.

Tori fought another frown. They'd just have to do the job without her shield. Kody could knock guns from the security guards' hands.

Tori's arm had become a smudge of blue. That's what she got for buying the expensive brand of eyeliner. This stuff wasn't coming off. She kept surreptitiously wiping. Both tissues were blue and her arm looked like she had a large bruise.

Dr. B wrote back *Where did Aaron get this information from?*

Tori glanced at the cameras and then answered. *He didn't say. He only mentioned he'd almost been caught finding it.* He also said he was going to have act like a dragon lord for a while. Although Tori couldn't bring herself to admit that part to Dr. B.

Dr. B didn't ask any other questions. Tori waited for ten minutes then fifteen. Finally she wrote *When are we going to Lock Haven?*

We've been studying satellite pictures, he replied. *The address is listed as the Energize Nutrition office building. Very rural, wooded area. We're currently debating the merits of a mission.*

Debating the merits? It shouldn't be a question of 'if'. This was the inside information they'd been waiting for. This was the whole reason she'd sent Aaron into enemy territory. He'd taken risks to get them intel that would give the Slayers an advantage. They couldn't ignore the lead.

The merits are obvious, she wrote back. *Six fewer dragons to fight. The debate should be about the best way to destroy them.*

A few moments later, Dr. B's answer showed up on her watch. *I'll let the others tell you about their concerns.*

A stream of messages made their way across her watch face in quick succession.

From Jesse: *Are you sure you can read Aaron well enough to tell whether he's telling the truth?*

From Ryker: *Aaron has only been a mole for a few weeks. How likely is it that Overdrake gave him important information and then left him alone with dragons—even though Overdrake knows Aaron could pass those details on to you? One or both are up to something.*

From Kody: *I say let's kick this pig. If you can't run with the big dogs, stay under the porch.*

Was that a concern or a vote of confidence? With Kody, sometimes it was hard to tell.

From Rosa: *Overdrake might have given false information to Aaron in order to see if he passes it along to you. If we show up at the building, Overdrake will know Aaron is helping us.*

From Lilly: *How stupid do you think we are? We already went on a mission to destroy dragon eggs, and we were nearly killed. Now you're suggesting it again? You might be able to read Aaron, but none of us can read you. This is the exact same thing that Dirk did to us. How do we know you haven't switched sides?*

Well, so much for Lilly and Tori's truce. It had probably been doomed from the start. Tori was too impatient to type out an answer to Lilly so she lifted her watch to her lips, pretending to scratch her ear while she whispered into it. "You know I haven't switched sides because if I had, the first thing I would have done is teach you some manners."

Aprilynne shot Tori a look. "What?"

"Nothing."

Tori lowered her hand, glancing at the message from Lilly that flashed across her watch face. *Try it and you'll have your ask handed back to you on a tray.*

The reply almost made Tori laugh out loud. Theo apparently hadn't programmed the voice recognition software to repeat swearwords.

Tori lifted her watch to her lips again. "Really?" she murmured. "What else will be on that tray besides my ask?"

A moment later Lilly wrote *Go to help.*

Priceless.

Aprilynne let out an exaggerated sigh and kept her voice low. "Is this some sort of cry for attention? Are you trying to get Mom and Dad to worry about you? Because if that's why you go through these episodes where you act insane, you're being selfish. Dad needs your support right now."

"Sorry," Tori said. And she waited a couple of minutes before she typed *I can tell Aaron isn't lying and I doubt Overdrake would feed Aaron false information. He realizes what the rest of you have forgotten. If I don't connect to an egg when I get close to the building, I'll know they're not there.*

Dr. B was the one who wrote back this time. *We need to investigate the building further. We'll contact you with our decision.*

Their decision. The phrase shouldn't have irked Tori, but it did. Granted, she knew the drill—decisions that affected the group were supposed to be made by the group. She was only one vote among many. She understood that. But why couldn't the rest of them see the opportunity Aaron had given them—six fewer dragons to fight.

And how were they going to investigate the building? She was the only one that would be able to tell them what they needed to know—whether or not dragon eggs were inside.

But Dr. B hadn't even asked her when she would be able to take a trip to Lock Haven.

He hadn't asked because he knew the Slayers wouldn't vote to attack the building. They were too suspicious of the source.

Frustration welled inside of her. She wasn't going to let Aaron's sacrifice be for nothing, and she wasn't going to sit idly by while six more dragons hatched. Each of those dragons was just another way for her friends to die. Whether they appreciated it or not, she would do everything in her power to save their lives. If that meant taking care of the eggs herself, so be it.

This weekend her parents were leaving for a campaigning trip to Iowa. Tori could invent a shopping date with friends on Saturday and be gone most of the day without worrying her sister.

Tori wrote back *I'm going to take a look at the building on Saturday night. Anyone who wants to come with me will need battle gear.*

A moment later, Dr. B's answer paraded over her watch. *We work as a team.*

We should, Tori answered. *But I'm afraid my team will be pretty small on Saturday.*

Big surprise, Lilly wrote. *Tori has decided her way is the best.*

Dr. B's response was immediate. *No one is going anywhere Saturday. Tori and I will discuss this later.*

That was the end of the messages, which was perhaps a good thing since Aprilynne leaned over. "Why do you keep playing with your watch? This is *live* television."

"I think it's broken," Tori whispered back.

"If it's dead, don't try to revive it. The thing belongs in the graveyard of bad fashion choices—right next to plastic shoes and headbands that go across people's foreheads."

Tori sat silently for the rest of her father's speech, attempting not to look frustrated, discouraged, or anything else a wandering camera could interpret as being sullen about her father's agenda.

What were the chances the Slayers would approve the mission? They didn't trust Aaron because he was a dragon lord. They thought he would betray them like Dirk had. When it came down to it, they wouldn't put their lives on the line for her plan. Or maybe they just didn't trust her judgment.

How had she gone from not wanting the responsibility of being A-team's leader to being angry because the Slayers wouldn't follow her?

 CHAPTER 15

Jesse switched off the display screen on his watch and shook his head. What was Tori thinking? And when had she become so reckless? The Slayers stood around Dr. B's golf cart, their practice momentarily forgotten and their horses making good use of the time to wander off and sample nearby bushes.

Willow's gaze circled the group. "Is Tori serious about going by herself?

Rosa sighed. "Probably."

Jesse scowled. "Definitely." Tori was putting too much trust in Aaron and her connection with him. The kid was twelve and probably couldn't tell real information from a set-up. Jesse needed to see her, talk some sense into her. "Even if she can sense a dragon egg in the building, that doesn't mean the information is legit. Overdrake might be willing to use an egg to bait a trap."

Kody's eyebrows dipped as he thought. "You think Overdrake would risk losing an egg?"

"Most definitely," Dr. B said. He held a tablet in his hands and zoomed in on the picture on his screen, getting a closer look at the building. "After all, he was willing to risk sending his son to camp with Slayers every year in order to trap us. An egg is a small price when he has nine others."

"But it could be the real deal," Kody pointed out.

Now it was Lilly's turn to snort. "We got this information from a dragon lordette, who got it from a dragon lordling, who got it from Overdrake. It's a trap."

Ryker leaned forward to get a better view of Dr. B's screen. "It's suspiciously similar to the first ruse Overdrake used. He knows we'll have a hard time resisting the chance to destroy dragon eggs. It's the lure of an easy kill. Maybe he fed information to Aaron in order to test him. That way he not only finds out if the kid is loyal, he also catches us."

Jesse nodded. "We have to be careful not just on our account, but Aaron's too."

Dr. B closed the site that showed the building. "I'll take Theo and Booker to Pennsylvania and see what sort of security the building has. We'll continue this discussion afterward. Meanwhile, I see no reason to delay practice further." He waved a hand at the Slayers. "Let's get back to work."

Jesse whistled for General and waited as the horse cantered over. Tori wouldn't like having her information called into question, but he would talk to her at school tomorrow and make her see reason. She couldn't go off half-cocked by herself on a dangerous mission. If Overdrake had the chance, he'd kill Tori. He'd already tried more than once.

For the rest of practice, Jesse's concentration was off. He couldn't shake images of Tori being captured, shot, or fed to the dragons.

He would have to convince her not to do anything rash. It was bad enough that he'd lost her to Dirk. Jesse wasn't about to lose her to Overdrake.

 # CHAPTER 16

Thursday, on the flight back to Maryland, Tori sat by the window. Since Overdrake's attack on the Slayer's jet Halloween night, being in planes had made Tori feel—well, not exactly claustrophobic. What she felt was more of the general variety of panic.

Now whenever Tori traveled with her family, she insisted on a window seat. She felt the compulsive need to look out it every few minutes and search for the dark shapes of incoming dragons.

Overdrake had contacts in the FAA who'd told him which flight the Slayers had been on. Despite Dirk's assurances that his father would leave her family alone, it was entirely possible that Overdrake might find out her dad's flight schedule and attack the plane.

She couldn't explain her fears to her family, just as she couldn't tell them why she'd acquired the habit of nervously tapping her foot on the floor.

Tori's mother sat next to her, answering emails on her laptop. Her father and Aprilynne were across the aisle. "Shouldn't you be doing your homework?" her mother asked.

Tori's book was open, but her pencil languished unused on her lap. "It's too hard to concentrate here."

What would she do if she heard a dragon in flight, if she felt her powers turn on? Even if she could manage to open a door in time, could she save all of her family? She would have no way of explaining to them that they needed to hold on to her while she leaped from the plane.

It was thinking of those sorts of scenarios that made calculus hard.

"Flying didn't used to bother you," her mother said.

"It's not the flying that bothers me," Tori said. "It's the possibility of crashing violently."

Her mother patted her hand reassuringly. "We've got an experienced pilot. We'll be fine."

"I know," Tori said, but perhaps her mother could still sense her nervousness.

Her mother didn't return her attention to her laptop. Instead, she leaned over and gazed out at the view. "That's an interesting cloud." She pointed at a bunchy one that was stretching out at both ends. "What do you think it looks like?" Tori's mother had played this game with her when she was little. They would lie out on the lawn and find shapes in the clouds. It had been a relaxing way to pass the time.

"A dragon," Tori said. A dragon with its wings tucked.

Her mother didn't comment, just gestured to another cloud. "What about that one?"

The cloud was long and mostly shapeless. "A stream of fire, I guess."

Tori's mother pointed to another cloud, this one C-shaped. "How about that one?"

"A mouth about to bite something."

Her mother turned and gave her father an are-you-paying-attention-to-this sort of look. He was paying attention, and the wrinkles around his eyes deepened in worry.

That's when Tori realized her mother hadn't been reviving a childhood game to keep her mind off of flying, she'd been giving Tori her own version of the inkblot test. She was checking for some sort of blossoming psychosis, and apparently she thought she'd found it.

Just great. When Aprilynne had said all of that stuff about Tori worrying their parents, Tori hadn't taken her seriously. But her sister hadn't been exaggerating.

Tori turned back to the window. "Now that I look at that cloud again, it seems more like a river. A nice river where people picnic. And that cloud over there totally looks like a flower garden. Oh, and that one is a rabbit."

Her mother turned to her again, speaking in the sympathetic tone parents used when they wanted to show they understood the problem. "Honey, a lot of people experience periods of anxiety. Being a teenager is stressful enough without the national attention on your family. I can understand why you might struggle with things. Sometimes it's best to talk about your issues with a doctor and learn coping techniques. Why don't I set up an appointment for you?"

No. Tori was not about to go to a counselor. What would she be able to say that wouldn't make her sound delusional? She'd have to make up issues just so the counselor wouldn't think she was holding out.

Not for the first time, Tori considered tracking down the blueprints Ryker had used to build his simulator and showing her parents that she had powers. It would be proof that Slayers were real and she was one of them. As soon as the idea passed through Tori's mind, she dismissed it. If her parents knew the truth, they wouldn't let her be a Slayer. They wouldn't let her fight dragons or

Overdrake. They would pull her out of the team the same way Bess's grandfather had. "I'm not crazy, Mom."

"I know you're not, sweetheart."

Her father leaned across the aisle, his voice filled with concern. "Going to a counselor doesn't make you crazy any more than going to a doctor makes you a hypochondriac."

"I'm fine, really." And then because she didn't think her parents would drop the subject, she added, "I guess I've been watching too many shows with plane crashes. They've made me a little tense. That's different than anxiety. A lot of people worry about flying."

Her mother and father exchanged another look, but they didn't say more.

Tori forced herself to work on a math assignment after that, or at least pretended that she was. This was one more thing she had to thank Overdrake for, one more way he'd made her life hard. She wouldn't feel badly about paying him back on Saturday at all.

 CHAPTER 17

On Friday morning, Jesse texted Tori that he wanted to talk to her, then went to her locker and waited for her to show up. He needed to convince her not to do anything rash tomorrow. She'd always told him the Slayers were much too willing to fight dragons, that it would be their downfall. Maybe she was right about that. But Tori's downfall would be fighting Overdrake by herself.

She may have decided that she didn't need Jesse, but that didn't mean she didn't need the rest of the Slayers. And they certainly needed her.

Finding a way to talk to Tori privately would be difficult because girls had a way of migrating toward her and forming little clumps of chatter around her. And then there was Roland, her ex from last year. Whenever he spotted Tori walking in the hallway, he barnacled himself to her side. Jesse had developed a profound dislike of the guy.

Still no sign of Tori among the stream of students drifting by in a sea of plaid and red polos. He kept watching. He knew the exact shade of her brown hair— golden brown with caramel highlights—and could have picked her out of crowd with only a glimpse of it.

After a couple of minutes, Tori appeared through the crowd, strolling down the hall, phone in hand. Alone for once. Her long hair swung around her shoulders and her mint green eyes were trained on her screen. Perhaps reading his text.

Even though she wore the same uniform as every other girl in school, she somehow still managed to make it look better. He wasn't sure whether he should feel happy or just tormented about seeing her every day. The emotions went hand in hand lately.

She slid her phone into her pocket, glanced up, and noticed him. "Hi." It wasn't an overly-friendly "Hi." Not like the ones she used to give him, full of personal subtext. She was professional, aloof. One more thing he had to live with now.

As she spun her combination, he began his speech. "I appreciate that you want to destroy the eggs. So do I. But we have to weigh the benefits of any mission against the danger. Even if you link to an egg inside the building, you'll still have no guarantee that Overdrake hasn't put an egg nearby to lay a trap for us. If the information is legitimate, then waiting a few more days or even weeks while we investigate won't matter. We don't need to rush into anything."

"I've already heard all of the objections." She opened her locker and slid her backpack from her shoulders.

"Good. Then you've had time to think about the merits of caution. Or the merits of teamwork, whichever seems most persuasive."

She took off her coat and hung it in her locker, hardly listening to him. "Do you think I act like I'm crazy?"

"I don't know," he said slowly. "Are you going to agree with me about Saturday or not?"

She put her backpack inside her locker with an unhappy shove. "I used to think the worst part of being a

Slayer was fighting dragons—and okay, it still is, but having to keep a secret identity sucks too." She pulled her journalism book from her shelf and tucked it under her arm with the air of a martyr. "This is why Batman and Superman don't live with their parents."

"What?" Jesse cocked his head. "What's going on with your parents?"

"They think I have anxiety issues because of the Slayer stuff."

"Why? Did you tell them you hear voices?"

"No. I don't explain any of it. That's the problem." She took a pen from her backpack and gave her bag a push further into her locker. "If Batman was real, trust me, people would wonder why Bruce Wayne was always talking into his bat-watch and disappearing at odd times."

"I don't think he had a bat-watch."

She shut her locker door with a clang. "Of course he did. He had bat-everything. The point is, the movies never show us the aftermath when Bruce Wayne is giving out lame excuses for his bizarre behavior and everyone is looking at him like he's had a nervous breakdown."

Jesse surveyed her silently for a moment. "So you're going to stay home on Saturday, right?"

Instead of moving down the hallway, Tori leaned against her locker. "My parents will be out of town on Saturday, and Aprilynne won't care if I'm gone. Those are rare events for me. I have to take advantage of them."

She wasn't taking this mission seriously enough. She hadn't foreseen all of the things that could go wrong, like gunmen shooting her or Overdrake capturing her. "An excuse to be gone isn't a valid reason for putting your life in jeopardy."

Tori folded her arms, still clutching her journalism notebook. "This morning at breakfast, my mother told me that there are lots of perfectly safe medications for anxiety."

Still no reason to act rashly. "We can come up with an excuse for you to make the trip later."

Tori sighed. "And later the rest of you will change your mind about intel from dragon lords? Why risk the possibility of Overdrake moving the eggs somewhere else when we know where they are right now?" Her green eyes found his. Those eyes, the same color as sunlight on sea glass, were asking for his support. It would have been easy to fall under their spell the way he'd done so many times—give her whatever she wanted just to make her happy. But he couldn't this time, not when her safety was in question.

"Waiting won't hurt," he said. "Not waiting could definitely hurt."

She arched a meaningful eyebrow at him. "Since when are you so concerned with whether I get hurt or not?"

She wasn't talking about the mission anymore, but he met the accusation and raised eyebrow without flinching. "Since always."

She leaned away from the locker, dismissing his words. "Taking no action isn't always the right decision." She seemed to be talking about more than Saturday, but before he could be sure of her meaning, the warning bell rang, announcing they had five minutes until class started. As they started toward their class, Tacy and another girl ambled up, putting a quick end to mission talk.

"Are you ready for the game?" Tacy asked Jesse, all smiles.

For a moment, he stared at her, not sure what she meant.

"The game against Maret," she clarified.

And then he remembered: basketball. The team was playing tonight.

When he first enrolled in Veritas, he hadn't wanted to join. He hadn't planned to play any sports this year because he knew after school practice would end up conflicting with Slayer training. But Jesse's parents had insisted. His father talked to the coach and told the man that Jesse had started for the varsity team at his last school. His mother went on and on about how colleges were bound to offer scholarship money if they saw him play. His father was already in contact with people from some universities.

Jesse could use scholarship money, although he couldn't help but think part of his mother's insistence he play was due to the fact that she wanted to keep him busy with sports so he didn't have time to hang out with Tori. Ironic. Turned out his mom hadn't needed to keep them apart after all.

"Yeah," Jesse told Tacy. "Should be a good game."

Technically he shouldn't have been playing in today's game since he missed a practice yesterday. He'd faked an illness so he could meet with the other Slayers. But the coach had seen his three-pointer enough times that he was playing him anyway.

That was the thing about being a Slayer. You had better aim, accuracy, and reaction time even when your powers weren't turned on.

"We'll be there rooting for you," Tacy purred, and then seemed to remember that Tori was walking down the hallway too. "Are you going tonight?" she asked.

Tori forced a smile. "I wouldn't miss it."

Jesse wondered what sort of meaning was behind that smile long after journalism class started.

CHAPTER 18

"Why exactly did we come to the game?" Melinda asked. She was one of Tori's Veritas friends. She sat beside Tori in the bleachers, mostly checking her phone and taking selfies.

The crowd around them had erupted in a cheer—Jesse had made another basket—and the guy next to Melinda jostled her, making her spill popcorn on her lap.

"School spirit," Tori said.

"Uh huh." Melinda wasn't a sports fan, which had always seemed like a good thing. For the most part, Tori avoided sports events. The yells from the crowd, the clapping, the sound of players thumping across the floor—and worst of all, the shrill referee whistles—it was a constant assault of sound.

But after Jesse had joined the basketball team, Tori had undergone a sharp increase of interest in the game. Tonight she'd told her parents she was going to Melinda's house and then dragged her to the game. That way, she didn't have to bring her bodyguard with her.

Melinda cast a glance at Jesse. "I thought you were over Jonathan."

"I am. Sort of. It's complicated."

Melinda rolled her eyes. "He's hot and acts all unattainable. That's not a complication, that's a challenge.

And you've fallen for it just like every other girl in the school."

At first, Jesse had acted unattainable to the other girls because he'd been seeing her. But even after their split, he wasn't seeing anyone. Was that because he still had feelings for her or because he didn't want any entanglements that would keep him from his Slayer duties?

The crowd erupted into another cheer, drawing Tori's attention back to the game. Well, not really to the game—she was only paying attention to Jesse. He ran down the court with a stride that had a grace and flow that made everything he did look effortless.

He'd stolen the ball from the other team and was winding his way around their players to the school's basket. He pivoted around the guard and went up for a layup. Two points. The crowd whooped its approval.

He didn't even pause before he headed down to the other basket to play defense. For a moment his gaze flickered to the crowd and Tori wondered if he saw her sitting on the bleachers.

Probably not. Jesse had a way of concentrating on what needed to be done and forgetting about the unimportant details. In this case: her, staring at him like some groupie.

The guy who sat on the other side of Tori was talking to a friend beside him. "We're going to bury Maret. That new kid is on fire."

He was. Tori hoped some of the scouts from local colleges would want him. It would be a pity if he had to turn down out-of-state offers because Dr. B had instructed the Slayers to stay in the area. She let herself wonder what Jesse's life would be like if he weren't a Slayer. He not only had athletic potential, the guy was smart and had a good head on his shoulders. He could go anywhere. He was the sort of person whose future should be wide open and limitless.

A familiar sensation bloomed inside of Tori, made her catch her breath. It was the feeling that a counterpart was close. *Dirk.* Her eyes searched the gymnasium. He was somewhere nearby.

Even as the thought occurred to her, she dismissed it. Why would he be at this basketball game? And yet that feeling of familiarity—of him—was there.

People were coming and going through the door. When her gaze turned in that direction, he wasn't hard to spot. He was tall, broad-shouldered, blond, and handsome. Those sorts of guys always stood out.

He wandered toward the bleachers, scanning the crowd, and the next moment his eyes connected with hers. He smiled but there was a tinge of worry, a hesitation in his expression. He crossed the floor, still holding her gaze.

Was this coincidence or had he come to see her on purpose? If it were on purpose, it could be good news—or very bad news. She peered at the area behind Dirk to see if anyone was with him. Overdrake maybe or an assortment of henchmen.

He seemed to be alone. No one who was burly, armed, or sinister trailed him. Eyes still on her, he made his way to her section of the bleachers.

How had he found her? Well, she shouldn't really wonder. He'd known she'd gone to this school before she moved. It wasn't surprising he would check here—but why had he come? Was he about to deliver some sort of ultimatum to the Slayers? That's what the bad guys in movies always did when they showed up unexpectedly.

Her breaths came faster, her heart pounded, and she wasn't exactly sure whether it was from worry or happiness—because, frustratingly, even though she was worried, another part of her was just happy to see him.

He climbed the steps, and people scooted over, letting him edge through her row. When he was still a couple feet away, she asked, "What are you doing here?"

He stopped on the bleacher beneath her, waiting for people to shift away from her to make room. "I came to talk to you, to make sure you were okay."

The guys on Tori's side didn't move. They were too engrossed in the game to notice Dirk standing there. Melinda didn't move either, but that was because she was staring, starstruck, at Dirk.

He spoke without sitting down. "Why didn't you answer any of my messages?"

She blinked at him, confused. "Your last message said not to contact you."

It was his turn to look surprised. "You haven't heard anything from me since then? You didn't hear my new contact information?"

She shook her head. Should she admit that she was connected to Khan now and not Vesta? If Dirk ever had another warning for her, she wanted to make sure she heard it. But at the same time, Overdrake hadn't let Aaron be alone with Vesta. If Dirk knew Tori could hear what Khan heard, would Aaron be kept from that dragon? Perhaps Overdrake's restrictions on the fledglings weren't only due to their unpredictable nature. Maybe he was making sure Aaron didn't leak anything to her.

Before she could decide what to say next, her attention shifted. The crowd had momentarily grown quiet, seemed to be suspended in a collective gasp. The ref's whistle chided a shrill complaint. Something was wrong.

She didn't see the basketball hurtling toward the back of Dirk's head. She couldn't see it because he was blocking her view of the court. But he turned—split-second fast—reached into the air and caught the ball before it hit his head.

Several people in the stands let out exclamations, some of relief that no one had been hurt, others in pure appreciation of the sort of skill it took to catch a ball going fast and hard when your back was turned.

But most of the crowd just gaped in disbelief, some at Dirk, some at Jesse.

Tori knew Jesse was the one who'd hurled the ball into the stands even before she tilted her head to see him standing in the middle of the floor glaring up at Dirk.

Jesse had apparently seen Dirk in the stands and his first reaction had been to stop the game and fling the only hard object he had at Dirk's head.

Jesse should have known it wouldn't work. The Slayers had done this sort of thing often enough at camp—pitched things at each other to test one another's reaction times. Dirk was hard to catch off guard.

"Well," Dirk said wryly, "look who's playing on your team."

Jesse stormed toward the stands, saying something that was drowned out by the ref's scolding whistle. Perhaps Jesse's teammates were close enough to hear him, or perhaps his look of determination was enough to announce his intentions because a couple guys grabbed Jesse's arms to hold him back.

Dirk smiled at Jesse, took aim at the opponent's basket, and threw the ball in that direction.

The ball swooshed through the net and the crowd let at an assortment of hoots and cheers. The guy sitting next to Tori raised his hand to give Dirk a fist bump. "Dude, that was so awesome!"

What it was, was proof that Dirk's powers were turned on. None of them could have so effortlessly landed that shot without their extra abilities, but it was the sort of thing all of them did at camp. Dirk had done it to make a point: He had extra strength and Jesse didn't.

Jesse stopped struggling against his teammates. His gaze went to Tori and the apprehension in his eyes made his thoughts clear. She didn't have extra strength right now. If she needed to fight off Dirk, she wouldn't be able to do it.

While the guy sitting next to Tori asked Dirk where he played, Tori held up a hand to Jesse, making the Slayer sign that everything was fine. Dirk wouldn't hurt her. She didn't sense any aggression or hostility from him. He'd come to make sure she was okay.

Jesse didn't look all that reassured, but at least he wasn't marching into the bleachers to confront Dirk.

Most people in the stands were still staring at both Dirk and Jesse, trying to piece together what had happened. Melinda was just staring at Dirk as if hoping if she waited long enough a priest would appear and marry them. "Tori," she chimed. "You haven't introduced me to your friend."

Dirk shook off his fanboy and turned back to Tori and Melinda. "I'm Dirk," he said with a forced smile. "I'm here to take Tori home."

She couldn't leave with him. They were, after all, enemies. "I can't," she said.

On the basketball court, the ref had retrieved the ball and was trying to get the game started again. The coach was at Jesse's side yelling but Jesse's gaze was still on the stands, a fact that was making the coach's face turn an unnatural shade of red.

She tapped the All's Well button on her watch and sent the message to Jesse so he wouldn't make things worse.

"We're old friends," Dirk told Melinda. "And we've got lots to catch up on. Sorry to take her away."

Melinda smiled back at him. "I'm one of her old friends too. Which means we probably have lots of other things in common."

Dirk took hold of Tori's wrist, a soft grip but an insistent one. "Let's leave. I'm blocking people's view of the game."

Tori tried to tug her wrist away from him, a pointless gesture against his strength. "You know I can't leave with you."

Melinda leaned toward him and giggled. "Hey, I'll leave with you."

Really, when had Melinda become this much of a flirt?

Dirk didn't let go of Tori's wrist. His voice went low, serious and teasing at the same time. "Don't make me carry you out of here."

"Don't even think about it," Tori said. "This is a public place."

She looked at Jesse again, and Dirk followed her gaze. Jesse was walking to the benched players, pressing buttons on his watch. No doubt, he was calling for reinforcement. Dr. B would bring a simulator so the Slayers could fight and capture Dirk. How long would it take them to get here?

"The watches," Dirk said in a tone that reminded her of Overdrake. Confident and plotting. When Dirk was a Slayer, he'd owned one, so he knew what they did and how important they were to the team's communication. Before she realized what he was doing, he hooked his finger underneath her watch and pulled. With the force of his strength, the band snapped and came loose from her wrist.

He held it up. "Do you want this back?"

She lunged for it and nearly toppled down the bleachers. He took hold of her waist, steadying her. He smelled of aftershave, a scent that brought to mind parties where men wore tuxedos. "Throwing yourself at me?" he murmured, then set her on her feet again. "This is a public place."

Melinda laughed, clearly missing the undertone of the conversation. "Are you okay, Tori?" She saw the watch in Dirk's hand. "Did that thing finally break? Good. Now she can get something decent."

Tori held her hand out to Dirk with an impatient wave of her fingers. "Give me my watch." Theo had recalled and changed all of their watches when Overdrake captured Alyssa and took hers. Tori didn't want to go through that again. As much as she hated the way her watch looked, it was handier than a phone and more secure. Her conversations with the other Slayers were automatically encrypted.

"I just want to talk to you," Dirk said, turning to go. "You can tell I'm not lying about that."

Without another word, he strode down the bleachers. His message was clear. If she wanted her watch back, she had to come with him.

She did want to talk to him, but not like this. She didn't like being forced into it or hurried so that she didn't have time to consider all the implications and dangers of going with him.

Still, he wanted to talk to her and he hadn't had a lot of ways to reach her since he didn't know she was connected to Khan. And what if he'd come to give her information or broker some sort of deal?

Her gaze went to Jesse again. He'd noticed Dirk moving to the door. Jesse had his wrist lifted, pretending to wipe sweat from his forehead. A practiced move to hide the fact that he was speaking into his watch.

Jesse was not going to be happy when he noticed her leaving the gym and realized what she'd done, but then she supposed that was par for the course. The Slayers didn't want her to speak to Dirk and she kept disappointing them. She would just have to live with whatever grief Jesse gave her.

She made her way down the bleachers, her footsteps tapping against the floor. She hardly heard them over the pounding of the game and the noise of the crowd. Most everyone had returned their attention to the floor. Only a few people watched her make her way to the door.

Dirk waited in the foyer, standing casually by the trophy cases and looking every bit the golden boy who could win them. He read her watch face, and without glancing up, said, "Jesse texted and asked what you're doing." Dirk spoke out loud as he wrote back. "I'm leaving the rest of you and running off with the man of my dreams. YOLO."

Tori marched over to him, hand out. "Give me that."

"Let's go talk first." He headed out the front doors, leaving her no choice but to follow him.

She reluctantly did so. She still sensed no aggression from him, no deceit. If he wanted a private place to talk, fine. The school steps were private enough. The cold night air pressed against her throat and face. She'd only worn a light jacket.

Dirk stood at the bottom of the school steps, had probably leapt down there.

She walked down them slowly. "What did you want to talk about?"

"Not here." Dirk sauntered out onto the parking lot, reading messages on her watch again. "Ryker will arrive in ten minutes. Fifteen if Dr. B gets held up in traffic with the simulator." Dirk shook his head as he ambled through a row of cars. "DC traffic. The bane of commuters and dragon Slayers alike."

Tori's watch buzzed and Dirk checked it. "Jesse says to stop being flippant and take the situation seriously." Dirk spoke as he wrote back. "Like when you chucked a ball into the crowd, Mr. Good Example?" He pointed to his black Porsche sitting in the back of the parking lot. "My car is over there."

He wanted to drive someplace. This just kept getting riskier. She stopped walking. "Where exactly did you want to talk?"

Instead of answering, he increased his pace, pulling further ahead.

She hesitated. She shouldn't get in a car with an enemy. But then again, if Dirk wanted to kidnap her, he could have already done it. He could have carried her off and she wouldn't have been able to stop him.

She grudgingly followed after him again. He was several yards ahead and wasn't slowing down. "Why aren't you waiting for me?" she asked.

"Because I need to do *this*." The Volkswagen bug he was passing had a window that was cracked down an ch. He slipped her watch through the opening, then checked to make sure the car doors were locked.

She reached the car and peered inside. Her watch lay on the driver's seat forlornly, one panel lit up to indicate she had a new message. "You said you were going to give it to me."

"You'll get it back," Dirk said. "As soon as Jesse tells Dr. B you left with me, he'll trace your watch's position and find it here. Ryker or Jesse will break into the car and get it."

Tori kept looking at the watch. "You were the only one who was good at breaking into cars. You remember that, don't you? Ryker is new and Jesse..."

"Is lacking in many skills. I do remember that." Dirk took her hand and led her toward his car.

She wondered if Dirk had somehow seen the Slayers breaking into Alyssa's car last October. Jesse hadn't been able to get the tool to work and they'd all ended up conspicuously crowded around the car while people strolled by giving them dirty looks. Tori felt the need to say something in their defense, or at least Jesse's defense.

"Jesse is trained to fight dragons. Breaking into cars doesn't come up much during those sorts of fights."

"Don't worry about him," Dirk said. "The Volkswagen's owner probably won't catch Jesse trying to jimmy his lock, and if he does—how tough can the owner be? He drives a bug."

They'd reached Dirk's Porsche. He unlocked the car, then held the passenger side door open for Tori.

"You know," she said, not moving to the car. "I don't think we have a very well-defined hero-villain relationship. I bet Wonder Woman never got in a car with...who did she fight, anyway?"

"Guys who could be stopped with a lasso. I see you didn't bring yours." Dirk kept holding the door open. "I only want to talk to you. Villains and heroes do that all the time."

Tori wrapped her arms around herself to keep from shivering. "You're not going to kidnap me, trick me, trap me—anything I'll regret later?"

He shrugged his shoulders in mock innocence. "How would I know what you'll regret later? What did you regret last time?"

She didn't want to answer that question. "Just promise me that you'll let me go anytime I want."

"I'll let you go anytime you want." He said the words with too much mischief seeping into his sincerity, but that was part of his personality—an underlying mischief and way of stirring things up for his own personal amusement. He wasn't feeling guilty enough to make her think he was lying.

She got in the car and pulled her jacket tighter around her. Once Dirk got in, he turned the heater on high, then drove across the parking lot. As he pulled onto the street, he glanced back at the school. "So you see Jesse every day. How's that working out?"

"That's not what you came to talk to me about."

"Yeah, but it's what I want to talk about now."

"I'd rather not talk about it."

"Hmm," he said with a smile. "Not so well then."

It was one of those times when she didn't like being Dirk's counterpart. He seemed to know all the things she wasn't saying. Tori watched the rows of colonial houses file past her window. A thin layer of snow covered the lawns, hiding the dead grass beneath. "Now that you know Jesse's location, Dr. B will probably move him."

Dirk nodded. "Bummer." Another smile.

Tori's cell phone dinged, announcing she had a text message.

"That's probably Jesse now," Dirk said.

It was. His message read *Are you okay? Where are you?*

She texted an explanation about the watch, reiterated that she was fine, and told him she would call him when she was done talking to Dirk.

Jesse was going to have a lot to say about that, was probably already composing a lengthy text. She planned on ignoring it.

"So where are you taking me?" she asked.

Dirk turned from the street they'd been on. "To a remote, secluded location."

She crossed her arms. "That sounds like you've planned my untimely death, not a polite conversation. How about we go to a restaurant instead? There's a good Thai place a few miles back."

He kept driving straight. "I know a place you'll like better."

"I'm not so sure about that. I prefer Thai to 'remote and secluded'. What will we be talking about?"

"My dad hacked my last account with you. That's why I told you not to contact me. So only post things there that you wouldn't mind him reading. I set up an untraceable account on the dark web. The login and password are on that slip of paper on top of the dashboard."

Tori picked up the paper. While she entered the information into her phone, Dirk said, "How come you haven't heard any of my spoken messages?"

There was no point trying to keep the truth about her connection with Khan from him. She couldn't come up with some other explanation for why she hadn't heard Dirk speak when he was near Vesta.

With almost a jolt, she remembered she should pretend to be angry that Overdrake had kidnapped Aaron. "I've heard you speak while you were with a dragon, but you never said anything that was directed at me."

She turned to face Dirk and concentrated on her worry for Aaron. She didn't have to fake that. "I know your father has Aaron. I didn't think you wanted that. Why haven't you done something to free him?"

Dirk's gaze snapped to Tori and look of surprised realization washed over him. "Your link is with Khan." He said the sentence with self-reprimand. "I should have figured that out." He released a slow breath as though figuring things out now. "Your default changed when you went into his mind. Before that, you were always connected to Vesta unless another dragon got a lot closer."

"Why Vesta?" she asked.

He shrugged. "Her egg probably turned on your dragon lord genes, so she became your default. But after you went into Khan's mind, you were more familiar with him so you've stayed there." Dirk drove in silence for a few moments, thinking about this.

Tori focused her thoughts on her worry for Aaron again. He was so young, so easily influenced, so unused to dealing with people like Overdrake. "Are you even going to comment on the fact that your father abducted Aaron?"

Dirk tapped his thumb against the steering wheel, unconcerned. "Aaron is fine. In fact, he's getting along better with my father than I am."

"Dirk—" she began.

"My father has parental rights. Any court in the nation would agree with him about that. And besides,

Aaron doesn't want to leave. He's never even asked me for help getting back to his mom."

"Your mom," Tori said. "She's your mom too."

Dirk grunted. "So I've been told."

Tori could feel the emotion stirring in him at the mention of her. Anger. Frustration. Pain. She hadn't expected these sorts of feelings, or at least not in the quantity he felt them.

"Have you talked to her?" Tori asked. "Aaron would give you her number."

Dirk hesitated. His grip on the steering wheel grew tighter. "I talked to her once for about a minute."

"Why only a minute?"

"I didn't have anything to say."

Not true. He had twelve years of things to say. "I wouldn't believe that even if I weren't your counterpart. If you squeeze the steering wheel any tighter, you're going to snap it in half."

His grip on the wheel lessened. He didn't say anything, though.

She waited. Finally, she said, "You can fake a lot of things. Apathy isn't one of them."

He hit his turn signal with a sharp flick, then stopped a bit too abruptly at a traffic light. "She chose to leave me so that she could be with Aaron. She can't undo that now and pretend she cares about me."

Tori worded her sentence carefully. She couldn't admit she'd talked to Bianca and seen the pain in her eyes. "Maybe she wasn't choosing Aaron over you. Maybe she knew she couldn't take you away from your father. She couldn't protect you from him because he knew about you and would make sure that no matter where she ran, he'd find you. But that wasn't the case for Aaron."

Tori didn't feel any softening in Dirk, just the continuing rumble of pain within him. He was determined not to forgive his mother, determined to hold onto his resentment as tightly as he'd been gripping the steering wheel.

She put her hand on his knee, half expecting to feel the intensity of his emotions buzz her skin like an electric pulse. "I'm sure your mom was brokenhearted to lose you."

Perhaps Tori said the sentence with too much certainty. Dirk took his eyes from the light to check her expression. "How would you be sure about that?"

"Because I can't imagine anyone not loving you."

Dirk laughed and his anger and pain faded into the background of his thoughts. "I can think of several people who don't love me." He glanced at the clock on the dashboard. "Some of them are converging on your school right now."

She placed her hand back in her lap. "Loving you and disagreeing with you are two different things."

His eyes cut to her again, reading her. "Do you love me, Tori?"

"Of course."

He returned his attention to the road. The light had turned green. "But not the way I want."

When she'd answered the question, she'd been thinking of him as her counterpart. She'd been thinking of how hard it was to see him willfully make bad decisions. She wasn't going to talk about the sort of love Dirk wanted.

He turned onto the freeway entrance. The spot he had in mind must be even more secluded and remote than she'd thought.

"You say Aaron is okay, but I'm not so sure. Face it, your father is a horrible parent. What sort of man tosses a twelve-year-old into a dragon enclosure, tells him to fly, and then leaves?" She eyed him. "Was that how he taught you to fly?"

"I was younger. It wasn't so hard for me." Dirk rethought his words. "Or maybe it was harder because I didn't know that my father was in the dragon's mind, that he had control of him."

Poor Dirk. She hated thinking of him as being young, vulnerable, and at the mercy of Overdrake. "Doesn't your father's ruthlessness bother you? You wouldn't treat your own children that way, would you?"

"No," Dirk said, as though he'd already given it thought. "I'm going to be like Dr. B. He's what a father should be."

The statement caught her by surprise and not just because Dr. B seemed entirely too willing to put the Slayers in danger. "How can you say you want to be like Dr. B and then fight against everything he believes in?"

She was prepared to elaborate on this topic, but Dirk lifted his hand to stop her. "I didn't say I would have the same beliefs, just the same methods. Dr. B taught us to be strong, but he never let us forget that he cared about us." Dirk picked up speed, weaving around a slow-moving car. "Although I don't suppose Dr. B cares that much about me now."

"He does," Tori said. "You know he still does."

"Yeah, I do," Dirk didn't sound like he was all that happy about the fact.

Tori glanced at the signs, noting the upcoming exits. "What restaurant are you taking me to?"

"We're not going to a restaurant. I'm taking you to see Minerva."

CHAPTER 19

Twenty minutes later, Dirk pulled into the empty Manassas National Battlefield parking lot. Minerva was close by. Tori could tell because her powers had turned on several minutes ago. She hadn't argued with Dirk about going to see the dragon because having her powers working would help Tori if she needed to protect herself or get away. She'd be on more equal footing with Dirk. And besides, she was curious to see Minerva.

There was no harm in scoping out her enemy. Going to see the dragon didn't mean she would go into its mind. She still had time to decide whether that was a good idea or not.

Dirk parked the car and the two of them stepped out into several thousands of acres of snow-covered grassland. A few trees lined the area, their lifting branches creating a lacy pattern against the night sky. Historic buildings, fences, and cannons dotted the area replicating what the land would have looked like during the Civil War.

Dirk took to the air, gliding a few feet from the ground, and motioned for Tori to follow him. She rose and skimmed along behind him, hair fluttering behind her. With her powers on, she no longer felt cold. The night air rushing over her skin felt as gentle as a caress and the moonlight that gleamed white on the snow seemed picturesque, not chill provoking. This was how flying was meant to be done—soaring, sliding, floating. No helmets and bulletproof jackets. No worrying that something was rocketing toward her, about to strike.

One small hill stood out against the field. No snow covered it. Tori's senses prickled and adrenaline coursed through her. That hill was a reclining dragon, tail curled around its body.

Minerva shifted, revealing in silhouette an angular head with pointed ears. The diamond shape in the middle of her forehead had a covering on it, something that no doubt blocked the dragon's signal from creating more Slayers. In the dim light, the dragon's scales appeared to be the color of drying blood. Since darkness muted and blackened the color, her scales were most likely bright red.

A red dragon—called *Y Ddraig Goch* by the Welsh. In English lore, Merlin had seen a red dragon fight against a white one and from that struggle, predicted the future of Wales. And here was an actual red dragon. Too bad there wasn't a wizard around to predict the future of this country.

The dragon turned two golden yellow eyes in Tori's direction, giving her an inquisitive look.

She hadn't known that dragons could look inquisitive. None of the other ones she'd met had. Or maybe she was just getting better at reading their expressions. She shouldn't go inside Minerva's mind. She'd already gotten to know this dragon as well as she should.

The thought made Tori slow in the air, pull up, and hover uncertainly. What in the world was she doing? Was coming here a good strategy or a terrible, terrible idea?

Although Dirk had been facing away from Tori when she stopped, he immediately flipped in the air and doubled back. He was in the dragon's mind and Minerva had seen Tori halt, so he'd known too. She had to remember that—when a dragon was around, a dragon lord could watch her with two sets of eyes.

Dirk took her hand and slowly guided her downward. "You're not afraid of Minerva, are you? You know I won't let her hurt you."

Tori didn't answer. Any sane person would be terrified of a fifty ton, armored carnivore. The fact that Tori was merely afraid and not stunned with panic spoke well of her bravery.

She swallowed and let Dirk pull her closer to the dragon. A familiar oily smell wafted from the beast, a scent like spilled kerosene. It stirred memories of past fights— the way Tamerlane's roar had cut through the night, his talons outstretched, jaws snapping at her. Kiha chasing Tori, gaining on her while burning trees cast jumbled shadows on the mountainside.

Tori took a deep breath and tried to slow her racing heartbeat. Dirk was right. As long as he had control of the dragon, she would be fine. Time to pull herself together and see what she could learn about dragons that might prove useful.

Dirk and Tori landed a few yards away from Minerva, their feet crunching into the snow. Still holding her hand, Dirk towed her to the dragon's side.

Minerva's breath rose, frozen in the winter air, and drifted upward. Her eyes—cat-like in shape—shone dimly as they watched Tori, tracking her every movement. One quick flick of the dragon's head and she could bite a person half.

Tori hadn't realized that she'd planted her feet until Dirk tugged her forward again. "Isn't she beautiful?"

"You have an odd definition of beautiful."

Minerva lowered her head to Tori, taking in her scent. Like a dog. Only dogs didn't have teeth as sharp as scalpels. Minerva blew out a breath. White from the cold, it surrounded Tori in a shroud before dissolving away.

"She likes you," Dirk said.

Tori was too tense to tell if he was teasing. "Do dragons ever like people?"

He shrugged, was definitely teasing now. "Stories from the Middle Ages say dragons had a thing for comely young maidens."

"I'm pretty sure their thing was they ate the maidens."

Dirk squeezed her hand. "We all have different ways of showing we care."

His hand around hers felt nearly as dangerous as the dragon in front of her. She could tell he wanted to kiss her again. Should she let him? The last time she'd kissed him, it had ended her relationship with Jesse. Kissing Dirk again would be like admitting that Jesse was right and she couldn't resist Dirk's advances.

Then again, what was the point of resisting Dirk now? Jesse had broken up with her. Dirk still wanted her.

He lifted her hand and put it on the dragon's side. Her fingers splayed out against the scale with a slight tremor. It was like touching a bomb: A calm hard shell that held something explosive.

"Here, feel how smooth she is." Dirk's hand stayed on the top of Tori's, intertwining their fingers together. "In the light, these scales are Corvette red."

An apt description. Minerva's scales were as smooth as metal. Sleek and fast. As the dragon breathed, the scale moved under Tori's fingertips. She was as aware of those breaths as she was of Dirk's proximity. His hand still rested on top of hers, experiencing each breath with her. He didn't want her to pull her hand away and she didn't. *See,* he seemed to be saying, *this is what you could have.* When he dropped his hand and wound his arms around her waist, her awe for the dragon kept her fingers sliding across the Corvette-colored scales.

Touching a dragon stirred some genetic place inside her, some place that she didn't want to awaken. But how could she move her hand away?

The feeling was like stroking the bottom of the ocean, like caressing something deep, mysterious, and undiscovered. A legend was beneath her fingertips. A dragon that had adorned the Welsh flag for centuries. Before the Welsh, the Romans had used the red dragon as their standard. Minerva was history and myth intermingled.

Dirk rested his cheek against Tori's hair. "Tell me you don't think she's beautiful."

"She's..." It was hard to think while Dirk was holding her this way. The warmth of his arms was distracting. Tori had known Dirk would do this and she'd let it happen anyway. Was she a good strategist or just hopeless? "...powerful," Tori said.

"Why don't you want to admit she's beautiful?"

"And captivating," Tori added.

"You're almost there. Keep the adjectives coming."

"And...what is it called when you know you shouldn't do something but you do it anyway?"

"Foolish?" Dirk supplied.

"Seductive."

He tilted his head, considering Minerva for a moment. "Are we looking at the same dragon?"

"Maybe power is always that way," Tori said. Or maybe the feeling stemmed from the way Dirk stood close with his arms wrapped around her waist. Her heart was racing again, and this time not with fear.

Dirk was her counterpart. He understood her. He had been there for her the last time Jesse broke up with her. It would be so easy to turn around, slip her arms around his neck and forget everything else for a few minutes.

She dropped her hand from Minerva and tried to rein in her thoughts. Forgetfulness wasn't something she could afford. She had to use this meeting to the Slayers' advantage. Should she go into Minerva's mind and learn about controlling her or not?

She remembered one of Dr. B's sayings, a quote from General Patton: *Take calculated risks. That is quite different from being rash.*

Was this a calculated risk or was it being rash?

Dirk's arms had coiled across her waist and she rested her own arms atop his. "After you took me to see Khan, you told me that if I met Minerva, you would teach me more about controlling dragons."

"Go inside her mind and I might."

"Might?"

"Life is always a gamble."

Was he teasing her or using her? The amusement he felt didn't let her know. Maybe he was amused she was so easy to use. She loosened his grip on her waist and stepped away from him. "You want me to go into Minerva's mind so I'll have a harder time killing her."

"True," he said, unrepentant. "But you'll do it anyway in the hopes that it will help you save the Slayers."

Perhaps he knew her better than she knew herself. She'd been debating the issue since she got here, but he was right—when it came down to it, she was willing to do whatever she had to in order to help them.

Without responding to Dirk, she let that ever-present thread of hearing she had with the dragon grow and strengthen until it pulled her into Minerva's mind. Her senses immediately expanded, joining with the dragon's. It had been so effortless to split her consciousness into two. She was both standing on the grass beside Dirk watching Minerva and also peering out of the dragon's eyes at the expanse of the deserted battlefield.

Tori could feel Minerva's thoughts, her casual surveillance of everything around her. Tori smelled the scent of the forest and tasted the blood on the dragon's tongue. Earlier, Minerva had spotted a deer in the park, flushed it out and devoured it. Now she was lounging in triumph and satisfaction.

Dirk's voice came from within the dragon's mind. "Welcome to Minerva. You won't find a gentler dragon."

That only meant the rest were even more fearsome.

Outside, he took her hand and smiled. She smiled back at him. "What are you going to teach me about controlling dragons?"

He spoke inside the dragon's mind again. "Spend some time getting to know Minerva. Ask her anything. Although, I've already told her not to give you any locations, so don't bother requesting those."

Tori didn't want to get to know Minerva. She wanted to find her control center and see if she could knock Dirk out of it.

Aaron had said that going along Minerva's path was like wading through a dark, thick river. Overdrake had shown him the path at first, but once Aaron had seen it, he only had to picture it again to get there.

A dark, thick river. She pictured the Potomac. She'd seen it at night from above.

Nothing happened.

"Don't you have any questions?" Dirk asked.

The Potomac had probably been too big. You couldn't wade through it. She imagined a creek she'd seen in a picture, small and winding through trees. Still nothing.

"Is Aaron okay?" She asked the question inside the dragon's mind, directing it to Minerva.

The dragon only felt confusion at her words.

Dirk ran his thumb along the backside of Tori's hand. "You can't ask a dragon to make judgments about someone's well-being. They don't have that sort of understanding."

Was she going to have to imagine an exact picture of a river she'd never seen? "Do you like Aaron?" she asked Minerva.

A scene flashed in front of her: Aaron tossing a lamb carcass into the air to the dragon. Tori felt Minerva's appreciation. So apparently that was a yes. Another scene of Aaron appeared. In this one, he'd brought a bag of thawed turkeys and dumped them out at her feet. More appreciation. The way to a dragon's heart was definitely with dead animals.

Picturing rivers wasn't working. With Khan, she hadn't visualized anything. She'd just been afraid and desperate. She'd instinctively reached out for anything that could help her, and she'd suddenly been in the next level of Khan's mind.

Fear and desperation. Instead of imagining rivers, Tori thought of Minerva bearing down on her school, talons outstretched. It could happen. Overdrake could attack that way. She envisioned the horror on her friends' faces. She saw herself there, unarmed, unable to stop it from happening. Her desperation blossomed into a sharp, frustrated need.

And then she was in the next level of Minerva's mind. She stood in a river of flowing colors: dark greens, blues, and reds. Not wading depth. The colors washed by all around her, over her head. They were the dragon's impulses, desires, instincts, pushing against her so firmly, Tori had the ridiculous urge to hold her breath. This wasn't real water and her avatar didn't need to breathe.

Aaron had said to wade through it, not follow it upstream or downstream. She pushed that way, cutting across. The colors parted revealing Dirk's avatar standing in a round dark room. He looked exactly as he did in real life and was even wearing the same clothes. One hand held something rectangular and black. His control object. As long as he held onto it, he controlled Minerva.

"Well," he said and the word came out with an echo. "That was too fast. If I hadn't caught you, you would have pitched face-first into Minerva's side."

"Thanks." Tori had lost contact with her body outside, didn't feel it anymore. She still could see out of Minerva's eyes, though. The dragon was considering the snow-covered field and the frosted fences stitching through them. Tori didn't want to pull back from this level to check on her body. She was afraid doing so would take her from this room.

She held out her hand and touched one of the dark walls. It gave way beneath her fingers as though it was made of a sheet of water. So it was more of a boundary than an actual wall. The floor felt solid enough. She wasn't sinking through it.

"If I come to the control center more slowly, will I be able to keep consciousness in my body?" With her fingers skimming the wall, she stepped around the room, circling to see what was behind Dirk. As far as she could tell, just more dark wall.

Dirk turned as Tori walked, making sure he always faced her. He didn't answer.

"You said you would teach me something about controlling dragons," she reminded him. "Were you telling the truth or should I stop trusting you?"

"Fine. I'll answer your question to show you I keep my word." He cleared his throat and put his hands behind his back, impersonating one of Dr. B's stances. "Controlling dragons is about balance. Think of it as riding a bike. You got on, leaned way to the left, and instead of straightening yourself, you kept pedaling harder."

She took another step around him. "How do I learn to do it right?"

"The same way you learned to ride a bike. Lots of practice."

"Will you let me practice a lot?"

"I will if you leave the Slayers."

She'd made a complete circle around Dirk without seeing anything else in the control center. Just the black walls surrounding the two of them. "As far as mind palaces go, this one is in need of serious décor help. Would it have been too hard to provide some chairs?"

"Tori," he said, his hands back at his sides, "You need to pull back from here and go into Minerva's senses." He raised his eyebrows for emphasis. "It's not safe to be unconscious."

"I know you won't do anything you shouldn't to my body."

"I meant it's not safe to be unconscious around a dragon, but good point." He gave her a mischievous grin.

"It's not safe to be unconscious around me either."

"I trust you to be a gentleman," she said pointedly.

He let out a scoff. "In the time you've known me, have I ever been a gentleman?"

She surveyed the object in Dirk's hand, tried to see it more closely. What was his control object? A remote of some sort?

"What do you have in your hand?" Tori asked.

"Tori," his voice was firmer, "leave, or I'll have to throw you out."

"Can we hurt each other in here?" They were, after all, avatars. Was it possible that she could hurt Overdrake inside a dragon's mind or vice versa?

"Well, I'll probably bruise your ego," Dirk said.

He was taller and stronger, but in a place like this, physical strength didn't matter, did it? This was all a mind game. Besides, even if she couldn't match him in muscle, she could take him down with a well-placed kick.

She ran her fingers across the wall again, watching the image shift like black oil. "You're the one that brought me to Minerva and told me to go inside her mind. You should be a better host."

He shook his head. "Don't think I won't toss you out of here. I will."

She smiled back at him. "Not if I can toss you out first." Without a pause, she sprang forward, leveling a at kick his chest.

He stepped out of the way easily enough. Her momentum carried her past him, out of his reach. She

ught herself before she went through the wall and spun
face him.

"You're not thinking this through," he said.

"But this is all thought, isn't it?" She lunged at him,
pivoting and kicking at his arm.

He barely dodged her in time and had to take a step
sideways to keep his balance. "Stop it, Tori."

"Why? So far, my ego isn't all that bruised."

She leaped upward, striking her foot into his chest. A
normal person would have gone down. Dirk only
staggered backward.

She pressed her advantage, following up with another
kick aimed at his hand. He regained his balance in time to
sweep her standing leg out from underneath her. She hit
the ground with a thud that knocked the breath from her
lungs and sent a slap of pain through her back.

"Ouch," she muttered. "That felt real."

"I never said you couldn't be hurt in here."

She rolled back onto her feet again. Before she'd
completely straightened, he plowed into her and flung her
over his shoulder. The room was suddenly upside down
and his shoulder was pushing into her stomach. In one
smooth motion, he turned, spun, and tossed her at the
wall.

She hit it with a smack and then felt it give way. The
sensation was like doing a back flop into a pool and she
instinctively gulped in a breath of air.

The next moment she was outside, blinking and
looking up at a sky full of dizzy stars. Not only out of the
control center, out of the dragon's mind altogether. And
she was still holding her breath. She let it out in a whoosh.

Dirk's arms tightened around her. He was sitting on
the ground and she lay on his lap, her head cradled in one

of his arms. Minerva sat not far away, twitching her head. The dragon growled, then glared at Dirk and Tori reproachfully.

Apparently, dragons didn't appreciate people bar fighting inside their heads. Well, that was one more thing she'd learned tonight.

Tori wanted to sit up but couldn't. She felt weak, spent, and the fact that Dirk was holding her sent tremors of guilt through her. While she'd been in the dragon's mind trying to kick him, he'd been here, tenderly watching over her.

Dirk shifted her in his arms, checking on her, and all the tenderness in his expression vanished. "That was completely suicidal. Did you bother to think what would've happened if you *had* managed to wrest control of Minerva away from me? She could have attacked us both, and you wouldn't have even been conscious enough to fly away."

"You would have flown me away from her."

He raised an eyebrow. "You fight me in one plane and expect me to protect you in another?"

She managed a shrug. "I told you we didn't have a very well-defined hero-villain relationship."

"That's the truth." He brushed a strand of hair away from her face, letting his fingers linger on her cheek, then bent down and kissed her. She didn't stop him. In fact, she wound her arms around his neck and kissed him back. And she wasn't going to feel guilty about this later.

Jesse had no claim to her and she was doing this to gain a strategic advantage. Sort of. Mostly. At any rate, Dirk had made it harder for Tori to fight Minerva, so now Tori would make it a little harder for him to fight her.

 # CHAPTER 20

Tori flew toward home, skimming through the air high enough to be unseen, but low enough that she wouldn't be picked up by radar. With her powers turned on, the stars shone so brightly, the sky looked like the entire galaxy had drawn closer. She would have liked to drift and loop and slowly glide with her hands stretched out, but she had to speed back to her house before her powers wore off. Otherwise she'd find herself walking. Or worse, falling.

Dirk had offered to drive Tori home, but she hadn't accepted. She couldn't let him know where she lived. He'd refused to drive her back to the school because he was convinced the Slayers would be waiting there for him. And they might be. He was still her enemy, despite the fact that she'd spent part of the night making out with him.

Granted, it hadn't been her best Slayer moment, but she'd also spent part of the night fighting with him inside the dragon's mind, so maybe those two events canceled each other out.

Man, what was wrong with her? When had her relationship with Dirk gotten so complicated?

The answer came to her even though she'd only been asking in a rhetorical way. Her relationship with Dirk had always been complicated, she just hadn't realized it at first.

Dirk had ended up flying her to Fairfax on Minerva's back so she'd be able to make it the rest of the way without losing her powers. While she soared over the highway, she texted Jesse on her phone. *I'm fine and on my way home. Were you able to get my watch?*

She knew he would answer right away, and she knew he would lecture her about going off with Dirk.

A few seconds later he called. Holding conversations was hard at high speeds since the wind had a way of blotting out words with its roar. Tori slowed. "Hello?"

"I can't believe you willingly left with him."

Cue the lecture.

"You put yourself in danger," he went on. "Do you realize what could have happened to you?"

"Dirk was worried because he kept trying to contact me through Vesta and I wasn't answering. Turns out, after I went into Khan's mind in November, I stayed linked to him. Dirk was checking to make sure I was all right."

"He could see you were all right. Why did you leave the school?"

"He wanted to talk and I could tell he didn't plan on hurting me. He's helped us before— saved our lives. We can't afford to cut off communications with him. He might warn us of something again."

Jesse didn't speak for a moment. She wished she could read his silences on the phone as well as she could in person. Was he considering her viewpoint or was this one of those times when he was fighting for patience? Below her, rows of townhouses looked like abandoned boxcars. She checked her direction and flew past them.

"So what did Dirk want to talk about?" Jesse finally asked.

"Um..." She struggled to remember their conversations. The kissing had pushed most of it from her mind. "We talked about Aaron. Dirk says he's happy with Overdrake. So that's good."

"Actually, that's not good."

"Good in that Overdrake trusts him. Aaron's giving us information, so he's obviously still on our side."

"Or he's setting us up for a trap. That is Overdrake's specialty."

She ignored this comment and picked up more speed. The wind fingered through her hair, occasionally whipping it into her face. "We also talked about what a horrible father Overdrake is—well, that was mostly me talking, but Dirk said that when he becomes a parent, he wants to be like Dr. B, so that means something."

"Yeah, it means he wasn't paying attention to any of Dr. B's teachings on fighting tyranny."

"It means Dirk isn't as far gone as we thought." She stared at the city spread out beneath her, so much civilization everywhere. Streetlights, window lights, car headlights, all dotting paths into the darkness. "If we could find a safe place for the dragons—"

"A safe place?" Jesse repeated. "As long as people like Overdrake can use dragons as weapons, there isn't a safe place for them. They're ticking time bombs, and we've got to diffuse them."

He meant kill them. Maybe Slayers couldn't see dragons differently. Maybe she'd have better luck teaching a bird dog to ignore pheasants.

She glanced at her phone's map, making sure she was still going the right direction. "Jesse, when dragons are controlled, they're amazing." This was probably the wrong angle to take with a Slayer. "They're an endangered species and a part of our history. Shouldn't we at least—"

"Dirk took you to see a dragon, didn't he?"

Was her opinion of dragons changing so much that Jesse could tell when she'd seen one? "Yes. I went into Minerva's mind and was able to learn a few more things. I couldn't push Dirk out of her control center, but at least now I have an idea how to do it."

To have a chance at pushing out a dragon lord, she would need the element of surprise on her side. She would need to appear and attack suddenly, pushing Overdrake through a wall before he had a chance to fight back. Getting to the control center undetected would be the hardest part. She would need to know the pathway there so well, she could zoom through it.

"I just need more practice," she said.

"And Dirk will never let you practice enough that you could become a threat to him. Why can't you see that? He's compromising your ability to fight. Now you won't be able to kill Khan or Minerva."

"I will," she said. "It will just be harder." She had been emphasizing this to herself ever since she went into Minerva's mind. She would do whatever she had to do to protect the other Slayers, even if that meant killing a dragon when she didn't want to.

She went on to describe her skirmish with Dirk inside Minerva's mind and what she'd learned. She left out the details about the kiss at the end. Since Jesse wasn't her boyfriend anymore, he didn't have the right to know that part.

When she finished, Jesse sighed unhappily and she wondered if he suspected anyway. "Look, I know you mean well, but please don't go off with Dirk again. He understands strategic manipulation as well as the rest of us, and when he realizes he can't persuade you to join him, he'll decide to take you out of the game like he's already done to Alyssa and Shang. Don't make it easy for him."

Was Jesse right about that? Maybe. Probably. "I won't make it easy."

There was another pause, then Jesse said, "I've worked out details for the mission tomorrow. Dr. B's already approved them."

"You're going with me?" That was a surprise.

"I need to keep you safe."

"Is that supposed to be a compliment or an insult?"

"It's a deep-seated fear of your untimely death. But I mean it in the most complimentary of ways."

"Oh. Then, thank you." She glanced at her phone. Ten more minutes until her powers wore off. She adjusted her altitude, flying higher.

"Tomorrow when we meet up for the mission, I'll give you your watch back. Location epsilon. Standard time plus five." Which meant five o'clock at the Manassas Regional Airport.

"Great," Tori said. "I'll contact Theo with a list of supplies we'll need."

"I already did that. That's how I kept busy while you were off with Dirk. That, and Ryker and I flew around looking for your discarded corpse."

Tori had expected a lecture, but not one so peppered with references to her demise.

"Dr. B made one stipulation," Jesse continued. "I have to be the one in charge of the mission. Are you okay with that condition?"

"Yes." Whatever would make the rest of them feel better about her chances of survival.

"Good." Another pause. Then his voice came over the phone, soft and earnest. "Tori, please be careful. If not for your sake, then for mine. If anything ever happened to you…"

"You'd be fine," she said. "You always are."

"I wouldn't be." His voice went low. "I really wouldn't be."

Just when it was becoming easy to put up walls between her and Jesse, one sentence like that could tear them down, could make her feel like the two of them might have a chance together after all. "Don't worry," she said, "I'll be careful."

 CHAPTER 21

When Dirk got home, he put Minerva in her enclosure, made sure she had enough water, and removed her saddle chair. Khan and Minerva were now about the same distance from Tori, but since she'd gone into Minerva's mind last, Tori was most likely still connected to that dragon.

"Send me a message," he said out loud. "So I know if you can hear me."

He used his new phone to check the site. A few moments later her message appeared. *I hear you. Home safe?*

Without seeing her expression or hearing her voice, he couldn't tell whether she was asking the question out of concern or whether she was fishing for information about where he lived. Probably the latter.

Talk about your doomed relationships, and yet he still smiled when he thought of her flying with him across the snow-covered battlefield.

"I'm glad you can hear me. I'd hate to have to show up to another basketball game and make Jesse look bad again."

Yeah, she wrote, *don't do that.*

"Next time, we'll have to meet somewhere more private." He was really asking if she would consent to another meeting.

A minute went by, then a message appeared. *Maybe.* He grinned. Maybe was as good as a yes. "Maybe I'll let you practice again."

Inside the house, he found his father sitting in the living room simultaneously writing on his laptop and watching coverage of the Democratic candidates' debate. Dirk braced himself for some sort of reprimand. He'd told his father he was taking Minerva out for some exercise and then stayed out much longer than the task required.

His father didn't seem to notice the time. He was intent on the debate, shaking his head with disapproval. "Ethington is going off script again. I've paid the best consultants in the country to tell him what to say, and he continues to disregard them."

Dirk padded tentatively over to the couch. He ought to warn his father that Tori was connected to Minerva now, not Vesta. But how could he do that without admitting what he'd just done?

His father probably wouldn't mind that he'd seen Tori, even though he hadn't gotten permission beforehand. Dirk had already said he was working on winning her over and his father hadn't objected. And by letting Tori go inside Khan's and Minerva's minds, Dirk had made it harder for her to kill them during future attacks. But he didn't want his father micromanaging his relationship with Tori. He didn't want to give him details about the evening.

It wasn't as though Dirk had compromised their security by switching the dragon Tori was linked to. His father never spoke of classified information near any of the dragons. He wasn't that careless.

On the other hand, maybe he should tell his father. Aaron practiced with Minerva. His father should know that Tori would be able to hear what Aaron said. The kid didn't have information about the revolution—their father didn't give those sorts of details to Dirk, let alone Aaron— but still, he might say something he shouldn't.

Dirk walked closer to the couch. How should he phrase this?

His father waved a hand at the screen. "Ethington is promising too much. Even as stupid as the population is, they won't believe the government is capable of solving every societal problem. He'll lose credibility."

"I don't know," Dirk said. "You might be overestimating the population."

His father grunted. "You're probably right. But still, when he disregards my instructions, he disregards me. I don't tolerate that. Not from anyone."

Then again, maybe Dirk shouldn't mention Tori was connected to Minerva. The less he brought her to his father's attention, the better. The best solution would be for Dirk to take Vesta out the next time he met Tori. Then she'd be joined to the right dragon again and Dirk wouldn't have to worry about Aaron messing up and saying something he shouldn't around Minerva. Problem solved, and his father wouldn't have to know any of the details.

"Politicians," his father said with disgust. "I won't mind destroying them all."

"All of them except Senator Hampton."

His father grumbled something that may or may not have been agreement.

Dirk didn't bother pressing the point. With his father in a bad mood, reminding him that he'd promised to leave Tori's family alone wouldn't do any good.

Still, as Dirk went to his bedroom, his father's response irked him. A promise was a promise. It shouldn't change every time his father got angry. He'd promised before that he wouldn't hurt Tori and then he turned a dragon on her plane.

A memory from tonight flashed through his mind: Tori lying unconscious in his arms. Even though he'd known she was fine, seeing her body so lifeless—hair spilling onto the ground in a brown tangle—it had bothered him more than it should have. She'd looked like she'd died, not fainted, and holding her had seemed like a bad omen, a premonition of things that might come.

Dirk pushed the image from his mind. He still had time to convince her she was more dragon lord than Slayer. He might not ever have to fight her. And even if he did, he would never kill her. He couldn't do something like that.

Of course, this thought led to the question: What *was* he willing to do in a fight? Although he tried to banish the question, it followed him around the rest of the night. "A war half-waged is a war lost," his father's voice echoed through his thoughts. "Empires have a cost, and the price will be paid with the blood of everyone who defies us."

His father had quite a few sayings about crushing the opposition. He probably made them up in his spare time.

How many people would die during the attacks? Ten thousand men had died during the Revolutionary War, forty thousand during the French Revolution, and six hundred and twenty thousand during the Civil War. Dirk's father had assured him their revolution wouldn't be nearly as deadly, but any unnecessary deaths were too many.

He wouldn't think about that. During the attacks, he was only going to fight people who were coming after him. Self-defense. No one would die by his hand unless they asked for it.

Before Dirk climbed into bed, his gaze fell on his nightstand and his phone plugged in there. For a moment, he had the irrational desire to call his mother. Not to ask her advice, just to hear her voice.

A ridiculous idea. What would he say to her?

Besides, if he called, she would ask for help getting Aaron back, and he wasn't spiteful enough to tell her that Aaron didn't want to leave.

CHAPTER 22

On Saturday, road construction delayed Tori and she was ten minutes late pulling into the Manassas Regional Airport. When she walked into the Slayers' jet, she found Dr. B sitting in the cockpit, laptop open, going over mission details with Jesse, who stood nearby.

Jesse nodded in greeting, his brown eyes lingering on her. She probably shouldn't read too much into that look.

"You're here," Dr. B said in the cheerful voice he always used during missions. "I'll get the door and we'll be on our way."

Tori checked to see if any of the other Slayers had come. Only one other person was onboard. Bess.

Tori blinked at her in surprise, then smiled and made her way to the open area in the back of the plane. If Bess hadn't been bent over a jackhammer, wrapping straps onto it, Tori would have hugged her. "You're coming on a mission?" she asked.

Bess tugged on a strap, making sure it was secure. "I don't really consider this a mission. I think of it more as an intervention." She dragged her attention away from the jackhammer for long enough to give Tori a reproachful gaze. "Did you actually go off with Dirk when he had powers and you didn't?"

"Not before he assured me he just wanted to talk." Tori scooted by Bess to reach the bin where the uniforms were kept. Might as well start getting ready now. The flight to Lock Haven would take less than an hour.

Bess wrapped straps around a second jackhammer with more force than the job required. "Even with your counterpart sense, you can't trust Dirk. He found ways to lie to you before, and he'll do it again."

Tori took her Kevlar pants, jacket, and boots from the bin. "Or maybe I'll convince Dirk to leave his father."

Bess rolled her eyes, letting Tori know what she thought the chances of that happening were. "One way or another," Bess said, "today's mission should serve as a reminder that you and Dirk aren't on the same team anymore."

Tori kicked off her shoes and stepped into the Kevlar pants. "Dirk hasn't left his father because he thinks he can temper him. He believes the revolution won't be as bad if he's a part of it. He's not a tyrant like Overdrake."

"Um, tyrant is as tyrant does."

Tori did up the pants' buckle. "Speaking of acting like a tyrant, how did you get away from your grandfather?"

Bess moved to the third jackhammer, attaching straps to it. "Grandpa doesn't keep me under lock and key. Since no dragons are attacking right now, he has no reason to prevent me from going Christmas shopping with my friends."

Tori nodded. "You lied to him. Welcome to my life."

"The hard part will be getting away during an actual dragon attack."

Tori sat in the nearest seat and pulled on one of her boots. "I've gotten really good at climbing out my window."

On the overhead speaker, Dr. B said, "Please fasten your seatbelts. We're fourth in line for takeoff."

Tori waited patiently until the plane was in the air before she got up again and made her way to the supply boxes in the back. She found flashlights, neck mics, earpieces, earmuffs, radar sensors, dust masks, and Dremel saws. Guns and explosives were in separate boxes.

Tori picked up a pair of earmuffs with an unspoken sigh. They were supposed to muffle the sound of jackhammers and explosives. They wouldn't help her as much as the others. She would hear both things from one of the unborn dragon's ears too.

Bess and Jesse joined Tori, dressing in their battle gear. The pile of helmets and gloves seemed so small with only three of them suiting up.

"I'm glad you guys came," Tori said, and tried not to let disappointment leak into her voice. "Didn't the other Slayers believe my information?"

Jesse paused from putting on his boots to send her a sympathetic look. "No one thinks you're lying about what Aaron told you. It was a captains' decision. Only three of us are going because if this turns out to be a trap and we take casualties, the Slayers will still have a healer, fire douser, flyer, and someone who can push guns away."

Bess tightened her holster around her hip. "And whatever Willow does."

A captains' decision. Tori hadn't been told about the meeting let alone consulted. How long was she going to be on probation for? Dr. B had said he'd reevaluate after a few weeks but a month had already passed.

She checked to make sure her tranquilizer gun was loaded, then slid it into her holster. "Maybe after this mission is successful, Dr. B will trust my judgment again and lift my probation."

Instead of agreeing, Bess and Jesse exchanged an uncomfortable look. It was only a fleeting glance, but it spoke volumes. Bess turned her attention to adjusting her boots, avoiding Tori's eye. Jesse checked the safety on his rifle.

"What?" Tori asked. They knew something they weren't telling her.

Jesse rubbed the back of his neck and turned his attention back to her. "Dr. B is going to have a talk with you about being captain."

A talk. That didn't sound good. Having a talk is what you did when you were delivering bad news. "What—he still won't lift my probation? Isn't he ever going to trust me again?"

"It's not that he doesn't trust you," Bess said quickly. Her insistence felt more foreboding than consoling. "He just thinks counterparts would have an easier time leading the teams, so he's making Ryker's position as captain permanent."

The air pushed from Tori's lungs in a disbelieving cough. "Dr. B demoted me?"

Jesse stepped toward her, hands out like he wanted to pull her into a hug. "Sorry, Tori. You were a great captain. I told Dr. B he shouldn't change things."

She pushed away from Jesse's hug, didn't want pity. She wanted to hit something. "Then why did he demote me? Was it because I had the audacity to make decisions on my own or was it because I'm part dragon lord?"

"Neither," Jesse said, his eyes soft with compassion. "When A-team and Magnus have to fight as one team, Ryker and I can lead more effectively because we're counterparts. And the way we're losing Slayers, fighting as one team may be our only choice."

It was true, and yet the explanation felt like an excuse anyway—like cold, hard rejection. Hadn't she and Jesse managed to kill two dragons? They'd worked as a team both times just fine.

She picked up her jacket and yanked it on. After the first dragon attack, she'd told Dr. B she didn't want to be a captain, but he'd made her one anyway. He said he believed in her. And now when she was actually using her position as captain to make decisions, he'd fired her. His belief, apparently, was a fleeting thing.

"When was he going to tell me?" Tori asked, waving a hand at the cockpit. "Why did everyone else know about it before me?"

"Everybody doesn't know." Jesse's voice was soothing. "Dr. B discussed it with me because I'm the other captain and he wanted my input."

Bess shrugged. "I just eavesdrop sometimes." When Tori raised an eyebrow at her she added, "Ryker and Willow stay at my house. I hear stuff. Or at least I did when I lived there."

Wait, that meant Dr. B had decided to promote Ryker weeks ago. Maybe as soon as he'd found out Ryker was Jesse's counterpart. The timing didn't really make a difference in the outcome, but she still wanted to know. She turned to Jesse, hands on her hips. "Did he talk to you about replacing me before I helped Aaron go to Overdrake's?"

Jesse hesitated, seemed to be judging her mood before answering. Slowly, he said, "He discussed the possibility."

In other words, yes. As soon as Ryker had come on the scene, Tori's days as the captain had been numbered.

The news should have made her feel better. Dr. B hadn't made the decision as a punishment. But all she felt was an irrational sense of betrayal.

Tori sunk into one of the chairs, put her elbows on the armrests, and rested her forehead in the palms of her hands. "This must be how Dirk felt when I replaced him." Used and so replaceable. Completely unappreciated.

Bess put her hand on Tori's shoulder. "Don't say things like that. You'll worry me."

Tori hadn't been trying to worry anyone. "Dirk didn't betray us because of his demotion," she reminded Bess. "It was in the cards ever since Overdrake sent him to camp."

"I know," Bess said. "But still, don't go all dragon lord on us."

She meant: don't go help Dirk. Which was ironic, since Dirk was the one guy who actually valued her help. A petty thought. The Slayers valued her help, even if Dr. B didn't want her as captain anymore.

Part of her felt like storming into the cockpit and demanding why—if Dr. B was so intent on the importance of discussing major decisions—he hadn't discussed this one with her. But Dr. B didn't have to consult with anyone about who he chose as captains. If she talked to him about her position right now, she'd get too emotional and do something stupid like cry or yell. Better to wait until she could act like it didn't hurt so much. She needed to take Jesse's advice and learn to set her feelings aside when she was fighting.

Tori lifted her head. She would get past this. "Let's go over the mission plans." She gestured at a laptop sitting with the supplies. "We've got the building specs?"

"Right." Jesse turned on the laptop and sat beside her. Bess plunked down on the seat across the aisle from them.

As Jesse brought up the satellite picture, he gave Tori a long considering look and his usual mission countenance—all business—flickered and softened into concern. Without a word, he reached over and hugged her. She didn't resist this time. She put her head on his shoulder and let his support seep into her.

"You deserve to be a captain," he said. "You are good enough."

She hadn't been questioning her worthiness—or perhaps she had, because otherwise, his words wouldn't have brought her so much relief.

She was good enough. The rest didn't matter.

Jesse's arms around her brought back memories of camp and dating, of all the times she'd laid her head on his shoulder like this. He was sunshine and safety. He was summer nights drifting under the stars. With his arms wrapped around her in sympathy, she could forget everything else that had transpired between them since then.

Only she shouldn't think like that because he didn't feel the same way about her anymore.

He held her for another moment, then let her go, checking her expression to make sure she was okay. She forced a smile to show that she was.

From the other side of the aisle, Bess let out a mock huff of offense. "I'd like to point out that *I've* never been put in as a captain and my dad is the one who chooses the position."

Jesse's eyes stayed on Tori, even though he spoke to Bess. "Your dad has been keeping you safe."

Bess waved a hand in his direction. "Don't try to make this better. If anyone deserves to be hugged, it's me."

Jesse leaned over and hugged her, which made her laugh and push him away.

He returned his attention to the laptop. "We've got plans to go over." And just like that, he was back to being a captain. Logical and precise. Summer was over. Tori couldn't decide whether to admire the way he could switch focus or hate it.

Jesse pointed to a building, a small brown rectangle ringed by snow and trees. "When we get close, Tori, you'll need to tell us if you connect to a dragon egg." He paused to let the weight of his words sink in. "Even if you do hear an egg, Aaron's information might be wrong. Overdrake could have hidden an egg somewhere nearby, and set up this building as a snare."

Tori nodded. "We'll be careful."

Jesse zoomed in on the picture, enlarging the structure and making shadows appear on the snow. "Theo drove out to Lock Haven two days ago and has been doing surveillance ever since. He hasn't seen any security guards outside, but the place has a dozen cameras. Some are noticeable, others are hidden. None Theo can't deal with. Once Dr. B drops us off, Theo will break into the cameras' signals and feed them a loop so the security guards won't see us approach the building. As far as our radar can detect, four guards stay in the building, round the clock."

"Our radar isn't sure?" Tori asked.

In another tab, Jesse brought up a blueprint of the building. A mid-sized room in the middle was completely black. "We can't get readings here. The walls are metal. It's probably a vault of some sort."

"Then that's where the eggs are," Tori said.

"Or the gunman waiting to ambush us," Bess put in. She'd apparently already gone over the plans with Jesse because instead of looking at the blueprints, she was messing with her earpiece.

"Even if Overdrake fed the information to Aaron," Tori pointed out, "Overdrake couldn't know when we're coming. It would be hard to keep a gunman in a vault for a long time."

Jesse swiped a finger across the screen, enlarging the blueprint as though this would give them more information. "Overdrake could have set up some other sort of booby trap. Explosives, maybe."

He could have, and Tori didn't like the idea. "When we break into the room, Bess will need to make sure she's shielding us from any projectiles."

"Agreed." Jesse returned the screen to the satellite view. "The building has two doors. One in front, one in back. Both are reinforced steel and controlled by facial recognition locks. It would be easier to blast a hole in the walls than to go through the doors."

Blowing a hole in the wall would be a quick way to alert the security guards and the police to the infiltration. "We go through the windows then," Tori said.

Jesse shook his head. "The windows are false fronts that cover brick walls. There's no way through them."

Someone had definitely taken precautions to keep out unwanted visitors—a sign the building was hiding valuables.

"Then how are we breaking in?" Hopefully the answer didn't involve kidnapping some off-duty security guard.

Bess smiled. "The building's strength is also its weakness. Theo whipped up a lovely canister of methanethiol to use in the ventilation system. Once we pump that baby into the air ducts, the whole place will smell like it has a deadly gas leak. It will just have the smell, not the actual gas, but the guards won't know that."

Tori saw the outcome. "They won't be able to use the windows, so they'll have to open a door."

Jesse sat back in satisfaction. "We'll hit them with tranquilizers as soon as they step outside."

Bess put her neck mic on and adjusted the microphone so it stayed inside her jacket collar. "The guards will probably report the gas leak to someone before they leave the building, which means we won't have much time to destroy the eggs before we've got company. My dad will place spikes on the road leading up to the building, but those probably won't stop Overdrake's men for long."

"We'll put our own chain on the gate," Jesse added. "It will make getting onto the grounds harder."

Not hard enough. "Why not jam their cell phones and cut the landline so they can't call for backup?"

"If the landline is cut," Jesse answered, "it automatically sends out an alarm. We're better off letting Overdrake think he has a gas leak. That will give us a few minutes more before he learns the truth and sends backup."

How many men did Overdrake have nearby and how long would it take them to descend on the building? Tori didn't bother asking. There was no way to know until they showed up.

"We'll blow our way into the vault," Jesse went on, "and jackhammer the eggs apart." Until dragons were ready to hatch, their eggshells were as thick as rock and as hard to break. "Once we're done, we'll return to the drop off point. Dr. B and Theo will be waiting for us."

Tori's training with explosives had mostly been with grenades she'd hurled at dragon-shaped objects. Plastic explosives were trickier and more dangerous to use. "What if you're right about this being a ploy and Overdrake has explosives of his own in the vault room?"

"Then we're going to see a big bang," Bess said.

"We'll be as far away as we can get," Jesse added, "and standing behind Bess's shield."

Bess's shield had limits to how much it could absorb. Although that shouldn't matter. The chances of this being a trap were slim. Overdrake thought Tori was connected to Vesta, and he never let Aaron go near the hatchlings alone. The information had to be legitimate.

As the plane was touching down at Lock Haven Regional, the noise in Tori's mind—the part of her brain that was connected to Minerva—changed. The echoing sound of the dragon moving around the enclosure faded and a new sound took its place. A slow thump of a dragon's heartbeat.

When Tori told the others, Bess smiled. "In the very least, this trip will be like an Easter egg hunt—supposing that the Easter Bunny wanted us dead."

Jesse nodded as though expecting the news, then looked at a map of the east coast on his cell phone. "If the other dragons are closer to your home than Lock Haven, they must be in the Maryland, Delaware, Virginia area somewhere. Perhaps New Jersey or another part of Pennsylvania. Otherwise you would have switched over long before now, wouldn't you?"

"I doubt it's that clear-cut. I think I stay in the mind of the dragon I've connected to last unless another one comes much closer."

And now, apparently, they were much closer to an egg. Probably more. Aaron's information about the eggs' location must be correct. Now they would see how well Overdrake had guarded them.

CHAPTER 23

At seven o'clock the Slayers pulled off of the main road and drove onto one not far from the Energize Nutrition building. Tori's mind was a forced calm. She watched the wall of trees that spread around them and reviewed the mission details.

This was no different than the drills Dr. B was always making them do. She'd used a jackhammer before, and Bess and Jesse had so much practice with the machines they could have used them to make ice sculptures.

When the van stopped—hopefully far enough away from any surveillance cameras—she, Bess and Jesse slid out into the cover of night. Their helmets were on, earmuffs around their necks, guns in place, and jackhammers strapped to their backs. Destroying the eggs wouldn't be pleasant, and wouldn't be easy for her to do, but that didn't matter. This had to be done. It meant six less dragons to fight later on.

The Slayers turned on their mics, took their tranquilizer guns from their holsters, and slunk off toward the building. It was a one-story, boxy, brick building. Small parking lot. Unassuming and unremarkable except for the tall fence surrounding the place that was rimmed with barbed wire. Trees concealed the area from passing traffic, but no vegetation grew on the grounds. Probably to avoid any surveillance obstructions. Four cars sat in a line in the parking lot. The security guards' vehicles.

Tori took in the information clinically, noting that if they had to fight outside, their only cover would be the cars.

Jesse flew Bess over the fence. Tori secured a chain on the gate, then followed them, gliding through the night air. Clouds were seeping across the sky, doing their best to erase the moonlight. Everything was silent except for the faint rustle of wind through the branches behind them and the occasional whoosh of a car on the main road.

Jesse dropped Bess off at the front door and then headed over the top of the building to position himself at the back. Tori flew to the roof, unhooked Theo's canister from her belt, and waited for the sign that both exits were covered. Once her watch flashed that the others were ready, she sprayed the contents of the canister into the vents.

Some of the gas smell wafted back in her direction, and she had to crane her head away to find fresh air. The stuff would undoubtedly linger in her clothes. Hopefully she wouldn't end up hiding from Overdrake's men during this mission because they would probably be able to sniff her out.

After she finished with the canister, she sailed off the roof and joined Bess at the front of the building. They stood at opposite sides of the door, weapons drawn, and waited. It was the first time they'd been together with Jesse out of earshot.

Bess muted her mic and motioned for Tori to mute hers. She whispered, "So what's really going on between you and Dirk?"

Tori hadn't been expecting the question. "What has Jesse told you?"

Bess tilted her chin in disapproval. "That isn't an answer. That's the sort of thing you say when you want to avoid admitting the whole truth."

"Sorry, but this isn't the best place for a heart-to-heart."

Bess put her hand on her hip. It was odd to see her that way—so serious. Usually she was joking around, even during the middle of missions. "I'm here because I believe in you, but so help me, if this is a trap..."

Bess didn't finish because the door burst open, and all four of the guards poured out. They wore bulletproof vests and had guns in their holsters but none of their weapons were drawn. They weren't scanning the area looking for enemies. They were just hurrying to get out of the building. Their mistake.

As soon as they passed by, Tori aimed at the men's necks and shot two in quick succession. Bess shot the other two while moving her foot into the doorway to keep the door from shutting.

The problem with using tranquilizer guns was that they took a minimum of sixty seconds to work. Longer if the victim had a large body mass or remained calm. That left a minute or two in which the guards could shoot back.

Each of the guards yelled and turned. Almost in unison, they reached for their guns and fired. Flashes of light sparked from the barrels and shots pierced the silence. Tori had expected more caution from the guards. Discharging your firearm in a place you thought had a gas leak wasn't exactly safe.

The bullets ricocheted off Bess's shield, sending the spray of bullets back at the men. If any of them had been hit by ricocheting bullets, they hadn't been incapacitated. Two turned and ran toward the parking lot and the cover of vehicles. The other two dived to the ground. One army-crawled toward the side of the building. The other stayed where he was, gun pointed at Tori. "Surrender or I'll shoot!" he yelled.

Apparently, Overdrake hadn't explained the concept of a shield to him.

"You go ahead and try that," Tori said. "It worked out so well for you last time." She held her radar sensor to the doorway. No people detected inside. If anyone had been in the metal room before she'd sprayed her canister in the air vent, they hadn't come within fifty feet of this wall. She didn't go inside yet. She and Bess were supposed to wait until Jesse was with them.

Bess unmuted her mic and spoke to him. "All four targets are tranquilized but still armed. It will be safe to join us in about thirty seconds."

"See you then," he said.

The guy who'd been crawling was halfway to the corner of the building. The man who'd threatened them stood up and darted that direction as well. Running only made the tranquilizer circulate faster in the bloodstream. He wouldn't last long. The men who'd run to the parking lot were already staggering. In a few seconds, they'd be splayed out on the parking lot.

One of the Slayers needed to stay outside to verify all the men had been neutralized. Tori held her hand out to Bess. "Give me the explosives. I'll go to the vault room."

Bess hesitated then shook her head. "Let Jesse set them up."

Tori felt a prickle of indignation. "Are you saying that because you don't trust me?"

"I trust you." Another hesitation. "I just trust Jesse more."

Ouch. "Okay," Tori whispered, "so I spent some time with Dirk. That doesn't mean my loyalties have switched."

Bess cocked her head. "I wasn't talking about trusting your *loyalties*. I was talking about trusting you with explosives. Jesse has years of practice and you've had one summer."

"Oh," Tori said, immediately feeling stupid. "Sorry."

One of the running men had begun stumbling around in drunken circles. The second stopped, swayed, and then toppled onto the ground.

Bess flipped off her mic. "What did you do with Dirk that would make you assume I was questioning your loyalties?"

"Nothing." Tori couldn't see Bess's expression through her helmet but still felt her stare.

"You made out with him, didn't you?"

Was she so transparent? "Um, it's complicated."

Bess huffed. "You totally did."

Tori was saved from having to answer further by Jesse's arrival. He flew over the top of the building and landed beside them. "T-bird, you're with me." To Bess, he said, "Make sure the men stay down, then follow us." Her shield would protect her if any of the men made any last shooting attempts.

When they were all motionless, she would hit them with a second dose and wait another sixty seconds to make sure none of them were faking unconsciousness. The Slayers didn't want any armed men following them into the building.

Although really, if the third man was faking it, he probably wouldn't have chosen to fall face first into the pavement.

Jesse checked his radar sensor. "It's clear."

At least what they could see of it. The device couldn't work through the metal of the innermost room.

Tori followed Jesse, gun raised, and glided across the sparse lobby. The stink of the methanethiol still saturated the room.

Except for a large desk that stood sentry, the place was bare of any decorations or furniture. Fluorescent lighting showed the way to a hallway in the back. Cameras perched accusingly on the ceiling. They shouldn't be recording, but even if Theo missed one, helmets and jackets hid the group's identity. Although Overdrake would still know the Slayers were responsible. Who else had the motive?

What would Dirk's reaction be when he found out what Tori had done to the eggs?

She didn't want to think about it, couldn't. The thought of facing him after this made her stomach feel like it had filled with sand. She pulled her rifle from its sling and made quick work of the cameras anyway. The less evidence of their time here, the better.

She and Jesse went down a hallway to their left, approaching every doorway and corner cautiously. They used the radar and kept their guns ready. If someone popped out and started shooting, hallways and doorways were the most dangerous places to be caught. The fatal funnel. Not much room to maneuver.

Jesse went into the room at the end of the hallway. An office. He swept the room then gestured for Tori to come inside. Theo's blueprints had shown the entryway to the eggs' location was through an entryway at the back of the room, but no door was visible. The wall appeared to be solid wooden paneling.

"Must be a hidden door," Jesse said.

While he held his radar to the paneling, Tori used hers to scan behind them, looking for any incoming men. She saw one figure approaching them fast through the hallway.

"Beta, what's your location?" Tori asked into her mic.

"I'm almost to you," Bess answered.

No one else was around. The thought should have reassured Tori, but her anxiety kept growing. What if she'd been wrong to bring her friends here? What if something horrible happened? Everything would be her fault.

Jesse slid his radar sensor over the wall. "There's metal behind the paneling." He took out his Dremel saw and put two holes in the wood.

Bess came into the room, gun at the ready. "Don't start without me."

"Wouldn't dream of it." Jesse used the holes he'd just drilled as handholds and ripped sections of the paneling off. It cracked and splintered, turning to kindling beneath his fingers. Behind the broken paneling, a steel wall and door appeared.

Jesse took a ribbon charge of C4 from his pack. With calm, steady movements he molded it around the doorframe, pushing it into every crevice. He taped what wouldn't stick, then jammed a shock tube into the blasting cap. Tori and Bess went back into the hallway, making sure it stayed clear. Jesse followed them, trailing det cord. They went all the way back outside.

Despite the assurance of Bess's shield, the further away they were from the blast, the better. When the three were out of the building, Jesse pulled the detonator pin to disable the safety. "Tell me when your shield is in place."

"It's up," Bess said.

Jesse nodded, the signal that the blast was coming, then yanked the ring from the top of the detonator. It made a small pop. A deceptively mild noise considering what it ushered in.

Tori shut her eyes and braced herself. The sound of the explosion was like a drum coming down on her head—so loud it seemed to vibrate all the way through her body. It had come at her from two different directions—the building and inside her own mind, the part of her brain that connected to dragons.

When she opened her eyes, she half expected to see that the roof had blown off the building and bits of shingles were falling like confetti. But the roof still held. No confetti in sight.

Tori spoke into her mic to include Dr. B. "I heard the blast through dragon's ears too. At least one of the eggs is in there."

"Good." Jesse put on his dust mask, tucking it beneath his helmet. "I've just changed my mind about Aaron's spying abilities."

Bess put on her mask as well. "And I take back all the things I said about this being an ill-thought-out suicide mission."

"When did you say that?" Tori asked, securing her mask.

"I didn't say it to you, just to everyone else."

Well, that was nice to know.

Jesse opened the door and smoke billowed out, a gray cloud that spilled around them and obscured everything. The place smelled of dust and destruction.

He turned on his flashlight and flew in. Tori picked up Bess, and shadowed him, making her way through the dark haze. All the electric lighting was gone. Debris plunked down like the patter of belated rain after a storm.

As they went through the hallway, a loose door fell backward as if fainting.

"Report?" Dr. B asked over the earpiece.

"Everything is fine," Jesse called from up ahead. "I'm almost to the room." A moment later he added, "Detonation successful."

Most of the hallway wall was gone. Inside the room, the vault door dangled lopsided from its hinges. No men with rocket launchers. Nothing that looked like a trap. Now it was time to do what they'd come for. Two eggs apiece. This shouldn't take long.

Gun drawn, Tori followed Jesse and Bess into the vault room.

Six sofa-sized eggs lay in cushioned bedding. All of them seemed to be made of dark gray rock, the exact color of the inside of the room. Dragons were the size of lions when they hatched, and there was no way to tell how developed the embryos inside these eggs were.

Jesse took a leaping step, landed onto the closest egg, and unhooked his jackhammer. Bess jumped onto the next, her jackhammer already out.

A spike of dread ran through Tori, a warning that this was wrong. "Wait," she called to the others. "Stop!"

Both paused and turned to her.

She wasn't sure how to explain her sudden fear. "What if only one egg is real and the others have explosives in them?" Overdrake knew that the Slayers had tried to destroy eggs with jackhammers in the past. What if he'd expected them to find this place?

Jesse motioned to her to come over. "Then you'd better tell us which one is the real egg."

Tori crossed to the closest egg, not sure how to make herself connect with it. She put her hands on the shell. It felt like a boulder warmed by the sunshine. She shut her eyes and forced her mind to go inside the egg until she heard the heartbeat. "This one is real," she said, then moved to the next.

It was easier to connect the second egg. As soon as her hands touched it, she felt the heartbeat, a thumping rhythm that was faster than its neighbor. "This one's real too."

And if two were, then they most likely were all real. Why bait a trap with more than one egg? But it was better to be certain. Tori went to the next egg to test it.

Real. The next one as well. She probably didn't need to check the last two but found herself doing it. She wanted to delay the sound of the jackhammers until she was sure. "They're all dragons," she said. Instead of feeling relieved by this fact, she felt sick.

 CHAPTER 24

Overdrake was sitting in his den, on the phone with a Colombian general when Hancock, his deputy in Lock Haven called. Overdrake ignored Hancock until his phone chimed, the signal that the call was urgent, then he grudgingly put the general on hold.

"What is it?" Overdrake asked, and didn't keep the irritation from his voice.

"Something is wrong at the Energize building. I got a message from the security head a couple of minutes ago. He said there was a gas leak in the building."

"That's impossible," Overdrake said, still irritated. "Everything there is electric."

"I know. I called them back for clarification. No one is answering their phones."

Overdrake's irritation was instantly replaced by fury. Someone was either trying to steal or destroy the eggs. Who was behind it? The government? The Slayers? Could anyone else have learned of the dragons?

Overdrake stood up, nearly tipping his chair to the ground in the process. Even if he flew fast, he was a good twenty minutes away. "I hope you're calling from your car," he said, "because you and every man you have should be on your way to the building right now."

"Yes, of course," Hancock replied, almost certainly lying. "We're on our way. I'll call you when I have more news."

"Do that. And then you can show me the prisoners in person. I'm on my way too."

 # CHAPTER 25

With helmets off and earmuffs on, Jesse and Bess started up their jackhammers, digging them into the hard shells. The jackhammers vibrated, danced almost, sending dark splinters fountaining to the floor.

Standing atop one of the eggs, Tori turned on her jackhammer. These deaths meant lives saved later. Six fewer weapons of destruction. She put the chisel to the egg, using the jackhammer's weight to hold it in place. She only had to kill two dragons. Jesse and Bess would take care of the others.

She shouldn't have been able to hear the sound of the dragon's heartbeat over the noise of the jackhammers. And she couldn't. Not really. But somehow, she could still feel it. An insistent thump, proof of life.

The jackhammer spat pieces of shell around her feet and would soon hit the dragon. She didn't want to see that, so she glanced over at Jesse. He'd made a large hole in his egg and was plunging the jackhammer inside, using the machine like a sword.

A wave of nausea gripped Tori. Did he need to do that? Wasn't it enough to break the shells and let the dragons die naturally?

But then, sometimes premature babies lived, didn't they? One of her mother's friends had given birth ten weeks premature and Tori had gone with her mother to the hospital to visit. The little girl had been so tiny, so fragile in her bassinet, but she'd grown up healthy.

Perhaps Tori shouldn't have thought of babies while she was killing dragons. Her hands were shaking so much it was hard to hold onto the jackhammer. Dragons weren't babies. They were dangerous beasts. Animals. Some had scales that shone like a starry night and some had Corvette-red scales.

She'd stopped pressing her jackhammer downward. It was just vibrating inside the hole, widening it.

This was wrong. She felt like she was strangling a puppy.

Tori had thought her dread about this room was a fear of the place being a trap. But that wasn't it. The feeling had always been a dread of this—of killing dragons. She glanced at Bess to see if she was having a hard time carrying out the assignment. Bess's expression was intent concentration. Her body language showed no regret. She was leaning hard on the jackhammer, driving it all the way through the shell.

Jesse moved to his second egg and bits of shell spit from the tip of his jackhammer. He would kill a second dragon soon.

Regret pulsed through Tori, sadness. *It's only because I'm part dragon lord,* she thought. *My genetics are making it hard to think straight.*

She still couldn't look down at the egg she was destroying. This would take forever. She would be trapped in this room of death and never get out.

The egg's surface beneath her feet gave way, making her stumble. She instinctively took to the air, hovering while she peered down to see what happened. The egg had cracked all the way through, revealing a pale, wet dragon who thrashed against the sides of the shell.

Tori had expected the dragon to be half-formed—more of a blob than a creature. But it was whole—too thin, too small, and with scales that looked more like wrinkles than armor, but it was still whole. The dragon blinked at her and stretched out its wobbling neck.

Tori didn't mean to go into the dragon's mind. In fact, she'd firmly planned on staying out. She was sucked inside though, and her vision immediately split into two.

She saw the dragon, trembling before her, and she also saw a blurry version of herself, floating with a jackhammer clutched in her hands. She wasn't in its control center, just its senses, but even that connection felt like too much.

The dragon was confused and cold. He opened his mouth and hissed in defiance, a sound that came out so squeaky the noise seemed more of a call for help than a threat.

What had Tori done?

The dragon raised his wings in panic, in an instinctual attempt to flee. His wings were so thin that their blood vessels stood out like spindly tree branches. He took a step forward and stumbled on legs too weak to support him.

She felt the pain that hit him, the fear that went through him, and she let out an involuntary cry. He was going to die and it was her fault.

Over her earpiece, Dr. B's said, "What's wrong?"

She couldn't answer. She could only gape at the dragon. He was still struggling to stand, fighting against the exhaustion of under-formed muscles.

Jesse flew over, his jackhammer raised like a club.

Tori opened her mouth to protest but didn't. The dragon was dying. It was better to put it out of its misery. She shut her eyes, desperately trying to disconnect herself from the animal before the blow came.

She didn't manage it. She felt the dragon's flash of pain and then the connection was severed, like a line that had been cut. Nausea welled inside her; she felt dizzy with it. The jackhammer dropped from her hands and clanged to the floor.

She opened her eyes and saw the dragon lying crumpled on the side of the room. Jesse had clubbed it so hard it hit the wall. One wing twitched. The handle of Jesse's jackhammer was covered in blood and his jacket was splattered with it.

He flew to her. "Are you okay?"

She shrank away from him, holding up her hands to stop him from coming closer. She could only focus on the blood drops dotting him.

"T-bird," he said, more concerned, "are you okay?"

No. Only she couldn't tell him that.

Bess was working on her second egg. The first looked like a pumpkin someone had smashed in. Jesse had made progress on his second egg, but Tori couldn't tell whether he'd finished killing the dragon inside yet. Although, with a large hole in its shell, it couldn't survive for long anyway.

Only one egg in the vault room was left undamaged. The one she was supposed to kill next.

Jesse took hold of her arm to draw his attention to him. "You don't have to do this. We can take care of the rest."

Her eyes went to the undamaged egg. It seemed so helpless lying there.

Jesse flipped off his mic then reached over and flipped off hers as well. Whatever he was going to say next wasn't meant for Dr. B and the others to hear. "I accused you once of not knowing whether you were a dragon lord or a Slayer. I was being a jerk and I'm sorry. I've always known you were a Slayer. I've never doubted that for a moment. I believe in you. This is hard for you, but you've got to remember, you're a Slayer."

She nodded. At least she thought she was nodding. "Don't kill the last one. We should take it with us."

"What?" he asked.

She turned her mic back on so Dr. B and Theo could hear her. "We'll take the last egg with us and that way we'll have a dragon on our side. I can control it. I can make it fight for us."

Jesse didn't move, just stared at her.

Dr. B's voice came over the earpiece, sounding disapproving. "How would you take care of a dragon? Where would you put it?"

"We have time to figure that out. It won't hatch for years."

Jesse shook his head. "You don't know how to control a dragon, but Overdrake does. He would end up taking it away from you and using it against us."

"We shouldn't kill it," she insisted.

"You're not being objective about this."

"I am. Don't kill it!"

Tori hadn't thought she was connected to the dragon in Bess's egg, but she must have been. She felt the moment of its death, felt its heartbeat being snuffed out.

She gulped back a cry and her hand went to her chest. She felt claustrophobic, trapped. A cloud of dust from the jackhammers and the remnants of the explosion filled the room, made it seem foggy. "I can't breathe," she said.

Jesse towed her toward the door. "Go back to the van. We'll finish."

"No. You'll need my help carrying the egg. It will take both of us to fly it over the fence. Bess can hold onto your back."

"Tori—" he started.

She shook off his hand. "You said you believed in me. We can always kill the dragon later if we change our minds, but we can't undo its death."

Bess had heard their conversation and was waiting, jackhammer in hand, for a decision.

Dr. B's voice came over the earpiece. "Sensors are picking up two vans headed your way. The spikes won't slow Overdrake's men down for long. Finish and get out of there."

Bess put her helmet back on. "Hurry. We've got to go."

Jesse flew back to the egg he'd been working on, wielding his jackhammer again to make sure the dragon inside was dead. Tori flew to the undamaged egg, stood beside it, and pushed it from the cushioned bedding. Slowly, it rolled forward.

Jesse watched her, then spoke out loud as he thought. "If we take the egg out of here, it will turn on the genetics of every unborn Slayer who comes within range."

Tori kept pushing the egg. "And that's a good thing."

"Let's hope so." He flew over to the egg's other side and helped her lift. "Because it will also turn on any dragon lord genes." He inclined his head in an apology. "Not that dragon lord genes are always bad."

"Let's hope not," she said. Genes don't matter, she told herself, choices matter. She could save this dragon and still fight against Overdrake.

Bess dropped her jackhammer and joined them lifting the egg. With the two of them helping her, Tori finally felt as though she could breathe again.

CHAPTER 26

The egg took up most of the back of the van. The seats had been discarded on the side of the road to make room for it. Tori, Bess, and Jesse were wedged into the edges at the corners. Tori didn't mind the squeeze. Possibilities always took a lot of room, didn't they?

Getting away had been relatively easy. Overdrake's men had been outside of the gate, working on breaking the chain that kept it closed by repeatedly firing at it. They turned their guns upward on the Slayers, but Bess kept her shield between them, and they were able to fly to Dr. B's van two streets over where it waited for them.

Once the danger was past and Dr. B was taking the back roads to the airport, the Slayers pulled off their helmets. Bess wrinkled her nose at the egg as though it smelled bad. It didn't; it smelled like the outdoors. Like rivers and canyons. Having it here in part wiped away the horror of the others' deaths. This one was safe and whole.

Bess gave Tori a pointed look. "This dragon is going to try to eat you. You realize that, right? It's not like a stray kitten."

Theo glanced over his shoulder nervously and nodded in agreement. "And don't expect me to help feed that thing. I'm not doing it. I've seen Jurassic Park."

Dr. B kept checking the rearview mirrors. "Studying our enemies is a sound tactic. And creating new allies isn't a bad strategy either. We should have considered it at the beginning of the mission and made it one of our objectives. Why didn't we?" He asked the question as much to himself as to the passengers. "Why weren't we thinking through all of the possibilities?"

Bess shifted, trying to find more room in her corner of the van. "Because keeping a dragon is inherently dangerous and probably stupid."

That wasn't it. Tori said the real reason. "Because none of you actually thought Aaron's information was valid."

Bess lifted a hand to stop Tori from saying more. "Okay, you were right about him and we were wrong. I hereby grant you gloating privileges for the trip home."

Jesse grinned at Tori, one of his real smiles—a bit of summer on a winter's night. "The kid helped us kill five dragons. You can gloat for an entire week."

Dr. B's voice was serious. "If Overdrake realizes Aaron betrayed him, the consequences will be severe."

Dr. B was right about that. How good could a twelve-year-old be at covering his tracks? "Should we find a way to get him out?"

"We don't know where he is," Bess reminded her.

"And we don't know that he needs our help," Jesse added. "Right now he's a valuable source. Tonight proves that."

Tori gazed outside behind the van. Clouds blotted out most of the stars, making everything seem shrouded, more dangerous. Somewhere, not far away, men were searching for them. "But if Overdrake realizes Aaron helped us and takes revenge..."

"We still won't know where he is," Bess said.

She was right, but Tori didn't like it. They would all have to hope that Overdrake didn't suspect Aaron.

Tori ran her hand along the egg's rough surface. It felt like rock, like something as ancient as cliff walls. Inside, the dragon's heartbeat was steady, its mind calmly oblivious, deep in sleep.

Her gaze was drawn back outside. Snow edged both sides of the road with jumbles of trees beyond that. It was hard to tell if any houses were behind them but they'd passed fields with homes earlier. Not many cars were traveling along this two-lane road, but still, they must have come within range of dozens of people. Were any of them pregnant, and if so, what percentage of the population had the right DNA?

"We should drive the egg around DC," Tori said, "then take it on a road trip. We'll create so many Slayers that eventually Overdrake won't be able to fight them all."

Having a new generation of Slayers and dragon lords wouldn't be a help for about another fifteen years, but the thought still lifted Tori's spirits. She and her friends would have help both in fighting Overdrake and controlling dragons. The responsibility wouldn't rest on such a small group.

She was deep in the happiness of this thought when the night grew a shade blacker.

Tori didn't understand what the darkness meant until she heard Dr. B mutter a stream of "No, no, no!" the way one might utter curses. The van's headlights were off. The car was slowing to a tired stop.

This had happened before. Last summer when Overdrake had attacked them with a dragon, he'd first disabled their van with EMP. He was somewhere close by, out in the darkness, searching for them. And it wouldn't take him long to find them disabled on this road.

Theo gripped his armrest and strained to see out of his window. "Tori, why didn't you warn us a dragon was coming?"

"I'm still connected to the egg," she said. "I didn't know." And that, she supposed was the disadvantage of stealing an egg.

Theo craned his head, still trying to see something outside. "I don't get paid enough for this."

Bess put her gloves back on, her hands slightly shaking. "How did Overdrake get here so fast?"

Jesse's movements were determined and edged with anger. Anger, Tori knew, that was aimed at Overdrake or perhaps fate, because neither was willing to let them have the upper hand for long. They'd just killed five dragons, but they might lose five team members for it.

"Overdrake must have the dragons stationed close by," Jesse said. "We should be able to use that information to help find his location. Theo, if the dragons are flying between ninety and one hundred and ten miles an hour and it's been thirty-five minutes since he was warned, what's the radius of his possible locations?"

"Seriously?" Theo asked with a grunt. "You want me to do story problems right now?"

Dr. B guided the car to the side of the road. "We don't have a healer with us or anyone who can douse fire. You'll have to decide whether it's tactically better to fight or to flee."

Jesse pulled his helmet back on. "We fight."

Tori put hers on with a groan. "You always want to fight. That can't be healthy. Or a good policy." It was Slayer genetics, she knew. The instinct seemed to outweigh common sense. "We don't have the equipment to fight." They had their rifles but not a lot of ammo. No grenades. They'd have to use the Dremel saws to cut through the dragon's Kevlar straps.

Jesse unwedged himself from behind the egg. "When have we ever had the right equipment to fight?"

The van slowed enough that Bess opened the back door and gazed around. "Grandpa is gonna be ticked about this."

"I don't plan on telling him," Dr. B said.

Jesse surveyed the land around them. There wasn't a lot of cover among the roadside trees. Their trunks were too thin to hide a person and their empty branches seemed raised in surrender. "Tori, we need to get Theo and Dr. B to safety. Let's fly them down the road where the trees are thicker. Then we'll regroup with Bess there." He pointed in the opposite direction at a bend in the road.

Tori tightened the buckle on her holster. "We should also take the egg to safety."

Jesse flew from the back of the van without answering her.

Carrying the egg would present a problem. If Tori and Jesse were holding onto it, how would they also carry Bess, Theo, and Dr. B?

Tori exited the van last. "Bess," she said, "You and the others will have to ride on top of the egg."

"Too slow." Jesse glided toward Dr. B. "We'll be caught. Overdrake won't just let us fly away. We'll have a better chance if we stake out a position and fight with our hands free." Without waiting for further discussion, he wrapped his arms around Dr. B's middle, lifted him off the ground and sailed down the street.

Tori only hesitated for a moment more. She hated to leave the egg, but Jesse had a point. Overdrake hadn't brought a dragon out here to negotiate with them. And if the dragon came close enough to catch hold of their scent, he'd be able to track them. She flipped on her neck mic, picked up Theo, and followed Jesse.

Over the earpiece, Dr. B said, "Beta, take cover until the others return."

The earpieces and the mics had been hardened to make them EMP-proof so the Slayers could use them during an attack. Whenever Tori questioned Theo about how this was done and why it couldn't be done to more electronics, he went on and on about resistors, capacitors, diodes, crystals and other things that made Tori's brain glaze over. Bottom line seemed to be that the procedure was too expensive to do on a wide scale.

As Tori skimmed along the roadside, her gaze constantly shifted between the trees and the sky—the jutting silhouette of trees against the gray night sky. How much time did they have? Overdrake must have hit the area with EMP to stop all the cars from leaving. He would search the roads and stalled vehicles. When he saw their van, he would know they were somewhere nearby.

Hopefully they still had time to hide Dr. B and Theo. With any luck Overdrake would be so intent on fighting the Slayers, the other two would be able to get away unnoticed.

Tori wasn't sure what made her look over her shoulder. Her Slayer senses must have picked up on the change in air currents or the beginnings of a smell. At first, she saw nothing.

Bess had moved behind the van into the foliage at the side of the road and was scanning the sky. "Bad news," she muttered.

A moment after she spoke, Tori saw the shape of the dragon. It had been flying low, barely visible against the trees down the road, not high enough to give them much warning. A huge black shape with flapping wings and a long tail. Khan.

The dragon's neck was stretched out, his golden eyes fixing on the Slayers. Nothing of the docile nonchalance Tori witnessed earlier remained in the dragon now. He was muscle and talons. Living thunder. Breathtakingly beautiful. Completely dangerous. And he was coming at them fast—heading toward Bess and the van.

Overdrake had found the Slayers too soon, hadn't given them a chance to regroup. Jesse and Tori were too far away to help Bess.

Tori dropped Theo. He'd have to find a hiding place here. "J-bird!" she called and didn't have to say more. Jesse turned and both of them raced through the air, high speed, back in Bess's direction.

A man was riding Khan, rifle raised. Had to be Overdrake.

Khan let out a cry of triumph. He'd seen the van and most likely Bess too. The sparse trees couldn't hide her well enough.

Tori automatically calculated the battle scene. Bess could only put the shield in one place. If she put it in front of herself, she left Tori and Jesse unprotected from Overdrake's rifle. If Bess put it in front of the other Slayers, she left herself vulnerable to not only bullets but the dragon.

Someone would probably die in the next few seconds. She, Jesse, or Bess. Maybe all of them.

Tori couldn't even shoot Overdrake. He wore bulletproof armor, and shooting at him would let him know where Bess's shield was. Tori and Jesse's best bet was to find cover and let Bess protect herself.

Khan dived downward—not thunder now, but lightning—toward the van and Bess. Her shield wouldn't hold up long against his force. Tori dodged into the trees, reaching out to Khan's mind even though she knew she didn't have time to find his control center. Was there any other way to distract him?

Her vision split in two. She saw through his eyes as he swooped down, talons outstretched. Bess leaped sideways, out of his trajectory.

Instead of pursuing Bess, Khan grabbed hold of the van and ripped off the roof as though it were annoying packaging. Bits of metal twisted and tore, shuddered and gave way. Fortunately for Bess, the dragon was after the egg, not her.

Jesse and Tori pushed their way into the thickets and trees, trying to find cover from Overdrake's rifle. Branches scraped against her suit, clawing at her.

Perhaps they would have been safer on the road. They would've had better maneuverability and the trees didn't offer much protection. Overdrake's armor-piercing bullets could chew the trunks into sawdust. Was all this underbrush just keeping them in place and making them easier to shoot?

Khan reached the egg quickly enough. With a threatening screech in the Slayers' direction, he picked it up and lifted into the sky, wings beating like sails in a storm.

Tori felt Overdrake's presence in Khan's mind, felt his rage directed at her. His words vibrated through the dragon's mind. "You brought this on yourself!"

Outside, Tori saw Overdrake swivel in his seat, pointing his rifle at Jesse and her. He shot off a round. Midair, the bullets thudded into Bess's shield and ricocheted back.

Now Overdrake knew where the shield was. It was typical of Bess to protect her friends when she was in immediate danger. Noble and foolish. With a sickening certainty, Tori guessed what Overdrake would do next. Shoot Bess. She wouldn't have time to switch her shield to protect herself.

Tori plunged deeper into Khan's mind, the second level. Strings of color hung everywhere. Where was the path that led to his control center? There—she recognized it and rushed to it, flinging strands away.

The sound of gunshot sliced through the air, sounding far away this time. Overdrake had shot again.

She could still see through Khan's eyes, but he wasn't looking at Bess, just the dull black street and anemic trees. More shots. Tori didn't want to go back to her body to see if Bess lay bleeding on the ground. The control center was on the other side of these last strings. She would force Overdrake out, make him pay.

Jesse's voice called to her, a distant sound. "Tori!" In his panic, he'd said her name, not her code.

And then Tori realized she had to leave the dragon's mind—should have already done it. If Bess had been killed, her shield was down and the rest of them were vulnerable to gunfire.

She opened her eyes with a jerk and was instantly gone from Khan's mind. Jesse leaned over her, checking her for wounds. "Are you okay?"

Her gaze snapped to the sky. She expected to see Overdrake somewhere close by, rifle drawn. But he and the dragon were flying away, disappearing into the night.

Tori attempted to sit up, but her body felt too drained to move. She turned her head toward Bess, could make her out through the crisscross of branches. Her friend wasn't lying on the ground, limp and bleeding. She was crouched behind the engine block of the upturned van, using it as cover.

The relief that washed over Tori was so strong, she nearly wept. Bess hadn't needed to move her shield for protection, she'd used the van for that.

Dr. B's voice came over the mic. "Status? Was T-bird shot?"

"I'm fine," she answered. Fine, but still weak. Her mind insisted she get to her feet, but her muscles weren't obeying.

Jesse took her hand and gently pulled her to a sitting position.

The world went dizzy for a moment, then cleared. "I tried to control Khan and passed out." Tori's thoughts reached out to the dragon, searching for his mind again. If she could stay connected to Khan, she could see where Overdrake took him and learn the compound's location— Aaron's location.

She heard what Khan heard—the rushing night air and the dragon's wingbeats, but she couldn't get further into his mind than that. Her attempts felt like she was grasping at smoke. Maybe a dragon had to be closer by for her to access it.

"Were you able to reach his control center?" Dr. B asked.

"No," Tori said wearily. "I was almost there but I came out too soon. I thought Beta had been shot and we were next."

Jesse helped her to her feet. Bits of wood and dirt tumbled to the ground around them. She wobbled as she got her balance back.

"Are you okay now?" he asked.

She nodded and pushed her way through the web of branches, breaking several in the process.

Instead of going out to the road, Jesse leaped upward, bursting from the underbrush. He left a trail of torn shrubbery shivering in his wake. "I'll get Beta and we'll go after Overdrake."

If Kody were with them, he could have knocked the rifle from Overdrake's hand. Pursuing a gunman and dragon with such a small team was dangerous. "If Beta's shield is protecting us," Tori reminded him, "we won't be able to get to the dragon."

"We'll wait him out." Jesse glided over to Bess, pausing so she could take hold of his back. Once she did, he soared in the direction Overdrake had gone. "As long as we're following him, he can't go home. And as long as the dragon is holding an egg, he won't be able to effectively fight. We should be able to at least make him drop the egg."

Tori reluctantly followed after them, liking the idea less with each moment. "Or Overdrake will circle back here and shoot Dr. B. He'll force Beta to decide who to protect. It will be dangerous for all of us." She halted, hanging in the sky while Jesse pulled farther ahead.

Dr. B's voice came over the earpiece. "Beta knows she needs to protect the Slayers. I'm expendable and you're not. Go after Overdrake. We'll be fine."

Tori lifted higher and caught sight of Khan skimming over the trees. A fight it was, then. Tori could do this. She could kill Khan. She wouldn't mess up and hesitate this time.

Theo's voice crackled through her earpiece, high-pitched with worry. "You're not fine. You're bleeding."

Wait, Dr. B was wounded? Tori stuttered in the air, suddenly unsure whether to keep pursuing Overdrake. The Slayers were trained to fight on despite casualties, but this wasn't a defensive battle, Overdrake had retreated.

"It's nothing," Dr. B insisted. "Just a small wound."

"Yeah," Theo said, his voice still too high. "Because bullets are small. The size isn't the point. What if it hit an artery?"

"It didn't," Dr. B said. "I can tell. I'm a doctor."

Not that sort of doctor. Up ahead, Bess twisted, nearly letting go of Jesse. "Take me back! We need to help him!" The panic in her voice matched the growing panic in Tori's chest.

"Priorities," Dr. B said. The word was tinged with pain.

Tori knew what Dr. B wanted her to do, what he'd drilled into the Slayers. But she couldn't leave Dr. B when he was wounded, even if it meant letting Overdrake get away.

Almost in unison, Tori and Jesse turned, mid-air, and headed back to the trees.

Tori reached Dr. B first. He was sitting on the ground, helmet off, and eyes shut while he leaned against a tree. Theo was tying his sweatshirt around Dr. B's upper arm with shaking hands. "Are we supposed to put the bandage directly on the wound? If I take off his coat, he'll get cold. We have to worry about shock—and further fire."

"Leave his coat on," Tori said. "I'll bandage him." With her extra strength, pulling the shirt tight against his sleeves wouldn't be hard.

Dr. B opened his eyes and shook his head at Tori. "Did I teach you nothing about priorities?"

"Yes." She knotted the shirt around his arm. A growing patch of blood immediately reddened the cloth. "You taught me that gunshot victims who reach a hospital within an hour are likely to survive. That's my priority." Before any mission, the Slayers always located the closest hospital. The one in Lock Haven wasn't far away. Less than ten miles.

Tori carefully picked up Dr. B, then took to the air with a gust that made branches wave at her departure. Dr. B seemed to weigh nothing, this man who was larger than life.

Jesse had been swerving down to land. He pulled up and flew along beside her, near enough that Bess could have jumped to Tori's back if she'd wanted.

"Is he okay?" Bess asked. "Dad?"

Dr. B's gray hair ruffled wildly in the wind. He forced a thin smile. "I'm fine. I already told you that." He held his breath during the last few words. "You should have gone after Overdrake. It was just bad luck that I was shot."

Probably not. Overdrake had been able to see through Khan's eyes and knew where Theo and Dr. B were hiding. He'd shot them in order to facilitate his escape.

"Hey," Theo said over the earpiece. "You guys left me. What am I supposed to do back here?"

They probably should have carried him with them to the hospital, but Tori wasn't going to go back now and she doubted Bess would let Jesse turn back.

"Walk toward Lock Haven," Jesse said. "When we get to the hospital, we'll call a car company to pick you up and take you to the airport."

"They won't think that's odd," Theo retorted. "A random shirtless guy who's splattered in blood, walking along the highway, carrying an assortment of weapons."

"We'll tell him you're into cosplay," Tori said.

Theo mumbled a few things about that, but Tori mostly ignored him. As the group flew, rushing toward the city, the wind shouted a long, high piercing note. Dr. B had to be freezing. She wished she could make him warmer.

Jesse kept looking over, checking on Dr. B. Theo's shirt was nearly completely soaked in blood. "Dr. B," Jesse said, "stay awake."

"Don't worry," Dr. B replied. "I'm awake and conscious of every throbbing pain."

He hadn't lost enough blood to pass out. That was a good sign.

Lock Haven came into sight, streetlamps glowing. House lights filled the area. Plenty of cars on the streets. The hospital was on the west side of the city, an oddly-shaped building that resembled an airplane from above.

Darkness hid the Slayers while they were high in the sky—making them appear as nothing more than a shadow that blotted out the stars. However, once they flew low enough to land, they would become visible.

Dr. B cradled his arm to his chest. "After you drop me off at the ER, call Booker, tell him what's happened, then fly to the airport. He'll see that you get home."

"I'm not leaving you," Bess said. "Not until I'm certain you're okay."

Tori didn't plan on leaving either, but there was no point in telling Dr. B this when Bess was already doing a fine job arguing the point.

"You won't have time to wait for me." Dr. B's voice wasn't loud, but was still firm. "Fly to the airport while your powers are still on. Otherwise you'll have to take a cab."

"I'll take a cab then," Bess said.

Dr. B shook his head. "I can come up with a story about being shot but I'm not going to drag you into it. You shouldn't talk to the authorities, and besides, you need to go home. Grandpa can't know about this."

"I don't care if Grandpa knows," Bess said.

"Bess," he said softly, "you have to think about what's good for the group." He looked at her so tenderly, with so much pride.

Her expression was unreadable under her visor, but her posture remained rigid. "Stop saying that." Bess's voice teetered between worry and anger. "You're not expendable. You never have been and you never will be."

They were nearly to the hospital. The parking lot was only half full so the ER shouldn't be crowded. Tori scanned the area for surveillance cameras and spotted them perched by the streetlights. The Slayers couldn't get too near to those. Tori gestured to get Jesse's attention, turned to avoid the cameras, and searched for a secure place to land.

"Grandpa says you have a death wish," Bess went on. "He says when Uncle Nathan died, you couldn't forgive yourself for being the one who didn't have powers. He thinks you're looking for redemption in a noble death."

"What utter nonsense." Dr. B struggled to sit upright. "This is simply one more reason I object to you living with your grandfather. Tell him he needs a different hobby than amateur psychoanalyst."

Bess shifted her grip on Jesse to better see her father. "I'm starting to think he's right. You seem pretty eager to bleed to death on the side of a road."

"We let two dragons go tonight," Dr. B countered. "Do you know how many people they might end up killing?"

"Yeah," Bess said, "Not you. That's the number I care about."

Tori and Jesse were still scouting the area, looking for a place to land. Jesse gestured to a road that led to the hospital. Unfortunately, it wasn't entirely empty. A middle-aged man sat in a parked car, perhaps waiting for someone. Still, they couldn't keep circling and waiting. Dr. B needed medical help. Tori began to descend.

"Think about what I'm saying." Dr. B tried to lift his hand for emphasis, then let it fall back into his lap.

"I know what you're saying," Bess said. "A bird in the hand is worth two in the bush—except for in this case, the bird represents your unnecessary death. So yeah, I don't really care about the ones in the bush."

Tori and Jesse landed behind the occupied car. Tori had hoped the man sitting inside wouldn't notice them in his rearview mirror. Perhaps with Bess and Dr. B's conversation going full blast that hope had been futile. Judging by the way the man jumped, then turned around, mouth gaping, he'd seen them land.

The guy grabbed hold of his wheel, gunned his engine, and drove off, lurching and screeching down the street.

None of the Slayers commented on his exit. They just hurried to the ER.

***

Despite Dr. B's protests, Jesse and Tori stayed in the waiting room with Bess. Jesse called Booker to report. Bess called her mother. "I don't think the wound is too serious," she said in hushed tones, "but we can't leave Dad here. If Overdrake realizes he shot one of us, he'll send men to search the local hospitals."

With Tori's sensitive hearing, she could make out Shirley's reply. "That's why your father has a fake ID. I'll call our doctor and have Dad moved as soon as possible. I'm arranging a flight there now and will be there in two hours."

"I'm staying until you get here," Bess said.

Shirley hesitated, then relented. "Fine. Tell your grandfather that your shopping trip has turned into a slumber party. If he says you can stay out, I won't make you come home."

Tori didn't hear the rest of their phone conversation because she was busy calling a driver to pick up Theo. Then she called the police and reported some cars stopped along the freeway. That way, anyone stranded out there by the EMP would get help.

On the walk to the ER, Dr. B had given them a story about how he got shot—random act of road rage. The story didn't explain why Tori, Bess, and Jesse were covered in a layer of ashy dust, but since Dr. B was conscious and the rest of the group was underage, the ER staff didn't ask them any questions.

After a while a doctor came out and gave them assurances that Dr. B was being treated and would most likely fully recover. The surgeon wouldn't give them any other details such as estimates on his recovery time.

Since there was nothing else Jesse and Tori could do for him, they called for a driver, hugged Bess goodbye, and left.

Their trip to the airport was uneventful, except for the driver's comment as he picked them up. "You're lucky I decided to work tonight," he said. "Crazy night. A bunch of cars in the area just stopped working. Left a bunch of folks stranded.

And what's more, the driver who's usually here has been telling everyone that a bunch of people dropped from the sky and pounced on his car." The man chortled at the idea, and Tori and Jesse forced out a couple of unconvincing chuckles in agreement.

The man shook his head. "Supposedly they were dressed in black like ninjas." He laughed again then seemed to notice Tori and Jesse wore black jackets and black pants. And carried black helmets. He may have also noted their disheveled appearance and the odd sooty dust that clung to them despite their best efforts to wash up in the hospital bathrooms.

The smile dropped from his lips and he drove the rest of the way silently, checking on them in his rearview mirror every few moments. He also sped fifteen miles over the limit.

Tori gave him a good tip anyway.

Well, at least the Uber drivers would have something to talk about tonight.

By the time the Slayers' plane took to the air, Tori was exhausted. She sat slumped in her seat, eyes shut while images from the night reeled through her mind: the feeble hatchling defiantly raising his wings in the vault room.

Jesse swinging his jackhammer. The dragon's broken body lying twisted on the ground. Khan diving through the night sky—much too close to Bess—talons outstretched. Dr. B wincing in pain while blood soaked through Theo's shirt.

All of it so violent. All of it because she'd insisted on this mission.

As soon as the plane leveled out, Jesse moved to the seat next to hers. He held out a bottle of Gatorade to her.

She shook her head, refusing to take it. "I feel sick."

He put the bottle in her hand anyway. "You're probably dehydrated."

She'd taken several long drinks at the ER water fountain. She shook her head again. Dehydration wasn't why she felt ill.

Jesse's gaze stayed on her. "Dr. B will be fine. In fact, I doubt his injury will even slow him down. He'll probably still call a Slayer practice this week. And if any of us complain about our injuries, he'll wave his bandaged arm at us."

"I know."

She must not have sounded encouraged. Jesse's brown eyes looked at her with understanding and then with sympathy. "Is this about destroying the dragon eggs?"

She shrugged and then nodded. "Maybe. I don't know."

He put his hand over hers. "You'll be okay."

She didn't reply to that.

He put his arm around her shoulder, pulling her closer. "Don't worry. You felt this way after we killed Tamerlane and Kiha. This is just your dragon lord side messing with you. You'll be fine tomorrow."

He was probably right. She had felt ill both times when the Slayers killed the dragons. Part of her relaxed. The dark images repeating in her mind wouldn't lodge there and stay forever. This would pass. She just had to get through tonight.

She leaned into Jesse, letting her head rest against his chest. She could hear the steady beat of his heart. So strong and reassuring. The two stayed like that, Jesse quietly holding her.

Theo, who sat in the chair nearest the cockpit, got up to rummage through one of the food bins. As he pulled out a box of zebra cakes, he glanced across the cabin, saw Jesse and Tori, and rolled his eyes. "Do we have to have PDA on the plane? I thought the two of you broke up."

Jesse kept his arm around Tori. "We did."

Theo snapped the food bin closed. "You don't seem to understand the concept of breaking up."

Jesse didn't move. "And you don't understand the concept of sympathy."

Theo ripped open the package and gave a dramatic shrug. "Oh. Excuse me. I guess some of my sympathy evaporated after the two of you flew off, abandoning me in the woods with a megalomaniac gunman and his fifty-ton, fire-breathing carnivore."

Jesse let out a not-so-patient breath. "Overdrake had already left. You were perfectly safe."

"He could have come back." Theo bit into one of the cakes. "You didn't know he was gone for good. Don't you watch horror shows? The villain and the monster always come back."

Tori lifted her head from Jesse's shoulder. "We were in a hurry to get Dr. B to the hospital, and we weren't thinking clearly. We're sorry."

Theo sat down sullenly. "You know when you'll be sorry—the next time you need to break into some high-security building. You never forget about me then."

"Sorry," Jesse said, although he didn't sound as sincere as Tori.

Theo held up a hand as though giving in. "Just go back to your PDAs. I'll sit up here and you can pretend like I don't exist again." He sat down with a thunk and made a show of putting in his earbuds.

"Tech guys," Jesse muttered. "I wonder if they're all such prima donnas."

Tori settled against Jesse's side and he put his arm over her shoulder again. It felt natural to sit like this, warm and comforting. Snug. "Theo isn't as smart as he thinks," she said. "He can't even distinguish a real PDA."

"I don't blame him for having a hard time," Jesse said with mock seriousness. "Women flock to men who've been wading through debris, underbrush, and have suspicious blood stains on their clothing."

The two of them *were* a mess: smudged with ash, dirt, and bits of bark. "Helmet hair is one of my best looks," she agreed.

He nodded. "We're practically ready for prom pictures."

Prom. It was so far off she hadn't given it any thought. Now she wondered who Jesse would take. Tacy? "Black is formal wear," she said.

Jesse wiped at a spot of dirt on his jacket. "And women love a man in uniform. This thing qualifies, doesn't it?"

"I'll let you know if I start loving it."

"Right," he said. "Let me know."

She wondered what exactly he meant by that for the rest of the flight home.

CHAPTER 27

Dirk hadn't heard his father leave. He'd been outside with Aaron, teaching him diving maneuvers. But Dirk heard his father come home. As soon as soon as his father stepped through the door, he called Dirk's name, loudly and repeatedly.

"Coming," Dirk answered.

What was wrong now? He walked toward his father's voice, intercepting him in the family room. He was dressed in battle gear and smelled of dragon and gunpowder. His face was flushed, either from riding without a helmet or from anger. Probably anger.

One glare at Dirk cleared up any doubt. Yep, anger. What had he found out? Dirk took a slow breath and kept his expression calm. He couldn't afford to do anything that would make him look guilty.

His father pulled off his gloves and flung them on the couch. "What did you tell Tori about the eggs?"

Dirk tilted his head in confusion. He'd given his father more than one reason to be angry with him but none of them involved dragon eggs. "What do you mean?"

His father stepped closer, looked like he was about to grab Dirk by the collar. "What did you tell Tori about the eggs?"

Dirk held his ground. "Nothing. She found out there were more eggs from being in Kiha's mind when you attacked her on Halloween." He added the last bit to remind his father that he was to blame for that part.

The reminder didn't curb his father's temper. "How did she know they were in the Energize building?"

Dirk didn't have to fake his surprise. "She doesn't know that. What are you talking about?"

"The Slayers broke in and destroyed five eggs." Dirk's father held up one hand, fingers splayed to emphasize the point. "Five. How did they know?"

A wave of sickness hit Dirk. Five eggs were gone. Years of breeding destroyed. Tamerlane, Dirk's favorite dragon, had fathered four of those eggs. To lose those—it felt like losing Tamerlane all over again. He had to sit down on the couch.

"How did they know?" his father repeated, louder this time.

"I don't know," Dirk insisted. Tamerlane's scales had been an orange-red, unusual for a dragon. Dirk had hoped one of Tamerlane's offspring would carry that trait, but if not, he'd planned on breeding the siblings until flame-like scales appeared again in their line. Seeing that color would be like bringing part of Tamerlane back to life.

Dirk's father paced in front of him, scowling. "Someone obviously told Tori where the eggs were, and you're the only one who had contact with her."

"I didn't tell her," Dirk said, his own voice rising now. "Why would I do that?"

"To save your friends."

"They're not in danger from the eggs. If I were trying to save the Slayers, I would have told them where the dragons were." He threw his hands up to show the ridiculousness of the argument. "Actually, I wouldn't have even done that. I would have just killed the dragons myself and fled. All four are still alive, aren't they? I'm still here." He ran a shaky hand through his hair. "Is the remaining egg one of Tamerlane's?"

His father must have heard the cautious hope in Dirk's voice, hope for that egg, and despair for the rest. He let out a long breath and with it some of his anger. "Yes. It's one of Tamerlane's."

At least there was that.

His father kept at his pacing, each step coming down hard on the floor. "You must have let the information slip somehow."

He hadn't, though. He knew he hadn't. "I've never talked to Tori about the eggs or mentioned the building. I couldn't have let anything slip."

A sick feeling settled in his stomach. Had his father said something around Khan or Minerva, thinking that Tori was connected to Vesta? No, that couldn't be it. His father would never be that careless. The leak was elsewhere. But Dirk decided not to mention Tori's change of dragon connections anyway. He wasn't going to let the blame for this be pinned on him.

Dirk shifted on the couch. "Someone in your organization must have told the Slayers."

"Who?"

Dirk shrugged. He didn't know all the people who worked with his father. How could he come up with the traitor? "Did you find out who leaked the information about the arms shipment?"

His father made a grumbling sound from deep in his throat. "I have my suspicions. But Ethington didn't know the eggs' location." He paused and his eyes narrowed.

"Although he knows Hancock." Hancock was one of his father's eagerly ruthless men who headed up the security of the building.

Another grumbling noise. "Ethington might have gotten the information from him and passed it on to Senator Hampton. Although why he'd double cross me…" His father trailed off as he considered this possibility. The slap of his footsteps against the floor was the only sound in the room.

"If you know the enemy and know yourself," his father said the phrase like it was a school lesson that needed repetition, "you need not fear the result of a hundred battles. If you know yourself but not the enemy, for every victory gained you will also suffer defeat." He looked to Dirk to say the last sentence of Sun Tzu's quote. *The Art of War* was just one of many books his father had studied like scripture.

Dirk obliged him. "If you know neither the enemy nor yourself, you will succumb in every battle."

His father nodded. "Perhaps we haven't known Senator Ethington as well as we should have."

Dirk had been so busy denying involvement in the killings, it wasn't until this moment that he processed the other fact his father had given him. If the Slayers had only destroyed five eggs, they must have been caught before they could destroy the sixth.

Panic took hold of his chest and squeezed. "Did you capture the Slayers? You didn't kill anyone, did you?"

Not Tori. She had to be safe. She wouldn't have gone with the Slayers—not to destroy dragons. Even as Dirk told himself this, another part of him was certain she was part of the mission. She was the only one who could connect to the eggs to make sure they were legitimate.

Dread clutched at his throat. *No,* he thought. And the word was meant for Tori as much as for his father. He knew he couldn't retroactively stop any of this from happening, and yet the word repeated over and over in his mind. *No. No. No.* Why had she gone?

Dirk's father grunted in disapproval at his concern. His words became clipped, accusing almost. "I got a phone call about the attack and flew Khan to Lock Haven. As I neared our building, Hancock called, reporting that the Slayers had flown off with an egg. I tracked the GPS chip embedded in the shell, hit the area with EMP, and retrieved the egg.

"Tori went into Khan's mind," his father added with irritation. "She was trying to reach his control center."

"She did what?" Dirk asked, incredulous. Why would Tori do something so foolish, make herself vulnerable that way when an angry dragon lord was right there? "Are you sure?"

"Of course I'm sure. I saw her faint. I felt her poking around."

Dirk stared at his father, alarm filling all the places the panic had hollowed out. "What did you do to her?"

"Nothing," he snapped, his anger shifting back to Dirk. "I flew away with the egg. Although if I had known then that the Slayers weren't just thieves, but murderers too, I would have tried harder to kill them." He pulled his phone from his pocket and yanked it from an EMP-proof case. "I was halfway home when Hancock sent this picture."

Dirk's father shoved the phone at him. The screen showed the carnage. Broken bits of shell everywhere. Cracked eggs. A pale, mangled dragon lying among spatters of blood. Its half-formed wings looked like canvases that someone had torn.

How had the others died? Stabbed, he supposed, before they'd taken their first breaths.

"One of the dragons tried to escape," his father continued. "They bashed in its head against a wall."

Dirk handed the phone back to his father. He couldn't bear to see the pictures anymore. Five dead. Five. Brutally killed.

How could Tori have been a part of this? Why did she let it happen? He'd shown her that dragons were majestic, powerful creatures. She'd seen them, ridden them, been in their minds. She should have protected those eggs, not slaughtered them.

And she'd done this, knowing how upset it would make him.

A shuddering breath pushed its way from his lips. He'd been trying to show her that she was a dragon lord. Instead, she'd shown him that she was a Slayer.

Dirk's father put the phone back in its case and snapped it closed. "This won't go unanswered. Two weeks from tonight, we'll take out our stage one military targets."

The sentence, spoken so easily, had implications that pushed all other thoughts from Dirk's mind. Did his father mean it? "I thought we weren't going to attack until Vesta and Jupiter were full-grown."

"Change of plans. The revolution starts January third. By then I should have everything in place." He shoved his phone case back into his jacket pocket. "I'll need your help preparing the dragons. Don't make other plans."

This was happening too fast. Dirk wasn't ready to make this sort of leap yet—a complete break with his country, with everything. "We shouldn't let the Slayers force us into acting prematurely. We need to make sure we have the best hand possible before we play it."

"It's too late for waiting," his father said. "I've already called operatives and put plans in motion. While most of the nation is busy with their holidays, our men will plant explosives in congress's bunkers. We'll destroy them the same night we take out the military bases."

Congress's protocol if DC came under attack was to move the leadership to secret bunkers and direct the nation's doings from there. Ethington had given the location to his father long ago, allowing his father to maneuver his men inside the government so that they had access to it.

"Why hit the politicians' safe spots then?" Dirk asked.

"They won't be there."

"Because I'm sending Congress a message. They have no place to run."

With that, Dirk's father stalked upstairs.

It was happening. Whether Dirk liked it or not, the revolution was about to start.

 CHAPTER 28

When Tori woke up in the morning, she checked the internet for messages from Dirk. She didn't find any. She hadn't heard from him near the dragons either. How angry was he? He must know by now what she'd done. Certainly, his father had told him not only about the dragons, but that she'd been one of the Slayers involved in the attack.

Tori held her phone, contemplating what to write to Dirk. She wanted to explain why she'd destroyed the eggs, but he already knew her reasons for being a Slayer. The two of them had talked about the subject enough times. Still, saying nothing seemed worse.

She wrote a sentence, erased it. Wrote another, then erased it too. Finally, she wrote one word—*Sorry*—and sent the message.

That word sat alone on the site all day. And the next day. And the next.

School let out for the holidays, and Tori's family went to Hawaii for Christmas to take a break from winter. She tried to keep her mind off Slayer things and did her best to be just another tourist—one with bodyguards trailing in her family's wake. But it was hard not to let her mind drift back to DC, back to the last few months of training, to stealing kisses with Jesse after practice, to kissing Dirk while dragons lounged nearby, and then to Lock Haven where she could still smell the dust and smoke—to explosions that had destroyed so much.

Sunshine, sand, and aqua blue water couldn't change who she was, what she had to do, or what she'd done already. Dirk and Jesse. Each so important to her, and yet she'd managed to hurt both of them so deeply.

She and her family flew back to DC on January second and she steeled herself to face school, practice, and everything else. Snow lined the streets, a cold, white reminder that made the tree branches droop. Winter had patiently waited for her.

# CHAPTER 29

At midnight on January third, Dirk was riding Khan over Hampton, Virginia. His father sent him to take care of the jets at Langley Air Force Base.

He had one goal for the night: disable as many fighter jets as possible.

The base spread out in front of him. Planes, jeeps, runways, homes—all lit up like so many birthday candles, waiting to be blown out. No wishes today, though, just darkness.

He circled near the base, hesitating. He'd known this moment would be hard for him—attacking his own country. But he didn't feel as much regret as he expected. Superimposed on the civilization down below him, was an image of battered eggs and a dead hatchling, one that lay crumpled on a floor, wings torn.

When the Slayers killed Tamerlane and Kiha, they'd been acting in self-defense. The attack on the eggs was different. The Slayers had killed the dragons for one reason: it was human nature to destroy things that opposed you.

The Slayers opposed him and so did the government. A government built on waste, corruption, and hypocrisy. Dirk would handle them in kind.

In Khan's mind, Dirk commanded the dragon to let out an EMP screech. Khan drew in a breath, chest expanding. He lifted his head and sent a high-pitched careening wave of sound that rolled through the sky. Below Dirk, the landscape blinked into darkness.

He turned Khan and headed to Andrews, the next target. It was going to be a long night.

 # CHAPTER 30

When Tori woke up in the morning, she dressed in her Veritas uniform and went downstairs for breakfast. School. Do not ask for whom the school bell tolls. The bells toll for thee and all the other students who didn't finish their English reading assignments over break.

Her father was gone but Aprilynne wasn't. Which was odd because they usually drove to his office together. Tori's mother was flipping through news stations on the TV and had her laptop open to another news channel.

Tori trudged over to the cereal cupboard. "Where's dad?"

Aprilynne cut a bagel in half and spread cream cheese on one side. "He was called in early. Government stuff."

"You didn't go with him?" It was worth going in early to avoid rush hour traffic on the beltway. Tori grabbed a cereal box and went to get a bowl.

"Dad left super early," Aprilynne said. "He told me to stay home and work on campaign stuff."

Tori's gaze went to her mother, noticing for the first time her serious expression and the crease of concern between her eyebrows. Whatever was on the news, she wasn't happy about it.

Tori poured her cereal, only half paying attention to it. "Is something wrong?"

Aprilynne glanced at their mother, then lowered her voice. "You're not supposed to tell anyone, but several military bases were hit with EMP last night."

Tori's hand froze on the cereal box. Flakes skittered unnoticed onto the table. It had started. Overdrake had attacked. That wasn't supposed to happen yet. She hadn't expected Overdrake to strike until Venezuela was doing exercises off the coast next April. Tori had assumed America would be safe at least until then. Had Overdrake attacked sooner as retaliation for the eggs? "How many bases?" Tori asked.

"Dad didn't say, and you're not supposed to go spreading it around. The government doesn't want people knowing some of the bases are crippled. Might give our enemies ideas."

Their enemies already had ideas. More attacks must be coming soon.

Aprilynne put her bagel slices on a plate. "The news gets worse. You know the secure locations the government moves politicians to if they're worried that DC will come under attack?"

Tori nodded. "Is Dad going there?"

"No. Those were attacked too. Explosives took out the bunkers. It had to be an inside job. Not many people know the bunkers' location. Dad still won't tell me where they are and they're inoperable now."

That sort of attack didn't make sense. "Why would someone hit bunkers when they're empty?" If Overdrake had wanted to take out Congress, he would have staged an attack on DC, then hit the bunkers once the leaders show up.

"Who knows," Aprilynne said. "I guess they don't want the leaders to evacuate. Although you can be sure the president is tucked away safely on Air Force One somewhere."

Tori's dad was one of those leaders. He couldn't go somewhere safe. Her stomach clenched. It felt hard to breathe. Were Overdrake's troops in place, or had he started the attacks without them? "Where is Venezuela?" Tori asked.

Aprilynne cocked an eyebrow. "Last I checked, still in South America."

"I meant their navy."

Aprilynne gave her a look that indicated she thought it was the wrong time to ask foreign country trivia. "Um, my guess their navy is in Venezuela."

Aprilynne obviously didn't know that Venezuela had asked to do exercises near the country, and Tori didn't bother explaining. "I need to talk to Dad." She took her phone from her pocket, crossed to the other side of the kitchen, and called his number.

"Good luck with that," Aprilynne said. "He'll be in meetings all day."

The call went directly to voicemail. Tori stepped into the dining room and paced while she left a message. "I know who's responsible for this. A man named Brant Overdrake. He immigrated here about seventeen years ago from the Island of St Helena. I don't know where he is now, but..."

She hesitated to tell her father the rest. "I know it sounds unbelievable, but he's using dragons. When they screech they create EMP. He's connected with the Venezuelans. More attacks will be coming. You're going to have to watch out for them both."

She hung up and walked back into the kitchen. Aprilynne stood by the door, staring at Tori with a raised eyebrow. "Uh huh. Dragons. And Venezuelans." She took a glass from the cupboard. "You know those are fictional, right?"

No good would come from arguing about it. "Venezuelans are real. Lots of people have seen them."

Their mother chose this moment to tune into their conversation. "What about Venezuelans?"

"They're going to attack the country," Tori said.

"Along with their dragons," Aprilynne added.

"I'm not crazy." Tori pointed to the TV as though it were proof. "Someone attacked. You can't deny that."

Their mother lowered the volume. "We're not supposed to spread that information around." She cast another glance at the TV. "Although I can't see how the news will stay a secret. Too many people know about the attacks."

Tori chewed on her bottom lip. Was there a way to prove she was telling the truth? If she got hold of a simulator... No, that would only prove she had powers. It wouldn't prove anything about dragons or Overdrake. And if her parents knew she had powers, they would keep tighter control on her, try to keep her from fighting like Bess's grandfather. Now, more than ever, the Slayers needed her help. So she couldn't prove anything.

Tori's mother sighed and looked Tori over again. Her voice softened and took on the parental tone she used to reassure her children. "We're perfectly safe. However, if you're feeling a lot of anxiety, you can stay home from school and help Aprilynne."

In case of more attacks, it might be tactically better for her to stay home, and yet Tori didn't like the idea of her family thinking she was having anxiety issues. Would they believe her about anything else if she let them think she was having some sort of nervous breakdown?

"I'm fine," she said. "I'll go to school."

When she got back to her room, she checked Dirk's site. He'd written one word back. *Sorry.*

He wasn't, she knew. He'd flung the word back at her because her apology for demolishing the eggs wasn't sufficient. No amount of apologizing would be. She'd killed something he cared about.

She ran her hand over the phone. Perhaps this wasn't really the beginning of Overdrake's attacks. Perhaps this was just his way of getting back at the Slayers. They'd destroyed his weapons, so he was destroying theirs.

Wishful thinking, probably.

She wrote a message to Dirk. *Please don't blame me for trying to protect people. I didn't want to do it, but your father didn't leave us many choices.*

Dirk didn't reply.

She was about to send Dr. B a message when her watch chimed with a warning message to the entire group. *Twelve key bases were hit with EMP last night. Be on alert today.*

The news had already made the rounds to Dr. B's people. He didn't mention the bunkers, so when she got to her room, she called him with that information.

"He's sending a message," she said. "The leaders aren't safe."

"True," he said, "but he's also sending a message that he doesn't want to hurt them. He could have, easily enough."

She hoped Dr. B was right about that. "Do you think this is an isolated strike or the beginning of his revolution?"

"Regardless, we should treat it as though his attacks will continue."

The answer didn't make her feel better.

"In light of these strikes," Dr. B continued, "we need to discuss your position as captain."

Well, he was finally getting around to breaking the news to her. His voice was casual, didn't show any hint of guilt. She didn't know whether to hold that against him or not—that he obviously thought demoting her wouldn't cause her any pain. Was it better to think him clueless or cruel?

"After much consideration and weighing the pros and cons, I've decided that Ryker should take your place as captain."

Tori swallowed and shut her eyes. It was official.

"You've done an excellent job as captain," he said. "A-team couldn't have asked for a better leader."

As far as breakup lines went, that one was too much. "Then why are you giving Ryker my position?" She hated that her voice sounded petulant. She shouldn't have asked the question in the first place. She knew what he would say: Ryker was Jesse's counterpart so the two of them could work better together. Blah blah you're not good enough.

"Because you're a dragon lord," Dr. B said.

The words were all the worse for being spoken so calmly. If he'd been yelling, she might have been able to convince herself he didn't mean them. But said in such a matter of fact way—yeah, he meant them.

He started to say more, but she cut him off. "You don't trust me?"

"Of course I trust you," he said as though she was missing the point.

"Just not enough to be a captain?".

"Tori, you can go into the dragon's mind. Despite what Jesse thinks of the dangers, a time may come when you need to leave the Slayers and fight for us there. If you're leading A-team, you won't have that luxury. I want to leave your options open."

As quickly as Tori's anger had spiked, it dissolved. "You think I should go into the dragon's mind?"

"I didn't say that. I said I want to leave the option open."

"Oh." It felt odd to have his approval. Her view of him suddenly shifted. Or maybe it was her view of herself. Being a dragon lord didn't seem like something she had to defend quite so much.

"Sometimes the best way to fight fire is with fire," he said. "That may be what you become—our fire."

Long after Tori hung up with Dr. B, the comment still echoed in her mind. If she was fire, she was a small flame at best. She'd never managed to control a dragon and Dirk wasn't likely to give her another chance to learn now. Had it been a horrible tactical mistake to kill the dragon eggs?

All day at school, her nerves were stretched tight, waiting for more news, for a message from Dr. B that another attack had happened. Pointless anxiety. Overdrake wouldn't attack during the day. He would wait until he had darkness on his side. He would wait until tonight.

CHAPTER 31

When Dirk woke up that afternoon, he checked his phone. Tori had written him. *Please don't blame me for trying to protect people. I didn't want to do it, but your father didn't leave us many choices.*

He grunted and wrote *Who were the eggs attacking?*

He erased the sentence. Sending it would only encourage her to defend her position. Instead, he sent the message *Don't blame me for trying to change the country. I don't want to do it, but my father doesn't leave me many choices.*

If she could make sweeping generalizations, so could he.

He went downstairs to get something to eat. Bridget and Aaron were in the family room playing Uno. When Bridget saw him, she loudly whispered, "Dad wants us to be quiet. He's in a grumpy mood."

Dirk walked through the room and into the kitchen. "That's because Dad was up all last night."

Bridget held her cards to her chest so Aaron couldn't peek while she talked to Dirk. "He's been in a grumpy mood since bad guys killed our dragon eggs. They just smashed up five of them."

Aaron put a card down on the pile. "Dirk already knows. That's why he was with Dad last night. They were getting revenge."

Bridget's eyes went wider as she watched Dirk. "Did you catch the bad guys?"

"Not this time."

She let out a disappointed breath and looked at her cards again. "Those poor dragon babies. I wanted Minerva's hatchlings to be red like her. She would have liked that."

Actually Minerva wouldn't have cared what color they were or that they were her children. When dragons had lived in the wild, they'd either steered clear of each other or fought over territory.

Dirk had explained this fact to Bridget a dozen times, but she insisted on believing that if given the chance, Minerva would lead her brood around like they were ducklings.

"Not all mothers love their children," Dirk said.

The sentence earned him a sharp look from Aaron. Dirk hadn't been talking about his own mother, but yeah, case in point.

Dirk opened the fridge and grabbed leftover pizza. "Khan and Minerva need to rest," he told Aaron. "So today you'll work with the hatchlings."

Bridget played a card. "The hatchlings are always grumpy. They tried to bite me once."

"Only once?" Aaron drew a card. "They must like you."

"Dirk saved me." Bridget slapped down another card.

Dirk didn't want Bridget telling that story, as his father didn't know about the event. It involved Dirk breaking several rules in order to warn Tori that a dragon was about to attack the Slayers' plane.

"Shouldn't you be doing homework?" Dirk asked. Cassie homeschooled Bridget. Although now that she was pregnant, she spent a lot of time resting. Bridget's study work was sporadic at best.

"I'm done," Bridget said proudly. "Aaron helped me do it because I played spy with him."

Aaron leaned toward Bridget. "Do you have more than one card? Because you didn't say, 'Uno.'" He said the phrase too quickly, with a surge of worry.

Dirk took a bite of pizza and eyed him. "How do you play spy?"

Aaron didn't answer. His attention stayed firmly on his cards.

Bridget drew a card and added it to her hand. "Aaron is a spy, and I start singing a song if I see anyone coming. Then I don't tell anyone."

Aaron sent her a dark look. "I think you forgot to do that last part."

"We're not playing anymore," she said. "So it's okay to tell now."

Dirk put his pizza on the counter and walked into the family room. He kept his gaze on Aaron so he could read him. "Did you play that today?"

With Dirk and his father sleeping and Cassie resting, only Norma, the housekeeper, would have been keeping an eye on Bridget and Aaron. And Norma was easy enough to get around. "How many times have you played spy with Aaron?"

"A few," Bridget said. "But I like hide-and-seek better."

Aaron shrugged casually. "It's just one of her pretend games. She makes me play pirates too."

Aaron might have pulled off the casual tone if Dirk hadn't been his counterpart. Aaron's emotions were bowstring-tense and he was trying hard not to show it.

Dirk put his hand firmly on his brother's shoulder. "Sorry to interrupt your game, Bridget, but Aaron and I need to talk." Dirk took hold of his brother's arm and yanked him up.

"Hey," Bridget protested. "We're not done with our game."

"Yes, you are," Dirk said, pulling Aaron out of the family room. "You won."

"Stop it!" Aaron jerked his arm away from Dirk. "You'll rip my arm off."

Aaron followed Dirk into the living room, grumbling. He was trying at anger but guilt and fear leaked from every word.

Dirk stopped and faced him, hands on his hips. "What were you doing that you needed Bridget for your lookout?"

"Nothing." Aaron rubbed his arm where Dirk had grabbed it. "She wanted to play and it was my way of keeping her busy while I went off and played computer games."

"I can tell when you're lying. You know that, right?"

Aaron rolled his eyes. "Then you can tell this next confession is true too: when Bridget and I play hide-and-seek, I do other stuff and take a long time to find her. So sue me for being a lousy playmate. Maybe you should go kidnap someone her age."

With that sentence, Aaron's anger overshadowed his nervousness. But neither emotion helped his case for innocence. What was he up to?

Dirk watched him carefully, judging his emotions. "I found you in Dad's den once. Why were you there?"

Aaron held his gaze, blue eyes stubborn. "I already told you. I was looking for Dad."

Not the truth. Dirk cocked his head. "Did I believe you when you told me that the first time? Because if I did, I was clearly not paying attention."

"Okay," Aaron said with a huff of confession. "I admit I was snooping."

Before Dirk could comment, he added, "Don't tell me you wouldn't do the same thing if you'd been abducted. I was hoping to find something that would tell me where I was. An envelope with an address or a bill."

This was the truth, even if Aaron was still holding things back.

"Did you find out where we are?" Dirk asked.

Aaron's shoulders slumped. "I've got no idea. There wasn't an envelope in the place. You guys don't even have a mailbox, do you?"

They didn't. His father had a PO box in the city.

Dirk didn't answer the question. He just studied Aaron. The kid was watching Dirk warily—afraid, but pretending he wasn't. Dirk couldn't help but feel sorry for him. Maybe it was because Aaron reminded Dirk of himself at that age—trying to please his father and at the same time trying to resist him. Come to think of it, Dirk was still doing that.

He ran his hand across the back of his neck, thinking. If Aaron wanted to escape, he would always be more of a danger than an asset. His father should have realized that in the beginning.

Eventually Aaron would figure out some clue to their location. Their father wouldn't slip up, but Cassie might. Norma might. Bridget would willingly spill everything she knew—which fortunately wasn't much. But if Aaron found a way to get information to their mother, the feds would show up on their doorstep.

As much as their father wanted another dragon lord around, losing Aaron now would be better than having to do damage control later.

Of course, his father was not going to listen to that sort of reasoning. "Look," Dirk said, lowering his voice, "if you want to leave, I'll help you. Just don't do anything stupid that we'll all regret."

Aaron returned Dirk's stare, weighing his words to see if they were true.

"I'll help you leave," Dirk said again. "But we'll have to do it my way." Dirk would blindfold him and drop him off somewhere far away so he wouldn't have any clue as to where he'd been. Dirk would also have to arrange the escape for a time when he had an alibi because if their father found out Dirk had helped Aaron leave, he would make Dirk suffer for it.

"I don't want to leave," Aaron said. "At least not yet."

Dirk hadn't heard Bridget come into the room, but she launched herself at Aaron holding onto him in a hug. "Don't make him leave!"

Dirk leaned down to hush her. "I'm not making him leave."

Aaron joined in making shushing noises. "I'm not going anywhere. We were talking about someday when I go off to college—that's a school for grownups. But I won't go there for a lot of years." The lie came off Aaron's tongue so effortlessly that it hardly even registered as an untruth.

Bridget's eyebrows crinkled as she tried to make this information fit with what she'd heard. "Promise?"

"Promise," Aaron said.

Dirk unpeeled her from Aaron's legs and bent down to be on her level. "Listen, Bridget, you can't tell anyone that Aaron and I were talking about him leaving. It would make Dad mad."

She nodded, a look of understanding in her large brown eyes. "He doesn't like regular schools. That's why I can't go to one."

Aaron took her by the hand. "Let's play Uno again." He led her out of the room without a backward glance at Dirk.

Well, Dirk had learned a few things about his brother today. He didn't want to leave right now and he was a better liar than Dirk had realized.

Could he be the leak?

The idea seemed absurd. He was only a twelve-year-old kid. And he was a dragon lord. Why would he help the Slayers, even if he knew how? And come to think of it, he did know how. All he had to do was pass information along to Tori.

The thought lodged in his mind and refused to leave. Aaron had met Tori. Was he getting back at their father for kidnapping him by finding out information and giving it to her?

His father most likely had information about the eggs on the computer in the den. His vets visited the eggs and sent him reports.

Dirk walked back to the family room, mulling over his theory. It was like a puzzle piece that didn't quite fit with the rest of the picture. Aaron thought Tori was connected to Vesta. Even if he found a way to sneak into that dragon's enclosure, Tori wouldn't hear what he had to say.

But there was one way to find out if Aaron was involved with the Slayers. Ask him.

Aaron and Bridget were sitting on the floor like they'd been before. Dirk walked over to the couch and sat down.

He kept his gaze on Aaron, waiting for him to turn and acknowledge his stare.

Aaron didn't. Which meant he was purposely avoiding Dirk. Counterparts could feel stares like they were a tap on the shoulder.

"Aaron," Dirk said at last. "How well do you know Tori Hampton?"

Aaron played a card. He was trying to push away a spike of anxiety. "Uh, hardly at all. I only met her once." His words seemed true, but the spike of anxiety was still there.

Bridget looked up from her hand and smiled. "I met Tori. She's pretty and she has a nice dog." Whispering, Bridget added, "Dirk likes her."

Aaron finally glanced at Dirk. "Does he? That's got to be an interesting relationship."

Interesting was one word. Impossible was another. Confusing was probably the best word. Half the time he wanted to cut her out of his life completely, the other half he wanted to call a truce and fly with her to some distant spot where neither of them had to think of war.

Dirk wasn't about to let the conversation get sidetracked in that direction, though. "Have you ever passed on any information to Tori?"

Aaron turned back to his cards. "You and Dad are always with me when I'm near Vesta. You've heard what I've said."

True. Aaron had no reason to believe that Tori was connected to a different dragon. But all the same, he was avoiding the question.

"Did you find a way to tell her about the eggs?"

"Why would you ask me that?"

Another avoidance.

Bridget's gaze was bouncing between her brothers trying to figure out what they were talking about.

"Did you tell her," Dirk asked again.

"No," Aaron said, offended. And guilty.

Dirk shook his head at him. Aaron wasn't such a good liar after all.

Dirk had to quell a sudden urge to haul his brother up by his shirt and slam him against the wall. Five eggs were gone. Three of them Tamerlane's. Dirk forced himself to speak calmly. "Why did you do it?"

Bridget cocked her head. "Do what?"

Dirk ignored her and waited, his stare boring into his brother.

Aaron held up his hands in frustration, presenting a picture of baffled innocence. "I didn't do anything wrong." He said the words with conviction. Aaron believed them, even if he was still scared. But then, there were a lot of ways to mean the phrase, "I didn't do anything wrong."

Bridget's frowned at Dirk. "What are you guys talking about?"

Dirk wasn't going to be the one to tell her. Not about Tori being a Slayer or Aaron being part of the dragons' deaths. "The next time Aaron asks you to play spy," he said, "tell me so I can play too."

***

Dirk was sitting in the family room eating and keeping an eye on Aaron when his father came down the stairs. He was shaved and dressed, with a duffle bag slung over his shoulder. "Dirk, help me with Khan."

His father was putting Khan on a cargo plane today and flying the dragon to his property in California. That way, he and Dirk could hit cities on both coasts tonight.

Dirk followed his father outside, still debating what he should say. Dirk was reluctant to rat out Aaron. Maybe it was because Aaron was his counterpart, or maybe it was because he was his brother, but he didn't want to see the kid hurt.

What would their father do when he learned Aaron was involved with the eggs' destruction?

Something horrible, probably.

Still, what choice did Dirk have? His father had been talking about using Aaron in some of the less dangerous ground operations. Dirk had to warn his father that Aaron might betray them.

Dirk didn't speak to his father until they were walking down the stairs of Khan's enclosure. The metal steps clanged underneath their feet, sending out two rhythms that were never quite in sync. "I need to talk to you about Aaron," Dirk said.

His father continued going down the stairs, unconcerned. "Why?"

"I like Aaron. He's a nice kid, but he's not old enough to understand what he's doing." Dirk kept his expression neutral, didn't want to reveal too much. "We can't trust him. We'd be better off sending him home instead of forcing him to stay here if it means we have to worry about what he's doing while we're gone fighting."

"This is his home," his father said the words like they were self-evident. "Besides, you were handling dragons at twelve. What makes you think he's not old enough?"

"We can't trust him."

His father looked over at Dirk, finally giving his words his full attention. "Why not?"

The question was an accusation by itself, one that hung in the air along with their echoing footsteps. There was no good way to break this news, but Dirk tried to do it gently. "A couple weeks ago, I found Aaron alone in your office. I didn't think much of it at the time. I figured he was searching for his cell phone or something. Today I asked him if he'd told the Slayers about the eggs' location. He denied it, but I could tell he was lying. I think he's the leak."

"Aaron?" His father slowed his pace. "How could he have found out about the location of the eggs?"

"I don't know. I can't read his mind. I can just tell when he's hiding something."

His father gave him a doubtful look. "Aaron's hiding something, so that means he's the leak? He certainly couldn't have leaked the arms shipment coming in. He wasn't even here when that happened."

"I realize he couldn't have had anything to do with arms shipment, but I don't see why else he'd feel a lot of guilt and fear when I asked him if he gave away any information about the eggs."

As they trudged down the last few steps, his father thought this over, seemed to be chewing on his next words.

"Don't hurt Aaron," Dirk added. "He's only twelve and you can't blame him for wanting to get back at you for kidnapping him."

His father's expression had turned severe, but he still didn't speak right away. He put his hand on the panel that recognized his fingerprints and unlocked the first door. It slid open with a swoosh like a knife blade slicing the air.

"The three of us will talk about this. I'll bring Aaron down here."

Instead of turning back, his father went with Dirk through the second door into Khan's enclosure. Dirk didn't have to ask why. His father was exposing himself to the dragon to turn on his powers. It was easier to fly up the stairs than to climb them.

"Start getting Khan ready," his father said. "I'll be back in a few minutes."

Dirk nodded and his father left. He stood there for a moment, unmoving, worrying about his brother. Dirk would have to emphasize to his father again that sending Aaron home, not punishing him, was the best option. You couldn't make someone be a dragon lord if they didn't want to be one. He'd already learned that with Tori, hadn't he?

Khan was spread out on the enclosure floor sleeping. He'd opened one eye when Dirk and his father walked in, sniffing the air to see if they'd brought food with them. When he saw they hadn't, he returned to sleep. The dragon was so used to them coming and going in the enclosure, Dirk didn't merit much attention.

As a precaution, Dirk took hold of Khan's mind anyway. It was never wise to be within striking distance of a dragon if you didn't have control. Dirk kept only a loose grip on Khan's will. He didn't need tight control here in the enclosure, and dragons liked to feel that they still had some freedom.

Dirk flew to a large hole in the wall where Khan's Kevlar shield sat and hauled it out. The thing was huge and heavy. Without his extra strength, it would have been too unwieldy for one person to heft around. Before Dirk made the command, Khan stood so that Dirk could maneuver around him. The dragon knew that when Dirk got out the Kevlar shield, they would be leaving the enclosure.

Dirk flew to Khan and began the process of strapping the Kevlar onto his underbelly. *I hate to disappoint you,* Dirk said in Khan's mind. *But you're about to be stuck in the back of a cargo plane for hours.*

Small talk was generally wasted on dragons. Khan didn't really understand what Dirk had said. He'd never ridden in a plane before and thought of them as large, tasteless birds he'd been commanded to stay away from. And Khan didn't ask what Dirk meant. Dragons never asked questions about the things people said or did. That sort of thought process seemed beyond their capability.

Instead, Khan swished his tail across the enclosure floor, anticipating stretching his wings and taking to the air. If thieves ever wanted to steal Khan, all they had to do was break into the enclosure carrying a Kevlar shield. The dragon would most likely happily stand there waiting to be suited up.

You'd be too tired if we made you fly the distance to California, Dirk said. *Don't worry, though. You'll fly around a lot once you get there.*

The dragon still didn't understand. He wasn't tired, let alone too tired to fly anywhere so the message made no sense to him.

Dirk phrased the information as basically as he could. *Wait. Fly later.*

Khan growled in disapproval, then sniffed at Dirk, checking a second time to see if he'd brought any food.

Dirk pushed the dragon's massive muzzle away. "That's all you think I'm good for: taking you out and giving you a meal. If you were prettier, it would be like we were dating."

Dirk flew to the dragon's back, first chaining the Kevlar shield in place, and then attaching bulletproof straps over the chains to protect them from being shot through. After that, he put a covering on the diamond-shaped scale on Khan's forehead so it wouldn't send out a pulse.

Back when dragons roamed the wild, the pulse acted as a warning beacon, alerting other dragons not to wander into the territory. The alchemists who'd created the first Slayers had used that pulse to their advantage. It was what turned on the Slayer genetics in unborn children.

Dirk was standing on Khan's back making sure the covering was secure when his father came back into the enclosure by himself.

"Where is Aaron?" Dirk asked. His heart lurched with worry. Aaron was probably locked in a room, beaten perhaps.

"We had a talk," his father said slowly. "He told me that you resent him and are trying to turn me against him."

Dirk flew from Khan's back and dropped down on the ground. "I guess he would say something like that."

His father folded his arms and sent Dirk a cold glare.

"You don't believe him, do you?" Dirk asked.

"Aaron said that just today you offered to help him escape and he turned you down. Do you deny it?"

Dirk let out an aggravated breath. His father *did* believe Aaron. His father had weighed their stories and decided to trust the son he hardly knew over the son he'd raised.

Well, it appeared that both of his parents favored Aaron.

Resentment twisted inside of Dirk. He'd given up his friends for his father. He'd given up Dr. B's respect and Tori's affection—and his father didn't even believe him.

"Do you deny it?" his father repeated, louder this time.

It was clear his father already knew the story was the truth. Aaron must have had Bridget verify it. A charming turn of events. Dirk had offered to help Aaron, and the kid was using that gesture as a weapon against him.

His father was still waiting for his answer. Dirk had no choice but to tell him the truth. "I offered because I figured it was better to lose Aaron than to have him lead the feds to us."

"And you weren't going to let me make that decision—his father. *Your* father." His voice was clipped and precise, bitten off with anger. "I won't stand for this sort of sibling rivalry between you and Aaron. I don't care what your personal feelings are, he's staying, and you won't try to sabotage him or turn me against him again."

Dirk's mouth dropped open. Sibling rivalry? That's what his father thought this was? He really believed that Dirk was trying to sabotage Aaron for some petty reason? "I saw Aaron in your den," Dirk emphasized. "He could have seen some information there about the eggs' location, couldn't he?"

"Even if that's the truth," his father said in a way that indicated he doubted it, "Aaron couldn't have found information about the arms deal. Ethington is the leak."

Khan paced across the enclosure to Dirk and his father, unfurling his wings to remind them that he was ready to fly. Dirk ignored the dragon. "I felt Aaron's guilt about the subject."

His father dismissed the claim with a shake of his head. "That isn't proof of anything. And I have no way to tell if you're right about that."

Dirk fought for inner patience. "You just refuse to believe me."

Khan growled impatiently and unfurled his wings again. Dirk's father raised his hand in a fist, the signal he wanted the dragon to sit.

Khan did, resentfully, even though Dirk hadn't forced him to.

His father lowered his arm, keeping his hand gripped in a fist. "Who do I have more reason to trust, you or Aaron? You're the one who betrayed me before. You're the one who wants to win Tori's favor. And you're the one who has unlimited access to Vesta. Now you're telling me Aaron's responsible for the leak and I should get rid of him. What should I think?"

The words felt like a slap. His father not only didn't trust him, he suspected Dirk had leaked the information to Tori in order to frame his brother.

Dirk's fingers curled. "I'm telling you the truth."

But his father was done with the conversation. He eyed the dragon, inspecting Dirk's work. "When you're finished getting Khan ready, load him on the plane. Put him into a deep sleep and make sure he's locked in. I'll be there with the rest of the supplies before he wakes. Aaron will come with me."

Dirk raised an eyebrow at that. Was his father making the point that he trusted Aaron enough to want his help or was he just worried about leaving Dirk alone with his brother?

His father turned to leave, then shot him one last look. "If you want to prove your loyalty, do your job tonight. That's how I'll know you're with me."

CHAPTER 32

At one in the morning, Dirk was soaring on Minerva's back toward Boston. He would hit the city and then move on to the next target. His mind was a churning mass of anger. Anger at Aaron for twisting things to make him look guilty. Anger at his father for not believing him. Anger at Tori for killing the dragon eggs.

Tori had told him once that he would feel awful when it came time for him to attack a city, and although he hadn't admitted it, he'd wondered if he would be able to bring himself to go through with it, but right now he wanted something to destroy.

Let the lights go out. He didn't care. Darkness was the natural state of things. It's what the world always ended up becoming.

Roar, he told Minerva.

And the dragon roared.

Below him, a wave of black swept across the city, extinguishing the lights like water on fire. Welcome to night.

The end of book four

Note to the reader: For those of you who skipped the dedication (Who reads those?) and are now irked that the series *still* isn't over—I know I said book four was going to be the end. But in all fairness, I also said book three was going to be the end. So there is a precedent for me changing my mind about that.

Once again, the story became too long so I broke it in half. But the good news is that book five *really* is the end. I know this because I've already written most of it. In fact, I would probably be done with it by now except that I decided to write two endings (who says you can't please everyone?) and also because that pesky family of mine keeps insisting that I come out of my room and attend to actual life. But hang in there, I plan to have the book out soon.

Thanks for your patience.

For any book to succeed, reviews are essential. If you enjoyed this book please leave a review on Amazon. A sentence or two can make all the difference.

Acknowledgments

I don't always put acknowledgments in my books. This is probably because I'm ungrateful. No, just kidding. After twenty-seven books, it seems redundant to thank the same people. Most of them are already in the dedications somewhere or show up as characters in the stories. And I'm more concerned about wrapping up the novel and getting through the mountain of projects, emails, and paperwork awaiting me than writing more to stick in the end. Plus, when I start thanking people, I always forget someone and then I feel horrible.

But I would be remiss if I didn't thank my friend Greta Bishop for going way above and beyond the call of duty to help me figure out the Village A complex at Georgetown University.

Usually, Google maps, a satellite image, and pictures from the internet will give me a good idea of what a building looks like. Not this complex. It is like a drunken Escher maze.

Seriously, I don't know how anyone finds their way around those apartment buildings. No amount of internet research or calls to the campus helped. (Despite being dubbed the Help Desk, campus folk are not eager to help strangers who call them wanting the layout of student buildings.) I even had a Facebook friend send me some pictures but I couldn't make sense of them. It was like looking at individual puzzle pieces and trying to figure out what the picture on the box was. I knew I needed more.

Why was I determined to use Village A? Well, if you look at the complex's staircases and catwalks, you can tell that it's a really cool place for a fight scene. Jumping between stairwells and from roof to roof— that's Hollywood gold. And although there are currently no plans for a film adaptation, the writer in me just couldn't let go of that awesome setting. Because maybe, someday...

Enter Greta who graciously drove half an hour to the campus and wandered around that maze taking pictures and video for me while I was on the phone with her. Twice. And then I sent her the manuscript and she drove to the university *again* and walked off the action to make sure I'd written things right. She even jumped across the stairwells and off the roof. Okay, I'm lying about that. She would have been arrested or hospitalized for such shenanigans. But still, it takes a true friend to meander around student housing with a camera. By the time she was through with the place, she knew it so well she was giving directions to strangers. The world needs more people like you, Greta!

Also thanks to Trent Reedy who answered my questions about the explosives needed to break through steel doors. Yes, I did try to research that subject online and I'm sure I have a new page added to my NSA file because of it but I needed info I wasn't finding. Trent served in the military and so had firsthand knowledge of det cords and such. The world also needs more people like you!

Thanks to Leslie Ethington for not only making sure I crossed my T's and dotted my I's, but for being my friend, allowing me to talk her ear off, and for not minding that I named the villain after her. (Bonus points if you can find Greta in the series.)

And speaking of awesome friends, I also need to acknowledge Sandra Udall because when I wrote the acknowledgments to *The Wrong Side of Magic*, I included everyone from my writing group except her even though she was one of the early beta readers for the book. (By the time I was writing the acknowledgments, she was on temporary hiatus from the writing group and thus I missed her name when I went through the group email.)

Forget the world, *I* need more people like my friends! And speaking of awesome friends (See how these acknowledgments just grow?) Thanks to my writing groups who give me feedback, make me laugh, and give me a reason to get out of my pajamas and join the real world.

I should also thank my beta readers. I won't name them all because I know I would forget someone. But I appreciate those of you who are cheerleaders, those of you who gently point out problems, and even you, Ryan, (AKA Darth Beta) who tell me that sections sound like I'm writing drunken poetry. All sorts of feedback helps the book become better. And that's the important thing.

ABOUT THE AUTHOR

CJ Hill is the pen name of author Janette Rallison. She lives in Arizona where she does her best to avoid housework and dragons. She still hasn't decided who Tori should end up with. Fortunately, Tori is only a teenager so she doesn't really have to decide who to spend the rest of her life with. Plus she's a fictional character, so there's that too. CJ is working on Slayers: Into the Firestorm and will decide soon. Probably.

.